Elisabeth writes romantic histori[...]
and historical folklore/fantasy r[...]

She teaches primary school a[...]
six year olds generally do what she tells them. She spends most of her spare time reading and is a pro at cooking one-handed while holding a book. She loves to travel and explore, looking for places to inspire her characters into life.

Elisabeth lives in Cheshire because the car broke down there in 1999 (though at heart she's still a Yorkshire woman). She has two almost grown kids, two cats, two dogs and a husband. The whole family are autistic. She dreams of having a tidy house one day.

elisabethhobbes.co.uk

X x.com/ElisabethHobbes
f facebook.com/ElisabethHobbes

Also by Elisabeth J. Hobbes

Daughter of the Sea

The Promise Tree

Writing as Elisabeth Hobbes

The Secret Agent

Daughters of Paris

My Fair Lord

DANCE WITH THE FAE

ELISABETH J. HOBBES

ONE MORE CHAPTER

One More Chapter
a division of HarperCollins*Publishers* Ltd
1 London Bridge Street
London SE1 9GF
www.harpercollins.co.uk
HarperCollins*Publishers*
Macken House, 39/40 Mayor Street Upper,
Dublin 1, D01 C9W8, Ireland

This paperback edition 2025
1
First published in Great Britain in ebook format
by HarperCollins*Publishers* 2025
Copyright © Elisabeth J. Hobbes 2025

Elisabeth J. Hobbes asserts the moral right to
be identified as the author of this work

A catalogue record of this book
is available from the British Library

ISBN: 978-0-00-863724-8

To my family who have put up with living with a writer for over a decade! Thank you xx

Chapter One

To truly be the hero of a fairy tale, a man should be a seventh son, or at the very least, the third.

Kit Arton-Price was neither, but then he was never intended to be a hero and had never wanted to be.

He should also have endured a trial or suffered under a curse, but it would have been churlish in the extreme to regard his engagement party as a curse.

He left that judgement for someone else to make.

'Watching you looking so unconcerned at your fiancée dancing so intimately with another man, could lead an onlooker to believe you don't care about the fact. Or the fiancée.'

Kit slid his gaze sideways to look at his cousin. There was nothing in Oliver Vane's expression to suggest malicious intent, so perhaps his observation was simply that.'

'Adelaide is a modern woman,' Kit said. 'She can dance with whomever she pleases.'

He swirled his glass around, inhaling the peaty fumes of the single malt he was steadily working his way through, before placing the tumbler on the mantelpiece of the great fireplace. This was already his third of the night and his brain was starting to feel soft around the edges. He didn't want to give anyone more cause to stare at him than they already had.

'I don't intend to limit Addie's social life after we're married so would not dream of doing it beforehand,' he said.

Oliver snorted. 'Even so, young Christopher, your engagement party is hardly the place to concede the floor.'

'I'm not conceding the floor,' Kit said a touch defensively. He bristled a little, too, at 'young'. Oliver, aged thirty, was only four years older than him.

'I'd rather be in the library with a pile of journals from The Royal Society than be gawped at by the gathered families from Dalbymoorside come to stare at the war hero.'

'God, you sound bitter,' Oliver muttered. 'At least you got to serve.'

Oliver was a veterinarian and though he had wanted to enlist, his poor eyesight had seen him remaining in his practice at home. The family had often joked that he was just about able to tell a cow from a horse but Kit wasn't in the mood for jokes.

He grimaced, his jaw clenching to the point of pain. 'Be glad you didn't. Besides, keeping the livestock fit and healthy probably did more for King and Country than me wallowing in mud-filled ditches among the dying did.'

Their eyes met, then Oliver dropped his.

'I'm sorry, Kit. I can't begin to imagine what you went through.'

Kit's mouth jerked into an uncomfortable smile.

'I'm trying my best to forget.'

Some nights he almost managed it and slept for four or five hours in a row without gasping awake in sweat-drenched sheets.

'I really would rather be standing here than dancing,' Kit said. 'I'm a terrible dancer; far too self-conscious. Adelaide deserves a partner who won't tread on her feet, and I get to admire her from the best position to watch her dancing. No one loses.'

Both men returned their attention to the dance floor where Adelaide Wyndham and her partner held court. They glided across the room, other couples moving out of their way, like the Red Sea parting. Adelaide had a look of utter ecstasy on her face, laughing with glee as the man dipped her backwards. He danced with much more of a sense of rhythm and flair than Kit had ever managed and, if anything, it was that which sparked his envy rather than seeing Adelaide in his arms. To be able to move with such freedom from inhibition was an attribute Kit didn't possess.

'Who is he, anyway?' Oliver asked, leaning back against the wall and wrinkling one of the ancient tapestries that adorned the brick walls.

Kit exhaled, frowning slightly. 'I haven't the foggiest idea, actually. I've never seen him before. Probably someone Father knows from the town council or some sort of war bureau that hasn't wrapped everything up.'

Oliver snorted. 'He doesn't look like any sort of councillor I've come across.'

Kit regarded the stranger with more interest. He was a tall man, dark-haired, slender-framed and dressed in an impeccably tailored suit of light grey. At the neck of his high-collared, white shirt was a purple silk cravat tied in an extravagant style.

Despite his assertions, Oliver's words had hit a nerve. Kit wondered if he was being too trusting. He wouldn't blame Adelaide if she was tempted by other men, especially one as flamboyant as this. Neither of them were the same people they had been before the Great War had left its mark. In Kit's case, literally as well as metaphorically.

He pushed those thoughts aside and forced himself to focus on the present moment. This was their engagement party, a time for celebration and joy, not only for the happy couple but for their families, friends and half the neighbourhood who had descended on Meadwell Hall ahead of May Day. The Long Hall, the oldest part of the original manor house, was alive with music, talking and laughter. The ladies wore long gowns in rich colours that seemed determined to prove the good times had returned, while their partners sported black dinner jackets.

As if the four-piece jazz band wasn't enough, at the furthest end of the room, a group of older guests stood around an old gramophone, singing along to its crackly tunes, while in the large, recessed fireplace sat a group of young children playing a game of Ludo with their nanny.

As the dance came to an end, Adelaide's partner bowed and murmured something close in her ear. She looked up into his eyes and smiled, then quick as a flash she dropped her gaze. The stranger walked away from the dance floor. His gait was slow and graceful as if he had all the time in the world to get where he needed to go.

Emboldened by the whisky that was slowly working its way through his system, Kit walked to Adelaide and offered her his hand.

'Come on, Addie, old thing. I owe you a dance.'

As Adelaide took his hand, the diamond engagement ring, which Kit had placed on her finger two weeks previously, winked, catching a beam of light thrown by the heavy candelabras hanging from the oak beams. They looked at it, then smiled at each other; a private moment in the tumult. The music swirled around them, and Adelaide wrapped her arms around his neck. Drawing him closer. Bringing him into reach of her scent and warmth.

'Are you having fun, darling?' Adelaide had to shout to make herself heard above the racket.

'Very much,' Kit replied.

Adelaide pulled back slightly and rolled her eyes. 'Are you lying, darling?'

Kit had to remind himself that he and Adelaide had known each other all their lives and were the closest of all the children in their generation. It was exceedingly rare for him to get anything past her.

'I'm only lying a little.' He gave her a sheepish grin.

If he'd been asked his opinion (which, he was learning, was subtly different to being *consulted* on matters when it came to being an engaged man) Kit would have said a quiet lunch with Adelaide and their respective parents and siblings would have sufficed to celebrate the engagement that had been on the cards pretty much since they had been born. However, it had been too many years since Meadwell Hall had seen so many guests and so much decadence, and Kit's parents, Charles and Ellen, had declared it the ideal occasion to open up the house again.

Adelaide seemed to read Kit's thoughts, as she so often did.

'We both know this party is to celebrate the peace as much as anything else.'

'I know.' It was never far from Kit's mind that while he had returned home, many of the men who had enlisted alongside him, had not. Icy fingers tore at his heart and belly, ripping them with grief. What right did he have to grudge their bereaved mothers and widows the opportunity for an evening of pleasure? Didn't he himself want a respite from the constant heartache that he couldn't even admit to?

'I just feel like a zoo exhibit. "Come and see the war hero returned home". I can feel everyone who has lost someone watching me and wondering why it was their son or brother, not me, who didn't return.'

Adelaide's embrace tightened. 'Do you blame them? If you hadn't come back, I'd have been feeling exactly the same.'

The song ended and another began. A familiar tune that had been popular throughout the war. He'd performed a bad tango to it in a dreadful regimental theatre revue, a mile or two outside Vimy, with a Canadian gunner named Andrew. Later, they'd met in the gloom behind the makeshift stage. Kit closed his eyes, lost in memories of Andrew's arms around his neck, the taste of cheap scotch on their lips.

"Don't suppose you've got a spare box of Lucifers? I dropped mine in the mud!"

He stumbled, fingers gripping tightly on Adelaide's shoulder.

She squeezed his hand. 'It's hard for you isn't it.'

'It is,' he admitted. But not for the reasons she would assume. How could he possibly explain that hidden, unlawful side of his nature. That he desired men in the same way as he wanted women was something he could never speak of, least of all to Adelaide.

'After this dance I'll go ask Father to do all the toasts and after that people can go on their way,' she said.

A feeling of affection swept through him.

'You don't have to do that if you're enjoying dancing,' he said. 'I'd better get used to making myself a presence in the area. I'm going to be Lord of the Manor eventually so I might as well start practising now.'

'I really don't mind,' Adelaide said, smiling at him. 'We can slip off into the gardens with a bottle of champagne. Just us two, or maybe Ollie and the Youngers if I'm still feeling tolerant by that point.'

Kit had to smile. The Youngers (as opposed to the Elders, who were their parents) was their childhood name for Kit's sister, Charlotte, and Oliver's sister, Millicent. Even though Adelaide was the same age as the two other girls – two years younger than Kit – she had always considered herself a contemporary (and equal) to Kit and Oliver.

'If you two are going to just talk, you should move to the edge of the floor! You're getting in the way of those of us who want to dance.'

The speaker was Millicent Vane, Oliver's sister. She and Reverend Keeth, the vicar of St Mary and the Holy Cross, appeared to be dancing a waltz despite the music being a foxtrot. Kit and Adelaide murmured half-hearted apologies and Millicent and the vicar moved off in the other direction.

'You would think that spending two years nursing would have given Cousin Millie a little compassion, but she's as sharp as ever,' Adelaide muttered, eying the other woman through narrowed eyes. 'That's probably why she can't find a partner her own age to dance with. I'm definitely not including her in the secret champagne drinker's confederation.'

'That's a little unfair. It isn't as if there are a bucket-load of young men to choose from,' Kit pointed out. 'Besides, Reverend Keeth is an old friend of the family and he deserves the chance to dance, too. Talking of partners, who were you dancing with before me? A tall gentleman I didn't recognise. He was wearing a purple silk cravat.'

'Lilacs,' Adelaide said slowly. 'He told me such sad stories. Something about lilacs and planting a seed to bloom later.'

Her eyes glazed, as if she was overcome with grief or pity for whatever he had told her. The man was standing at the edge of the dance floor close by one of the alcoves. His arms were folded across his chest and one hand was raised to support his chin. He was alone and gave Kit the impression of a cat deciding which of a nest of fledglings to pounce upon.

'There he is,' Kit said, manoeuvring Adelaide around.

'Oh yes, 'Adelaide said. Her cheeks reddened. 'He's very distinctive.'

'What do you know about him?'

'I don't really remember.' Adelaide blinked and an expression of unease rippled over her face. 'I think I forgot to listen.'

Kit and the stranger made eye contact, and a shiver danced lightly down Kit's spine. It was completely understandable that she'd find the man attractive (Kit did too if he was being honest with himself), but she didn't need to fib about it.

'Perhaps you should lay off the champagne,' he suggested lightly.

'Nonsense!' Adelaide lifted her chin and gave him a determined look. 'You know I can hold my drink and I won't be too tired in the morning. When I worked in the convalescent hospital, they used to give me the night shift especially, as I'm so good at staying up late and still rising early. Do you know, I never once let my alarm clock ring more than three times before I stopped it. It was a point of honour.'

'Lucky you,' Kit said, giving her a grin. 'I'd happily lie in bed until nine if I had the chance. Every day I was in France, I'd dream of the day I could do just that.'

'Well, now you're home, you can do as you please,' Adelaide said. She tilted her head to one side, looking up at him boldly. 'After the wedding, we'll have to work out a timetable of sorts to make sure we have some hours when we're both awake.'

Kit's stomach scurried. They hadn't discussed matrimonial sleeping arrangements and he wondered whether Adelaide would favour twin beds or the rather old-fashioned double. He assumed she was a virgin, but these days, when women had had so many interesting opportunities during war, she might well not be. He'd almost lost his virginity to a buxom Dutch nurse with whom he'd had a brief romance in 1917, but before they could consummate it, orders had sent them separate ways.

They reached the edge of the dance floor, close to where Oliver stood, just as the song ended.

'Wait with Ollie. I'll go and speak to Father,' Adelaide instructed Kit, before dashing off towards the far end of the room where the Elders were gathered.

'You were right,' Oliver said, handing Kit the glass, which he'd refilled in Kit's absence.

'Right about what?'

'That you're a godawfully bad dancer.' Oliver laughed. 'The only couple worse were Millicent and the vicar, and he's got the excuse of an arthritic knee. Are you sure they didn't miss a piece of shrapnel stuck in your foot?'

A chill ran down Kit's back. The explosion that had taken him out of action had left his legs mercifully uninjured. All the damage had been done to his face. The visible damage, that was. He felt his arm jerk, fingers instinctively reaching for his cheek.

'Oh lord, I'm sorry,' Oliver gasped, mouth dropping open in dismay. 'I'm making a complete ass of myself this evening.'

Kit swallowed. 'Let's go face the audience.'

They wandered down the hall to join Adelaide and the Elders. Adelaide's mother, Sarah, and Kit's mother, Ellen, were efficiently organising the staff who stood with trays bearing champagne flutes. Their fathers were discussing the toasts they were about to give, and their grandfather, Christopher Price, ancient in his wheeled bath chair, was tolerating his wife, Sybil, who was fussing with his bow tie. Kit put the uncomfortable exchange with his cousin to the back of his mind as he greeted them all.

He met his father's eye and nodded. Charles tapped the

small gong which had stood at the end of the hall for centuries. Silence descended across the gathering in a wave, spreading out from those closest to those at the back until there was silence.

'My dear friends, I'm delighted so many of you could be here to celebrate the engagement of Kit and my dear niece, Adelaide. Almost as much as I am glad that that branch of the family will be returning to the correct part of Yorkshire.' Charles paused for the inevitable laughter.

Richard Wyndham had returned to his native Halifax taking Sarah Price with him. Adelaide had been adopted there, but the Wyndhams had spent every summer at Meadwell Hall.

Kit smiled into the gathering crowd. It was good to see faces he recognised: immediate and extended family, neighbours in whose gardens he had played, the doctor who had nursed him through childhood illnesses, women who furnished the church with flowers, the nursing mothers with soups and the households with gossip.

There were strangers, too; men and women who had arrived between his departure and return. He really should make an effort to introduce himself to them. Some faces that should have been there weren't: the men Kit had known since childhood, whose bodies were now mouldering in French cemeteries and whose absence made his heart ache to bursting point.

Uncle Richard gave a speech along the same lines as Charles: families creating stronger bonds, the love between the cousins, et cetera.

He felt Adelaide slip her hand into his and he gave it a reassuring squeeze. Her lips were fixed into a wide smile. The marriage had always been inevitable and no one making a toast was crass enough to mention the huge dowry or the vaster sum Adelaide would inherit eventually. Charles had inherited the estate. Sarah's wealth through marriage to Richard would provide the money it needed to keep going. Kit considered himself lucky that it wasn't Millicent's father who had made the fortune.

After the applause died away, Christopher Price motioned for Kit and Adelaide to help him from his wheeled chair. Despite being eighty, he still stood tall, eyes piercingly blue and clear. He gazed fondly at his grandchildren then faced the guests and spoke in his rasping voice.

'Reverend Keeth, I intend to live long enough to witness this marriage being sanctified in holy matrimony at St Mary and the Holy Cross, so I suggest you start considering appropriate hymns once you have sobered up tomorrow.'

From the timbre of his voice, a listener might assume Christopher was vexatious or short-tempered but as a matter of fact he had a wicked sense of fun and had taught the male grandchildren some of the dirtiest limericks Kit had ever heard. There was good-humoured laughter, not least from the vicar himself.

The servants had been moving through the guests, distributing champagne during the speeches.

'Three cheers for Kit and Adelaide!' Christopher announced, raising his flute.

'And good luck to them both!' shouted Kit's younger brother Alfred, which caused a burst of laughter.

As he raised his glass in acknowledgement, Kit scanned the crowd again. His eye fell on Adelaide's mysterious dancing partner. His arms were crossed and his glass was still full. He had been staring into the bubbles that rose and fell in the pale liquid, but now he raised his head and looked directly at Kit with eyes that pierced him with cold. Remembering the way the stranger had danced with, then watched Adelaide, Kit wondered just how much he might need Alfred's blessing of luck.

Chapter Two

After the toasts, the floor was commandeered by the older generation who demanded waltzes. Kit and Adelaide moved through the room talking to guests eager to offer their congratulations.

'Odd isn't it,' Kit remarked to his future bride as they left the doctor and her elderly sister and headed towards Oliver and his mother. 'Nearly everyone here has already congratulated us, but they're compelled to do it again now in something like an official capacity. It's as if the engagement wasn't official until the Elders had done the speeches.'

'Rituals are important. They consecrate the ordinary and elevate it into something with higher meaning,' Adelaide murmured, stepping forward to hug Aunt Josephine Vane.

Kit stared at her in astonishment. The words sounded like they came from someone entirely different. She saw his bewilderment and gave him an airy smile.

'It'll be good practise for the wedding breakfast.'

Kit grimaced, anticipating another event where he would be the centre of attention.

'Can't we just elope to Gretna and do things on the quiet?' he murmured.

'Scotland!' Adelaide gave him a horrified look. 'If we elope anywhere, let it be somewhere hot and glamorous. The French Riviera or the Italian Lakes. I need to be somewhere dazzling again.'

She tossed her head back, the teardrop gems in her ears swaying back and forth. She looked far too glamorous for the antiquated hall, with its faded tapestries and portraits of long-dead ancestors. When she'd adopted Adelaide, Aunt Sarah had wanted an accessory or travelling companion as much as she'd wanted a daughter. From childhood, Adelaide had spent her time visiting fashionable spa towns and travelling down to London with her mother, attending theatres, galleries and restaurants.

Even before the war had left him averse to crowded places, Kit had been happier walking or riding across the Yorkshire Moors or absorbed in a book. How would Adelaide adapt to the quiet life they would inevitably end up living, on an estate equidistant between two market towns with barely anything to entertain them? A little worm of doubt began to wriggle in his lower belly. The whole marriage might be a dreadful mistake.

'I'll go and find us a bottle of champagne and we can head outside,' he said, before the worm bred and he became incapable of thinking clearly.

Adelaide was already waving at a fashionably dressed couple that Kit didn't recognise. He watched her sashay away, effortlessly picking her way through the dancers to reach them, then headed back to where the drinks were being served. Adelaide's earlier mysterious dance partner was now gracefully waltzing with a short, slight woman in a moss-green gown with a purple ribbon in her hair. The man caught Kit's eye and inclined his head an almost indiscernible degree. Kit nodded back before the couple were swept off into the melee of dancers. His partner gave Kit an initial haughty look, but followed it with a smile of such gentleness that he was unable to take offence.

His grandparents were lingering by the long oak table where the Meadwell staff were handing out refreshments. Sybil Price was on her second flute of champagne, while Christopher was nursing a large whisky in his claw-like hands. A couple of Adelaide's young cousins on her father's side were being ushered off to the nursery in the company of a rather frazzled looking governess. Kit checked his watch. It was almost nine. Far too early for him to turn in.

Sybil gazed after them fondly.

'It's lovely that the nursery wing is occupied again.' She gave him a mischievous look. 'Of course, within a year or two I expect it will be filled with the fond cries of babes in arms who'll occupy it more permanently.'

She spoke in such a convoluted way that it took Kit a couple of minutes to work out what she meant.

'Oh, you mean mine?' he said.

'Of course, dear.' She patted his arm. 'Oh, I know Adelaide pretends to be a modern young thing, with all this dancing and smoking and that new-fangled way of dressing her hair, but I firmly believe that a woman is only truly happy when she is nursing a babe or two. I know I was. Do you think you'll want three or four?'

Kit was saved from admitting that at the moment he had no plans for even one babe in arms, by Adelaide's arrival, accompanied by Sybil's sister, Great-aunt Merelda.

'Three or four what?' Adelaide asked, sweeping towards them. 'If you mean cocktails, then yes, please, the more the better, don't you think, Merelda.'

The old woman gave a high-pitched giggle then covered her mouth and glanced around with mischievous eyes. She let go of Adelaide's arm and drifted over to the table.

'Children, dear,' Sybil said. 'We were discussing how nice it will be to have the nursery filled with Prices again.'

'Were you indeed?' Adelaide arched her eyebrow at Kit.

'Not exactly,' he said hastily, 'And I was about to tell Grandmother that we are in no hurry.'

'Absolutely right,' Adelaide said, clapping her hands. 'Babies can wait. We have lots to think about, such as how we're going to improve Meadwell, and I can't be swelling to the size of a zeppelin while I'm trying to organise plumbers and decorators. Every bathroom in the house will have hot running water if I have anything to do with it.'

'I had a baby once, you know.'

Great-aunt Merelda had spoken. She tipped her head to the side and her bright hazel eyes glinted like a bird's. A robin or a blue tit, or something equally small. Great-aunt Merelda lived in the grounds of Meadwell Hall. She had never married and was described by kind people as extremely eccentric. Kit's mother described her as being 'away with the fairies' or 'slightly touched'. She dressed in the clothes of her youth, when she had presumably been a great beauty. Even at the age of sixty, Kit could see the traces of a beautiful woman etched on the paper-thin skin and the white hair, which she wore in thick curls down her back.

'Merelda, dear, you never had a baby,' Sybil said, taking her sister's hand and smoothly removing the bright green cocktail she had acquired. 'You were ill, but it was only a fever from being caught in that dreadful rainstorm.'

'I'm sure you would have made a wonderful mother, Great-aunt Merelda,' Adelaide said. 'I remember how you used to sing to me and play hide-and-seek in the maze whenever I visited as a child. Do you remember, Kit?'

'Of course. We used to make marzipan flowers and leave them on the stepping stones near the bridge. They were always gone by morning, and you told us the fairies had taken them.' He grinned at the long-forgotten throb of childhood disappointment. 'It took me years to realise it was probably hedgehogs or foxes.'

Merelda smiled wistfully. 'Everyone liked the songs. They promised me I'd be able to charm the birds from the trees but the birds never came. The guns scared them all away. Only the crows liked it when I danced.'

She held out her skirts. Kit and Adelaide exchanged a glance. Merelda had a club foot and had walked with a stick since the age of fifteen as a result of the illness Sybil had referred to. Dance partners had probably been few and far between.

'Merelda, would you like me to fetch you a glass of punch?' Kit offered. 'There's lots left over now the children have gone to bed.'

She fixed him with a hostile stare. 'I don't want the stuff the children are drinking, young man. I'll have the one with gin in it. Walk with me.'

She held her arm out and Kit obliged by slipping his through it. Looking over his shoulder, Kit saw Adelaide helping herself to a bottle of champagne. 'I'll go and find Oliver,' she mouthed to him.

Kit nodded.

'I did have a baby,' Merelda repeated as he escorted her to a chair. 'Only they took it back and left a stone instead. One day I shall have words with the gentleman.'

Kit poured her the punch without gin. She was behaving very strangely tonight. He wondered where her companion, Enid, was. He left Merelda with her punch, humming along with the music and went in search of Enid but couldn't find her, and when he returned to the chair, Merelda had gone. Feeling his obligation was behind him, Kit walked outside.

The night was warmer than usual for early May. The Long Hall had been filled with myriad colognes and perfumes and the air smelled of night-scented stock, mingling with freshly mown lawns. He took a deep breath and walked halfway to the maze before he looked back at the house that would one day be his. His heart swelled at the sight of the structure cast into shadows beneath the waxing moon. The damage to his right eye; the result of concussion, meant that the silhouette was slightly blurred at the edges, giving it a green tinge. He doubted he'd ever become accustomed to seeing people and objects with a touch of double vision and he blinked, trying to resolve the aura into one outline.

'It's an odd-looking house isn't it.'

Kit jumped in surprise. He'd thought he was alone. The voice was deep and husky and in his mind he imagined someone of his parents' age, but his eyes settled on a young woman leaning against one of the statues that lined the long path. The statue was of a woman carrying an urn on her shoulder. Her Greek chiton fell in carved drapes to the plinth and the live woman was leaning in such a manner that she appeared to be a continuation of the sculpture. Her hair was sandy blonde and her dress was pale green, which was why Kit almost hadn't seen her in the shadows.

He scowled, not liking the thought he was being spied upon, before allowing his more reasonable side to admit that she must have been there before he had arrived and he had simply failed to notice her.

'It is rather odd,' he admitted, turning to look back at the building.

Meadwell Hall had started life in late Tudor times as a simple, rectangular building and home to a wool merchant. In the late sixteenth century, it was extended by Robart Tessincham, an influential businessman who had grown tired of waiting to be given a title. Since then, it had been passed down through generations of the same family, each adding their own touch of splendour and elegance to the structure in accordance with current taste, or developments in engineering or technology. The result was an odd amalgam of architectural styles, from Gothic to Georgian.

'You're Kit and it's going to be yours one day,' the woman said, walking to his side. He recognised her then as the waltz partner of the enigmatic man. She sounded as if she might be

Scottish, or perhaps from Northumbria. 'But you aren't happy about it.'

She sounded Irish now. Kit looked properly at her, surprised and unnerved at how she had gleaned the information. It couldn't be from reading his expression, because the shadows were deepening, and besides, she was standing at the side of his face that wasn't capable of showing much expression. He had a horrible thought that his reticence might be common knowledge and the subject of gossip.

'It's a lot of responsibility,' he admitted grudgingly, in what he considered to be a grave understatement. Meadwell Hall had been an integral part of the local landscape and economy for centuries, and if the Price and Arton-Price families had their way, it would remain so for generations to come. The prospect of taking the reins from his father weighed heavily on Kit's shoulders. At least with Adelaide by his side, it might stand a chance of surviving for the next decade or two.

'I would like to congratulate you on your engagement.'

She looked downcast. Was she yet another poor soul who had lost a husband or lover in the war? Kit's heart throbbed.

'Is there anything I can do to help you?' he asked.

She smiled. 'An offer so ill-defined can be a dangerous thing!'

'I just meant… I don't know what I mean really,' Kit said.

She pursed her lips. 'My homeland isn't free, and I need it to be. Will you help me?'

'I meant more along the lines of if you need me to fetch a friend, or if you want a drink of water.'

'I think my friend is busy,' she said, 'but I appreciate your kindness. A heart as good as yours gives me hope.'

'I'd better go, I'm meeting someone,' Kit said, feeling her words were slightly excessive. 'You should probably go back inside the hall. These gardens are private, after all.'

She tilted her head to one side and gave him a serene smile. 'We've been invited.'

'Yes of course you have,' Kit replied. 'Who asked you, by the way? I'm afraid I don't know who half the people here are. I didn't have much say on the guest list.'

She nodded sagely. 'Yours is not that role. The consort is there to look pretty.'

Whoever the woman was, she wasn't close to the family if she thought Adelaide was the daughter of the house he was marrying into.

'I'm not the consort,' he said, leaving unsaid the fact that he could never be described as pretty. 'Well, it's been nice talking to you, but I have to go. I'm sure I shall meet you again,' he said.

'Yes. Soon.' She looked up at him. 'May I have your permission to go down to the water for a minute? The moon looks especially beautiful at this time of year.'

'Of course. Though it's getting rather dark so watch where you put your feet. The edge is a bit crumbly when you go along from the bridge and the river is faster than it looks.'

He walked off and by the time he looked back again she had vanished. He shoved his hands in his pockets and strolled towards the maze, hoping Oliver and Adelaide had left him something to drink.

The maze had been planted at some point in the early days of the house, though no one was quite sure which ancestor had been responsible. It was hardly challenging, given that the hedges were only six feet high but when they had been too small to peer over the top, Kit and the other children had spent hours at a time squealing with mock (and sometimes genuine) fear at being unable to find the centre.

Now Kit was the same height as the laurels and yews that formed the walls, and if he were to raise himself onto his toes he would be able to peer over the top. Not that he needed to, given that he had a perfect memory of the route through the winding pathways that curved, spiralled and twisted around themselves. He could have walked to the heart whilst wearing a blindfold and not missed a turn.

At the centre was a grove containing a small pergola with five slender columns, up which roses had been trained to climb. Inside the structure was a low bench and as he walked into the gravelled area of the heart, Kit saw that Adelaide was not alone. Her companion was the gentleman she had been dancing with earlier. Kit's skin fluttered with annoyance. Dancing with a stranger was one thing, but inviting him to join the champagne party was entirely another. Kit began to whistle the tune of 'The British Grenadiers' as he stuck his hands back into his pockets and strolled into the clearing, determined not to show his irritation.

The occupants of the bench both turned, and Kit stopped whistling. The woman was Great-aunt Merelda. There was a resemblance between her and Adelaide in terms of height and build, but it was probably the hair that had deceived him. Adelaide was wearing hers so that it cascaded down her back in the same way that Merelda's did every day. Adelaide's hair was pale blonde and Merelda's was white, so in the moonlight the shade appeared the same.

'And here, of course, is my great-nephew,' Merelda said in her sing-song voice.

'I'm sorry, did I interrupt something?' Kit asked.

'We were discussing the old times,' said Merelda.

'The old times and the old ways,' the stranger said. His eyes settled on Kit as he spoke. They were deep pools of a green that was extremely rare. Most people who claimed to have green eyes had a sort of brownish, mossy colour, but these were quite startlingly green with no trace of hazel in them.

He was exceedingly handsome, with an angular chin, sharp cheekbones and black, glossy hair, which was slightly longer than was fashionable but framed his face in a way that meant Kit couldn't imagine him with any other cut. Why a man who looked barely thirty was sitting alone with a woman of Merelda's age was highly suspicious. She wasn't wealthy, so if he was hoping to take advantage, he had picked the wrong woman.

'Old ways of what?' Kit asked, strolling a little closer and trying to keep the misgivings out of his voice.

'The old ways of being. The old ways of doing,' answered the man, bestowing a wide smile on Kit that positively brimmed with charm. His silhouette glimmered but when Kit blinked, it resolved itself.

It wasn't even close to an answer.

'We haven't been introduced,' Kit said curtly.

The man rose to his feet, demonstrating the same smooth movements he had when he had been dancing.

'Isn't the customary phrase "I don't believe we have been introduced"?'

His voice was very soft and deep. There was a touch of accent to it that Kit wasn't able to place.

'In this case, I know we haven't.'

The stranger laughed. 'I appreciate your directness. You are a truth teller, I see.'

Kit blanched. Adelaide had called him a poor liar already that evening and now someone else was making claims about his relationship with the truth. It felt rather odd to have his character remarked on, so to hide his feelings of unease, he held out a hand.

'Christopher Arton-Price.'

'Yes. Kit, I believe.'

'To my friends,' Kit answered, giving a not-quite smile that he hoped suggested he didn't count this man as one of them.

The stranger's eyes gleamed as if he understood perfectly. He took Kit's outstretched hand in one that was very warm. It came as something of a surprise to Kit who had, for some reason he couldn't explain, expected it to be ice cold.

'Silas Wilde.'

It was a very English-sounding name and contrasted with his distinct accent. Kit looked at him with more interest. In his time in France and Belgium he had encountered men from the lowland countries as well as a few from eastern Europe, and of course Britain was still teaming with displaced persons whose homes had been destroyed. It would have been too rude to ask who had invited him and where he was from in the same breath, so he just smiled.

'I saw you dancing with my fiancée,' he remarked. 'You're exceedingly good.'

'Yes, I hope you didn't mind me stealing her away.' Mr Wilde gave a vulpine smile.

'Not at all. It was a pleasure to watch you dancing. I'm afraid I have two left feet myself.'

Mr Wilde glanced down as if expecting to see evidence of such a claim, adding to Kit's conviction that English might not be his first language.

'I did dance once,' Merelda said with such longing in her voice that Kit's heart ached.

'I'll ask you to dance at the next opportunity, Merelda, and damn anyone who might laugh at the pair of us,' he said.

'A gallant offer.' Mr Wilde raised his eyebrows at Kit, then nodded with apparent satisfaction.

Merelda rapped her cane on the floor sharply.

'Mr Wilde, I am growing tired and we should leave Kit to wait for Adelaide, shouldn't we. Will you escort me back to my house?' she said firmly, making it clear that refusal would be looked upon most unfavourably.

'Oh yes, the young lovers.' Mr Wilde smiled at Kit. 'We shall leave you to your assignation. Thank you again for giving your blessing to my dancing with Miss Wyndham. You must tell me if you have any objections to me stealing her away in the future.'

'Not at all,' Kit said, feeling it was the only polite response.

Merelda started to speak but was interrupted by a cough. Kit darted forward but Mr Wilde had already struck her between the shoulder blades.

'Miss Tersingham, you have a toad on your tongue it appears,' he said with concern.

He'd got the expression wrong – another suggestion that he

was from foreign parts – but it did indeed sound like the elderly woman was croaking rather than choking. Her watery eyes gazed at Kit and she looked as if she was still trying to speak. Mr Wilde reached out a hand and plucked a white rose from one of the columns.

'I say, some of those bushes are older than I am,' Kit exclaimed, eyeing the partially closed bloom.

'But not older than I am,' Wilde said, holding the flower to Merelda's nose. 'Breathe deeply, Miss Tersingham, and the toad will return to sleep.'

Merelda did as instructed. Against Kit's expectation, but to his relief, her wheezing began to fade.

'I believe fair Adelaide is approaching,' Mr Wilde said, tilting his head. 'Come along, Miss Tersingham. A little walk will help you recover fully.'

The maze had a trick exit that led straight out from the left-hand corner of the grove. From most angles it looked like an unbroken hedge, but on approaching it obliquely, the walker would see it was in fact two overlapping hedges, with a gap that was only visible at the correct angle. Watching visitors puzzle over how to leave without returning the same way had been one of the things Kit had most enjoyed growing up here. He expected Mr Wilde to look around in confusion, but he simply guided Merelda gently, one arm under her elbow, and they left that way as if he knew exactly where he was going.

Chapter Three

No sooner had Merelda and Mr Wilde exited the grove than Adelaide, with the timing of an actress following her cue, walked into it through the archway. She was carrying a bottle of champagne in one hand and clutching her silk shawl around her shoulders with the other. She swept towards Kit.

'Kit, darling, there you are. I'm sorry I took so long getting here. Do you know, I actually took the wrong turning and went right instead of left almost as soon as I came in. I don't know what's wrong with me.'

'Never mind,' he said, taking the bottle of champagne that she waved in his direction. 'You're here now. Where's Oliver?'

'He was busy being quizzed by some old dear about her pregnant goat, so I didn't bother asking him. Millicent spotted the bottle, but I pretended I couldn't see her. I couldn't find your brother or sister, so I came by myself. It will be nice to spend some time together alone, won't it. We can catch up properly now.'

He'd been back in Yorkshire for nine weeks but had only

seen Adelaide twice before the engagement party. They were long overdue some time in each other's company. The air was strongly scented with roses, and some of the flowers winding up the pergola were fully open. It was unusual for them to be so awake at this time of night. Kit inhaled deeply, as a pigeon flew over and settled on the top of the hedge, staring down at him.

He sat down on the bench, beckoning Adelaide to join him and drummed his fingers on the edge.

'Do you find it odd to think that one day this place will be ours?'

Adelaide sat beside him and kicked off her shoes. Her toenails were varnished bright red. As she flexed her feet, they looked like beetles trying to burrow into the gravel.

'I suppose it's a little odd, but we've always known it was going to happen. It could be decades in any case until you inherit it properly. Not that we want that to happen too soon,' she added.

'No of course not,' Kit agreed. 'Though Father has told me that when he is sixty he will hand over all the responsibilities to me and go off to play golf in Scotland for six months of the year. I'm not sure he has shared that plan with Mother, however, so we'll have to see.'

Adelaide made a non-committal noise.

They sat silently for a few minutes. Kit had discovered some silences were amicable, where the people present were comfortable enough in each other's company not to need to speak. Others were more awkward in nature, brought about by having nothing much to say. He was aware that it was the second type that they were now observing.

Adelaide looked as if she was feeling it too from the way she was twisting her engagement ring back and forth around her finger.

'I was talking to Merelda and Mr Wilde before you got here,' Kit remarked.

'Mr Wilde? Who is that?'

'The gentleman you were dancing with.'

Adelaide's eyes widened. 'Do you know, I had completely forgotten his name! I'm going to be such a terrible hostess when we are married. I shall have to give all our guests little buttons with their initials on whenever we do a Saturday to Monday party.'

'You won't be a terrible hostess,' Kit said loyally. 'You'll be perfect.'

'We'll have hundreds of parties, so I'll get lots of practice,' Adelaide said.

She leaned forward and kissed him softly on the cheek. Not the cheek with the puckered scars, that would involve a level of courage that he'd expect from no one.

'That's for being so brave my love,' she whispered before leaning back and taking a deep breath. 'I'm so very proud of you, Kit, you deserve all the honours that comes your way for what you have done for our country.'

He nodded at her words, all the while knowing how greatly he was undeserving of them, no matter how much Adelaide might think otherwise.

Shells. Guns. Screams. Pleading.

He blinked rapidly in an attempt to rid himself of the ghosts that flashed before his eyes.

He was such a hypocrite. Such a damned, undeserving fraud.

He pulled his hand away from Adelaide's and reached for the champagne.

'Let's have a drink,' he said, twisting the cork and letting it shoot off into the air.

There was a fluttering of wings and he looked up to see the pigeon flying off. The poor thing must have been startled by the cork. Adelaide hadn't brought glasses, so he drank from the bottle then held it out to her. But she was sitting on her hands, gazing at him solemnly.

'What's wrong?' he asked.

'The way you change the subject. At some point we'll have to talk properly about our experiences in the war,' she said. 'Tell me what it was like for you.'

Kit drew in a juddering breath as his stomach clenched. *Bursting shells. Screaming voices. Flashes of artillery in the blackness.*

'You've read the newspapers I'm sure you know what happened. You must have heard what happened to the men who came back, too. Raving and weeping. Insensible with shellshock.'

'I know. I saw them when I nursed,' Adelaide snapped.

Kit half-lifted his hand to his face then forced it down. 'Then what more do you need to know?'

'I need to know what it did to *you*,' she whispered. 'Because we're going to be married and we shouldn't have secrets.'

Kit slumped against the back of the bench. She really wouldn't want to know his secrets. 'Maybe in a couple of years I'll be able to face talking about it, but it's too soon now.'

'I understand,' Adelaide said quietly. 'That is, I don't because I can't imagine. You're right. Nursing was an adventure. Taking responsibility. Having freedom. It sounds dreadful to say it, but my life expanded and I did things I never believed I was capable of. Some of the men I nursed spoke of friends in the trenches, and fun in between the battles. There were good times for me. Were there no good times for you, at all?'

A boyish grin beneath a barely there moustache. "Don't suppose you've got a box of Lucifers?"

Kit dropped his head. Already feeling tense, his throat filled with a bitter taste that the bubbles from the champagne did nothing to help. 'There were. But all my friends are gone. Everyone I loved over there died.'

'I'm sorry,' Adelaide said. She leaned against him, her shoulder pressing up against his. 'You'll make new friends and of course I'll be able to introduce you to new faces at the wedding and afterwards. All my friends will be able to visit us, and I do need to stay in touch with them.'

There was pain in her voice that Kit had never heard before. It occurred to him that although the marriage would be a bit awkward for him, it would be harder for her; she would need to uproot herself from everyone and everything she knew.

Meadwell Hall had been a feature of Adelaide's life since birth and Kit was so used to her coming and going that it had never occurred to him it had never actually been her home. The villagers and neighbours were acquaintances rather than friends, and the leisurely pace of village life was no substitute for a thriving town and the frequent trips to the capital she took. It wasn't the same as knowing his friends were dead, but he could see how, in a slightly clumsy way, she was trying to cheer him up, and he was grateful.

'We can have as many parties as you like,' he said.

'And of course we can go down to London very often,' Adelaide said, reviving slightly.

'Well perhaps not *both* of us so often,' Kit said hesitantly. 'You know I am rather a country mouse. The local players doing a spot of Gilbert and Sullivan is enough culture for me.'

Adelaide pouted then laughed. 'I don't imagine you'll want to come to fashion shows, but you can go sit in the reading rooms at the British Library or go to the museums or galleries, and then we can spend the evening doing exciting things.'

Kit bristled slightly at the implication that the museums and galleries that he loved weren't exciting. 'You'd probably have more fun taking Charlotte or Millicent,' he suggested.

He meant it helpfully, but she frowned at him. 'I don't want to be taking my spinster cousins around London when all my friends will be there with husbands or fiancés. Do you know, in some cultures when a husband dies the widow is buried alive with him, or thrown onto his funeral pyre.'

'I have heard of such a thing,' Kit said.

'Well, I don't intend to be buried alive before you're even dead! Even the country mouse visited the city.'

'I haven't said that I won't,' Kit snapped. 'Just not as frequently as you'll want to. I'm going to be busy running the estate, and I'm hoping to continue some of my studies in my spare time, too. I want to learn about advances in biology for cultivating new crops and perhaps strengthen the breeding pedigree of the deer. Besides trips to London will cost an awful lot.'

Adelaide tossed her head. 'Lucky we're going to have my money then, isn't it!'

It was the first time she'd ever openly referred to her wealth. Kit drew a sharp breath.

'Addie!'

Adelaide gathered her shawl around her shoulders defensively, fingers tightening in the silk. 'Well, it's true, isn't it. We can dress it up as much as we like, but even though your branch of the family tree owns the orchard, my branch has got much more fruit.'

'That's a dreadful metaphor,' Kit retorted.

She snorted and reached for the champagne bottle that Kit was still holding, tugging it from his hand. She lifted it to her lips, swigging quite a lot of it in one go.

'Steady on,' Kit cautioned.

She lowered the bottle and gave him a contemptuous look. 'Yes, far be it from me to want to have some fun,' she sneered, emphasising the final word heavily. 'I'm going to go back to the house. There will still be some dancing. Are you coming?'

'Not yet.'

'Then I'll have to find a different partner!'

She tossed her head and stalked off. Kit leaned back and closed his eyes. The argument had erupted from nowhere and he felt quite in shock. Remembering Adelaide's temper tantrums in childhood, he suspected the best thing he could do now was give her some space.

He gave it ten minutes, then went back through the

ornamental gardens. Although much of the land belonging to Meadwell had been given over for wartime food production, the grounds immediately surrounding the house were well kept and beautifully landscaped with hedgerows, flower beds, fountains and statues. He walked past three statues before something caught his attention and he spun around.

Someone was standing in the shadow of a statue – this one was a youth dressed in an indecently short tunic that showed off the muscles in his well-formed thighs, while he reached over his shoulder for an arrow with a knowing look on his stone face. Kit's first thought was that the person was male but then Mr Wilde's companion stepped towards him and he realised he'd been mistaken.

'Why are you still lurking around in the garden?' Kit asked.

'I saw your fiancée return but you weren't with her.'

'And what is that to you?' Kit snapped, wondering what Adelaide's expression had been like. It was bad enough that they'd rowed, without a complete stranger knowing of it, especially when the woman was connected to Silas Wilde.

She pouted. 'It's nothing to me. I just saw her. She didn't see me. In answer to your first question, I wanted to be quiet for a few moments and listen to the night birds.'

She tilted her head and looked up at the sky. Kit followed her gaze. There were no birds but a dozen or so stars had emerged from behind the clouds while he'd been in the maze. He took a deep breath and smelled mimosa, the scent momentarily transporting him back to a childhood summer in Nice.

Her eyes glinted. 'Do you favour the youth or the woman?'

Fire coursed through Kit's veins, heating his cheeks. Had someone been spreading gossip, or was this woman particularly perceptive? 'I'm not sure what you mean.'

She gestured around. 'The statues. I was beside a woman before. Now I'm standing beside a man. I wondered which statue you preferred.'

Kit swallowed and his heart began to resume normal speed. 'I've never given it much thought. They're just garden ornaments.'

'Would you like a nut?'

The question was so unexpected that Kit assumed he must have misheard, but the woman held her hand out.

'Will you take a nut from me?' She uncurled her palm and cupped in it was a single walnut, the shell unbroken. Even if Kit had wanted to accept, walnuts were notoriously annoying to crack and he had nothing with which to do it.

'No thank you. I'm not hungry,' he answered.

'It isn't for eating,' she said, looking at him from beneath her lashes.

'What is it for then?'

She closed her palm and drew her hand back to her side. Kit could have sworn that it was already empty and glanced at the ground in case she had simply tossed the nut away but he couldn't see it.

He'd met a Welsh corporal in the trenches who could do tricks with cigarettes and empty shell casings. He'd tried to teach Kit how to make them disappear, but Kit never had the knack. He was grudgingly impressed at the woman's dexterity.

She put her hand to his chest, the movement quick and unexpected. Her fingers pressed into the soft cotton of his shirt and a blush of heat crept across his torso. He gulped.

'What do you think you are doing?'

She looked pained, then contrite.

'I'm sorry, I can be a bit over-familiar at times.'

'I'll say!' He imagined the hand twisting at an angle of ninety degrees, so the fingers were pointing downward, slowly walking their way lower, over his abdomen, down to the waistband of his trousers.

She took her hand away and stepped back. 'Sometimes when I like people, I forget that they may not like me back. Where I come from, we are a little bit more passionate in our actions.'

'And where do you come from?' Kit asked. 'I've been trying to place your accent.'

'Oh, quite far away. From a long way. I doubt you would have heard of it.'

So it did seem as if she might be a refugee from the war. Poor thing. Little wonder that she and her devilish friend were trying to charm themselves into local society.

'I'm going inside,' he said. 'Don't stay out here too long.'

He walked away, purposely not looking behind him. The party sounded still in full swing, but the thought of being in company was unbearable and he decided to return to his rooms in the Second Tower (oddly named, because as far as anyone knew there had never been a First Tower).

The tower had been added in the early seventeenth century and was accessible from the grounds as well as from inside the

Long Hall. Kit was grateful, given his uneven emotions, that Meadwell was a house of many exits and entrances, so it was easy for him to slip back inside unseen. Perhaps he should suggest that he and Adelaide took a flat in London. It couldn't be in one of the fashionable areas, because even with Adelaide's money that would be a stretch, but they could manage somewhere that they'd be able to travel into the centre on the underground. He often pondered what his parents and grandparents would do if he announced that he intended to rent a property in one of the nearby towns of Helmsley or Malton.

The subject had never arisen, because the entire family assumed that as heir to the house and estate, Kit would live at Meadwell his entire life. His father had, and his father before him, and so on, back as long as Kit was aware. It was how things were done. Younger sons were expected to enter the church or military or law, or otherwise find a respectable profession. Daughters, obviously, would marry and leave to join their husband's household but the eldest son was expected to stay at Meadwell.

The family resided in the North Wing at the other end of the Long Hall but at the age of sixteen, Kit had been shown to the second floor of the Second Tower, where the heir to the estate traditionally resided in what was known as the Buck's Apartment; a suite of rooms comprising a pair of linked bedrooms, a sitting room, bathroom and study. Kit loved the independence it gave him. He'd spent all his holidays from St Peter's School there, and had continued to do so throughout his studies at Oxford.

Naturally, he had returned after being demobbed from the

Green Howards after the war ended. Once he was married, he expected Adelaide would move in with him, and claim the study as her personal sitting room.

He set a pan of water to boil on the small spirit stove in the sitting room and walked into the bedroom to undress. As he unbuttoned his shirt, he caught a glimpse of himself in the cheval mirror and his stomach heaved at the monstrous vision that stared back.

One half of his face looked boyishly handsome, the other not only aged him but transformed him into a ghoul. He raised his left hand and his reflection did the same, fingertips running over a cheek that was mottled red and white, the skin puckered and stretched. When the bandages had first been removed and he was handed a shaving mirror, he had screamed at the sight for a full five minutes. The scarring caused by the mustard gas and shrapnel would never fade.

He took hold of the walnut frame with both hands, tilting it back on the stand. Closer, his uneven vision gave the mirror-Kit a halo of greenish purple. He blinked and the skin beneath his right eye drooped at the corner, the eyelid taking longer to return to fully open. The mirror-Kit's nails dug into the cheek, stretching and pulling it. Though Kit could see his reflection doing it, felt the pressure with his fingertips, he felt nothing on his face. There was barely any sensitivity to his skin.

He wouldn't blame Adelaide if she preferred to furnish the third-floor rooms, currently used to store junk, and live up there, rather than sleep next to him and have his ruined face be the first thing she saw as she opened her eyes. He wouldn't even blame her if she chose to live in a London flat most of the time rather than in the countryside with him.

The room became unbearably oppressive. Kit wiped his eyes harshly with the back of his arm, walked to the window, flung up the sash and leaned out, letting cool air whip around his bare torso.

The party guests were starting to leave. Cheerful voices rang out and silhouettes swung torches back and forth as neighbours made their way to the bridge. Others were leaving in motorcars, sounding discordant horns. Soon the noises died away, leaving only the distant clattering of the staff stacking bottles outside the kitchen door.

Adelaide and her family were staying below Kit, in the guest wing on the first floor of the Second Tower. The inner door opened and closed, and their voices rose in laughing whispers as they went into their rooms.

The water in the pan had boiled away almost to nothing and there wasn't enough for a cup of tea. Kit's well of tolerance for what should have been a pleasant evening had boiled dry, too. He went back into his bedroom. He left the window fully open and threw himself onto the bed without bothering to undress further. Somewhere in the distance he heard the distinctive barking of a fox, followed by howls from every dog in the area.

Kit closed his eyes and eventually fell into a fitful sleep. He had been plagued with nightmares for months but tonight the usual shrieks of pain and bursts of gunfire were replaced with foxes cracking walnuts and pigeons drinking champagne.

≈

'Walnuts and sympathy? Is that the best you could do?' Silas's voice dripped with disdain. 'A pretty boy like that and you couldn't capture him? Not even a dance? The touch of your hand on the back of his wrist to make his blood rush? An enticement to ease his sorrows in your lap?'

'He didn't dance, other than with her.'

She had touched him of course. His heart had practically left his chest when she'd laid her hand over it and he'd so clearly wanted her to touch him more intimately. It was both pathetic and endearing how prim and proper he was. That was none of Silas's business.

'He stood and watched and glowered, full of pity and anger. You saw that. His mood wasn't fit for anything else. Especially not after he argued with her.' She smiled smugly. 'But you didn't know about that, of course.'

Silas cocked an eyebrow, digesting that new information. 'A lovers' argument. Thank you for telling me.'

He narrowed his eyes. 'Were you only Valentine?'

'I think he saw me in between, though I expect he thought he had imagined it.' Valentine recalled the flash of shame that had almost exploded from Kit when she'd mentioned the statues.

'Perhaps you should try being Valentin," Silas suggested.

'Perhaps you should try for him yourself,' Valentine retorted, with a glint in her eye that contained the barest trace of rebellion. She was no longer a common doxy to be used as her master commanded.

Silas peered down his nose. 'I thought about it, but that side of him is closely buried. Very wise, too. Their kind sniff out difference and call it an atrocity. No matter. He is not necessary. She is the one I came for. I want her. I need her.' Silas smiled at a nugget of knowledge Valentine wasn't party to. He rolled his head back and growled deep in his throat. 'She captivates me. I will know no peace until I have won my lady.'

Trophies and conquests. Valentine sniffed contemptuously. Silas turned to her with a scornful look.

'You do want him, though he is of no use?'

'He's pretty,' she muttered.

'Pretty, but so consumed with self-pity that the spark of courage in him isn't hot enough to singe a feather. What good would he do you? Could he fight for us?'

She recalled the gentle smile as he offered to get her a glass of water and cautioned her against the river. Valentine bit her lip, keeping to herself the offer of help Kit had selflessly given. It would have been so easy to entwine him that it had felt unfair.

'I rather think he is done with fighting for now. He's full of grief and anger. There is strength beneath it but he resists the call.'

Silas laced his fingers, looking thoughtful. 'He is a truth-teller. He has a brain. I saw a little of it tonight when we spoke in the maze.'

'There we go, then. He thinks the world he lives in wants nothing of him, and he wants nothing of it. But given the time he could be changed.'

Silas laughed good-humouredly. 'You still have the capacity for optimism. How heartening. But time is running short, and I cannot waste it searching this world any further. We will have to make do with the resources at our disposal. I shall continue to work on my path, you on yours. He released her tonight without really understanding what he agreed to.'

He began pacing around the room. She watched him striding back and forth, flowing like water, then he paused at the window and stared in the direction of Meadwell.

'Time for bed, my child. Tomorrow we will walk the countryside, speak to whom we meet and recuperate. We will return to Meadwell on the day of the fete and see if the seeds I have sown have bloomed enough to be picked. A fateful day it will be.'

He laughed at his own pun then walked back to her and lifted her chin, fingers gripping tightly enough for her to feel the power coiled in him. His eyes flickered from violet to deepest emerald.

'You'll have to try harder at the fete if you want him.'

'If I want him.' Valentine shrugged indifferently. 'He's rather pathetic, truth be told.'

Silas rolled his eyes, obviously not fooled by her protestations. He let his clothes drop to the floorboards until he was naked. The moonlight caressed his long, lean form, lightly tanned from head to foot. She paid no attention, having seen his body enough times to be unmoved to desire. He sighed then climbed into his bed and drew the furs over himself with a rustle.

'Sleep well,' he murmured.

She threw herself back on the narrow cot and watched Silas long after he fell asleep. She had never needed more than three or four hours of it a night since she'd been a child. This was her own time, when no one could command her. The scent of fresh grass and the humming of night insects on the breeze called to her. She slipped from the cot and tiptoed to the open window and leaned out, tempted to leave the ground behind for a while. An owl hooted, answered by its mate and she drew back inside. Too dangerous to go out there when she might become easy prey. One day, if Silas's plan worked, she might be her own woman again, and then nothing and no one would keep her tethered to the form she wore.

Chapter Four

Adelaide was late to breakfast. Kit was on his second helping of scrambled eggs before she even appeared in the North Wing at the other end of the Long Hall, where the dining room was located.

She picked listlessly at a plate of kedgeree, which she usually devoured, but Kit thought it best not to mention that after their argument the night before. He shouldn't have minded too much because they'd always argued, growing up in the same way siblings and close family did. It was probably unrealistic to expect to get through a lifetime of marriage without having quarrels, so he tried his best to put it behind him.

'Tea or coffee?' he asked, wandering across to the sideboard where the breakfast dishes had been laid out. In a house with multiple generations, breakfast was a relaxed meal.

'Tea for me,' Alfred said.

'Nothing for me,' Charlotte replied. 'I'm trying a new diet, which involves foregoing all stimulants.'

'Addie?' he asked.

Adelaide yawned, open-mouthed. Her tongue curled like a cat's. 'I'm sorry. I was a hundred miles away. I think, coffee, please, and lots of creamy milk.'

He took the cup and saucer and placed it down before her.

'What happened to "I can stay up all night nursing and never miss my alarm", sleepyhead?' he asked, despite his intentions not to provoke her.

She pouted but then gave him a smile.

'I don't know. Maybe I had forgotten how strong champagne can be. It's been such a long time since we've had any after all.'

'Lucky you. Mother says I'm still too young for more than a glass,' Alfred grumbled.

'I hope you're not sickening for something,' Charlotte said. 'We were going to visit Lady Burroughs today.'

Adelaide swallowed her toast. 'Oh yes, of course. The bitch.'

Alfred snorted. His sister gave him an impatient look.

'Fred, you know we're talking about dogs. Don't be infantile.'

'What a dreadful lot I have in life. Too young for champagne, but too old to make silly jokes,' Alfred said theatrically.

Charlotte stuck her tongue out at him, proving that at twenty-four she was not too old for a bit of sibling antagonization.

'Do you think Lady Burroughs will let you stud Maxie?' Kit asked hastily in order to avoid another round of bickering.

Charlotte took a long drink of coffee before answering. 'I

think so. He's got a good pedigree and Lady B says that she is keen to develop the lineage a little.'

The wire fox terrier, Maxie (or Maximum Myles Travelled, to give him his full name) was Charlotte's pride and joy. She intended to start seriously breeding the dogs now the war was over.

'Well, I have some chemistry and arithmetic to wade through,' Alfred said gloomily. 'If I want any hope of getting into Oxford, I really need to mug up on it.'

Both subjects had come easily to Kit. He would have liked to have read them at university, possibly even become a scholar, but his father had made it very clear that given his future role as owner and manager of the estate, something more useful was appropriate. Alfred's interest in the estate and towards animal husbandry made him a far better choice for successor, but of course Charles was a traditionalist.

'Cheer up,' he said. 'As soon as the estate is mine, I'll make you manager and abdicate to live on a yacht off the coast of Devon.'

He was lying of course – to himself at least. There would be no abdication for Kit.

'I need to look over finances with Father when the fete is done with,' he said gloomily. 'Now I am back, I need to try and get a sense of what shape the estate is in after the war. We need to hire a new gamekeeper, too.'

'Not before time,' Alfred said through a mouthful of crumpet. 'I swear, last night I heard the sound of dogs howling in the park.'

'I don't think you did. I would've heard it, too. Probably

too much champagne. Oh no, you didn't get very much, being so young,' Charlotte crowed.

Kit let them bicker. It was an extra layer of worry, however. Meadwell Hall was famed for the quality of its venison, but the animals came at a hefty price. Even the loss of one fawn would have an effect on the estate's income.

'I dreamed of dogs last night.' Adelaide put down her cup and looked towards the windows. Her blue eyes were troubled, causing Kit's heart to catch.

'There, see,' Alfred said triumphantly. 'There must have been something out there, and their howling worked its way into Addie's subconscious mind. It does that, you know.'

She blinked and her eyes lost their glazed look.

'I tell you what, I was planning to test out the new gelding,' Kit said. 'I've not had the chance to get to know him, but he comes from a good stud and I think he might turn out to be good at hacking. Alfred, get your work finished, then we'll have an early lunch and ride over to invite ourselves for afternoon tea. Sophie might be there and I haven't said hello properly.'

'Oh Sophie!' Charlotte cooed, giving him a wink. 'Better watch yourself Adelaide.'

Kit blushed. The honourable Sophie Burroughs had been an early crush of his. Adelaide frowned but after the way she'd carried on with Mr Wilde the night before he didn't really care.

Alfred brightened and the plan was agreed. It was immediately thrown into disarray when there was a soft knock at the door and Enid walked in.

'Young Kit, Merelda would like you to come visit her this morning,' Enid said. Kit didn't mind the rather outdated title.

Enid had lived with Merelda since long before Kit had been born. She was a Scotswoman with copper-coloured hair that was turning grey now that she was in her late fifties but she was still extremely pretty in an ethereal sort of way.

'Of course. Is anything wrong?' he asked. He had never checked whether Mr Wilde had seen Merelda home safely after her choking fit.

Enid pursed her lips. 'I'm not sure. Best come as soon as possible. She's got one of her moods on her. Been awake since five.'

She helped herself to a piece of toast and left.

Once he'd finished breakfast, Kit strolled across the grounds to Merelda's residence. The Tersingham women were generally beauties with more intelligence than most husbands needed, and Merelda staying a spinster was surprisingly rare. She and Enid lived in a converted dovecote that suited their eccentric nature well. Merelda was tying up the trailing roses around the door when Kit approached. On seeing him, she flung down her ball of twine and put her hands on her hips.

'What were you thinking?' she demanded.

'About what?'

'Agreeing to allow that … that man to steal Adelaide away from you.'

'Do you mean Mr Wilde? It hardly matters what I said,' Kit said. 'She can choose whether or not to dance with him if she meets him again.'

'You think that was just about a dance, do you?'

Merelda's cane bashed onto the flagstones like a thunderclap. Kit often wondered why she didn't glue some rubber or suede to the tip to deaden the noise, but presumably she enjoyed the effect it made.

'You don't make promises like that to them.'

'To whom?' He wasn't aware that Mr Wilde fell into a particular category of person.

'To that sort! From *away*!'

Kit's mouth fell open. There was a great deal of hostility in the country towards the refugees who had arrived since the start of the Great War, and who were still arriving, even though it had ended. Where else could they turn but to the countries that had helped to free them, and in the process left their homes as trenches and rubble? Hearing the words coming from Merelda was truly shocking, however. She was good-natured, and from what Kit had gathered, she had helped organise collections of clothing for the displaced women and children.

'Aunt Merelda, I don't think I've ever heard you sound so unwelcoming. Mr Wilde was a little odd, and perhaps his manners aren't exactly British, but what harm can he do?'

'Ha! You have no idea. Oh yes, he seems harmless and of course he's charming, but once you're tangled up, it becomes hard to escape!' She punctuated her exclamation with an extra hard strike of her cane. A bird of some sort exploded from the nearby apple tree, flying overhead in a swoosh of alarm.

'If you didn't think I should have agreed then why did you not say anything at the time?' Kit retorted.

She gave him a baleful look.

'I tried, didn't I, and you saw what happened to me: a coughing fit and a toad on my tongue. Let me tell you about Mr Wilde and his sort.'

She took a breath but began to cough, wheezing as she had done the night before. A frog in her throat, as the mysterious Mr Wilde had said. Kit dashed forward to support her in case she fell. She waved the hand that wasn't holding her cane and shook her head in an irritable manner.

'I don't need your help to stand. If you want to make things right, keep him away from Adelaide.'

'Let me get you a drink,' Kit offered, taking a step back. 'Or shall I call Enid? She could bring you some tea.'

Enid's face appeared at the window so promptly that Kit wondered if she had been listening. She waved the teapot.

'Bring her into the kitchen, Young Kit.'

Ignoring her previous instruction, Kit took Merelda by the arm and led her into the kitchen-cum-dining room that made up half the ground floor. Enid took hold of her hand, stroking it gently.

'Let the breath out, Merry. One more and it's all done and dusted. Young Kit, you mustn't try to get her to talk of things she shouldn't.'

Some of the colour returned to Merelda's cheeks but still Enid held her hand until she stood fully upright and was breathing regularly.

'He's a good lad,' Merelda said, as Kit helped her sit in the winged Chesterfield by the fireplace. 'He's just been too educated.'

Enid bustled about the Welsh dresser in the furthest corner, collecting the kettle from the chain above the open fire and pouring water into the teapot.

'There are things in motion,' Merelda said.

Kit smiled. She was an old woman and prone to confusion.

'Everything is going to be fine,' he said. 'Don't worry about me and Adelaide. I know it's what you might call a marriage of convenience, but it is convenient for both of us, and we are genuinely fond of each other.'

His jaw tightened. After the quarrel he hoped that was still true.

'You're a good boy. Have you a good heart?' Merelda patted his cheek. It took him a moment to realise she'd touched his scarred cheek. Another to realise that he hadn't flinched.

'I hope so.' He dropped his eyes.

'If you have a good heart then all will be well,' Enid said, passing him his tea. No dainty porcelain cups for these two, just solid earthenware mugs with a decent amount to drink. Enid mixed her own leaves from varieties she ordered from Jacksons, so the blend was never the same twice. He took a swig then cradled his mug.

'What do you think is going to happen, Merelda? The war is over and we so thoroughly trounced the Hun that it'll be another century before they try anything else.'

'Wars don't just end. Wars beget wars,' Merelda said seriously.

'What do you mean? And what has that got to do with me having a good heart, or my engagement to Adelaide?'

Merelda took a deep breath. Enid clicked her fingers briskly.

'Don't you go asking questions anymore, you'll start her off coughing again,' she warned him.

Merelda was old, but she seemed to be really taking it to heart that Silas Wilde had a bit of a hankering for Adelaide. He thought back to the night before when he had happened upon them in the maze. He rather suspected that they knew each other already.

'At least tell me why Mr Wilde shouldn't dance with Adelaide? He's probably lonely, being all alone in a strange country.'

'You think he's alone, do you? Haven't you seen the other one? She'll have some undertaking, I'm sure. Sly little piece hiding in the shadows. Big, sad eyes and no bust to speak of.'

'Do you mean the girl who was wearing green?' Kit asked. She'd had an attractive, boyish figure and yes, her eyes had been disarmingly soulful. 'If she's Mr Wilde's wife or something then it hardly matters if he dances with Adelaide, does it? I don't believe it will do any harm.'

'And that shows what little you understand about the ways of folk like them.' Merelda snapped. She coughed again and took a deep swig of tea.

Kit swallowed down his surprise. Merelda hardly lived a conventional life, so had no place being so scathing about the affairs and liberties of others.

'She seemed perfectly pleasant, if a little odd. She asked if I wanted a walnut.'

'Did you accept?' Merelda faced him, and Kit was shocked to see how pale she had become.

'Of course not. I was going back to the house,' he said.

'Well, Kit, you can't say I didn't warn you, and don't come running to me when you discover your lady love has vanished in the morning mist.'

Kit sighed. 'Merelda, you've known Adelaide as long as I have. She's not the type of woman to run off with a stranger. If she wanted to break her engagement – which of course she's perfectly entitled to do – then she would have the honesty and courage to speak to me about it.'

'Assuming she has the means to speak,' Merelda muttered cryptically.

Kit stared at her. Was she losing her mind more than she already had? He'd have to speak to his parents and see what they thought.

'Best go now and do whatever else you need to be getting on with,' Enid told him.

Kit took the hint. 'Yes, I'd better go. I'm sorry if I've upset you in any way.'

'What's done is done, and all that's done is done,' Enid tutted. 'Watch your heart and watch your lady. That's all I can say.'

The two women left the room, which was slightly odd as it was their house, leaving Kit to see himself out. He put the tea things back on the dresser, tidied up a little, and hung the kettle on the chain. As he passed the sitting room, he overheard Merelda speaking.

'He has no idea and I can do nothing. It's hopeless. I am helpless.'

He paused. He wouldn't have done, except the words were so cryptic and must have referred to him.

'No, you're not, Merry, love. You've set him on the path. That's all you can do. Besides, nothing might come of it.' Enid said, as sensible and reassuring as ever.

'He won't stop. You know that as well as I do.'

'Well, then, we'll just have to hope that young Kit can keep his wits when he needs to. Now sit back and let me rub your head.'

'You're too good to me, sweetness.'

Kit left. Listening in while he was the subject of discussion was one thing, but this was a private moment between the two women, and it was not his place to intrude. He sometimes wondered if anyone else suspected they were lovers. They bickered and talked like any married couple, but to many it was inconceivable that women could love each other in that way. Of course, it was considered an abomination that men could love each other in that way, too, but Kit knew otherwise.

"Got another spare Lucifer? Do you fancy a mug of tea?"

Kit's eyes grew moist, remembering Andrew and the tentative approach he'd made. Both sizing each other up, trying to gauge the safety of an admission. Knowing the penalty. Knowing the risk. Balancing them with temptation.

He left the dovecote, misery swelling inside him but perturbed by what he had overheard. Whatever path had been set in motion, he had no idea, because Merelda's words had been far too cryptic.

~

Kit didn't get to speak to Adelaide in private, what with one thing and another, until they were driving back from Castle Francombe, the home of Lady Burroughs. Charlotte offered to ride back with Alfred, having already packed her boots, hacking jacket and jodhpurs in the car in anticipation.

'Last night—' Kit started to say as he eased the Vauxhall Prince Henry up the hill, after leaving the long driveway.

'You don't need to apologise,' Adelaide interrupted with a sweet smile.

Kit suppressed an eye-roll. Naturally she had assumed he was going to apologise.

'It was a very odd evening, wasn't it? I didn't feel quite myself you know,' he said.

'Neither did I! I didn't mean to make you jealous.'

'I wasn't jealous. What would I be jealous of?' Kit asked, again taken aback at her misinterpretation. It had been the way she had thrown her wealth in his face that had mattered.

'Of me dancing with that Mr Wilde, of course.' Adelaide twisted in her seat and placed her hand on his upper arm. 'I know it must be hard for you seeing me in the arms of others. And, of course, you mustn't think that I want to go to London to have affairs.'

'That has never occurred to me.' Kit pulled over into the entrance to a field and switched the engine off. 'Addie,' he said. 'I got touchy last night about the money and you flinging it in my face that it's all yours.'

'I hardly flung it in your face,' she said, frowning.

'I don't want you to think I intend to plan what you do with your money.'

He looked down at his hands. He genuinely hadn't cared about her dancing, but after Merelda's grilling and her talk of affairs he was beginning to wonder if he was an idiot.

'Look, Addie, I know it's always been planned for us but we're old enough to make our own minds up,' Kit continued. 'If there's somebody else you'd rather marry, or if you'd rather just not marry me then I really don't mind. I'll release you from the engagement.'

Adelaide's eyes widened. She pouted then smiled. 'Well,

that's very sweet but I don't want you to do that. It would positively kill Mother if we didn't marry.'

Adelaide's fingers twitched to her hair. Kit wondered if she was aware of the habit. All the Price family had dark hair – ranging from deep chestnut to a muddy brown. The only one who was different was Adelaide whose hair was so fair it was almost white. That might have passed as a slight aberration, but her skin was porcelain, too, like an old-fashioned doll's. Kit had often wondered why Sarah and Richard (who were both dark) had adopted a child whose colouring was so different. It seemed unfair to Kit, because it would only ever draw attention to the fact that she was not of their blood. Then again, if the child needed a family, perhaps that was more important than finding a family where it would blend in.

'Do you ever wonder about your other parents?' he asked.

She pressed her lips together and shook her head before looking at him with a flash of anger on her face. 'No. I was given up. I don't care to think why, or by whom. I don't want to appear ungrateful when Mother and Father have been so good to me. Marrying you is my way of paying the family back for adopting me.'

'That's no reason to marry me if you don't want to,' Kit said. 'It isn't an obligation you agreed to.'

She patted his hand. 'I don't see you as an obligation.'

If she was lying, she did it well.

'What do you think they would have done if we'd hated each other,' Kit mused. 'Or if you'd been a boy.'

'They'd have married me to Charlotte and you would have been my best chum,' Adelaide said breezily. 'I don't think you and I could ever have hated each other, even though you were a little rag at times and put salt in my porridge too often.'

'Well, you used to try to make me wear your hair ribbons,' Kit retorted.

They laughed.

'We'll make it work, I promise you,' Kit said. 'I'll never make you unhappy or make you do anything you don't want to.'

'Of course you won't. You're too sweet for your own good.' Adelaide leaned against him. 'We'll be good for each other. Come on, let's get back to the house. I want to pick out a dress to wear to the fete tomorrow. It'll be my first event as almost lady-of-the-manor and I want to look breathtaking.'

'You always do,' Kit said gallantly.

He started up the motor and drove home, pondering that at least with Adelaide at his side few people would care what he looked like.

Chapter Five

May Day had been the day of the village fete for over a century. The grounds of Meadwell Hall were separated from the village of Dalbymoorside by a river, over which there was an ancient, stone footbridge. It had been a tradition since the mid-1800s for the gardens to be opened up by the owners. When Kit had been young, his mother had put forward the idea of opening the Long Hall up to visitors for the cost of tuppence, but this had been roundly rejected by Charles and his parents who felt that treating it as an exhibit was undignified for the old place.

This year the rain looked as if it was going to be so bad that Reverend Keeth had hinted that maybe some of the traditional games could be played inside the hall. Though they obviously had reservations, Christopher and Sybil compromised on allowing it to be used to serve refreshments. Merelda was vocal about her misgivings as she and Kit hung garlands about the windows on the morning of the fete.

'Inviting them to the engagement party was a bad start, but

now we're giving them the freedom of the building,' she grumbled. She was wearing a long gown as always, but this one was slightly floaty and made her look like the subject of a painting by Waterhouse. She had braided rosebuds into her hair, along with some pale green leaves that Kit identified as sage when he got close enough to smell them.

'The doors to the rest of the house will be watched to ensure nobody goes where they shouldn't,' he reassured her, indicating the presence of Millicent laying out crockery on a table by the door to the tower. 'And no one visiting is going to try to steal the family silver.'

There were a few valuable pieces of small plate, but they were locked securely in a room off the butler's pantry with an iron grille on the window and iron bands fixed to the inside of the door. The full display came out rarely, and the next time wouldn't be until Kit and Adelaide's wedding breakfast. He smiled at Merelda, thinking he'd been rather harsh and gestured to the walls.

'If anyone wants to take some of these old antlers, they're more than welcome. They always slightly scared me.'

The deer in the park often shed them and the branches were hung along with stuffed heads of animals from days long past. Kit had already decided that as soon as the house became his, he would remove all of them.

The fete began at midday, with a parade of children from the local school escorting the May Queen and her attendants, their clothes decorated in colourful ribbons and flowers, accompanied by the remaining members of the brass band. The musicians were sadly depleted, and the sight of the reduced numbers gave spectators a moment's pause for solemnity. Kit's eyes misted. His childhood friend, Clarence, who'd died in action three days after arriving in Mons, had played the cornet. There was a glaring space where he should have been.

Silas Wilde was strolling through the crowd. Adelaide spotted him first, squeezing Kit's arm then waving to Mr Wilde who wheeled about to join them. At his side was the woman Kit had spoken to.

Her hair was cut into a short, layered style that framed her face, emphasising her delicate features. Where the sunlight caught it in places, it became copper, in others corn, occasionally chestnut. It was as if the locks couldn't settle on which colour and were battling for ascendency. It was a remarkably modern-looking cut, given her slightly old-fashioned yellow summer dress.

'Miss Wyndham and Mr Arton-Price, how delightful to see you both joining in the ceremony. May I introduce my companion to you. Miss Alexandra Dove.'

'What a pretty name,' Adelaide said, taking Miss Dove's hand.

'Thank you.' Miss Dove flashed a glance at Mr Wilde.

Kit wondered if Miss Dove was going to admit to their encounter in the garden. He wouldn't claim prior knowledge unless she did, thinking it a lady's prerogative.

'How nice to meet you again,' Miss Dove said, when she shook his hand.

'You've met?' Adelaide asked sharply.

'Yes, we were walking in the garden and came across each other the night of the party,' Miss Dove answered. If she noticed Adelaide's response, she ignored it. She spoke very quickly in her low, husky voice.

'When you say companion?' he asked, leaving the question tailing off.

'You might call her my ward,' Mr Wilde said.

Miss Dove looked to be around Adelaide's age, whereas Mr Wilde didn't appear to be much over thirty. It was an unusual situation for a guardian to be so close in age, but who knew how the terms could be dictated. At least, Kit assumed, that meant they weren't also lovers.

'Shall we walk together to see the crowning of the Queen?' Mr Wilde suggested. 'We know very few people in this area.'

Kit looked at Adelaide and raised his eyebrow. She nodded eagerly. Possibly too eagerly in his opinion.

The procession ended at the village green where the maypole had been erected and the queen was crowned with a circlet of rose and ivy by two youths dressed in green wearing leafy crowns.

'It's all rather pagan, isn't it,' Miss Dove said.

'Is it?' Adelaide asked.

'Pagan? Rather,' Kit said. 'Worshipping old fertility symbols and suchlike while dressed as a Green Man. And as for that thing…' He gestured to the maypole.

'Do you know about the old ways?' Mr Wilde looked at him keenly.

'I used to devour the stories of King Arthur and Merlin when I was a child, and of course at school we read Caesar's accounts of Britain and druids.'

'Well, that's all fascinating,' Adelaide said in a voice that strongly suggested otherwise. 'It's delightfully provincial.'

'Just because you never got to be the May Queen,' Kit said

with a laugh, hoping to lighten the mood. She just stared at him.

Mr Wilde tilted his head to one side. 'And would you be a queen if you could, Miss Wyndham?'

'Of course. Who wouldn't,' she replied.

'Then let me be your courtier. Shall we walk?'

He held out his arm to her but looked at Kit. 'Mr Arton-Price, do I have your permission to steal away Miss Wyndham?'

Kit met Adelaide's eyes. She looked at him with a challenge. 'Oh, I rather think it's up to Miss Wyndham to give her own permission for that.'

Mr Wilde's eyes glinted, then he laughed. 'How very modern of you both. Well, then, Miss Wyndham, will you let me spirit you away?'

'Gladly,' Adelaide said sweetly, taking his arm. 'Let's leave the children to their dressing up and paganism. Kit, I'll see you for cake later. Have fun.'

They walked off, leaving Kit standing with Miss Dove.

'And would you be a knight, swearing fealty to your king and your devotion to a fair maiden?' she asked, looking up at him through thick lashes. 'Does the romance of that appeal to you?'

'I swore my loyalty to the King and fought for my country. It was not remotely romantic. I'm in no hurry to do it again,' Kit replied quietly.

'A wise man would answer such,' she said. Her brown eyes shone with intelligence and he had the distinct impression she was mocking him. 'Though would a wise man let his fiancée go with Mr Wilde?'

'Why not? She's a modern woman. I shall be as devoted a subject as my wife requires me to be but I'm not going to stand in her way.'

'Then how much do you really love her?' Miss Dove's smile was definitely mocking now.

'Why would letting her walk with another man suggest I don't love her? Love isn't about possessing.'

She looked at him as if he were stupid. Her eyes lingered on his face. The last time they had met it had been dark but now his cheek was clear to see. He gestured to it.

'Of course, we've been unofficially engaged for years but that was before I came back looking like this.'

Usually, any reference directly to his disfigurement meant the topic was swiftly changed, but Miss Dove just carried on looking at his face. Kit tried to suppress the shiver that ran down his neck, feeling rather like a prize bull at market. Finally, she dragged her gaze from the remains of his face and looked into his eyes.

'I've seen worse. You came back alive. That's more than many. And you're still half-handsome, which is more than some get to start out with.'

Her smile softened, and Kit was about to return it when she jabbed her forefinger at him. 'You just need to stop being so self-pitying. That's what diminishes a man's charm.'

'I—' He scowled. 'I'm not self-pitying.'

She lifted her chin belligerently. 'Yes, you are. You were skulking around in the dark by yourself at the party and feeling sorry for your lot in life. You even confided in a complete stranger that you think it's too much responsibility.'

Kit stared at her. Adelaide had a forthright nature, but Miss

Dove was something else entirely. Well, if she could dispense with politeness, so could he.

'Miss Dove, I'm afraid I'm going to be awfully rude now. I haven't been back in the area very long and I'm afraid I have no idea where you and Mr Wilde have come from or how long you've been living here.'

'I don't think you're afraid, at all,' she said candidly. 'Nor should you be. It's astonishing how susceptible people can be when they don't want to appear impolite. A person can invite all sorts of trouble into their lives.'

'I see impoliteness doesn't worry you. Speaking of which, who invited you to the party?' Kit asked.

She glanced over her shoulder in the direction of the house. Adelaide and Mr Wilde were quite a long way ahead. For all her assertions that she had no interest in Mr Wilde, Kit could see Adelaide was holding onto his arm and laughing at whatever he was saying.

'Shall we follow them? I would not want to be too far from Mr Wilde,' she said.

Kit held out an arm and she linked hers through it.

'Why don't we go look at some of the stalls and see if we can be polite to each other for the next ten minutes.'

They strolled towards the river. Her arms were bare from wrist to elbow, and she was wearing a bangle of some sort of pale pink gemstone. It had a pearlescent sheen to it where it caught the sunlight, and the surface was carved into intertwining swirls that made Kit think of old Celtic jewellery he had once seen in a museum. It was tight-fitting and looked to have been carved from one single piece of rock. There appeared to be no way of slipping it over her hand and he found that fascinating. Presumably, some of the swirls covered a hidden catch. It reminded him a little of the maze with the concealed exit.

Miss Dove must have noticed his interest because she twisted her hand and withdrew it from his arm.

'That's a very interesting piece. I'm sorry if I was being indiscreet by staring,' Kit said. 'Is it a family heirloom.'

'No. I'm the first one to wear it,' she said, slightly brusquely.

'It's a clever design. I can't see at all how you take it off.'

'You can't.'

She put her arms behind her back and walked a little faster.

They reached the footbridge. Miss Dove stopped halfway across and leaned against the low parapet. She craned her head round to look down at the water that rushed beneath, scurrying around rocks. Her silhouette shimmered thanks to a combination of the sun behind her and Kit's troublesome eye. He had to blink and force himself to concentrate.

'I never answered your question,' she said. 'Mr Wilde and I have come here because our land has been ravaged by the Great War.'

Her expression grew heavy. It was a familiar tale. Desperate and traumatised people displaced from their homes and with nowhere else to turn. Women and children who had been forced to leave with nothing but what they could carry on their backs. Miss Dove's dress was simple but of decent quality, and she had worn an evening gown when she had attended the party. That didn't mean that friends of hers were equally fortunate.

'I'm sorry. I've seen the devastation in France and Belgium

with my own eyes, and it was shocking for me. It's inconceivable what that must be like.'

'Then give us your aid, Mr Arton-Price. We are searching for support in our quest to restore it to the glory it once was.'

'Do you need a donation to a fund? I'm afraid I don't have access to much as it's mostly in trust, and I'm between jobs.'

She smiled warmly. 'Not gold or silver.'

'What, then?'

She turned to him and placed both hands on his arm, gazing up at him in entreaty. Her fingers were warm against the soft flesh of his inner wrist and the pressure sent moths dancing across his skin. It was distractingly pleasurable and when she looked up into his eyes, the world receded.

'How brave is your heart? How true is your soul?' she murmured. Her lips were the pink of early strawberries and looked just as tempting. 'Will you cross over and journey with us to help restore what needs to be restored?'

'I'm afraid I can't leave everything here and come to Belgium,' he said.

He didn't think what he said was that funny, but she gave a rippling laugh that struck him as rather absurd.

'Not Belgium, then? You still haven't told me where you're from,' he prompted.

Her eyes became dreamy. 'The land of great lakes and mountains. Where fruits grow in abundance and the grasses are so soft you can make a bed of them.'

'It sounds wonderful,' Kit said. His family had visited the Italian Lakes when he was nine, then journeyed until they reached the French Alps. His mind filled with visions of the mountains fresh with the first dusting of winter snows, and spring flowers budding through the bleak wildness.

'It is. Or was. It can be again. A place where the dreams of mankind can come true.' She gazed up at him, her lashes fluttering, causing his heartbeat to grow feathery.

'Do you have dreams, Kit Arton-Price?' she breathed.

Screaming rockets. Screaming horses. Screaming men.

Nights thrashing in sweat-soaked sheets that clutched him like desperate hands.

His back grew clammy.

'Not pleasant ones,' he muttered.

She touched his shoulder, resting her fingers so lightly this time he could barely feel the pressure. 'Would you like them to be better? There are ways and means to ensure that.'

He couldn't quite believe she was intending to seduce him in broad daylight, but her eyes were intoxicating and he was falling into them.

'Miss Dove, you lack subtlety.'

They both turned at the voice. Mr Wilde and Adelaide were walking back towards them. Miss Dove dropped her gaze to the floor, biting her lip, then glanced at Mr Wilde.

'We were just talking,' she muttered, withdrawing her hand from Kit's shoulder and giving him a rueful look. 'I was telling Mr Arton-Price about our home.'

'It sounds like a beautiful country,' Kit said, trying to break the awkwardness.

'I too am trying to impress the beauty of our land upon Miss Wyndham,' Mr Wilde said. 'I hope I'm being slightly more persuasive in my efforts to recruit her.'

'I'm sorry,' Kit said. 'I don't believe either of us will be able to help you with what you need. Not that I'm very sure what that is.'

'We were on our way to admire the gardens when we spotted you two,' Adelaide said to Kit. 'Come with us.'

'We'd be delighted,' Mr Wilde replied, giving a reverential bow of his head.

It seemed natural at that point to swap partners. Miss Dove fell in beside him. As Mr Wilde took her arm she fixed Kit with a piercing stare.

'Perhaps on another occasion I can impress upon you just how subtle I can be.'

She winked and walked away.

He opened his mouth, but catching Adelaide's look of astonishment, he closed it again. He didn't have any particular intention or expectation of meeting Miss Dove again, and with Adelaide turning scarlet it would probably be just as well.

Kit and Adelaide strolled slowly together while Mr Wilde and Miss Dove walked ahead. Wilde seemed rather cross with her, striding with his hand around her waist in a manner that almost forced her to keep up. She glared at him in profile. He whispered something in her ear and her face softened. She laughed and they slowed to a more leisurely pace, allowing Kit and Adelaide to overtake them. Miss Dove had one of the most expressive faces Kit could remember ever encountering.

'What were you talking about? She seemed awfully close to you,' Adelaide muttered.

'She was trying to persuade me to go to wherever they're from and help to rebuild it. I don't know what exactly she thinks I'd be any use doing. They'd be better off going to the cities and asking factory workers or looking for employees on the farms, though I'd rather they didn't because we need them here.'

Adelaide wrinkled her nose. 'Mr Wilde was asking me the same thing, but I got the impression he wants people with ideas rather than manual labour. Aren't you tempted, at all?'

Kit dropped her arm and stared at her in astonishment. 'Not at all. I have enough to do here. Are you?'

'A little.' She smiled dreamily. 'It sounds such a beautiful place. Wild moors and rivers, and snow-capped mountains.'

'We have moors and rivers here,' Kit said, feeling slightly aggrieved on behalf of Yorkshire. 'Besides, what about cities and theatres and restaurants? Do they have those?'

'I don't know, but I can't imagine anywhere that doesn't. Why don't we go together and find out?'

'Yes, both of you come. That would be wonderful,' Miss Dove said brightly, joining them. Her hearing was very sharp.

'We can't and that's the end of it, I'm afraid,' Kit said.

Adelaide's mouth turned down. 'Is this what marriage to you is going to be like?'

'Keeping you from doing something rash when you have no idea what the consequences would be? You make it sound like a bad thing. It's what all good husbands would do,' Kit replied, remembering Miss Dove's earlier comments.

'Deciding for both of us? You're not in the army any longer, and I'm not one of your men to command,' Adelaide snapped.

Kit stepped back at her words, which had been hurled with force. The prospect reared up of their having a full-blown quarrel with an audience. From the corner of his good eye, he could just about see Mr Wilde and Miss Dove both watching and not concealing their interest, Mr Wilde with a slight smile that Kit found intolerable.

'I'm not going to lay down the law to you, Adelaide,' he said levelly, standing straight and trying to look dignified. 'If you wish to go off to help then I will not dream of stopping you.'

'Well, then. I'll consider it.' Adelaide tightened her lips then gave a curt nod.

Mr Wilde looked quite satisfied, which gave Kit a small degree of pleasure. Adelaide would change her mind as soon as she realised what it would be like going somewhere that had recently suffered the devastation of war. He could almost smell the fire and decay just thinking of it. The burnt-out houses and piles of rubble that half-revealed remnants of everyday life. The thick ash that covered everything, so that one might think the trees and grass grew grey naturally.

Aware that the quarrel had been narrowly averted, Kit felt suddenly disinclined to spend any more time with the odd couple.

'Adelaide, I promised that I would go and judge the children's sack race,' he said. 'Will you join me?'

'Of course.' She adjusted her gloves and gave him a thin smile that suggested if the battle wasn't over, she was content to call a temporary truce. 'I was rather hoping we could take some tea as well.'

'If you will excuse us,' Kit said.

'Of course.' Mr Wilde held out his hand and after a brief hesitation, Kit shook it. Then Mr Wilde raised Adelaide's hand to his lips.

'I hope we'll meet again soon.'

Miss Dove was looking at the ground. She twisted the bangle back and forth around her wrist, worrying at it.

'It was nice talking to you,' Kit said to her. She looked up briefly and her mouth jerked up at one side into a sort of smile.

'Was it? I'm glad you think so. Goodbye, Mr Arton-Price. Or perhaps it's only *au revoir*.'

The two of them walked away.

'If I didn't know better, I'd say she was trying to enamour you,' Adelaide murmured.

Kit glanced over his shoulder to check they weren't within earshot, storing away the comment about *knowing better* for later. He wasn't overly vain, and was painfully aware of how little he had to offer a woman in the way of company or charm, but there was something in Adelaide's casual sureness that was wounding.

Chapter Six

As the couples parted, the pressure in Kit's head lifted. He hadn't realised how twitchy he'd been feeling. Adelaide yawned audibly. Seeing him watching her, she put a hand over her mouth.

'Excuse me! I feel very tired all of a sudden, as if I'm just waking up. I seem to be tired all the time at the moment.'

'I feel odd, too. I wonder if we're in for a storm?' Kit brushed the hair back from his forehead, feeling clamminess. 'Addie, I don't want to be one of those husbands who treats his wife like a child or a chattel, but I really don't think getting involved with Mr Wilde and Miss Dove is wise. We don't know them from Adam, and I have no idea what their credentials are. I don't even know where they're living here, never mind where they're from.'

Adelaide's brow furrowed. 'I'm sure he told me. I got the impression he's a minor nobleman of some sort. He mentioned the gentry at one point. He's very respectable where they come from, but now in exile.'

'Did he happen to mention where that is?' Kit asked. 'I still haven't managed to pin them down to a country.'

'I'm sure he did but I can't remember that, either. I really am very sluggish today.'

Kit glanced back over his shoulder. Mr Wilde and Miss Dove were on the bridge. Miss Dove caught his eye and waggled her fingers towards him, giving him a pert smile. Mr Wilde was staring up at the house, his hands spread wide on the parapet of the bridge as if he was a duke surveying his realm. He did look quite majestic, much to Kit's annoyance. He'd risk Adelaide growing bored of a penniless refugee, but a member of the gentry might be a different matter entirely.

'He's very handsome, isn't he,' Kit observed.

'Very.' Adelaide sounded quite dreamy. She blinked twice. 'Of course, looks don't matter to me in the slightest.'

She reached a hand up as if she was about to touch Kit's cheek but then closed her fingers and drew back.

'You are handsome, too.' She took his hand and squeezed it reassuringly, possibly even fondly.

Kit swallowed. He hadn't been a bad-looking chap before the explosion. Still wasn't, from some angles.

'If you stand on my right-hand side in the wedding photos so that I can turn my left to the camera I might be able to fool everyone into believing that.'

Adelaide looked him in the eye. 'Christopher Arton-Price, I don't care in the slightest about your scars! You should look at the world face-on. You're far from being the only soldier who has come back from the front with proof of his time there on his face. You should be proud of what that signifies. What you gave for your country.'

Adelaide sounded more impassioned than he had heard her for quite some time and it warmed Kit's heart to hear it.

'I suppose so.'

'And you are a war hero, my darling,' Adelaide continued, in the sort of soothing voice that one might use with a child. Her words were meant kindly, but there was an air of condescension about them. His brain was unaffected and he didn't need to be spoken to like that. It was in stark contrast to Miss Dove's abrupt assessment, and he found that, oddly, he preferred that response.

'You have a medal. Why on earth would I not be proud to be married to you?'

Kit smiled and tried not to clench his jaw at the description. He wondered if Adelaide would have been so eager to marry him had he not returned with the Military Cross and she couldn't call him a hero. But he was being unjust, and it was his own bitterness that was whispering these treacherous messages to his brain. He would trade all the glory and medals in Britain for a face he could look at in the mirror without wincing, and above all, to undo the circumstances under which he'd been awarded them.

~

The sack race was more eventful than expected. The child widely believed to be the favourite appeared very sluggish from the off, and though he rallied slightly, he then lay down six feet from the finishing line, curled into a ball and appeared to go to sleep. His mother shouted encouragement from behind the ropes while his father just shouted. When it became clear that the child was intent on having his nap, the father stepped over the rope, walked to his child and picked him up, sack and all.

The winner and runner-up skipped over to Kit to claim their prizes of an ounce of sherbet pips each. He handed them out with the required congratulations, trying not to mind when the winner – a small girl with long pigtails – stared openly at his face in horror.

Kit found Adelaide standing with Oliver, his wife Helen and their baby.

'I do hope the boy isn't sick,' Adelaide murmured, watching the mother hurrying along anxiously after her husband, while the boy lay limply over his father's shoulder, still in the sack.

'It's rather odd of a child that age,' Kit said.

'Probably just eaten too many iced buns and was overcome with fatigue,' Helen said. She was a cheery woman with a practical nature; an ideal vet's wife, who took everything in her stride when her husband was called out to birth a lamb at three in the morning. She jiggled her baby over one arm while the infant stared with solemn eyes at Kit.

'There's that nasty Spanish Flu, though,' Adelaide said, furrowing her brow. 'We were relatively lucky here during the worst of it. I know it's supposed to be all done with but what if the government is wrong?'

'Then we'll find out soon,' Oliver said quietly.

Contemplative silence descended over the group. Helen drew her baby tighter to her chest and stepped closer to her husband. The influenza had ravaged the country and barely a village had escaped losing some members.

'Do you know the family?' Kit asked.

Oliver squinted into the sun, looking at the departing family. 'He's a labourer on Dad's farm. Not the nicest fellow from what I've heard. More often in The Nag's Head than his house.'

'If the child is still ailing, his parents can consult a doctor,' Helen said. 'There's a new one in Helmsley who is cheaper than Doctor Fulford. Odd fellow.'

Curiosity piqued; Kit was about to ask why when he caught sight of Merelda limping across the lawn with a determined expression on her face. Enid could barely keep up.

'Oh lord, I think I'm in for another scolding.' Kit sighed. 'Tell Merelda I've gone to the tea tent. I'm going off to try my hand at the archery.'

He slipped off towards the butts that had been erected next to the stables. Kit's father was overseeing the competition and greeted his son with a raised brow.

'Coming to have a shot?'

Kit strapped on the wrist protector and took the yew-wood bow and three blunt-tipped arrows. It hadn't occurred to him how his vision problems would affect his aim until he lifted the bow. He'd become quite proficient as a child, going through a Robin Hood obsession, but that had been a long time ago.

His hand trembled as he fitted the nock onto the string. He closed his left eye, assessing the target. The paper sheet, pinned against a hay bale, shivered before coming into focus and the circle at the centre appeared to glow. If anything, the effect made aiming much easier than he had anticipated, because the colours shone brighter than the surroundings and his first arrow struck the centre. He gave a little cry of triumph and grinned at his father. The next arrow went slightly wide but hit the red, just on the boundary to the gold.

He was drawing the string back for the final time when he became aware of a movement at the corner of his vision. Silas Wilde stood alone in front of the ancient oak tree. His eyes slid to the target, then back to Kit and he raised one brow questioningly. Kit gritted his teeth and took a deep breath, releasing it slowly through his lips as he drew the string back, only uncurling his fingers from beneath the fletch as his lungs fully emptied.

The arrow flew true and landed in the inner circle beside his first.

'Not a bad effort, at all,' Charles said as Kit handed the bow back. 'I'll add your scores to the list. Could you bring me a slice of fruit cake and a cup of tea? It's getting quite warm now.'

Kit agreed, both with the request and the assessment of the weather. It was growing warmer and as clouds gathered overhead the atmosphere was starting to feel oppressively humid. He walked away in the opposite direction to the oak tree but wasn't surprised when Wilde caught up with him.

'Impressive. You have an excellent eye and a steady hand. What would I need to offer you to join my crusade?'

Kit carried on walking. 'Mr Wilde, I don't know what *crusade* you mean, but neither I nor Adelaide are going to come on a vague expedition to somewhere we have never heard of. I'm not going to get involved in another battle as long as I live.'

'And yet you pick up a weapon,' Wilde said softly.

During the war Kit had fired bayonet rifles and pistols. Had taken lives. This was the first time he had picked a weapon up since being demobbed. He knew at a visceral level that if it had been a gun, he wouldn't have touched it. Wouldn't even have ventured into that area of the grounds. The bow was different. No one fought with medieval weapons any longer.

Kit swung round, stepping into Wilde's way. 'Will you please leave me and my fiancée alone before I have you thrown out of the grounds.'

A slow smile spread across Wilde's handsome face and his eyes crinkled at the corners. Damn him, he looked amused rather than concerned by Kit's outburst.

'I shall take my leave, Mr Arton-Price. Perhaps our paths will cross again. Perhaps they won't. The Fates will decide that, not I. Allow me to wish you well in your future marriage.'

He walked off. Kit curled his hands into fists, fighting the urge to go knock the man to the ground. Instead, he turned away and went round the perimeter of the house to the entrance to the Long Hall.

A little later, armed with a large slice of date and walnut cake and a cup of tea, Kit made his way back to the archery butts, taking the long way around the back of the house.

Miss Dove was sitting on the lawn close to the entrance to the deer park, throwing cake crumbs to pigeons. They flocked around her, looking almost tame. He glanced around to see if Silas Wilde was there, too, but he wasn't. Possibly Wilde had heeded Kit's warning.

A particularly daring pigeon jumped onto her outspread skirt and chirruped. She cooed at it and it squawked. The birds scattered as he drew close, taking to the sky in a cloud of greys and greens. Miss Dove looked up as he approached, eyes watching him steadily and never wavering.

'A dove among the pigeons. You looked like you were conversing,' Kit said.

'Maybe we were,' she answered, brushing her skirt down.

She looked so serious that Kit laughed kindly. 'You should meet my great-aunt. She'd love to think that was true.'

'But you know better? You have the soul of a sceptic.' Miss Dove sighed. 'What if such things were possible?'

'Then the world would be turned upside down,' Kit said with a shudder.

'Shall I read your fortune in the tea leaves?' Miss Dove asked, flicking her hand towards the tray in Kit's hands.

'It's my father's cup and I don't believe in that sort of rot, any more than I believe in talking birds,' Kit said.

She snorted. 'You don't have to believe for it to be true. Look with the eyes you've been given.'

'What does that even mean?' Kit asked. 'And what was all the business with the walnuts the other night?'

'It could have been an egg, I suppose,' she said, throwing the remains of the cake into the air. 'All the worlds and all the possibilities can be contained within a shell. You never know what you'll get until you choose to break it open.'

'You have an annoying habit of talking in riddles,' Kit said.

'They're only riddles to those who won't untangle them. Sometimes they're all one can speak. You have to listen to what they're not saying as much as what they are.'

A gust of wind, sharp and cold blew around Kit's legs. After the muggy, dense air that had been descending since noon, it came as a relief.

'Miss Dove, I came over here to say how sorry I am that I

can't help you. It's not that I don't want to, but circumstances are such that—'

She held up a hand to stop him. 'Circumstances are such that you lack the wherewithal and the resolve. It's a shame for you, and a greater shame for me.'

She looked over Kit's shoulder towards the house, then stood.

'The rain is coming.'

As she spoke a clap of thunder ricocheted off the walls of the buildings, and without further warning the clouds burst and heavy rain fell. People hurried across the lawns for refuge, crying out in surprised laughter or annoyance at being unexpectedly drenched. Kit pushed himself to his feet and hunched over. He tugged his collar up, fruitlessly attempting to keep the back of his neck dry, but compared to the greatcoat he'd worn in the trenches, the light tweed might have been a sheet of tissue paper.

Miss Dove appeared unaffected by the rain, though her frock was flimsy. The lemon-yellow fabric clung to her frame, giving life to the contours of her narrow torso and slender hips. Water trailed down her face and neck. Kit tried not to stare at a rivulet that had taken a route in the shallow valley between her breasts.

'You need to get inside somewhere before you're completely drenched and catch a cold,' he said.

'Thank you for your concern, but he'll be here before long and I'll be inside soon enough. I'll wait in the open.'

He was presumably Mr Wilde. Kit felt a stab of dislike, coupled with frustration that she was prepared to stand in the rain. Aside from a group of young children who were delightedly jumping in puddles, they were the only two people who hadn't found shelter.

'Come into the house,' he said. 'Mr Wilde can find you there.'

'Do you mean that?' Her eyes gleamed. She bit her bottom lip and gestured to the tray. 'Your cake is ruined.'

Kit looked down at the tray. Sure enough, the plate was swimming in water and the cake had become mush, with a few stray pieces of walnut floating amid the sludge. Any tea leaves worth reading were now swimming in the saucer where the cup had overflowed.

'It doesn't matter. My father can get some more cake. I think the fete is probably over, judging by the state of the weather.'

Miss Dove nodded, looking serious. 'Yes. Everything that needed to be done has been done.'

She put both hands on his chest and gently but firmly pushed him backwards.

'Go now, Kit Arton-Price. Find shelter and don't waste any more time getting wet. Keep dry and keep well.'

He shivered at the contrast of her warm hands on his cold shirt. His heart thudded, the swelling of desire taking him by surprise.

'Do the same yourself,' he said. He stepped backwards three paces then turned and walked away as if he was leaving the presence of royalty, only wondering as he reached the door to the Second Tower why he'd done so.

Kit took a long bath to warm through, changed into dry clothes then strolled across the Long Hall to find the rest of the family in the North Wing. A fire had been lit in his parents' sitting room and the remaining cakes and sausage rolls were piled high on plates. Sarah, Charles, Charlotte and Alfred were playing Bridge. Adelaide, Ellen and Sybil stood by the window staring out at the gale that twisted and bowed the trees. The three women regarded Kit as he approached, momentarily conjuring an old painting he'd seen of the Furies. Wisely keeping his observations to himself, he kissed them each in turn, catching a heady, almost cloyingly sweet scent as his lips brushed Adelaide's cheek. She was holding a small bouquet of lilacs, surrounded by leaves and grasses.

'They're pretty,' he said, though it wasn't exactly the daintiest arrangement.

Adelaide looked down and touched one of the many petalled, light purple flowers.

'Yes, they smell lovely but make me quite tired.'

Ellen had decreed there would be no formal dinner and that cold cuts and salads would suffice while everyone ate on laps. The mood was jovial, as the fete was judged a success by everyone.

Kit excused himself not long afterwards and went to bed, where he read until the words began to vibrate on the page and his eyes began to complain, leaving him no choice but to surrender to their demands. He discovered he was unable to sleep, and it was probably for that reason that he heard the distant, melancholy howling of a lone dog just as the clock struck one.

$$\sim$$

They stood on the grass, damp underfoot and smelling of sweet growth.

Three of them.

'Everything that can be done has been done. It's time to return home.'

Silas had changed out of his suit and was now dressed in more familiar clothes: a long cloak, immaculately tailored calfskin breeches, a cream, high-collared shirt and a green brocade waistcoat. His hair was back to its usual shoulder-skimming length, caught at the nape with a velvet ribbon beneath a tricorn hat.

Valentine wondered what Adelaide thought of the change from respectable gentleman to something so clearly *other*.

Adelaide stood beside Silas, her right hand in his left. Their wrists were linked by a plaited thread of gold, silver, and blood-red silks. In her left hand she held the small bouquet of lilacs that she had accepted from him, and which had sealed her fate. Did she truly understand where she had agreed to go? Briefly, Valentine felt a pang of frustration that they had to resort to trickery and half-truths.

'Are you ready, my dear?' Silas asked. It took Valentine a moment to realise that he was talking to Adelaide and not her.

'Of course.' Adelaide's voice was dreamlike, slow and slight. It was only to be expected. The moonlight shone through her hair and in her flowing nightdress and rose-pink satin dressing gown she looked as delicate as dandelion seeds about to blow away.

It was almost midnight.

'Are you sure Kit won't be coming?' Adelaide asked.

'I'm afraid not.'

Silas sounded genuinely regretful, though Valentine had been with him as he had crowed triumphantly about his success at parting the lovers and his intention to make Adelaide love him in her fiancé's absence.

'Miss Dove will remain here for a while longer. She will watch over your beloved and, if possible, persuade Mr Arton-Price to follow us.'

'I will as best as I can,' Valentine assured Adelaide. She motioned to Silas with her hand.

'Wait here my dear,' Silas instructed Adelaide. He let go of her hand and walked away, the thread binding them together, stretched to its full yard span.

'You don't mind me staying?' Valentine asked.

Silas stroked her cheek.

'I'll admit you were right about Mr Arton-Price, there is something in his nature that is of steel, and his prowess with a bow was unexpected. Bring him if you can.'

'How long may I stay?' Valentine asked.

'No more than a week. By that time, either you will have persuaded him, or he will have completely lost heart. After that time is up, I cannot guarantee a way back will be open for you.'

Silas looked thoughtful at this point, as if the concept of Valentine being stranded in the human realm was an interesting concept rather than a dreadful sentence. Fear tightened like iron in her chest. If she lost her means to return, or the gateway failed to open, she would be forced to remain here, alone and friendless, until Silas returned. *If* he returned.

'I cannot honestly say which I expect. He's a strange one. But I want to try.' Valentine's innards twinged with apprehension. Kit should have opened to her easily. He'd been very close when they had stood on the bridge, speaking of dreams. What darkness held him, that made the light surrounding him dim?

'If he does come, it won't be peacefully,' Silas warned. 'He is brimming with anger beneath the self-pity.'

Cold wings fluttered over her, causing a shiver to run the length of her spine. Silas took her face between his hands, tilting it back tenderly.

'Don't fear, little one. I wish you luck. We cannot fail in this, and then our land will be free. You want to be free, don't you?'

He took her hand, held it tight, then moved his hand further up until it covered the bangle on her wrist. She fixed her eyes on it. Over here, the power it held was not so strong, but there was still enough for it to pulsate with light from within. It gave her the determination she needed to see everything through.

'My fealty is yours and I will serve as best as I can,' she said boldly.

'I know you will.' Silas sniffed the air. 'Five minutes until midnight. Adelaide, my dear, are you ready to travel to my land?'

'Of course I am.' She smiled with the listlessness of the barely awake. Her eyes drifted to Valentine. 'Look after Kit for me, please.'

Valentine's jaw tightened. A request under the circumstances was practically a command and could not be refused.

'Of course,' she answered, as if she had any choice in the matter.

From the village came the sound of church bells pealing midnight. Silas waved his arm in the air, drawing a complicated sigil, and the bells were joined by another timbre of resonance from far away.

Hand in hand, Silas and Adelaide walked towards the river and waded in. Valentine had wondered which doorway he would use and was surprised to see he had chosen the bridge. The water came to their waists. As they reached the stone arch that was now the threshold, Silas threw his head back and howled in triumph. The Wild Lord at full strength.

He extended a hand and blew a handful of lilac petals at the bridge, and the stones began to pulsate with silver light. They stepped under the bridge and did not emerge from the other side.

Valentine's legs wobbled, a moment of foreboding incapacitating her. She almost ran after them in fear but stood firm. She was alone, but with no one to command her and almost no restraints placed upon her for the first time since her youth.

The horizon gleamed like diamonds. She ran towards it on light feet and then spread her arms wide. Her laughter became a cooing as she changed form and took to the sky, ascending higher towards the stars until she was only a silhouette against the night.

Chapter Seven

Charles Arton-Price's study was on the ground floor of the North Wing, with windows facing east. The balmy sun cast the room into soothing light as Kit and Charles pored over the accounts of Meadwell's income and expenditure, going back to the first year of the war.

'Great-aunt Merelda seems very suspicious of a couple of the guests who were here yesterday and the night of the party,' Kit said when they took a well-earned break for coffee. 'One of them danced with Addie, and now Merelda believes he is planning to spirit her away.'

Charles frowned. 'Who is the chap? We can't be doing with that. We need the money.'

He gestured to the ledgers, which unfortunately confirmed his words.

'A man by the name of Silas Wilde. His companion was a Miss Dove.'

Charles lit his pipe, which Kit recognised as an indication he was thinking deeply. As a child he'd always loved the comforting warm smell of his father's pipe tobacco when it was shredded and kept in the leather wallet. Since the trenches, though, the smell of ash and exotic places just made memories of mustard gas and flames scream through his head and he couldn't bear it. He walked to the bay window to slide open the sash. A pigeon flew across, settling somewhere in the maze.

'Tall man? Pretty girl with a bit of pertness to her face but no figure to speak of? Looks like she could play Cesario more convincingly than Viola,' Charles said.

'That's the pair,' Kit said, struck by how good the description was. Miss Dove would make an excellent Shakespearean youth. He could imagine her as Ariel in *The Tempest*. But would that make Mr Wilde Prospero, and did Kit's distorted face make him Caliban?

'Did you invite them?' he asked.

'Not I. Your mother, perhaps.'

Kit raised his eyebrows in surprise. Mr Wilde didn't seem the sort of person Ellen would know or approve of.

'So, he wasn't somebody who could have been a patient convalescing here during the war? Or perhaps one of the staff?' he asked.

'No, I don't think so, but speak to your mother.' Charles's expression darkened. 'The village has remained reassuringly the same as it was before you went away, but the towns are changing. They have struggled to replace the men who were lost. I know some of those who came back ... well ... what they saw has clearly affected them.'

Charles joined him at the window, and surprised Kit by putting both hands on his shoulders.

'I'm not the most demonstrative man,' he said, in what Kit considered was the biggest understatement of the new century so far. 'But I am so very glad you returned safely.'

He paused and dropped his hands. 'Are you… Your face is… Has your mind been affected? You won't end up in an asylum, either comatose or raving like those poor souls I've read about? You will cope with the pressure of your responsibilities?'

Kit hid his disappointment. The consideration was not for Kit as a son, but as an heir.

'I have bad dreams, of course, but my mind is unbroken,' he said curtly. His heart was his own business, he thought ruefully.

"Please don't leave me!"

He swallowed before he choked on misery. 'I don't think any of us will ever forget what we saw. How could we. Why should we?'

'You did us proud,' Charles said. 'My son a war hero. Mentioned in dispatches twice, and a Military Cross. It's such a shame you wouldn't wear it at the party or the fete—'

Since returning home, the Military Cross had remained in its case, which had remained in a locked drawer in Kit's bedroom. As far as he was concerned it could stay there, slowly being buried in dust. He needed no reminders. The hellish sights and sounds of that night haunted his nightmares. They made him want to pick up the ugly glass paperweight his father kept on the desk and hurl it through the window just so that the visions in his mind would be slightly altered by something new.

'Are we done here?' he asked abruptly.

'Do you have somewhere to be?' Charles asked.

'I promised Fred I'd take him out on another ride,' Kit lied.

Charles clapped him on the back. 'That's the spirit. Your brother chafes at the bit a little, being younger than you. Poor chap, missing out on the chance to fight for King and Country. He was fully prepared to step into your shoes here while you were away, you know.'

'Of course.'

If Kit had been in any doubt where his father's priorities lay, he knew now. Keeping Meadwell going was all that mattered. He almost regretted, for his father's and Alfred's sakes, that he had come back.

He gathered his notebook and pencils and headed back towards his own apartment, taking the route through the upper floor of the Long Hall. There were rumours of secret passages and hidden rooms, though the children had never succeeded in finding anything. Some people claimed that the building was haunted by the ghosts of previous occupants, or the monks who had been cast out of their home, but again, there had been no sightings in Kit's lifetime. And as Miss Dove had recently told him, he had a sceptic's soul, so without seeing one himself he'd have disbelieved any reports.

Never mind, he had brought his own ghosts back from the trenches with him and though they weren't visible, he carried them with him everywhere.

He'd been in his sitting room for less than five minutes when there was a knock on the door. Aunt Sarah stood there. She looked frantic, twisting her hands together.

'Is there something wrong?' Kit asked.

'Yes, with Adelaide. I can't get her to wake up and it's almost noon. She's never slept this long.'

'It was quite a busy day yesterday, she's probably just having a longer lie in,' Kit said. 'Open the curtains and let the sunshine in.'

'I did that an hour ago.' Aunt Sarah's face crumpled. 'I really can't get her to wake up. I touched her hand, pulled the covers back, even shook her, but nothing will wake her.'

Kit's nerves jangled. 'Do you want me to come?'

He followed his aunt down to Adelaide's bedroom. The rug was strewn with discarded clothes and shoes that he recognised from the day before. Her dressing gown was in a pile by the side of the bed and her slippers lay crooked beside them. Adelaide was lying in the bed with her hands neatly folded over her belly.

'Come on, Addie, wake up,' Kit said cheerfully. 'Too much booze last night?'

There was no response. He walked to the bedside, terrified for one moment that she wasn't breathing, but when he held the back of his hand to her mouth, the soft even breath fluttered across it, causing the hairs to stand up.

'Addie, this isn't funny,' he said sharply. He took her wrist. Her pulse had a steady rhythm but was faint and slower than seemed possible.

'She was lying like this when I came in,' Aunt Sarah said feebly.

'Why not ask Mother to telephone Doctor Fulford,' Kit said.

He tried to speak calmly to suggest there was no need to worry, but Aunt Sarah gave a slight moan and fled from the room. Kit stood back and studied Adelaide. Her face was serene and there was even a slight smile on her lips. She didn't look ill; no pallor that suggested a cold, no flush that spoke of fever. He bent over and sniffed at Adelaide's lips, wondering if there was any chance she had taken some drug or other, but there was only the faint smell of rosemary, which he assumed came from her tooth powder.

Rooting through her bedside drawers felt intrusive, but he opened the top one, just in case there was something to explain her heavy sleep. There was only a diary, a pencil and a few bundled handkerchiefs. He drew up a chair and sat beside the bed.

❧

'She is in a state of catatonia,' Doctor Fulford announced, almost perfunctorily, after listening to her heartbeat, lifting her eyelids, tapping her wrists and knees with a small hammer, and lifting her arm to let it flop back into place.

'Why?' Sarah asked.

'No reason I can diagnose, I'm afraid.' He closed his bag with a snap of the clasp and shook his head. 'I have read about cases like it, but usually they are of men returning from the trenches whose minds have overreached their ability to cope.'

'What shall we do? We should be returning home tomorrow,' Aunt Sarah said. She began to cry.

Doctor Fulford picked up his bag and walked to the door. 'Wet her lips hourly and ply her with smelling salts. With luck that will rouse her. I'll return tomorrow if she hasn't woken up.'

'Is that all?' Kit asked in astonishment.

'For the time being.'

'A young lady falls asleep unexpectedly and with no warning, and all you can say is… Well, you haven't really said anything, have you.'

Doctor Fulford sighed impatiently. 'I'm a country doctor. My patients usually come to me for matters like whooping cough or day-to-day ailments, not sudden episodes of catatonia.'

'It wasn't sudden, though; she's been tired for a few days. She was yawning half the afternoon at the fete.'

'Well, then, it's probably a cold. Or possibly she has been overtaxing herself.' He leaned close to Kit and dropped his voice to a confidential whisper. 'There's no chance she could be in a… delicate condition?'

'Absolutely not!' Kit retorted, temper flaring so that he forgot to speak quietly. He drew a deep breath. At least, not that he could lay claim to, and he was not going to cast aspersions on Adelaide's principles by suggesting anyone else might have got her pregnant.

'Then try not to worry, Master Arton-Price.'

'Did you treat a young boy for excessive sleepiness yesterday?' Kit asked, suddenly remembering the child who had fallen asleep in the middle of the sack race.

'No. However if the child exhibited similar symptoms, then it lends to the theory that there is an illness of some sort going round. I do hope it won't be another influenza.'

The doctor made his farewells and left, leaving the family with no answers and more worries than before he had visited.

Kit hugged his aunt and sent his mother to make tea, then went down to the dining room and shared the news of

Adelaide's illness with his siblings. They were as worried as he was, and everyone agreed that she must have been sickening for something.

'I think I'll motor into Malton in search of another doctor tomorrow,' Kit announced.

It felt disloyal to Doctor Fulford, but he was not happy at the thought of waiting another day to see what the outcome might be.

~

Aunt Sarah spent the day with Adelaide. Kit took her place through the evening, firmly steering his aunt to her own room and sending for soup and crackers.

He dropped off to sleep at about ten but woke with a jerk of his limbs to the beating of wings against the window. The curtains were still open and the sky had a faint summer glow to it. A pigeon was walking back and forth along the window ledge.

'Damned thing!' Kit shouted at it. 'Nearly scared me to death!'

The bird gave him a daring look and then flew off. Kit opened the window. It settled on the branch of a magnolia bush and stared at him with bright black eyes, giving him as haughty an expression as a bird could muster. It gave a low, whooping call.

'Well, I'm not going to talk to you,' Kit shouted, before realising with annoyance that was exactly what he was doing.

A sigh came from the bed behind him.

'Addie?' He spun around.

The moonlight was falling upon her face in a wide beam. Her eyelids fluttered. Kit dashed to her side and squeezed her hand tightly.

'Addie, wake up!'

There was no further movement or sound. He soaked her lips with the sponge as Aunt Sarah had shown him, letting a little water trickle into her mouth. Her lips moved but that meant nothing. Babies a few days old suckled in their sleep instinctively, after all. He waved the smelling salts beneath her nose.

'Silence.'

The word was barely intelligible, but his heart leapt.

'This is rather quiet isn't it,' he said, trying to sound normal. 'I do wish you'd wake up and then we could chat properly.'

The bird chose that moment to return to the window ledge, wings beating in a flurry as it settled. He'd left the sash up and he almost expected it to hop inside. It cocked its head to one side. A ring around its foot glinted in the moonlight. A pet, or a homing dove? Possibly the braver one that had hopped into Miss Dove's lap the previous day.

Something inside him clicked at the name and his stomach churned.

Adelaide hadn't said silence.

She had said Silas.

He swore aloud, jealousy finally getting its claws into him at the realisation she had called for another man in her sleep. He stared back at the window, but the dove had gone.

Adelaide hadn't woken up by the following morning. Kit left her in Sarah's care once more at a little after seven, intending to drive to Malton in search of an alternative doctor.

He didn't make it past the front door before being waylaid by Enid.

'There's a problem with Merelda. She's turning over the sitting room.'

'Turning over?'

'Pulling books off the shelves.' Enid wrung her hands together. 'She's been behaving very strangely ever since she heard the news about Adelaide yesterday evening. We're all deeply concerned about her, and Merry can be a little … eccentric. Can you spare a minute or two?'

'I'll come now,' Kit said. He followed her out to the dovecot.

Merelda had indeed been busy. She had tipped over one of the small ladders in her haste to reach something and was busy sorting through books, discarding some by simply tossing them onto the floor, but placing others on the table. She turned at the sound of his footsteps.

'There is none as blind as those who won't see,' she snapped. She glared at the pile of books on the floor.

'Do you think we are going to find a cure in these books?' Kit asked gently. 'I think most of them are poetry and fiction. I'm not sure there's anything scientific enough.'

'There is none as blind as those who won't see,' Merelda repeated. 'Look in there!'

She tapped the end of her cane on one of the volumes she had placed on the table. Kit cocked his head to the side to read the title. It was a collection of poetry by Robert

Browning. He gave a weary groan, but he had a brief glimmer of hope that she'd found something useful. Hadn't Elizabeth Barrett Browning been inflicted with some sort of illness? Did Merelda believe that Adelaide was suffering from the same? Perhaps there was some method in her madness after all. He didn't remember any poems about it though.

'Thank you,' he said, thinking it best to humour her. 'I'll take it with me and study it carefully.'

He reached an arm out.

'Let me help you down from there. Enid, perhaps you can take her other arm. Would you like some tea? Both of you can come up to my flat if you'd like. I can get one of the housemaids to come and tidy your room.'

'Thank you, that's very kind, yes we'd like that,' Enid said gratefully.

Merelda appeared a little bit calmer now.

'Bring the books,' she instructed, smoothing down her hair and adjusting the seam on her left glove.

She gave her arm to Enid as Kit scooped up the books from the table, including the book of Browning's poetry and followed them. If it kept Merelda happy, he would read it later.

'Tell me everything that passed between you and Silas Wilde,' Merelda commanded as soon as he sat down in his sitting room.

Kit sucked his teeth. He'd dropped off to sleep with that name at the forefront of his mind, thanks to Adelaide's muttering. Merelda had warned him against the man, but he'd disregarded it.

'When I came across you in the maze on the night of the

party, I got the impression you knew Mr Wilde already. Am I right? Did you know Miss Dove as well?'

'No not that one,' Merelda answered. She leaned back and closed her eyes. 'Yes, I knew Silas Wilde, when I was younger. He tried to do me a service but wasn't able. He's dangerous.'

The pronunciation resulted in another bout of coughing.

'So, was it you who invited them?' Kit asked, when she had finished. He was surprised at the degree of outrage on Merelda's face at what he'd thought a simple question.

'Absolutely not! I'm surprised you could even contemplate it after my warnings. I know better than to invite them into my home. No, I imagine you'll find it was my foolish sister. Your grandmother has no sense and far too much compassion for a pity story. All their talk about restoring their homeland, and now look where it's led.'

'Yes that's what Miss Dove said to me. She wanted my help but I don't quite know how I could've given it. I know Adelaide and Mr Wilde had been having the same conversation. I thought at first they wanted a subscription to some sort of charity but they actually hoped we'd go halfway across Europe with them.'

'They said Europe, did they?'

'Not exactly,' Kit admitted.

Merelda and Enid exchanged a glance. 'I suspect Adelaide agreed, and now this is where it's got her.'

'She did agree, though I think it was mainly to spite me.' Kit avoided their eyes, hating to admit to the quarrel. 'I hoped that her enthusiasm would wear off when she learnt what it would entail. I hardly think you can blame him for her illness.'

'No, you don't think,' Merelda said, her exasperation clear.

'It's not your fault, I suppose… But I can't help you. And when I say that I don't mean that I wouldn't like to, I mean I can't. You'll have to work this one out for yourself. Remember the games you used to play and look at what I've given you.' She craned her head round to the table where the books lay. 'Read them and learn from them. I can't tell you, but when you think you know, I can answer.'

'Of course,' Kit said. He glanced at the top book. 'Fairy tales?'

Enid tutted. 'A modern young man like you doesn't believe in matters of fancy and fable.'

'No, I don't. Or tea leaves,' he added, thinking back to the conversation with Miss Dove.

Nevertheless, it clearly mattered a great deal to the old women, so he picked up the volumes put them on the table beside the chair and resolved to look at them that evening. He escorted them down the stairs. Halfway down they almost collided with Aunt Sarah who was walking up.

'Kit, it's wonderful. She's awake!'

'Well, that is wonderful,' Kit said. 'We'll come and say hello. See, Merelda, there was nothing to be concerned about.'

'We'll reserve judgement on that, won't we Enid,' Merelda said darkly, sweeping past Kit and leaving him to follow on, increasingly impatient with the old woman's foibles.

Chapter Eight

Merelda's reservations were unfortunately correct. 'Awake' was a very loose definition of Adelaide's condition. She was on the chaise longue in the window bay with her eyes closed when they entered the room.

'Kit is here to see you,' Sybil said in a voice she might have used for a toddler.

Adelaide's head lolled to the side. Her lips formed a wan smile, but she didn't speak. Her eyes opened but they had a glazed air. Her hands flopped loosely in her lap. The sight of the usually vibrant woman was staggering. Kit glanced at Merelda and Enid, conscious that this was the first time they would have seen her. Merelda looked furious.

Kit took Adelaide's hand.

'Hello, Addie, it's good to see you awake. We've all been concerned for you and hope you'll be feeling a lot better soon.'

She did not respond to Kit's greeting instantly, only turning her head and blinking slowly after perhaps seven or eight seconds. It was almost as if a stage hypnotist had put her under his spell.

'You make sure you read those books,' Merelda hissed. 'Enid, come along.' She turned on her heel and stalked out, Enid following behind.

Adelaide accepted a little beef broth by spoon but made no attempt to feed herself. This progress however, and a telephone call to Doctor Fulford, was enough to reassure Aunt Sarah that she was recovering.

'I'm sure by tomorrow she will be perfectly well again and we will be able to travel home. We have a dressmaker's appointment on Thursday.'

'Well, you are welcome to stay as long as necessary,' Kit told her.

He rode over to visit Oliver at his practice in Helmsley and told him of Adelaide's progress.

'That little fellow from the sack race seems to be suffering from the same thing. There's a child who needs a bit more nourishment,' Oliver said.

'I'll have cook send some beef broth over,' Kit said. He thought for a moment. 'I know Doctor Fulford didn't treat him. Can you tell me which doctor he saw.'

The physician in question lived in a small, disconcertingly dilapidated cottage in a back street close to the castle. It was identified only as a surgery by the brass plate proclaiming it the home of *John Smith, MBChB.* He was an older man with wide, deep-set eyes, a beaked nose and a shock of curly, greying hair. He greeted Kit with a firm handshake and offered him a boiled sweet from a paper bag.

'Yes, I saw the child. You say there's another sufferer of the same condition? How interesting.'

Kit recounted Adelaide's situation. 'Do you think they might be suffering with the same illness?'

'Almost certainly.' Doctor Smith muttered something beneath his breath and swept along the passageway, past his consulting room and into a cluttered study. He tipped a pile of newspapers onto the floor, pulled out a box that had been buried beneath them and began rooting through it.

'The latest name is Von Economo Disease – named for the neurologist who managed to get his name attached to a monograph – ha! I was in Paris during the war for a time and cases were rife. It's older than that, though. Much older.'

'So it can be treated?' Kit asked, hope rising.

'Not by any method known to medicine.'

The doctor placed a slight emphasis on the final word. Kit seized upon it the way a man submerged to the waist in quicksand might clutch a straggle of seaweed.

'Any method known to anyone else?'

The doctor popped a sherbet lemon in his mouth and crunched it noisily. When he'd finished, he licked his teeth and looked at Kit.

'Throughout history there have been unexplained epidemics. The dancing sickness in Medieval times, the writing tremors half a century ago, the plagues of Egypt.'

'The last one had divine causes,' Kit interjected.

'Who's to say the others didn't, or don't,' the doctor said darkly. 'Or beings other than divine.'

'Thank you for your time,' Kit said politely, standing.

'If you discover anything else, please let me know,' the

doctor said. 'Or if you encounter any persons who might offer more enlightenment, I'd be interested in meeting them.'

'Of course,' Kit said.

Outside he let a long groan erupt. It was no wonder this doctor came cheap; he was clearly a quack whose scientific methods were as sophisticated as Merelda's explanations.

He set off home. The new gelding was an easy ride and already broken in. Kit trotted down the bridleways he had ridden since he'd first climbed into the saddle as a child. An impulse for something more challenging to release some of his frustration saw him turning off across the Home Farm meadows in search of more interesting terrain, with a stream or fences to jump. He cleared three low, stone walls with ease. The gelding found his head, whickering in delight. Spurred on, Kit dug his heels in to take the stream when he saw a young man emerge from the bushes at the other side.

Too late, the gelding had leapt, and it was all he could do to cry out in warning. The man threw himself to one side as Kit tugged sharply on the reins to turn the gelding in the other direction as soon as it landed on the bank. It neighed in frustration and reared up.

Kit jumped down, holding firmly to the reins, trying to bring the spooked animal under control.

'Are you alright?' he asked, looking over his shoulder. 'You!' he exclaimed.

The young man was not a man at all, but Miss Dove. She was dressed in a calf-length shepherd's smock and a felt hat that had confused him.

She climbed to her feet (bare, Kit noticed) and walked to the horse, holding out a hand and whistling in a low tone until the gelding settled and bowed his head. She ran her hands over his nose and the horse blew out a warm breath. Through the veil of alarm that still caused his heart to race, Kit had to admit he was impressed. He let go of the reins, knowing instinctively that the animal would stay put and gave his attention to the woman.

'What are you doing here?'

'These are public ways. I'm not breaking any laws by being here,' she said giving him a hostile look. Small bits of moss were stuck to the front of her smock and flew off in all directions as she brushed her hands briskly over it.

'That's not what I meant,' Kit replied. 'I would swear there was no one around when I started the run up. I could've killed you.'

'That's unlikely,' she replied with dignity.

'Are you alone? Where is Mr Wilde?'

'He has journeyed on.'

'Leaving you alone here?'

'Yes.'

Just for a moment, her voice sounded small, and she looked apprehensive, causing a flicker of pity in Kit's stomach. She rallied, smoothing back her hair with a flicker of her fingers.

'But I shall follow soon. How is Miss Wyndham faring?'

Kit's subconscious tapped at him. There was something odd in her voice, as if she knew something was slightly askance, though he couldn't say what.

'She's a little ill, as a matter of fact. Just under the weather I think.'

'Yes.'

Faring. That was the word. If he hadn't visited the odd

doctor, he might have let it pass but he was beginning to wonder if there was something slightly more sinister at play.

'Do you know something?' he asked sharply.

'I know lots of things,' she replied.

It wasn't the answer he was looking for.

Not divine means, but something else. A bell chimed in his head.

'Do you know anything about Adelaide's illness?'

Her lashes flickered, batting like moths against a window. That she didn't immediately deny it was enough to assure him that she did.

'I did nothing to her.'

'But he did? Wilde?'

He was alert now to the subtleties of conversations with Miss Dove and Mr Wilde. Merelda, too. It seemed everyone was saying things without meaning to, and not saying the whole truth.

'Look here, if you know something you have to tell me. Or tell the doctor. Not necessarily Dr Fulford, but that other chap in Helmsley. I think he's quite interested, and he doesn't think the causes are entirely natural.'

'And what do you think?' she asked, eagerly. She leaned forward, hands on her hips and gave him a coquettish look. 'Would you like to come and find the answers with me?'

Fury fizzed inside Kit. 'This isn't a game. I want the answers, but why the hell would I want to go anywhere with you? Can't you see, with everything going on here I have even less time to go rushing off on a mission of mercy. Adelaide is barely alive. She could die!'

'She won't die.'

'There's a local child who won't wake, either,' Kit said. 'More people, for all I know. Whatever it is, it isn't an isolated case.'

Her brows knitted and she looked genuinely furious. 'That should not have happened. It was nothing to do with us.'

'What shouldn't have happened? Tell me.' Kit grabbed her by the wrist and pulled her to face him. She was wearing her pink bangle and the stone was cold against the edge of his thumb and finger. She looked up at him, her face contorted with anger.

'Release me at once!' she hissed.

'Not a chance. You've just admitted now that you know something. I'll drag you straight to the police unless you tell me. They won't take kindly to suspicious foreign types drugging people.'

'No one's been drugged,' she said. 'There's no need to be hasty. You're so close to the answers now.'

'Then give them to me,' Kit bellowed.

'That's not how it works.'

She smiled infuriatingly, then kicked him on the shin.

The assault was completely unexpected, and as a consequence he let go of her. She fled, leapt across the stream and landed in a crouch. Kit ran to the gelding, which had sauntered to the stream to drink, clambering into the saddle to give chase. But by the time he looked up again she was nowhere to be seen.

～

Adelaide had resumed her sleeping state by the time Kit got home. Furious that he'd let Miss Dove slip from his grasp, he received the news with a grimace. The temperature had dropped dramatically and the wind was blowing an unseasonably cold gale. Twice, he caught sight of a statue lining the pathway outlined with the shimmering that resembled a heat haze, and jumped in alarm, believing it to be a living person.

After dinner – a sombre affair which not even his favourite trout croquettes and curried lamb chops could save – he went back to his apartment. His windows were wide open and the curtains billowed, forming shapes like the shroud on an unquiet banshee. He walked to the window and stared out. The grounds were too quiet, with not even a flurry of wings as birds settled for the night but he felt eyes raking over him.

He slammed the sash down and pulled the curtains closed. The pattern in the heavy brocade had always resembled comforting lions' faces when he was younger. Now they smirked and twisted, as if wishing to be free from their prison.

He took off his shirt and replaced it with a comfortable old sweater. The weather had no business being so cold in May. He made a mug of cocoa, staring blankly at the milk while it shuddered to a boil in the small pan then took the drink to his favourite chair and sat down. Something jabbed him in the small of the back and he reached round to rearrange the cushion and found he was sitting on a book. He unearthed it and glanced at the title.

Virgil's *Georgics*. He'd studied it at school, but this wasn't his copy, which, last he saw it, was dog-eared and full of jottings, doodles and rude notes as befitted a book owned by a sixteen-year-old. He recognised it as one of the volumes that Merelda had hurled from her shelves. A feather was slipped into a page and he opened it curiously. It marked the story of Orpheus in book four. Something inside Kit's brain twanged like a rubber band, snapping against his temple. He put the book on the table with the others, glancing with a smattering of weariness at the pile that he hadn't even looked at.

Craving something sweet to eat, he fetched a tin of ginger biscuits from the shelf. Something twanged in his brain again and on the way back to his chair he paused and studied the titles in more detail. *The Green Book of Fairy Tales*, the Orpheus story again in Virgil, as well as a copy of *The Tale of Orpheus and Erudices his Quene* by a poet called Henryson that he was unfamiliar with. The Browning anthology, *Men and Women*, that he hadn't read before.

One in particular caught his eye – *The Science of Fairy Tales*. He didn't know that one so took it back to his seat and flicked through it as he dipped the biscuits into his cocoa. It was a book of fairy law that appeared to be a serious academic work, rather than the children's stories he was expecting, detailing ways of dealing with the Fae, how to avoid entrapment, how to seek favours. One whole chapter was devoted to humans taken by the fairies, only to return when everyone they knew had grown old. Another listed examples of men and women who journeyed to the Fae lands to rescue stolen loved ones. It was very similar in fact to the story of Orpheus who followed Euridice into the underworld.

Browning's *Men and Women* contained the poem of Childe Roland, whose sister was snatched by the Elf king. A book of fairy tales contained the same story, along with countless others of people beguiled into following a dazzling man or woman into a land of fantastic beings. Keats' *Belle Dame Sans Merci* was a not unexpected inclusion. There was a common theme running through them all. Bewitchment or the stealing of someone to fairyland.

Merelda had told him with some force that the books held the explanation, but she could not genuinely believe that fairy enchantment or the work of ancient gods was behind Adelaide's illness.

Kit laughed aloud.

Something thudded against the window, causing him to jump and drop the book. He crossed the room and flung open the curtains. A dove was beating at the panes, buffeted back and forth by the wind. The pink band on its leg suggested it was the same tame one from the previous day. It landed on the sill and folded its wings, gazing at Kit with a calmness that was disconcertingly sentient. Without knowing quite why, he lifted the sash. The dove remained where it was, cocking its head and giving a soft, warbling coo. He'd quite liked the carrier pigeons that had taken messages from place to place during the war. They were undemanding company. If this one was lost it would naturally gravitate to humans.

'Hello, little bird,' Kit said. 'It's a bit rough out there. Do you want to come in?'

The dove had something in its beak and when it dropped it, Kit saw it was a portion of walnut shell. The shell wobbled as it landed, then settled. The sight shouldn't have unnerved him, but a shiver washed over Kit, cold sweat gathering in his armpits and between his shoulder blades.

'Is that for me?' he asked with a shaky laugh. 'I'm not sure what I can give you in return, unless you'd like a ginger biscuit.'

The dove cooed again.

'Shame Miss Dove isn't here to talk to you,' he said, with a laugh that he would later look back on and curse himself for his dullness.

He walked back to the chair and broke off a section of biscuit, crumbling it in his hands as he walked back to the window, but by then the bird had gone.

It was almost ten. He yawned and caught himself, nervous that he might be falling ill, too, but told himself to stop being foolish. He'd spent the previous night sleeping in an armchair in Adelaide's room and the few before that feeling restless. He craved a good night's sleep, though couldn't remember one that hadn't been plagued with the usual nightmares of war and his last fight with Andrew.

He finished his cocoa, extinguished the lamps in the sitting room then got ready for bed. He took the Browning with him and began to read but before long, his eyes grew too tired and he closed them for longer intervals at a time.

The church bells were ringing eleven when he awoke, book face down on his chest, aware by some primordial sense that he was not alone. He opened his eyes with a start to discover Miss Dove was standing at the end of his bed, shafts of moonlight illuminating her like a stained-glass window.

He jerked upright.

'What the hell! How did you get in here? The door's locked.'

'You invited me. I didn't come through the door,' she said.

She stepped closer to the end of the bed and gestured to the book. 'You are almost there. So close.'

'Stop where you are!' Kit held out his palm and sat up. The book slid to the floor. Miss Dove ignored his instruction and dropped to her knees at the side of the bed. When she stood, she had the book in her hand.

'I never liked this poem, it's gruesome and unsettling,' she said, holding it out to him. 'Only the worst of us would behave like that.'

'I don't care what you like,' Kit snarled. He threw the covers back and snatched the book from her. 'I don't know how you got into my apartment, but I want to know exactly what you know about Adelaide. And tell me the truth, in plain words. I'm done with cryptic conversations and nonsense about fairy tales. It feels like everyone but me has become addled.'

'You aren't addled,' Miss Dove said. 'You just need to let yourself believe the truth.'

'The truth being that Adelaide is under an enchantment. That Silas Wilde is a fairy and at any point she might wake up and follow him to fairyland.'

'Almost right. Well done. Though we prefer to be called Fae not fairy and our land is known as the *Faedemesne*.' Miss Dove's lips curved into a delighted smile. 'And your bride doesn't need to wake up to follow him there. She's already gone.'

Chapter Nine

For a moment, Kit said nothing, far too astonished to form the thoughts, let alone the words, that would articulate his sense of confusion. He walked around Miss Dove and kicked the door shut, keeping his eyes on her face at all times as he walked back to her. Of all the things she claimed, one stood out to him more than the others.

'Adelaide hasn't gone anywhere,' he said slowly.

'Her body, no. Her … being… Yes. She travels with him now. I was there when they left.'

Miss Dove sounded perfectly rational for someone who had just admitted to being a fairy. Convincingly so.

'You're a fairy and—'

'A fae,' she interrupted. 'I just told you that.'

'Fae. Let's say I believe you, and that Silas Wilde has magically stolen away Adelaide's soul because she accepted something from him – that's what you're expecting me to believe, isn't it?'

She didn't answer but her eyes darted to the door and a

subtle tensing of her frame made Kit sure she was about to run. He took a step between her and the door.

'Tell me the truth!' he yelled.

She jumped and, as he had suspected, she darted round him, but not to the door, to the window. He was quicker and seized her by the back of her dress, jerking her to a standstill. She tried to wriggle free, but he held tight, fury overcoming his scruples about handling a woman in such a manner.

'No, you don't! Whatever you claim to be, you're an accomplice to abduction. I'm sending for the police.'

'Abduction? Miss Wyndham is ill in bed.' Miss Dove looked smug. 'What will you tell the police?'

Her words gave him pause. What would he say? Admitting to his outlandish suspicions would see him laughed out of the police station or admitted to an asylum.

He took her by the arms and brought her face close to his. She was panting and her eyes gleamed. She looked as if she was enjoying herself. Kit wasn't a violent man, and the idea of striking a woman was abhorrent to him but he could quite happily have shaken Miss Dove until her teeth rattled.

'I will tell them that you broke into my flat – and I'm not exactly sure how you got in, which is something we can discuss later – and that you admitted your guardian is responsible for Addie's state. I'll mention that you might be supplying her with drugs, and they can start from there.'

She laughed. 'Might as well tell them she pricked her finger on a spindle or ate a poisoned apple.'

Kit let go of her and raked his hands through his hair. He looked at her bleakly.

'Why don't you tell me the truth, rather than all the nonsense from fairy tales.'

'That is the truth,' Miss Dove said, sounding frustrated. 'Why couldn't you have accepted it as easily as Adelaide obviously did? I can see you need to see for yourself. Go to Miss Wyndham's room. Silas will have given her something to use as a key to the gate. Finding *that* might convince you.'

'Something? Don't you know what?'

She looked shifty. 'I do, but I'm unable to tell you. It's not my settlement. You need to hunt for it yourself.'

She was so earnest that he was starting to believe her, despite the nonsense it clearly was. Kit heaved a sigh. He felt fully awake now after only an hour of napping, and he might as well do something productive with his time. He put on his dressing gown and slippers.

'All right. I'll go and look.'

'Let's go now.'

She turned towards the door. Kit caught her by the arm again.

'You aren't going anywhere near Adelaide.'

'Then I'll stay here.' She looked unsurprised, and he wondered if she had ever expected him to agree. He looked her up and down. What to do with her while he searched was a conundrum. He didn't want her alone in his rooms, yet he didn't trust her enough to let her leave the house. He thought briefly of tying her to a chair but disregarded the idea as improper. He needed somewhere secure, and the perfect place flashed into his mind.

'Come with me,' he commanded, tugging her with him.

'Where are we going?'

She pulled against him, but he took firm hold of her arm and put the other around her waist. He marched her through the building until he reached the servant's wing where the butler's pantry was located. Leading off from that private domain was the plate room. It didn't contain as much silverware as it had at the height of the family's wealth, because over the years various members had sold it off to meet debts. What it did have, however, was a door that comprised two layers of wood with iron bars inserted between them, and a grille on the small window. Everything too large to be stored in the locked cupboards was so obvious that if Miss Dove tried to steal anything while he was gone, he would spot its absence immediately.

Kit had expected the pantry to be empty, but the butler was sitting at the table in his shirtsleeves, poring over the racing pages of a newspaper and eating a sandwich. He jumped to attention when Kit walked in, closing the pages hastily.

'Good evening, Mr Crossle. I'm sorry to disturb you so late but this woman knows something about what has happened to Miss Wyndham. Until I can find out I want to put her in the plate room. Do you have the key?'

'Of course, sir.' Crossle flashed a nasty look at Miss Dove. He'd worked for the family for decades and had always had a soft spot for Adelaide. He produced a ring of keys, slipped a large, iron one off the ring, and unlocked the door to the plate room.

Kit led Miss Dove to the door. As soon as she saw the room she let out a piercing wail and began to struggle against Kit.

'You can't put me in there!'

'It's perfectly safe and you'll be able to breathe. The

window is small, but I can open it a crack, and there are air holes so that the room doesn't get damp.'

She was creating such a fuss, her eyes wide with genuine alarm, that it occurred to Kit she may suffer from claustrophobia and his determination briefly wavered.

'Mr Crossle, will there be any handcuffs about the place?' he asked. 'The table here would be too heavy for her to move if I cuffed her to a leg.'

'Unlikely to find any in the house, sir, but I could go out to the gamekeeper's cottage and see what I can find lying around.' Crossle's eyes fell on Miss Dove. 'There may be a mantrap we could repurpose,' he said nastily.

'That's enough,' Kit said sharply. 'Well, Miss Dove, what is it to be? The plate room or Mr Crossle's rather archaic suggestion?'

He was being a little disloyal to the butler, but really, mantrap, indeed!

'But the iron,' Miss Dove whimpered. 'Please, no, I beg you!'

Her eyes filled with tears but Kit steeled his resolve and prodded her gently in the back to propel her forward into the room. He had been careful not to use excessive force, but as soon as they crossed the threshold she stumbled and collapsed in a ball on the floor, clutching her head.

'It hurts,' she moaned.

'If you have hurt yourself then it's your fault for flinging yourself to the ground in such a manner,' growled Crossle from the doorway.

'Fetch her something to sit on,' Kit asked.

Crossle provided a low chair and Kit took it into the room, placing it against one of the cupboards.

'Here, there's no point sitting on the floor.'

She didn't move so he put his arms under her armpits and lifted her. She weighed almost nothing. Her head rolled backwards and he almost dropped her with shock. She felt hot to the touch but her complexion was ashen, as if she'd lost a couple of pints of blood.

'I'll be as quick as I can searching Miss Wyndham's room and come back once I've found whatever I'm looking for. If you're ready to tell me the truth, we can talk.'

He lowered her onto the chair, whereupon she slumped against the door of the cupboard with a sigh.

'Please Kit, don't go. Don't leave me here. I'll die.' Her voice was a whisper. Her words an echo too painful to be endured. Guilt drove a fist into Kit's ribs and he almost changed his mind. He couldn't have her blood on his hands. Then he pictured Adelaide lying on the chaise, her eyes fixed blankly on nothing. He had no choice but to commit to his plan. He balled his fists and pressed them hard against his temples then took a breath and turned back to Miss Dove.

'You're being melodramatic. The sooner you tell me what's really going on, the sooner I'll let you out of here.'

Her eyes rolled back as she focused on him. It looked to be taking a lot of effort.

'My truth is told. If you can't see it, then there's no more I can do in the telling.'

'It would really help if you gave me a hint what I should be looking for,' he snapped.

'Find the thing that doesn't fit in the room.' Miss Dove's

voice was slurred and barely audible. She dragged her head up and focused on his eyes. 'Something she's been given.'

It wasn't much of a hint.

He walked out, closed the door behind him and locked it. He thought about leaving the key in the lock, in case Crossle needed to open the door, but given the butler's animosity towards Miss Dove, he wasn't sure that would be in anyone's interests so he stuck it in his pocket, informed Crossle that he would be back as soon as possible, and left.

≈

Aunt Sarah was dozing in the chair by the bed. She woke up with a start when Kit tapped her shoulder.

'Is it morning already?'

Kit looked at his watch. It was just after eleven. No wonder he felt weary.

'No, I just came to check on you.'

He glanced around the room but there was nothing untoward that was immediately obvious. No magic spinning wheel or glass slipper.

He hugged his aunt. 'Aunt Sarah, why don't you go and sleep in your own bed? Addie looks peaceful and nothing is going to happen to her tonight.'

'Will you stay?' Sarah asked.

'For a little while, but really the best thing we can both do is keep well. You don't want to become ill yourself.'

Sarah nodded and made her way wearily out of the room.

'Right, Addie,' Kit murmured once the door was closed. 'Tell me what you've been hiding.'

It would have been helpful if Adelaide had been a neater person. Her discarded clothes were now hanging in the wardrobe, or had been taken by the laundry maid so the floor was clear. The bookshelf was cluttered with trinkets and photographs, while magazines covered the shelves. The dressing table was strewn with pots of creams, bottles of scent and a large bottle of setting lotion. Her jewellery box was open, but there was nothing unusual that he didn't recognise. He checked the wardrobes and drawers, past caring about his intrusion into her privacy. A bitter taste filled his mouth. How stupid, how gullible must he be to have believed what Miss Dove had said to him! Of course, there was no such things as the Fae, it was all a huge joke on her part.

Except…

Merelda had thought so. The doctor did, too. Was Kit being stupid by refusing to allow the possibility?

Kit dropped to the floor and looked under the bed but there was nothing except a pair of slippers and a discarded paper tissue. He was about to stand, when the scent of lilacs filled his nose. It was unusual enough to catch his attention because he was familiar with the various perfumes Adelaide wore for daytime or evening, summer or winter and none of them smelled of lilacs. So where was the fragrance coming from?

Taking as much care as possible not to disturb Adelaide, he slid a hand under the pillow. His fingers brushed against petals. A ripple of triumph caused him to grunt but the sound didn't wake her. Carefully, he drew his discovery out. It was the posy Adelaide had obtained at the fete. One of the three flowers was missing all the petals, leaving only a bare stem.

The flowers were days old. By now they should be wilted

and crushed almost beyond recognition, especially after being beneath a pillow, but they were as fresh as the day he had first seen them. Even as he watched, the largest flower unfolded itself slightly, creased petals smoothing and plumping up. The scent pounded into his senses with a voluptuousness that was overbearing.

Kit swallowed, his mouth drying. Up until then he hadn't genuinely believed there was any truth in Miss Dove's words, but now his faith in the rational laws of the world were eroding by the second. He felt as though he had stepped onto an icy pond and seen the zigzag lines breaking on its surface under his weight. One more piece of impossible evidence would see him plunging into the depths.

'What have you done, Adelaide?' he muttered, crushing the flower in his palm.

She gave a long moan that vibrated with pleasure.

Miss Dove was waiting but she'd have to wait longer. Kit needed to talk to Merelda. It was too late, really, to go traipsing across the grounds, but he wanted to be sure he was not going slowly insane. He slipped the flowers into his dressing-gown pocket and walked to the dovecot, picking his way in semi-darkness. Tongues of damp grass lapped at his bare ankles unpleasantly.

Enid answered his knock. She was dressed in a red and gold smoking jacket and her hair was in papers. She looked him rapidly up and down.

'Come in,' she said, before he'd even spoken. 'We haven't gone to bed yet. We were about to have some cocoa.'

The dovecot was lit only by candles and smelled of chamomile and sage. Merelda was stirring an iron pan hanging over the fire suspended on the kettle chain. Her hair trailed down her back as it always did which contributed to the otherworldly effect. She looked at Kit and her eyes twinkled. It was undoubtedly Kit's already warped imagination, but tonight he felt convinced he was walking into a witch's cottage.

She tapped the spoon against the pan then walked to the sofa. 'You read the books.'

'I read the titles. I've skimmed through a couple of them.'

Merelda smiled.

'Will you tell me why you gave me them now?'

She shook her head.

'Why not?' Kit asked tersely, flopping down onto a low, overstuffed armchair. Enid came back into the room carrying a small bottle. She sat down beside Merelda and the two women held hands.

'Have a guess,' Enid said. 'I thought you were supposed to be the clever one.'

'Don't be harsh on him, dear,' Merelda scolded gently. 'He's so clever he doesn't remember how to be intelligent. He doesn't believe what he sees. I gave you those books in particular because…'

She gave the familiar coughing croak and stopped talking, gesturing to the bottle. Enid passed it to her. Merelda swigged from it.

'That's better. Kit, I can't answer your questions, I've told you that already.'

Miss Dove had told him she couldn't help him, either. He sat back, trying to piece everything together. 'Whenever you try to talk about it you start coughing.'

Merelda smiled. 'True.'

'Is there a reason for that?'

She looked away.

'There's a reason you can't, isn't there.'

Merelda smiled again. 'True.'

Kit suspected he was getting the idea now. 'You can only answer if the question requires a confirmation or denial.'

Enid beamed. 'Finally!'

Merelda smiled and took another swig from the bottle. Kit tried to frame his next question. 'Is there a limit on the number of questions I can ask?'

Enid snorted. 'If there was, then that was a particularly stupid waste of one, wasn't it?'

He acknowledged it with a bashful grin, thinking that Enid had given him the answer. No limit. It posed interesting questions about Enid and what she knew.

'You gave me these books because the characters get taken by the Fae and this has happened to Adelaide.'

A tear trickled down Merelda's cheek, travelling a path along the wrinkles. 'Yes,' she whispered.

'But she's still here in body, even though her soul has gone somewhere else.'

'You seem remarkably at ease with the idea. More than I'd expected,' Merelda said. 'Why?'

The milk in the pan chose that point to boil over, causing a hiss that made Kit jump. Enid put on an oven glove and poured it into the cocoa jug. She whisked vigorously then added a generous quantity of what Merelda had been drinking. The scent of honey filled the room.

'What is that?' Kit asked.

'Mead,' Merelda answered. 'The libation that gives our home its name, though the origin is long forgotten I fear.'

Enid handed him a mug and he took a drink. His mind filled with the image of an autumn forest. Of tired bees crawling their slow way to the hives where they had laboured throughout the summer. Sadness wound through his veins, strangling him like ivy claiming a house.

'Why do you believe?' Merelda asked. 'It's not just the books. It would take more than that.'

'I'm not at ease, at all. I want to think the whole thing is a joke or some sort of delusion, but it seems that I might be wrong about that.' Kit took a long breath and pulled the flowers out of his pocket. He placed them on the table where they lay, innocuous enough but with a sharper edge to their outline than should be possible.

'I found these beneath Adelaide's pillow. I think Silas Wilde gave them to her on the day of the fair. I think that somehow they did what you suspect.'

The two women stared at them. Merelda extended a finger and prodded the blooms then sniffed dismissively.

'What you're telling me is unbelievable. It's completely impossible,' Kit said. 'The only reason I'm even contemplating it being true is because I've had the same explanation from Miss Dove.'

Merelda and Enid exchanged a glance.

'When?' Merelda asked.

'Tonight. I found her in my room. I don't know how she got there without being seen.'

The dove sitting on the windowsill bobbed into his mind, but he dismissed it. One outlandish thing at a time.

'She told me a story that is beyond belief. She told me that both she and Wilde are fairies. Fae,' he corrected. He looked at Merelda to gauge her reaction, but she merely waved a hand, indicating he should continue.

'It was Miss Dove who told me to look for something strange in Adelaide's possession.'

'Where is she now?' Merelda asked.

'She's secure,' Kit said. 'I locked her in the plate room.'

Merelda dropped her cup. Cocoa splattered her nightgown, but she didn't seem to notice.

'You enclosed her in iron! Whose wrath are you trying to provoke? You have no idea what you're dealing with, and if she dies you'll rue it.'

'She's not going to die,' Kit said, startled by the reaction.

"Don't leave me here, Kit."

He folded his arms defensively. 'There is plenty of air and it's warm enough.'

'It's bound by iron, you wantwit,' Merelda sighed.

'A touch of it is as painful to her as mustard gas is to you,' Enid added.

'That's nonsense,' Kit said.

Merelda scoffed. 'Nonsense, is it? Take her my kettle and ask her to pour it. She won't even lift the handle. I bet she didn't want to go in there, did she.'

'Of course she didn't. She was being locked in a cupboard under threat of me calling the police.'

'And I bet she swooned,' Enid muttered.

Kit couldn't meet her eye, remembering the lolling head and pallid skin.

'If you don't want a death on your hands, you'd better

release her quick, and if you don't want a curse on you, you'd better make apologies,' Merelda said.

Kit scowled. 'I'm not apologising for anything. She's an accomplice to a kidnapping. Well, a kidnapping of sorts, hell, I don't know! I don't understand any of this. You don't even seem surprised at what I'm telling you. How do you know all this anyway?'

Merelda opened her mouth and only croaking came out. The same awful croaking that came whenever she tried to answer his questions. He took a breath.

'Merelda,' he asked carefully. 'Are you under a spell?'

'The truth,' she breathed.

Kit balled his hands into fists, remembering the curious phrase Silas had used. He'd assumed Silas was getting the expression wrong because English wasn't his native language but perhaps he'd been wrong. 'Merelda, do you have a toad on your tongue?'

She shut her eyes tightly and opened her mouth. Kit looked. It was a normal tongue, as far as he could tell.

'Silas Wilde is a…'

Merelda got no further through the sentence before the shape of her mouth changed and a squat, bulbous shape lay where her tongue should be. Small eyes caught the candlelight, turning the creature's old, black pupils orange as they stared at Kit. It gave one, long croak.

Kit's stomach heaved and the taste of bile filled his throat. He jerked to his feet, trying to escape the stifling room, but too late. He dropped to his knees and threw up expansively on the rug.

Chapter Ten

Kit vomited relentlessly, heaving up cocoa and ginger biscuits until only stomach acid remained. Throughout, Merelda rubbed his back, her palm moving in slow circles as she murmured words of comfort that did nothing to ease his revulsion at what he'd just seen. When his stomach had nothing left to surrender, he gazed up at her, his eyes swimming from the exertion. Genuine tears weren't far behind, he suspected.

'That's… Who did that to you?'

Merelda looked at him, impatience writ large over her face.

'Of course, you can't answer. Oh God, Merelda, you poor thing, it must be torture. Does anyone else know?'

Enid handed him a handkerchief and a glass of water. He wiped his mouth then took a long drink.

'Only me. And the man – the creature – who did this to her. I guessed within minutes of meeting her. My great-grandmother was raped by a kelpie so I've a touch of The Sight, you see.'

'This is madness.' Kit sank back on the chair, his legs no longer supporting him as he struggled to comprehend what had happened to his world. His ears buzzed, making everything sound distant and muffled, reminiscent of the after-effects of a bombing raid.

'You, casually talking about fairies and spells and whatever that thing you mentioned. If it's true, it turns everything we know about the world on its head.'

'*If* it's true? I'm starting to get a little impatient that you don't accept it after what you've seen and what you've told me tonight,' Merelda snapped. 'Did you weep and wail with denial like a child when you were faced with the battlefield and the folly of men?'

Kit shook his head. He felt his mind let go of his doubts and the relief that came with it. Merelda's expression softened.

'Go back and talk to Miss Dove. For the sake of all of us release her from her prison before the entire force of the Unseelies descends on us. I've set you on the path as much as I can. The rest is up to you. If it leads to Adelaide being unenchanted, then that's to the good.'

'Take this,' Enid said, holding out the bottle of mead.

'I've got whisky in my room, thank you,' Kit replied.

She looked at him pointedly. 'Mead is always a good thing to have for emergencies.'

Obediently, he slipped it into his dressing-gown pocket beside the lilacs. He walked to the door, but before stepping outside a thought struck him.

'Was it Silas Wilde who cursed you?' he asked Merelda.

'No. I have no doubt he's as duplicitous as the rest of his

species and I wish you'd heeded my warnings, but he has never harmed me.'

'Good. That's one less reason to take vengeance on him.'

He bristled with anger as he returned to the butler's pantry.

Crossle was sitting on the comfortable chair smoking his pipe and reading the newspaper. He sat up sharply as Kit entered.

'Any trouble?' Kit asked. He squared his shoulders, the memory of Merelda's toad galvanising him to take no nonsense. His stomach rippled with loathing and disgust once more. He pushed the image from his mind, though he knew in truth it would never leave him and would join the catalogue of mud and blood-soaked trenches and battlefields that taunted him at night.

'Been as quiet as a mouse.'

That should have been reassuring but after Merelda's threats his hand shook as he reached for the key. The reason for the silence became immediately obvious. The chair had been knocked sideways and Miss Dove was lying in a heap, her face hidden from view and one arm stretched to the door. The room was filled with the scent of mimosas. Not the fresh, dewy, honey-like scent that he'd experienced before, but overripe and pungent. He was past the point of caring about odd occurrences by now.

'Miss Dove!'

He dashed to her side and dropped to his knees beside her.

'It could be a trick,' the butler said darkly.

Kit glared round at him. With Merelda and Enid's dire warnings in his head that thought hadn't even occurred to him.

'Crossle, don't just stand there, get me some water!'

The butler looked outraged at the lack of use of his title, but he backed out of the doorway. Kit unearthed Miss Dove's arm, checking for her pulse. It was regular, though very faint and rapid.

'Miss Dove, can you hear me?'

He rolled her onto her back, cradling her head in his lap. Her face was alabaster pale, and her lips bloodless. She didn't respond, so still holding her wrist, he pinched between her thumb and first finger as he'd been taught in the army. The soft spot was so painful to a firm touch that if she was faking, she wouldn't be able to hide her response. Her eyelids fluttered and she gave a soft moan. Crossle appeared at Kit's shoulder with a glass of water. Kit tried to tip a little between her lips but most of it trickled down her chin and neck.

She murmured a word.

'Out.'

Kit had to strain to catch it, she spoke so quietly, but he recognised what she was asking. He didn't hesitate, scooping her into his arms and carrying her out of the unintentional torture chamber.

'I'll put her in your chair, Mr Crossle,' Kit announced, remembering to use the butler's title.

'Miss Dove, can you open your eyes? Alexandra? Can you speak?' Kit asked loudly.

'She's acting, sir,' Crossle said.

'I don't think so.'

She had barely flinched when he had pinched her hand. He gently stroked her cheek and she gave a gentle moan.

'Do you have anything stronger than water?' he asked,

before remembering the bottle Enid had given him. 'Never mind. I have.'

He took the bottle of mead from his pocket and uncorked it. To his intense relief, Miss Dove sniffed and partially opened her eyes.

'Neat or in water do you think?' he asked Crossle. On the battlefield he wouldn't have hesitated in giving a soldier neat liquor, but Miss Dove looked so delicate. Throwing caution to the wind, Kit put the bottle to her lips and tilted it.

She opened her eyes, straining her head forward. He let her sip then withdrew it. Her lips glistened and a single drop of mead lay on the indent in the centre of the bottom lip. Not quite knowing why, Kit reached his finger out and brushed it into her mouth. Her lips tightened around his fingertip and her tongue flickered over the underside of his nail. It was intensely erotic and unnerving. He pulled his finger out.

Miss Dove opened her eyes fully. 'Thank you,' she murmured. 'How did you know about mead?'

'I just happened to have some,' he said. He sat back on his haunches, considering what he'd just said.

He hadn't *just happened to have some*; Merelda and Enid had known it might be useful and pressed it on him. His throat tightened, he still found it hard to believe any of what he was learning, and if it hadn't been for the toad he most likely still wouldn't have. His stomach heaved again, reminding him that for all the sympathy he felt for Miss Dove, she was his enemy.

'Can you walk?' he asked curtly.

'I'll try.'

Kit gave her space to stand. She was a little uncertain on her feet as they walked through the house. He wasn't entirely sure that she wasn't play-acting so he slung one of her arms around his neck and held her wrist. He put his other arm around her waist and caught the scent of mimosa again, but now there was none of the over-sweetness.

It was perfectly logical. When she was ill she smelled of decaying flowers and now she was recovering she smelled fresh because she was a fairy. At this time of night, he was prepared to accept anything. Back in his room he lowered her into a chair in the sitting room, hauled another over and sat opposite her.

'Are you feeling recovered? You can have some more mead if you like. Personally, I'm going to have a large whisky.'

'Does the mead come with conditions?' she asked. Her eyes were starting to look less dazed. 'I don't want it, if that's the case. I'm under enough obligations already.'

She was sounding better too, more belligerent.

'The only condition is that there are more questions I need to ask you.'

'That will do,' she said, and held her hand out for the bottle.

Kit clicked his tongue, wondering about how to phrase them, and also how many he may ask.

'Honestly, I don't even know how to begin,' he said finally. 'What you told me shouldn't be possible. It can't be and yet… And yet, I spoke to my great-aunt. She appeared to confirm some of the things you have said.'

She raised her eyes, lifting a brow questioningly. Otherwise, she sat perfectly still, hands neatly in her lap.

'I saw a damned toad!' he blurted out. 'Your Mr Wilde told her she had a toad on her tongue, and I saw one.'

Far from looking unnerved, Miss Dove smiled and took a swig from the bottle. 'I knew there was something affixed to her, but not all of us can read each other's bedazzlements.'

'Then who did it?'

She looked down at her hands, twisting the bracelet around her wrist.

'Caul Gilling likes to stymie people in that manner.'

'Who is that?'

'No one you'd want to meet,' she said quietly.

'You're going to tell me how to get my fiancée back.'

'I can't. She needs to be where she is.'

'She needs to be *here*.' Kit leaned over her, his heart beginning to thump. 'Because if you don't, I'll surround you with iron until you beg for mercy. Handcuffs, horseshoes. Even Crossle's damned mantrap if I have to.'

'No, you won't, you don't have it in you,' she said, giving a dismissive wave of the hand.

'Oh, really?' He walked away to the window, putting his hands in his dressing gown pockets and his fingers closed around the iron key. He hesitated. If everything he'd learned was true then this would amount to torture, but how could he not do everything within his power to get Adelaide back?

He turned back to face Miss Dove.

'Catch!' he commanded, throwing it at her head.

She reached out as he'd anticipated. It was a natural instinct, especially when coupled with an instruction. Her fingers closed around it and she let out an ear-piercing shriek that could have been surprise, pain or anger, or a mixture of all three. She dropped it immediately and it fell into her lap. With hands like claws, she brushed it off as if spiders played on her gown. She looked up at him with eyes full of accusation and pain.

'You cullion! You waggot!' she spat.

'You didn't think I would be capable? Then you don't know what I suffered in the war.' Kit snarled. His stomach curdled with remorse and he walked back to her side and spoke a little more gently.

'Show me your hand.'

She held it out, curled into a fist. Kit eased her fingers open. There was an inflamed red mark across her palm, the thickness of the key, and the same on the second fold of each finger. Kit winced with guilt. The iron had done this. Everything she said was true.

'That looks painful,' he said quietly.

'Oh, do you think so? How observant!' Her voice dripped with sarcasm, and he couldn't blame her. She turned her wrist over and held it up to the light.

'A crack! Look, the band! It's cracked!' She held her arm out towards Kit. He had to peer closely to make out the almost invisible hairline crack between two of the swirls. It was about the length of his little fingernail and about as thin.

'Don't worry. It's barely noticeable.'

'But it's there,' she whispered, so quietly he could barely hear her. When she raised her head, her eyes were brimming with tears. 'It cracked. The iron did it. And I never even considered that.'

She laughed, loud and wild, then before Kit could react, she had leapt from her chair, thrown herself into his arms and kissed him. Not just a peck on the cheek but full on the mouth. Her lips were soft, skimming his with a lightness that was agonisingly insufficient. He tasted honey from the mead she'd drunk and he kissed her back, hooking an arm behind her head to pull her close while he crushed his mouth with hers. His mind caught up a moment too late and he released her with a cry. Flames danced across his face.

'Why did you do that?' he gasped.

'Because you believed me,' she said. Her eyes filled with tears but she smiled. 'You threatened me with iron. You wouldn't do that if you didn't believe me.'

Kit licked his lips. The lingering trace of mead sent shivers running down his spine and curling into his belly.

'I believe you. After what I've seen tonight I can't not. Now you're going to take me to where Adelaide has gone and you're not going to play any tricks and there aren't going to be any curses or bewitchment.'

'I don't bewitch,' she scoffed. 'That's for witches.'

'Then tell me what you call it.'

'Bedazzlement,' she said sourly. 'Or entrancement.'

'Then I want your word on whatever scrap of honour you have that you will attempt nothing against me.'

'Why do you assume my honour is less than yours,' she sneered.

'Because you associate with an abductor and you would have condemned me to the same fate had I been foolish enough to accept a walnut from you,' Kit said coldly.

'I swear.' She put her forefingers together, then rested her thumbs in the hollow of her collarbone making a sort of triangle shape. 'I swear by the codes to which I am bound, the moon I was born under and the rock I was birthed upon, that I shall not enchant, entrap or bedazzle you.'

'And you won't let anyone else do that to me,' Kit added. 'Swear that, too, that you'll keep me from harm.'

Her eyes glinted. 'You've cunning in that pretty head of yours as well as sweetness on your lips. Yes, I swear I shall be your patron and protectress and your counsel. I will not play you false in this. There, will that do?'

'I think so,' Kit said. It was the best he was going to get, and he'd followed men into battle with less assurances.

She nodded in satisfaction. 'Now, there are things I need, and they are where we've been staying. I'll be back soon. You should probably take a few things with you, too, and change out of your pyjamas.'

Kit glanced down at himself, having completely forgotten what he was wearing. Miss Dove took advantage of his distraction and began to walk to the door, but Kit caught her arm. She looked at his hand pointedly then rolled her eyes. Slightly shamed, he released her.

'I swear I will come back. It's to my advantage to take you there, not only yours. I won't be gone more than a quarter-hour.'

Despite everything, Kit was intrigued. 'Where have you been staying?'

'There's an old house at the furthest end of the village from here that has been a wayfaring house for centuries. The landlady kindly let us have a room.'

'The Pipe and Drum? You won't get there and back in that time,' Kit pointed out. 'It'll take you ten minutes at least to cross the grounds and the bridge, and that's in daytime when there's nothing to trip over.'

'Let's say I'll take the route as the crow flies.'

She laughed and Kit felt, as with so much recently, that he was missing something. The flavour of an idea tickled his mouth; a suspicion so outlandish that he needed time to think it over. Miss Dove clapped her hands and he lost the threads.

'Fifteen minutes in front of where the maze opens.' She left the room.

Kit went to his bedroom, changed from his pyjamas into trousers and a shirt and pulled a sweater over the top. He still owned a canvas rucksack from his teenage years when he'd gone camping, and it had less unpleasant associations than his army knapsack. He had no idea how long he would be gone for, so packed two changes of socks and underwear just in case; the experiences of soaking wet feet in the trenches having made him determined never to suffer that again. His toothbrush and pot of tooth powder joined them, along with the bottle of mead.

His stomach growled and he made himself a pot of tea and toast to replace the food that his stomach had evacuated, then put the half-eaten packet of ginger biscuits into the bag, thinking they'd be useful for keeping hunger at bay.

His heart gave a thump and he shivered. What was the point of all this preparation, when he would most likely be lying in a stupor on his bed like Adelaide was? Did his possessions go with him in whatever dreamlike state he was in? He hoped so. He thought about scribbling a note to his parents telling them not to worry but decided against it on the basis that no one would believe him. Except, of course, the two people who would. He checked his watch. Only seven minutes had elapsed. He slung the bag onto his shoulder and ran out to the dovecot.

This time it took three knocks before Enid opened the door. Without waiting to be asked, Kit rushed in. Merelda was making her way slowly down from the bedroom.

'I'm going with Miss Dove. I need you to tell me everything I need to know to be safe. I'm sure there are lots of rules in the books, but I don't have time to read them.'

Merelda completed her descent.

'Words have power. Be respectful. Don't make a bargain unless the terms suit you, and make sure you ask bravely. Don't make a promise without something in return. Don't stray from the path, however tempting.'

Enid had gone into the kitchen as soon as Kit had spoken. Now she returned and handed him a couple of apples and a slice of tea bread wrapped in waxed paper.

'Take these to ward off hunger. Don't take food or drink offered without ensuring it places you under no obligation – ask that specifically. Freely given and no obligation. Remember the words. You don't want to end up like Proserpine, trapped because of your belly.'

'Is this freely given and with no obligation?' Kit asked.

The women nodded. 'That'll do.'

Both of them embraced him and kissed his cheeks.

'Good luck,' Merelda said. 'Bring Adelaide home, but remember that if you fail it won't be from want of trying.'

Kit raised his head, feeling a little like he had on the day he'd joined the regiment. They'd left as young men with nervous bellies but optimistic hearts and had won the war but at a cost that sometimes felt too high to have paid.

'I don't intend to fail.'

Miss Dove was waiting for him outside the maze. She was

wearing a rather worn grey cloak that fell to her knees. She pulled a long thread from out of the embroidery at the hem, then reached to Kit's jumper and pulled one out, ignoring his objection. She had a satchel across her body and took out a small spool of silver thread and broke off a long piece. She plaited the three strands together into a long thread, her fingers moving deftly like a spider testing a web. She tied a knot in each end then held it out.

'Give me your wrist, I need to bind us together.'

'Like hell you will,' Kit said sharply. 'You're not putting any enchantment on me.'

She gave him a patient look. 'It's not an enchantment. We have to travel together, and we could become separated if we're not careful. If that happens, you'll never find your way backwards or forwards and you could end up taking a minute to travel or a year, or never get there at all.'

Kit's mouth dried out. His face must have showed his apprehension because Miss Dove patted his shoulder in a comforting manner.

'Don't worry, that almost never happens and if we're joined then whatever happens we'll be together. As soon as we reach our destination, I'll undo it.'

Cautiously, Kit extended his arm. Miss Dove took hold of his hand and gave it a gentle squeeze before tying the thread around his wrist. She did the same with the other end. Side by side they walked to the exit of the maze. Kit expected her to pause and ask if he was ready. To check that he truly wanted to go with her. Or tell him it wasn't too late to turn back. She did none of those things and he was quite thankful for that, because he was not sure what his answer would have been.

'Hold this,' she instructed passing him a walnut. He held it in the palm of his hand and she took a short-bladed knife from her satchel and used it to cut down the grooves between the two halves of the shell and wiggled it. The two halves fell apart neater than Kit had ever managed to crack walnuts at Christmas, revealing the brain-like meat of the nut. Miss Dove took the two kernels and crushed them between her palms, murmuring words that Kit could not catch. She raised her palms and blew on them. The fragments of nut curved into the air and hung in an arc that ignored the law of gravity.

It was nearly midnight and the air was chilly but it began to shimmer as it did on a hot day when the heat haze rose. The greenery took on a luminescence, guiding Kit to where the exit emerged. His flesh crawled and his eyes began to smart with the wild urge to weep.

He was witnessing magic.

'Let's go,' Miss Dove said briskly.

She linked her fingers between Kit's and he was glad of the reassuring pressure grounding him. He blinked away the unshed tears and took a deep breath. Hand in hand, they walked forward into the maze.

Chapter Eleven

The pathway that led to the centre, where Kit and Adelaide had met less than a week before, should have been no more than eight or nine paces, but they kept walking. This was not the same maze and after the glowing lights Kit was not surprised. There was no pergola, and the shrubs were unfamiliar with gently moving fronds and clusters of berries the colour of venous blood. The walls were curved and Kit suspected that from above it resembled a giant thumbprint or spiral. Now he understood the reason and was thankful for the thread linking him to Miss Dove.

Eventually, they emerged into sunlight and Kit's sense of disorientation was complete. There was nothing familiar about where he was and disconcertingly it appeared to be daytime.

'This is impossible. We left in the dark,' he murmured. The air was completely silent. No birds sang. No cattle lowed. Not even the susurrus of leaves caught by a breeze. The world seemed dead. He shivered even though it was warm.

'And yet here we are,' Miss Dove said spreading her arms.

Kit turned back to look at the maze, only to discover it had changed. Shimmering light hovered above an ancient and gnarled oak that had grown out of a cluster of moss-covered rocks, the branches curving downwards to make an arch. As he stared at it, the light ebbed away, and he saw that what he had assumed was one tree were separate branches laced together with delicate strands of ivy leaves. The ivy withered, and with a creak like an elderly woman pushing herself from her chair, the branches collapsed and the archway vanished. There was no way home.

'I think I'm going to be sick,' Kit murmured.

Miss Dove lowered her arms and gave him a sympathetic look. 'Breathe slowly and look at the horizon. Count to ten.'

He did as she told him. The sky was a pale magenta and tinged with buttercup yellow; colours no sky should be, which didn't help, but eventually the nausea passed. When he was capable of standing upright, Miss Dove untied the threads and rolled them onto a bobbin that she slipped into her bag.

'Miss Dove,' Kit began, but she cut him off with a sharp wave of her hand.

'I hate that name. It's the one Silas gave me to walk in your world. It does not follow me here.'

'Then what should I call you? Alexandra?'

'That's not my name, either.'

She lifted her chin, straightening up. Her appearance had changed. Not a great deal, but subtly. Her eyes more catlike and her jaw broader. Her hair was lighter and shorter; spiky waves flecked with the colours of walnut shell.

'You may call me Valentine.' She waved a hand around her. 'Kit Arton-Price, welcome to the Faedemesne.'

He could do little more than nod and follow the direction of her hand. They had emerged on the edge of a forest. The colours of the trees were brighter, more vibrant, than anything he had seen before. The tree trunks glowed with a soft, golden light, so thick that Kit felt sure it would feel like velvet if he were able to somehow touch it, and the air smelled of honeysuckle and cinnamon.

A figure appeared before them, tall and lithe. It wore a cloak of leaves with the hood pulled close. Kit's nerves twanged and he stepped forward, hands curling into fists.

'Silas Wilde?' he snarled.

Valentine caught his arm, pulling him back.

'For Mab's sake, what are you thinking?' she exclaimed.

The figure lowered its hood. It was not Silas, though there was a similarity to the features and the golden skin. Kit knew without a doubt he was in the presence of a fae. As Kit stared, the figure tilted his head and looked at him, pupils sparkling like stars against a backdrop of violet. It smiled, and it was as if a hand had reached into Kit's chest and taken hold of his heart. The fae's face shimmered between male and female, changing from angular and slender to plump and heart-shaped, full-cheeked to wide-jawed, smooth to bearded, broad to narrow, all equally captivating.

It slowly licked its lips and Kit felt his penis throb and swell. He heard a groan of longing erupt from his mouth, knowing deep in his consciousness that he should be embarrassed about such unconcealed arousal but he took a faltering step towards the fae, reaching his arms out. He'd die happy if only he could kiss the full, sensuous lips that were now smiling at him so enchantingly.

'Enough!'

If Valentine's shout had not been enough to jolt him from his reverie, the slap she delivered to his cheek did the trick. The sharp pain made him blink, breaking the gaze between him and the fae.

'Be off! This one is mine!' Valentine snarled, stepping towards the fae. 'He is under my protection, and you will not have him.'

The fae looked at Valentine and became a man with an unshaven jaw and wide, honest-looking eyes.

Valentine spat on the ground with clear disdain.

The fae turned back to Kit again, still wearing the same face. It raised a sculpted eyebrow and stroked a finger across rosebud lips, but the glimmering of arousal Kit had felt was gone. There was something glassy about the eyes now; the stars cold in irises of dull mauve and Kit shivered.

'No, thank you,' he said. He stepped back to Valentine's side. The fae opened its mouth and hissed, revealing a long tongue and too many sharp teeth, then drew its hood over its head and vanished.

Kit took a deep breath, his lungs ached as if he'd been swimming underwater for too long. 'Thank you for saving me,' he panted.

'I did it because I need you and I swore to protect you, not because you deserve it!' Valentine turned to him, hands on hips and a scornful expression. 'That's not a good start, is it! Less than five minutes here and you're about to give your soul to a *buareadh*.'

'Not just your soul either,' she said, glancing down at Kit's crotch then met his eyes and winked. 'Impressive. Miss Wyndham is a lucky woman.'

Kit's hands rushed to cover the area in question and she laughed then scowled.

'Why did you think that would be Silas under the hood?'

'I don't know. I thought he'd be meeting us here. What's a buareadh?'

'That was.' Valentine indicated to the place where the fae had recently stood. 'They turn themselves into what you want them to be and promise to give you what you want. Of course, what they really do is enslave you, body and soul, for entertainment. If I hadn't intervened, you'd have swived it then woken up tomorrow morning in an amphitheatre, chained hand and foot and digging through mounds of dirt in search of poppyseeds while the clan placed bets on how many you'd find. And you'd be doing it willingly.'

Kit shuddered at the image, remembering how close he'd come to giving into his hunger for the creature. His knees buckled slightly, and he had to concentrate to remain fully upright. 'Then, thank you even more for saving me.'

Valentine was looking at him with eyes narrowed.

'It didn't know how to appear to you. Female or male.'

Hot blood rushed to Kit's cheeks and crept beneath his collar. It was disconcerting that someone could spot the shameful aspect which he did his best to deny.

'If that wasn't Silas, where is he? Where is Adelaide?' he asked harshly. 'I thought they'd be waiting for us.'

'What, The Wilde stand and wait by the roadside on the off chance that we follow? No, he'll be at the castle by now.'

'Where is that?' Kit asked, scanning the landscape but seeing nothing other than distant hills beyond the forest.

'About three days walk in that direction.' Valentine pointed toward the hills. She sounded irritable, which gave Kit no reassurance, at all.

'Three days! I can't take that much time to find Addie.'

'Did you think we would arrive exactly where we wanted to be, going straight there?'

'Well, yes.'

'Can you catch a train to Meadwell directly from London or do you have to walk part of the way?' She laughed at the answer written on his face. 'It's the same with our gateways, and this one is the safest if we're to avoid trouble.'

'Avoid trouble?' Kit folded his arms. 'We walked straight into something that would have kept me as a pet! Besides, I don't think Adelaide will have enjoyed a three-day walk.'

'Oh, Silas had his coach waiting. We could've travelled that way if you hadn't been stupid enough to refuse him and come when she did.' Valentine crossed her arms and glared at him, clearly very unhappy. 'We could have driven to the castle in style but instead we're on foot. I hope you're happy with yourself.'

'I'd rather be a free man on foot than a slave in a coach,' Kit snapped.

She rolled her eyes. 'Oh, well done, free man. I hope you've got good shoe leather.' She indicated a well-trodden, rutted track that led, to Kit's growing unease, directly into the forest.

'It'll be sunset soon. We can get beyond the worst of the forest before it becomes completely dark if we hurry. Believe me, you don't want to be too deep in after dark.'

She picked up her bag and stormed off towards the forest, following the track. Not wanting to be separated, even by a few feet, Kit heaved his rucksack over his shoulders and followed. His body still throbbed with the occasional remnant of desire caused by the buareadh, though knowing what would have happened to him, he felt sullied and filthy at feeling it. He wished he'd brought a knife or cricket bat so he could defend himself against further assailants. He'd memorised Merelda's and Enid's rules but there was precious little he could do against an enemy he didn't even know existed.

The air grew thick. The trees seemed to stretch higher, their branches intertwined to form a canopy that blocked out the sunlight, and he wondered whether he'd even know when the sun had set. The ground beneath his feet felt spongy, covered with moss that suggested the path wasn't well used. Valentine set a fast pace, walking in long, easy strides and swinging her arms. She'd changed – not just physically – she moved with more assurance and seemed to occupy more of a space in the world. It was an intriguing change and one he quite liked.

Despite her diminutive size, she strode along with a sense of purpose, her steps quick and efficient, seemingly unburdened by the terrain, whereas his back and calves ached in a way they hadn't since he'd been in France, marching from location to location – something he'd thought he would never have to do again once he'd returned home. He did his best to keep up with her, gritting his teeth against the discomfort, and before too long he felt his muscles ease back into a comfortable gait. The long trudges through France and Belgium had been relentless but at least he'd had friends at his side to make it bearable. There had been crude songs and even cruder jokes to make the miles speed underfoot, but occasionally he'd found companions to confide in. He missed them. He missed those days, though he would never have imagined he would.

"We could always have another go at the tango. If you'd like to, that is..."

He stopped and closed his eyes for a moment, pressing his quivering lips together. Missing Andrew. Missing Adelaide. Missing not knowing that places like this or people like Silas existed.

'Is there something wrong?' asked Valentine from up ahead.

Kit shook his head. There wasn't much right.

As the Sun descended, the air grew cold and clammy. Birdsong gradually became replaced with the hooting of owls. Valentine slowed down and she and Kit walked closer together. He refrained from asking whether it was for his benefit or hers, but she moved with a touch less swagger, eyes darting from side to side.

They reached a stream and followed it. Kit's throat was parched but the water looked stagnant, and he'd die of thirst before drinking from it. Will-o'-the-wisps danced before them, ducking and weaving, darting about, leaving trails of dust that lingered in the few shafts of sunlight that broke through the dense foliage.

'They're beautiful,' Kit remarked.

Valentine waved her hand and hissed, and they scattered.

'Lightmares. They're little wretches,' she said, in response to Kit's raised eyebrow. 'The males are the worst. They buzz as they fly around, and when you're disoriented from the sound they lead you off into the marshes.'

'And then what happens?' Kit asked. He wrinkled his nose. 'It's going to be something horrible, isn't it?'

'They lead you deeper until you trip and then they descend and mob you until you sink. Most likely you drown or suffocate. Then the females lay their eggs in your corpse.' Valentine shuddered. 'I saw them hatching once out of a greyback stag that had broken his leg. He screamed in a way I'd not heard before, and never want to hear again.'

'It was alive?' Kits stomach churned. 'I thought you said they drowned their prey.'

She grimaced. 'If you're lucky. If not, well, it's mercifully quick. The whole cycle from laying to hatching takes no more than a day, and then of course the newlings feed so—'

'Stop!' Kit held his hands up. 'I don't want to hear anymore. This place is monstrous.'

'More so than your world? There are places there that were once beautiful and no longer are, thanks to the destruction wreaked on it.'

Kit pursed his lips to ward off the bitter taste of memories.

'Your face has changed,' Valentine said quietly. 'You're thinking dark thoughts.'

Kit looked at her, slightly flustered that his emotions were so clear to see.

'After what you've just told me that's hardly a surprise,' he said, making a feeble effort.

'No, you went somewhere else,' she said, looking at him with an expression that suggested she could see into the pain in his soul.

'A friend of mine broke his leg once in the trenches. It was a whole day before the stretcher-bearers got to him. When they got his boot off the stench was unbelievable. There were already maggots growing. It was just outside a town that had once been a spa where people went to taste the waters and bathed. I find it hard to think of those places being somewhere people would go to visit for their beauty.'

'Is that when you got your injuries?' Valentine asked quietly.

'No. I don't talk about that.'

He hefted his rucksack and increased his pace and she fell in behind him as they picked their way through increasingly unpleasant dense undergrowth.

'This is really the land that Wilde persuaded Adelaide to come and help rebuild?' Kit growled, after plunging to the calf in a pool of stinking brackish water.

Valentine shook her head gently. 'It isn't all like this. It's not very pleasant here but when we get through the other side of the forest you'll see what we're fighting to reclaim.'

Valentine walked to a fallen tree trunk and clambered on top of it, sitting with her legs crossed. Kit sat by her side, leaning back, but very soon inside him there grew a disconcerting sense of something unpleasant around his ankles and he too lifted his feet up, drawing his knees to his chest.

Valentine grinned.

'You sensed something then, didn't you? You feel it sometimes when your feet are dangling. I bet as a child you used to hate the thought of anything under your bed.'

Kit laughed genuinely for what felt like the first time in weeks. He dipped his head in acknowledgement.

'That's what the sickness here feels like,' Valentine said. 'A wrongness that you can't explain. We think your war has affected our world. Some of the folk say it's the blood that was spilled that has caused our air to grow rotten, but others think it's the deluge of sorrow and hate. In any case we felt it here and it's just getting worse.'

'The war is over now, won't things go back to how they were before?' Kit asked. 'God knows we're all trying to do the same back home.'

He ran a finger along the tree trunk and it came away moist and dirty. As a visual illustration of sorrow or hate it was a good example.

'Some factions are happy for it to continue.'

Valentine hugged herself tightly, her expression darkening. It was probably the same back home in some quarters. There was money to be made from wars, after all.

She heaved her shoulders and stared upwards. 'We'd better keep moving. The light will be going soon, and I want to be clear of the swamps before we find somewhere to camp.'

She lowered herself off the log. Kit's eyes caught something scuttling underneath his feet. His jaw clenched and he suppressed the feeling of revulsion, telling himself it was only a beetle or grass snake.

'Shall I go ahead and see what I can find?' Valentine suggested. 'You can follow at your own pace.'

'Not a chance. I'm not letting you out of my sight,' Kit said hastily, growing cold at the thought of being abandoned in such an eerie place. Not wanting to appear cowardly he cast his face into a frown. 'For all I know you intend to abandon me here to the wisps or whatever else there is. We stay together.'

'Why would I do that?' Valentine asked. 'It's in my interests that you get where we are going *and* I swore my oath. You are being deliberately insulting to suggest I'd break it.'

She sounded genuinely offended. Kit owed her nothing, but the injury in her voice succeeded in penetrating deep enough into his conscience that he held a hand out and apologised.

The trees began to thin and although the sky was darkening with impending night, there was still more light than there had been in the depths. A thick layer of greasy, grey clouds covered the moon, but a silvery edge to the sky meant that they could pick their way reasonably easily. The area beyond the marshland was desolate. The trees looked ill, with parched leaves and mottled trunks.

Kit was close to dropping by the time they found a small structure that looked like an animal shelter of some sort with a low roof and three sides. There were no animals but the straw was sweet smelling and looked clean, so they lay down end to end and huddled next to each other for warmth. Valentine wriggled around until she'd created a satisfactory dent in the straw, lying with her back to Kit. He lay on his back, letting the knots in his shoulders begin to loosen. Although night had only recently fallen, they'd left Meadwell at midnight and his body assumed it must be about four or five in the morning.

If anyone had told Kit that morning that he would end the night lying beside a fairy in a field, he'd have laughed at them, assuming he had the strength. He tried to keep watch but before too long his eyes refused to stay open. He didn't trust Valentine, far from it, but with her back curved against his side and the scent of mimosas mingling with the smell of the hay, his anxious thoughts began to disperse, giving his mind enough ease for sleep to come.

And thus ended his first night in the Faedemesne.

～

Kit snored gently. Valentine had feigned sleep until she sensed his body relaxing into slumber. Now she lay awake staring through the gaps in the wooden roof at the midnight-blue sky spiralling away. Even though night was the time she took for herself, when the moon cast her placid flame over the land and no one had claim on her, the warmth of another body beside her was welcome in the chill of the evening. How could she explain to the man beside her that the cold was abnormal; yet more evidence of her world dying.

Despite herself, Valentine was impressed with Kit's resilience and acceptance of what he had seen. She'd been right to follow her instinct. He already stood taller and prouder as he walked, watching out for dangers, though she doubted he would be aware of that. Just as well: the next two days would involve a lot of walking and it would be tiresome having to warn him of everyone who might decide to prey on him. The buareadh had got far too close.

It didn't stop her hating him for his treatment of her back at Meadwell. Her whole frame shivered violently as she remembered the suffocating feel of the iron doors and bars of the room where his meagre hoard of valuables was stored. She would have revenge one day for the discourtesy he had shown, she swore on her mother's blood.

She folded her arms and cradled her bangle. The hair-thin

crack in the stone had healed as soon as she stepped through the gateway, but it had been there. That would be something to report to Silas; either there were ways around enchantments that hadn't occurred to him, or the powers of her world were fading in Kit's. A link or a coincidence?

Her explanations of the sickness had been poor and she wasn't sure how bringing more humans to the faedemesne would help.

'Blast you, Silas Wilde. Why must you keep things so close to your chest?' she muttered.

Kit stirred and rolled onto his back; no doubt disturbed by her movement. She wondered if he ever slept with someone at his side. She assumed the beautiful Miss Wyndham was saving herself until they were wed in that ridiculous way humans did. They seemed to place such a curious emphasis on virginity, which meant nothing, whilst throwing away favours and bargains without even knowing what they were worth.

She leaned up on her elbow and studied him. His head lolled to one side and his scarred cheek was upright, giving her the opportunity to examine it in a way he would never sanction otherwise. It mattered a lot to him, she could tell. It was the source of his self-effacing behaviour and his unease in the world, which was stupid because the balance of his face was barely affected, and the other side was handsome enough. A glamour would fix it easily. Valentine wasn't powerful enough, but if she felt so inclined, she might intercede on his behalf to Silas as a kindness.

She stretched out her legs, luxuriating in the space. No doubt Silas would even now be courting Miss Wyndham. Had he made her love him yet? Surely so. He was charming, vibrant and so utterly dashing. How could she not give in to his persuasions. Poor Kit. He'd gambled on his fiancée refusing Silas's appeal when he'd given his blessing and he'd lost. If Valentine ever loved someone, she would not be so cavalier with her claim. Silas would definitely succeed in seducing Miss Wyndham, so the best Kit could hope for was to mop up her tears when Silas eventually tired of her.

She must have sighed out loud because Kit mumbled in his sleep and rolled over. The crook of his armpit looked like an enticing place to rest her head and she might as well be comfortable. The membrane of darkness that stretched over the sky was beginning to take on a lighter hue. Morning would be here soon enough and Valentine needed some sleep. She pulled her cloak a little more snugly around her, ignoring the impulse to lean against Kit. He was so innocent.

He was learning, though. He had demanded assurances from her, which had been unexpected. The old one who was under the enchantment had helped him with the knowledge and thank goodness for that! Without the mead he had given her, she would have taken much longer to revive. She licked her lips, recalling the taste, which in turn made her remember the kiss. Oh yes, Miss Wyndham had not granted Kit many favours. He was filled with a suppressed thirst that was just pleading to be released like the cork from a bottle of champagne.

Even though she had promised not to, just a small drop of Heartswell Moss tincture slipped into his food or drink would buy her an hour or two of pretending she was the one he had chosen. He'd be completely convinced his devotion was genuine and he'd have no memory of it afterwards. She'd resorted to taking it herself on occasion, when she'd had the prospect of an unpleasant evening ahead of her and couldn't fake desire convincingly enough to please whoever her master had gifted her to.

She shook her head and rolled over. She couldn't do it. Taking advantage could so easily turn to actually caring. She didn't give her affection lightly and wasn't going to waste it on someone who would be gone from her life in a day or two.

Chapter Twelve

Kit woke to bright sunshine and the worst stench he had ever smelled. He was lying in a foetal position and something was looming over him and stabbing him in the ribs. He cried out, scuffling back against the end of the shelter.

He looked up to face his assailant and locked eyes with the most malevolent-looking bird he'd ever seen. He sagged back, relieved that he wasn't actually being attacked, and let out a long sigh. The bird honked at him, sounding like a goose with a sore throat, and let out another belch of foul breath. He pushed it away and it waddled off on squat legs.

Valentine was still asleep, smiling serenely. He had ended up huddled in a corner because she was spreadeagled across most of the straw. Aching and stiff, he begrudged her the easy sleep she was obviously having.

His stomach growled. His wristwatch had stopped at midnight, and he had no idea what time it was here. He'd been hoping it would keep track of the time in England but apparently not, unless the reason the hands had barely moved was that no time had passed at all. His body might by lying on his bed while the dregs of his cocoa cooled in the cup.

He hoped that was the case. He'd find Adelaide, deal with Silas Wilde (quite what that would involve, he hadn't yet decided) and return home before anyone noticed his absence. He hauled over his rucksack, deciding not to wake Valentine just yet, and ate a couple of ginger biscuits and an apple. It wasn't much considering he was ravenous. He should ration the food, but with luck he'd be home before dinner and it was best to be satisfied now.

The bird returned while he was finishing a third biscuit, and it wasn't alone. With it was another, larger, of its species, along with three chicks in a neat line. The original bird stared at Kit with eyes that were more intelligent than a bird's had any right to be. It clacked its beak a couple of times then gave itself a shake, ruffling feathers all over its dumpy little body. Something clicked in Kit's brain. He'd seen one identical to it stuffed and mounted in the Natural History Museum.

'A dodo!' he exclaimed. 'It's a bloody dodo!'

His words roused Valentine, who mumbled something and rolled over. The bird looked meaningfully at the remains of the apple in Kit's hand. There wasn't much left. He'd gnawed almost down to the core, but he broke it in half and lobbed both pieces a little distance away. The birds immediately began squawking and scurried over to it.

'Stop feeding them,' Valentine mumbled. 'Otherwise we'll have the entire flock after us for the next week.'

'They're dodos,' Kit said.

She sat up, brushing a little straw from her fringe. 'Yes. Stupid things that they are. As birds go, they aren't too bright, but they're very determined.'

'Never mind their relative intelligence, why do they exist at all?' Kit asked. 'They went extinct hundreds of years ago.'

Now he knew what they were, he couldn't tear his eyes away. All five of them stood in a semicircle: parents on the outside, chicks in between, with expectant glints in their eyes. They were taking cautious steps closer to the shelter.

'No, they didn't.' Valentine clambered to her feet and walked towards the noisy birds, trying to shoo them away, but they skirted around her and resumed their vigil. 'When it became apparent that your kind was determined to wipe them out, The Parliament brought most of the colony here.' She smiled. 'It was actually Silas's great, great-grandmother who first tabled the motion. I believe in some circles they are quite valued as pets, though their cry sets my teeth on edge.'

'But this is wonderful,' Kit breathed, crumbling a biscuit and throwing it to the dodos. 'We could take this whole family back and re-introduce them.'

'And what right would you have to do that?' asked Valentine. She put her hands on her hips and glared at him. 'What arrogance do you possess to think that you have any claim on this bird, given how your species treated them?'

Her voice dripped with contempt. Kit flushed defensively as he struggled for a retort, but then he caught himself and stared at the family of dodos.

'You're right. We don't.'

The youngest chick cocked its head on one side. It was

about the size of a Yorkshire terrier. It bobbed over to him and he threw it a couple of the gingerbread crumbs. It made a trilling noise and he reached out a hand. The dodo allowed him to scratch it at the side of its beak. His fingers came away slightly oily. Emboldened, the chick's siblings rushed forward.

'I haven't got anything else, I'm sorry,' he said, holding his empty palms out as proof. The birds warbled in collective disappointment and the parents began to gather them round, hissing angrily.

'We should leave,' Valentine said, picking up her bag. 'We've got a long way to go today. I know where we are now, and I think there's a pool we can wash in a little down the road. Come on.'

Kit gathered his things. The dodos, presumably realising no more treats were on offer, waddled off, hooting disappointedly. By the time Kit and Valentine were packed and ready to go the birds had moved on to a field, pecking at corn that a young boy with hairy feet was throwing to them from a bucket. Roughly a dozen more birds were flocking around him. Kit paused to look. They appeared as contented as chickens on farms. He had a brief vision of thousands of the birds strutting around the farm at home.

'I would love to show these to Oliver. Before you say it, yes, I know that's not possible, and I understand why.'

Valentine looked on him with slightly kinder eyes than she had the first time he had mentioned taking them home.

'You want to because you're genuinely interested in them, aren't you? Not for what fame or fortune it could bring you.'

'Yes. They're not exactly beautiful but they have a lot of personality.'

'And there's a lot to be said for that.' Valentine smiled.

Kit dropped his eyes. He assumed she was referring to his ruined face, and not for the first time he found her matter-of-fact attitude refreshing. He shifted his bag to a more comfortable position on his shoulder. 'Let's go and leave these birds with their friends. You can tell me what other strange species you have rescued.'

'Well, unicorns of course,' Valentine told him as they walked along the path that climbed gently upwards. 'A couple of packs of lyam-hounds, and I believe someone tried to reintroduce basilisks, but finding blind men to watch them isn't easy.'

Kit shook his head. 'Basilisks and unicorns. If I ever tell anyone about this, they'll assume I have gone mad.'

'Very true,' Valentine said cheerfully. 'That's the usual outcome for those who encounter us, assuming they don't actually go mad. Look to some of your artists and poets, if you want examples.'

She sounded so blasé about it that Kit's hackles raised.

'My great-aunt, Merelda, is under a spell. For years we've all assumed she's feeble-minded, and have treated her with pity or condescension, but she isn't. She's been horribly treated by one of your kind and it makes me feel sick to think of it. Now you have the audacity to laugh about causing madness! Don't take the moral high ground with your talk about the harm my kind cause when yours can inflict such suffering.'

'Neither Silas nor I had anything to do with that,' Valentine shot back at him.

'That doesn't matter. I had nothing to do with the extinction of the dodo, yet you speak as if I've gone round stamping on nests. You came to my world to steal people. You disgust me!'

He was breathing hard by the time he finished ranting. Valentine's mouth had fallen open, and she stood dumbstruck, her eyes brimmed as if she was about to cry but he didn't care.

'Come on,' Kit snarled. 'Take me to Silas and let's get whatever we have to do over and done with.'

He spun on his heel and carried on walking. Presently he heard Valentine's footsteps and she fell in beside him. She didn't speak and he continued to ignore her, keeping his eyes fixed on the way ahead. The path joined another and became a road that reminded Kit of the Roman ones he'd learned about at school. At least it made walking easier because the company left a lot to be desired. They stamped along in uneasy silence but when Kit thought it was probably time for elevenses, he unearthed the biscuits and offered one to Valentine out of politeness.

'No conditions,' he said pointedly.

She curled her lip but ate it, then gave him a wide-eyed smile. 'Oooh, I could grow fat eating those, they're lovely. You should have at least tried to gain an advantage before offering me something that nice.'

Kit stared at her, the rage which had been ebbing catching up with him again.

'I don't want to try to gain an advantage. Unlike you, I have some honour and I don't see everything as a way of getting what I want.'

She tossed her head. 'Well, then, that makes you a fool.'

'No, it makes me a decent person by not seeing everything as a bargaining chip. You just listen to yourself.'

'What else can I do?' she asked. 'I have barely any power and every moment of my existence must be earned by what I can offer or accept.'

'Wouldn't it be better to be poor but not beholden?'

'You listen to *yourself*.' Valentine laughed bitterly. 'Don't think for a minute that you are any different to me. The bride you are coming to rescue is only your chosen wife because of her money. Would you choose her without it? More to the point, without your land and status do you think she would choose you?'

'Oh, get to hell,' Kit snapped.

Valentine visibly paled. 'Don't say that. Never say that.' Her voice was actually shaking. 'Hell has claimed enough of my kind.'

Kit stared at her in bewilderment.

'It's just an expression,' he said.

'Nothing is just an expression.'

She carried on walking, stumbling slightly. Kit followed in dismay, the expression on her face and the horror in her voice eating away at his conscience. She'd been genuinely scared, and his mind whirled with implications he didn't really want to contemplate.

The morning grew hotter and more oppressive. Kit's throat dried out and his belly felt shrunken. He removed his sweater, but his shirt clung to him uncomfortably.

Valentine turned off the road as it wound downwards through a valley and walked across a field to a shallow pool surrounded by trees, with a narrow strip of sand at one side. She dropped her bag at the edge and took off her shoes. To Kit's mortification she unbuttoned her dress and slipped out of it, so that she was standing only in what appeared to be a short vest that came barely below her bust, and a pair of drawers that barely reached halfway down her thighs. He averted his eyes hastily and heard her snigger. Already feeling intolerant from the heat and their previous argument, he scowled.

She walked past him, straight into the pool, not turning back to Kit until she was waist-deep.

'Aren't you going to come in? It's wonderfully cool.'

'I don't know if it's safe,' he said sullenly. 'From what I've learned of this place, there might be anything lurking under the surface to drag me down and enslave or eat me.'

Valentine laughed and let herself fall backwards, the water billowing around her and swallowing her. She swam a few strokes on her back beneath the surface, kicking her legs boldly. The water was clear enough that he could see her shape perfectly. She resurfaced and looked at him.

'I shouldn't have laughed,' she said. 'That was a fair point. I give you my word that I'm the only thing in the pool.'

The breeze licked around Kit, drawing his attention to the dampness beneath his armpits and on his torso and back. The pool looked inviting, and his resistance was weakening.

'So, the only thing I need to worry about is you,' he grumbled, not yet ready to bend.

Her face grew earnest. 'You don't need to worry about me hurting you.'

He sneered. 'Forgive me if I show doubt.'

'I mean it. I gave my word.'

Her hair was plastered to her cheeks. She lifted her arms and ran her hands through it, pushing it back off her forehead – a movement that gave Kit a glimpse of the soft, golden hair beneath her armpits and raised her breasts a little. He tore his eyes from them, acutely aware of how much he wanted to touch the small mounds. Her chemise was pale pink, and now that it was wet through, didn't conceal anything. If he could see below her waist would there be a triangle of gold at her crotch, visible only in silhouette? He grew warm thinking of it, and his collar appeared to shrink around his neck. He unbuttoned it, trying to be discreet, but Valentine's eyes glowed.

'I knew you wanted to come in,' she said.

Kit gave up the pretence that he was resisting it. A cool dip would put an end to the completely inappropriate fantasies his brain was currently spinning for him.

'Turn your back for a minute,' he said.

'Don't be so coy,' Valentine purred. 'I don't care.'

'Just do it, please,' Kit said, wishing he was as uninhibited as she was.

He stripped down to his underclothes then waded into the pool. The water was intensely cold and he gasped as it reached his groin, goosepimples breaking out all over his body.

'You made it look so warm!' His teeth were actually chattering.

'Isn't it? I don't really feel the cold,' Valentine said, lowering herself beneath the surface.

Kit counted to three, lifted his feet and threw himself backwards, letting himself sink under the water and resurfacing quickly beside Valentine.

'There, you're braver than you knew,' she said, giving him a smile.

Once he'd got over how cold it was, it was very

invigorating. Valentine dived under and swam the width of the pool. Kit followed and for a while they raced each other. When he tired of being beaten, he lay back and floated, letting the tension in his muscles ebb away. Small waves lifted him to and fro, caused by Valentine's gentle strokes as she swam in circles around him.

He could gladly have stayed there all day, but when Valentine tapped him on the shoulder to get his attention, he reluctantly followed her to the shore.

They had no towels, but the sun was warm so they lay on the sand to let their clothes dry. Valentine stretched out like a pedigree cat luxuriating on a sunlit cushion while Kit extended his arms and legs like a starfish. He couldn't imagine Adelaide doing such a thing. She had always hated bathing in open water, practically needing to be forced to paddle when they'd gone to Whitby or Scarborough as children. She might consent to lie by an outdoor pool somewhere like the French Riviera and occasionally dip in to cool off, but that would be about the extent of her aquatic adventures.

'Kit, I'm sorry for what happened to your great-aunt, and for making light of what can happen.' Valentine spoke quietly. 'My kind can be blasé at times. We are fickle and wayward by nature.'

He looked at her in surprise. 'Thank you.'

She sat and propped herself up with her elbows.

'I haven't treated you well since we arrived. I'm still furious at the way you treated me when you locked me in that room and it'll take me a while to get over it, but it isn't your fault that humans behave the way they do. I can't blame you for all their ills.'

Adelaide wouldn't have apologised. Valentine's frankness was quite disarming.

'I want to apologise, too,' Kit said. 'I know neither you nor Silas were responsible for Merelda's situation. She told me that herself.'

He rolled over onto his front to let the back of his clothes dry and propped himself up, head level with Valentine's.

'I think if we're to get along, you need to tell me everything I need to know. What's going to happen when we reach Silas? I'd appreciate honesty. Will there be danger?'

He tried not to let his voice shake, but heard a slight quiver at the edge of it.

'There is always danger. That's one of the terrible things that has happened since the changes. I can't guarantee it won't come from Silas, but he won't be the main source of it. I don't expect you to believe me, but he is not your enemy.'

'He made himself my enemy when he stole Adelaide,' Kit said harshly. His chest constricted. Here he was, sitting by a pleasant pool while she might be suffering goodness knew what indignities and torments, sunbathing with her abductor's accomplice.

'Yes, I know. And I know that is something he regrets,' Valentine said quietly.

'Please believe me, Kit, neither of us want to be your enemies. We are generally a peaceful people, but desperate times cause even the mildest person to do things they find anathema.'

She put her hand on his upper arm. Her fingers were cool from bathing and felt acutely sensitive on his slightly damp skin, causing the hairs to rise on end. Immediately the flare of anger subsided, replaced by escalating desire. He had to assume she wasn't using magic against him because she had vowed not to but the shock of such an unexpected reaction was immense. He'd kissed her once and that was more than he should have done.

'I'm getting hungry,' he said, using the comment as an excuse to pull away and reach for his rucksack. 'I'm nearly out of biscuits. What here is going to be safe for me to eat? Merelda said it's an easy way to get trapped.'

'Food growing wild is fine. That belongs to no one. For example, the berries on the bushes over there are safe to eat,' Valentine said, pointing to a cluster of foliage that looked a little like blackberry bushes but with lime-coloured leaves. She jumped to her feet and pulled her dress on, completely indifferent to whether he was watching or not, then strolled around the pool towards them. By the time Kit had dressed (a little less self-consciously than he'd undressed) and joined her, she had picked a handful of deep purple, swollen berries.

'Here.'

She held one up to his lips. When he hesitated, she frowned.

'What?'

'I only have your word that they're safe.'

Her frown deepened into a scowl. 'When will you believe you can trust me?'

She threw the berry up into the air and caught it in her mouth, swallowed, then licked her lips.

'Perfectly safe, see.'

She held out another between thumb and forefinger. He took it into his mouth quickly, still mindful of how her earlier touch had set excitement racing through him. Sharp, sweet juice exploded in his mouth, running down his throat. He moaned in appreciation, which caused Valentine to grin.

He picked a handful himself and they ate as they walked, only speaking to bid other travellers a good day. Unlike before, the silence was companionable. The swim and the rest had done wonders for Kit's mood.

The road passed through a few settlements, mainly straight, occasionally winding, but always with a gentle incline. When it reached a crossroads, Valentine turned left.

'Tomorrow we'll have to climb the path through the mountains and it's not a place to be at night. We'll stay at the next inn we see. There's bound to be one this close to the crossroad, and with luck it will be a Safe House.'

Kit wrinkled his brows and before he could ask for clarification, Valentine explained, 'That means every traveller is welcome and no one will trespass on another's privacy or business. No one will care that you're a stranger.'

'I didn't bring any money for a hotel,' he said with dismay.

Valentine smiled. 'I'll pay. You can owe me a box of those delicious biscuits, and I'll take payment when you return home.'

He stuck his hand out. 'I accept your terms, Valentine.'

She shook it. 'You'd still better observe the courtesies regarding obligations, and for Mab's sake, be polite to other guests, because the protection only lasts a certain distance from the Safe House and you don't want someone catching up with you on the road to settle scores.'

She looped her arm through his and gave it a reassuring

squeeze. 'But on the whole we'll be able to sleep easily and in a bed for a night.'

Considering the last couple of days, Kit would risk an awful lot of scores to be sleeping on a mattress rather than straw and not to be woken up by extinct birds. Besides, if there was the assurance of safety from the inn itself, then even if he didn't completely trust Valentine, what harm could possibly come to them?

Chapter Thirteen

The inn they came to reminded Kit of the chalets he'd seen travelling through the Alps. A painted sign above the door proclaimed it to be the *Parsley Flower Safe House*.

The guests looked mainly human, but some had ears that were too pointed or long, eyes too large or hooded, colours that were unnatural. Figures ranged from unnaturally slender and tall, to tiny and childlike. A couple had wings and one wide-eyed young man had a cat's tail that wafted softly as he walked through the room, and Valentine had to jab Kit sharply in the ribs to stop him staring. It was as if he'd tumbled into an Arthur Rackham illustration and he drew closer to Valentine's side, regretting agreeing to stay there.

'Will it be the dormitories or the bind-bench, or can you fine travellers stretch to a room?' the ginger-bearded landlord asked, when Valentine enquired if there were vacancies. He looked like a schoolboy's idea of a Viking.

'What's a bind-bench?' Kit asked.

The innkeeper raised his impressively arched eyebrows as

if this was the oddest question and Kit wondered if he'd revealed himself to be an outsider.

'You all sit on the high-backed benches, all packed in together. We pass a rope beneath your armpits, and tie it nice and tight behind so you don't slide off before morning. If you don't have your own pillow, we can rent you one, or you can use a neighbour's shoulder.'

Kit got a sudden flash of memory: five nights in the trenches in his ninth month in France, where there had been no chance to get horizontal and the detachment had all slumped against each other upright, grabbing what sleep they could.

'It sounds dreadful,' he muttered to Valentine.

'Those are for the poorest travellers,' she said haughtily. 'Which we are not!'

This last comment was addressed to the innkeeper.

'We will have a private room,' Valentine said. 'It doesn't have to be big, doesn't have to be luxurious. But it has to have a bed and a lock on the door.'

The innkeeper raised his brows again, giving them a salacious look that strongly suggested he had an idea what they'd be needing the bed and lock for.

'Four rings. Top floor, room with the circle on the door.'

Valentine whistled beneath her breath but fished a handful of coins out of her bag and counted out four. They were about the size of farthings but copper coloured.

'Five Rings to a Hand, two Hands to a Head, four Heads to a Crown,' she explained to Kit as they made their way up a grand staircase that became considerably less impressive as they reached the top floor. 'Though most people outside the towns rely on bartering.'

So, ten Rings to a Head, Kit worked out. Matching the denominations to body parts and counting in tens seemed a remarkably sensible way of counting coins.

'Were we charged too much for the room?' he asked.

'We were charged what you get charged,' she said. 'Beggars don't get to choose and it's the only Safe House around.'

'What is the equivalent? What would I be able to buy in my world with them?' he asked.

'Nothing.' Valentine laughed. 'They dissolved into dust as soon as Silas tried to take them across. He was very upset, though he knows enough stories of humans stealing fae treasures only to find them vanishing. I wonder if they appeared back in his scrip when he came back through?'

Kit wished he'd carried some money so he could see if the same thing happened in reverse.

They found the room, one of three in the attic of the inn that reminded Kit of Meadwell. There was one bed big enough for two, if the occupants were prepared to sleep close. The only light came from a high, triangular window at the top of the wall in the eaves, which had oiled paper nailed over it. He suspected that at some point this had been open to the elements and the builders had just given up on the brickwork about a foot from the apex. There was a decent-ish looking leather armchair with a high back and arms.

'You can take the bed,' he said to Valentine. 'I'll have the chair.'

He would drag it in front of the door in case she decided to abscond in the night. He was fairly certain she wouldn't, but a healthy dose of paranoia never did anyone any harm. His mind went back to the bind-bench briefly and the memory came flavoured with loss. Hands tightly clasped, shoulders to lean heads on, lips whispering reassurance as the skies rained death. He wondered how many others had found comfort in those dark times like he had, and an unbearable pang of grief for Andrew tore through him.

A hand touched his shoulder and he tumbled back into the room.

'Kit, are you all right?' Valentine was looking at him with concern in her eyes.

'Fine. Just tired,' he lied. He dropped his rucksack on the floor, wondering whether to put on a fresh pair of socks now or in the morning. 'I want to wash. I feel filthy, even though we went swimming.'

'In there.' She motioned with her hand to a pair of thick velvet curtains covering what looked like a wardrobe, then kicked off her shoes and threw herself back onto the bed with her arms wide. She sank slightly into the thick eiderdown and Kit momentarily regretted being a gentleman.

He opened the curtains and gasped with astonishment and delight. The space was a whole bathroom, much bigger than the depth of the wardrobe would suggest. There must be a false wall. There was a sink with a wash basin, and over it a hand pump, like an old-fashioned well. The walls were decorated with mirrors, and there was a tray of glass bottles with interestingly coloured contents. Beside the sink, was a wooden chest – and beside that, a seat with an inlaid chamber pot.

He walked to the bedroom door, took the brass key from the lock and put it in his pocket.

'Don't you trust me?' Valentine asked from her position on the bed.

'You know I don't,' he said as he returned to the bathroom, though he couldn't muster the energy for much animosity. He pulled the heavy velvet curtain across the door (the lining was tartan for some reason, which made him laugh) and used the toilet with relief. The water that came out of the pump was perfectly warm and one of the bottles contained bright green liquid soap that smelled of parsley.

When he came out from behind the curtain, Valentine was sitting on the edge of the bed, barefoot.

'This room is marvellous,' he said, 'I hope I remember it when I wake up. I'd like to work out how to replicate it in Meadwell.'

Valentine stiffened. 'What do you mean 'wake up'? You're not dreaming. You're not like Miss Wyndham. You're really, completely here. Can't you tell?'

Kit crossed his arms defensively. It was something that he'd tried not to think about.

'I don't know. It does feel real,' he said slowly.

'That's because it is.'

He remembered going to the garden, meeting her, walking into the maze and out again. The scent of night-damp grass, the brushing of the bushes against his clothing. The chill of the pond and the warmth of the sun on his bare back. Valentine's fingers on his skin.

It was all so clear in his mind, but he couldn't escape the lingering worry that he was lying in his bed with his parents stricken with worry as he refused to awaken.

'I imagine whatever Addie's going through feels real, too,' he said.

A shadow crossed Valentine's face. 'I wish I had the power to lock away your thoughts of her, but that sort of bewilderment is far too difficult for me.'

'Why would I want thoughts of her locked away?' Kit asked, anger creeping into his belly and coming out in his voice.

'Because you'll be at peace,' Valentine said. 'I don't think you're often at peace, are you.'

Her eyes searched his face. He dropped his gaze, alarmed at how well she appeared able to read him.

'I don't want to be at peace. I want to know she's well,' he snapped.

'Of course you do. But if you could trap that little maggot of anxiety inside a shell, wouldn't that make your journey easier? It won't stop you loving her if you don't think of her constantly, will it?'

'Of course not,' Kit said, far too quickly. There had been times when he'd not given Adelaide a thought for days. Most of those times had been in wartime, true, but the war had not been the only reason.

'Perhaps I don't deserve to be at peace,' he muttered.

Valentine reached out a hand but stopped an inch from Kit's arm. She looked into his eyes and withdrew it, leaving him wondering if she'd seen his shame.

'I think I'll go and wash,' she said quietly.

She slipped off the bed and took her bag into the bathroom with her. While she was in there, Kit removed his shoes and socks and sat in the chair. It was as comfy as he'd hoped and he yawned once or twice. A strong smell of vanilla drifted out from the bathroom that made him even sleepier. He only meant to close his eyes for a moment, but when he opened them again the room was darker and Valentine was standing over him, furtively easing her hand into his pocket. He sprang awake, the need to be alert at short notice coming back to him in a rush, and he grabbed her by the wrist.

'What are you doing?' he snarled.

'I was just trying to get the key. There's no need to be so angry,' she protested.

'There's every need,' he growled. 'The minute I'm asleep you try to pick my pockets and run off.' He sank back into the chair, disorientated at having slept too deeply for not long enough. Her deviousness incensed him. He should have moved the chair to the door immediately.

'I wasn't going to run off,' she said haughtily. 'I'm hungry. I was going downstairs to get some supper. I was going to bring you something back up.'

'I don't need anything to eat. You can wait until morning, too.'

His belly chose that moment to growl loudly. A smug look settled on Valentine's face, but she controlled it and instead gave him an imploring smile.

'Come down with me. Food and company are always better in the evening than in the morning. Everyone then will be hurrying to leave. Now no one has anywhere else to be. I know you're hungry and so am I.'

He couldn't deny that, especially now that he could catch the faint aroma of roasting meat in the air. But spending an evening among the strange people he had seen as they arrived was unnerving.

'It's safer here. I might find myself bewitched,' he said.

'I told you, it's a Safe House. Listen,' Valentine said, cocking her head towards the door. 'Pipes and lutes and drums. Doesn't it make you want to dance?'

He hadn't been aware of the music until she'd mentioned it but now, listening carefully, he could hear the strains of something that sounded a little like an Irish jig or a Scottish reel.

'I don't dance,' he said.

'Then you can drink and watch while I dance,' Valentine said. She took him by the hands and attempted to pull him to his feet. 'Please. I need to be merry.'

Her eyes had grown wide and pleading and he found himself unable to think of any more reasons to resist.

'Only for a little while,' he said. 'And we don't speak to anyone.'

He reached for his socks and sniffed them, then reached into his rucksack for another pair. He laced his shoes and caught Valentine smiling to herself.

'It's odd how little things mark you out as different. Your footwear is one. If you pass through a town tomorrow, I will buy you a pair of boots. Or you could try win a pair from someone tonight,' she said.

He couldn't disagree. His brogues weren't particularly good for hiking. Valentine wore a light pair of dancing slippers with low heels that looked like they should be uncomfortable to walk in, but she seemingly had no problem. His army boots had taken a while to break in but for a time between then and when they became so waterlogged they refused to dry, they had been the most comfortable things he'd worn. He wished he still had them.

Theirs was the furthest of the three rooms on the floor. From the next room came the sounds of panting and gasping that could only be a couple making enthusiastic love. A third voice joined in. Kit blinked, and Valentine laughed.

'So innocent!'

'Come on,' he said sticking her arm into the fold of his. 'Let's eat and go back to our room as soon as we can.'

The voices reached a crescendo that showed no signs of abating.

'Or perhaps not,' he added and, when she laughed, he joined in.

Just before they reached the bottom of the stairs, Valentine paused. 'You're safe unless you do something foolish and I can't prevent it. Try not to.'

She took his hand and led him forward. The room was pleasantly warm with a large fire burning in a round grate in the centre of the floor. The landlord appeared at their side.

'A table for the two of you, Gentle? Or will you join the congregation of travellers?' he asked, indicating the long trestles and benches that were set around three sides of the fire.

'The congregation,' Valentine said, just as Kit asked for a private one. 'You hear the best stories at the communal tables,' she explained. Kit was about to retort that he didn't care for stories but surprised himself by agreeing to her plan.

They walked to the closest trestle, where there was room for two to sit side by side. Valentine nodded to the travellers, who were already eating, as she sat down and gestured for Kit to do likewise.

A barmaid was noting on a pad what the diners asked for. Her hair was pale green and fell to her waist in a thick braid. Her skin was light brown with markings that looked like tree bark.

'It's rude to stare,' Valentine hissed.

'I'm sorry, I know. It's just her skin looks like tree bark.'

'What do you expect? She's a dryad,' Valentine said.

'I've never seen anything so odd,' Kit whispered. 'And yet she's beautiful.'

Valentine smiled. 'You have half a face that looks like it was in a bonfire, and yet you're passably handsome, too.'

Kit flinched and raised a hand to his cheek.

'I don't say it to be cruel,' she said, shrugging. 'Just a reminder that oddity is as it appears.'

'Hogbelly stew or fried cockletails?' the barmaid asked, finally arriving at their end of the table.

'We'll have a plate of each and a flask of rosy wine,' Valentine replied.

'It's pronounced rose-ay,' Kit whispered to her.

'Aren't I lucky that I've got you to educate me,' she replied sweetly, rolling her eyes, and the old woman sitting next to Kit cackled.

The food arrived almost at once, along with a plate of something resembling thin crumpets and a dish of green beans that glistened with melting butter. The smell that rose from the bowl of stew made Kit's mouth water. He caught a whiff of aniseed and cinnamon, along with garlic in the brick red gravy, but there were more scents he couldn't identify. The other bowl contained small fried clumps of something in batter, with sprouting fronds – at least, he hoped they were fronds rather than legs. The wine came in a clear flask and had rose petals floating in it.

'Rosy Wine,' Valentine said, breezily. She poured two cups and held one out. Kit had it halfway to his lips when he caught himself.

'I can't drink this. Or eat anything,' he added, casting a regretful glance at the stew.

'This is a public inn,' Valentine said. 'A Safe House. What sort of business would it do if your dinner placed you under servitude? Besides, you're going to pay for it so there's no exchanging required.'

Kit felt for his wallet before remembering he didn't have it. 'Your money won't work here anyway,' Valentine explained. 'I'll have to pay for both of us.'

'But then I'll owe you,' he pointed out.

'You're too quick a learner, that's your problem,' Valentine said, scowling. 'It would serve you right to end up owing me something.' He got the impression she was quite pleased, though.

'You can entertain the congregation with a song or a story or a poem. That's usually good enough,' said the old woman who had laughed earlier and who was making no attempt to hide the fact that she was listening in. She pointed her long fork at the two men who were playing the trombone and fiddle on the fourth edge of the fireplace.

'I can't sing very well and I don't know any stories,' Kit said.

'Ridiculous! Everyone knows a story or two,' the old woman said. 'Can you dance?'

"Shall we have a go at the tango? Or should we go for a drink?"

Kit shook his head, both to banish the memories and answer the question.

'He can't dance. I've seen him,' Valentine confirmed with a wicked grin.

She speared a large piece of hogbelly, brick-red and with gelatinous fat running through it, and popped it into her mouth. Kit's stomach tightened with hunger. He needed to eat and entertainment would be his only way of paying but he cringed as he remembered the regiment's revues. He'd only gone onto the stage because Andrew had wheedled and coaxed, and Kit would have done anything for him in the first few weeks they'd known each other.

The charming grin. "Now you've given me some matches, don't suppose you've got a cigarette?"

For the first time he could remember, he smiled at the memory of Andrew.

'I know a few poems,' he said slowly. 'They're not my words but I can share them with you.'

'If the owners don't mind,' the woman said.

'They're long since dead and it's something schoolboys have been taught to do.'

'Then that's your payment,' the woman said. The musicians finished and left the performance area to loud applause. Valentine elbowed Kit sharply in the ribs and he jumped to his feet with a small cry. She pointed at him.

'He's going to give us poems,' she shouted. An expectant lull descended on the diners and Kit realised he had no choice.

He coughed to clear his throat as he made his way across the room. He wasn't a stranger to recitals. He'd won a prize when he'd been in the fourth form but that had been long ago. He stood straight, shoulders back and took a deep breath.

'I... I met a traveller...' he began hesitantly, but then the words to Shelley's *Ozymandias* came flowing back. He straightened his shoulders, took a breath and began again. When he finished he became aware of a collective release of breath, then some applause. Valentine was beaming and applauding.

'Another,' she called.

'I'll have a morsel of that stew first.' Kit grinned. She speared a piece of hogbelly on her long fork and held it out. Kit accepted it. The meat was velvety soft, collapsing in his mouth as the flavours rolled over his tongue, aniseed, cinnamon, a hint of ginger. It was delicious.

'What will you do for us now?' the old woman asked.

'You don't have to,' Valentine whispered.

'I know.'

But the exhilaration was a spell of its own. He looked around the patrons. What would they like to hear? He could probably sing or say almost anything and they wouldn't know it. What had they sung in the trenches? He gave them a verse of *Pack Up Your Troubles*, which went down even better than the poem had, then *All the Nice Girls Love a Sailor*.

'Sing it again!' someone shouted from the back of the room; a person of indeterminate gender with heavily made-up eyes, a long beard woven through with silver ribbons and teeth that were slightly too pointed when they smiled.

Kit sang it again, this time marching up and down, and by

the time he'd finished, half the room had taken up the tune and were banging on the tables with their palms. Kit looked at Valentine. She was laughing hysterically.

'What?' he asked, giving her a grin.

'You are a true Caster of Words,' she answered. She walked to Kit and threw her arm around his shoulders, planted a kiss on his cheek and raised his hand in the air like a prizefighter.

'Gentles and travellers, has he earned his dinner?' she shouted.

The chorus that responded assured him that yes, indeed he had.

'Has he earned his drink?'

'One more song for a bottle of Rosy Wine,' shouted an unbelievably buxom serving maid standing at the bar. 'And if he makes me dance, I'll throw in a kiss for free.'

Valentine's fingers tightened on Kit's shoulders. 'Keep your lips to yourself, you old snatch-maggot!' she yelled, to a resulting chorus of 'Ooohs!' from the diners.

'Don't be rude,' Kit said, appalled. He had no idea what it meant, but it was clearly an insult.

'You really don't want to tangle with her,' Valentine murmured discreetly. 'Get yourself caught in that web and you'll never come free.'

'Even so, there's no need to be offensive.' He bowed to the serving maid. 'Fair maiden, I have taken the vow that no thought of lust shall pass through my mind, until I have kissed the lips of my fair betrothed who has been cruelly stolen from me.'

This appeared to go down well with most of the audience,

but declaring the reason for his presence might not have been wise, so he stood upright quickly.

'A final song,' he called. He gave them a rousing rendition of *A British Tar* from HMS Pinafore, finishing with a flourishing bow to wild applause.

He sat down and Valentine passed him his cup.

'*Tchovikste*,' she said, raising hers to bump the lip against his.

'What does that mean?'

'It means, may your health and happiness be what you deserve.'

'That sounds double-edged,' Kit remarked.

'A reason to be virtuous, I'd say,' Valentine answered with a grin.

Kit drained his cup in one. His heart was beating with exhilaration! He'd actually enjoyed himself.

'I hope you've left me some hogbelly, Valentine.'

She pushed the bowl to him with a lazy smile. 'Yours is a gift of taking men with you in spirit. Silas will be pleased when I tell him of this night.'

Kit's smile grew brittle. 'I don't care if he is pleased. Why does he want us? He said the land is in trouble, but from what I've seen it looks perfectly pleasant and the people here seem content.'

Valentine's smile grew fixed. 'I'm sure in your war you found moments of happiness, but that does not mean everything was good. Besides, we're only on the outer lands. Closer to the seat of the capital, things are darker.'

'And you need to steal humans to heal it?' Kit snapped.

'Not steal, borrow. Stealing suggests we would take those who weren't willing,' Valentine said, with dignity.

They could quibble about that all night, Kit suspected, and she wouldn't see anything wrong with the deception she and Wilde had perpetrated.

'Silas will explain more when we reach him. I don't know much about it, only that somehow it coincided with things that happened here. There must be a link.'

He was getting a little tired of having to wait for Silas to explain but what else was there to do.

'It could be a coincidence,' Kit suggested. 'They do happen.'

'After everything you've learned you still believe that?' she smirked.

'I suppose you're right,' Kit agreed. 'Look, someone else is going to perform.'

A man clad in a heavy grey cloak had taken the stage. As he raised his arms for silence his sleeves fell, revealing black and gold tattoos that encircled his arms from wrist to shoulder.

'My tale shall not be so humorous,' he said, gazing slowly around the room, his pale, watery eyes unsettling as they lighted upon Valentine and Kit. 'I speak of sorrow and of betrayal.'

'Well, that's a good way to kill the atmosphere,' Kit whispered.

Valentine frowned at him, but she had giggled softly just before she did, so he wasn't too worried about offending her.

The storyteller waited until the room was perfectly quiet before lowering his arms. He glanced once again at Kit, smiling in a way that set Kit's teeth on edge, and then began his tale.

Chapter Fourteen

'Once upon a time there were three brothers,' the storyteller said. 'Noble children of noble parents, although they were changeable as their nature dictated. They had a sister. A maid as fair and free as the birds in the sky.'

'They always are,' grumbled the old woman opposite Kit, and was shushed by the man at her side. She scowled at him.

'The sister was fairer than the brothers, fairer than their mother, fairer than any maiden for a hundred miles round, as quick and bold as the salmon that darts upstream. Every man wanted her for her lively nature and her comely figure.'

'Never have a nose like a hoof pick or tits like pebbles on a dinner slate,' the old woman muttered.

The speaker dropped his voice to a low whisper, causing the audience to lean forwards. Entranced, Kit let his fork fall into the bowl.

The man waved his arms around, creating shadow puppets. There had to be magic in his artifice because the pictures were more real than they had any likelihood of being.

'The maid was haughty. She knew her worth and the value of what she had. Poor men came and tried. They failed. Rich and powerful men failed, too. The maid was free in spirit and in body and intended to stay that way, until one day there appeared a man with eyes that danced like violets in a rainstorm.'

Valentine hissed sharply, drawing breath in. Kit slid his eyes sideways at the sound. Like everyone else, she was sitting forward, watching and listening.

The storyteller lifted his hands and the shadows became a box. Jewels cascaded from them in the shadows but nothing fell from his hands.

'The merchant came not to woo the maiden but to sell his wares to her.'

There was a clattering. Kit, who had been as spellbound as anybody else, looked round. Valentine had been toying with a fork and dropped it. Her hands shook.

'I'm tired. I'm going to bed.'

'Wait a little longer,' Kit urged. 'I want to hear what happens next.'

She stood. 'Do you really? Do you? Don't you know this story?'

'I don't think so,' Kit said, taken aback by her vehemence.

'I do.' She looked at the storyteller with intense hatred. 'I know and everybody here knows, and I will not suffer to listen to it.'

Kit reached for her hand, but she snatched it back and pushed past him. She ran towards the stairs. A man with the ears of a spaniel reached out to grab her, but she spat something in a language Kit didn't understand. The dog man laughed. Kit was halfway to his feet before Valentine had kicked the man between the legs and he doubled over, whining. The storyteller had momentarily lost his audience in the quarter of the room where Kit was sitting, as many had turned to watch the disturbance. The rest appeared not to have noticed, but the storyteller himself stood still with an unpleasant grin on his face.

'I have offended. A thousand apologies.' He didn't sound remotely sorry.

The old woman sitting opposite Kit snorted, clearly thinking the same. 'Best go comfort your lady.'

'She's not my lady,' Kit said, thinking that even if she was, he'd give her time to calm down before attempting to talk to her. 'What happens in the rest of the story?'

'The usual.' The old woman dipped a piece of crust in her wine then sucked at it. 'The maiden either falls for him or falls for what he's selling and lets herself get seduced. Too proud to pick a poor man who loves her, too prideful not to realise she's getting herself trapped.'

Kit poured another glass of wine and sat back to listen. The story played out exactly as the old woman had predicted. The peddler showed the maiden his wares and she tried to bargain a price with him for a necklace but when she could not afford the cost he offered the exchange of a kiss from her lips. When she obliged and he gave her the necklace, he clasped it around her throat and it became a shackle, trapping her as his servant. It was rather horrible, no wonder that Valentine hadn't wanted to listen to it. It left Kit feeling slightly tarnished having done so himself. It seemed he wasn't the only one because there was only a smattering of applause and not as much enthusiasm as Kit's songs or the previous tales had generated.

'My story is done,' said the storyteller. 'Who goes next?'

'Sam Cole,' the innkeeper cried, looking around to find a means of lightening the atmosphere. 'Give us the latest verse of yours, if you will.'

An old man sitting in an armchair in the corner of the room stood up and cleared his throat. 'Gladly, I will oblige.'

'Not more of this,' the old lady groaned. 'Bloody wedding guests and bloody shipwrecks and bloody canyons. It's never ending. I'm off for a piddle in the compost heap. Good luck to you and your lady fair. I'm sure with bravery in your heart you will free her from her servitude.'

The old lady picked up her skirt and walked out. She had the clawed feet of a chicken and somehow this did not seem at all odd to Kit. Certainly not as odd as the fact she appeared to know about Adelaide. He mopped up the rest of the stew and ate the last few cockletails, which turned out to be some sort of flower in batter. There was half a flask of Rosy Wine left so he took it with him. As he neared the bedroom door, he heard the sounds of the trio still (or again) having sex. His stomach curled. He shouldn't have let Valentine go off alone in such a place when she had been so upset.

The room was lit only by moonbeams slanting through the high window. They cast everything into greys and mauves but there was enough light to see Valentine's huddled form beneath the bedspread. Kit put the wine flask on the table, planning to drink it as he sat in the chair. He moved around the room stealthily, trying not to wake her up. It was only after he'd finished brushing his teeth, changed into the night shirt and put his discarded clothes inside the chest, that he became aware of the sound of muffled sobbing. Valentine might not have been awake the whole time he had been clumping about, but she was now, and she was definitely distressed.

His heartstrings tugged.

'I hope I didn't wake you,' he whispered. There was no reply, but the bundle shifted slightly.

'I brought the rest of the wine. Would you like a glass?'

She still said nothing and the sobbing became more audible and more violent. Kit sat on the edge of the bed and cautiously patted what he hoped was Valentine's shoulder. He wasn't prepared for the long string of obscenities that resulted, and pulled his hand back sharply. She emerged from beneath the covers. Her hair was in disarray, sticking up all over her head, and her eyes almost glowed.

'What do you want?'

'I wondered why you are crying.'

'Why do you care?' She pulled the cover to her chin. 'Go away and leave me to be.'

'Leave you to cry, you mean? I'm not going to do that.'

'Why not? You owe me no kindness,' she said, rolling over in an eiderdown cocoon.

Kit sighed deeply. 'I suppose I don't, but I owe you no unkindness either. I can't bear to see anyone cry, but if you'd rather spend your night sniffing under a blanket then don't let me stop you.'

He fetched the flask of Rosy Wine from the table.

'I'm still thirsty. Let's drink this.'

She rolled over and looked at him suspiciously.

'It's the one we opened before, so there's no obligation or trickery involved,' he said.

She gave a half-smile. 'You're starting to learn, aren't you.'

'I've had to!'

Valentine took the flask and swigged from it then passed it to Kit. There was an extra taste of sweetness on the lip of the flask that hadn't been there before, and he assumed it had come from her lips. He sniffed the top suspiciously.

'What are you doing?'

He slid his eyes to her. 'Did you put something in this? It tastes different. More floral than before.'

'You saw me take it from your hand, put it to my lips and hand it back. When would I have put anything in it? You go from kind to insulting so quickly.' She rolled her eyes. 'And my kind is supposedly capricious! I didn't put anything in it.'

'I'm sorry I meant no offence,' Kit said, floundering.

'Then choose your words more carefully!' She tugged the flask out of his hand and tilted it back. Her lips plucked at the opening. Kit couldn't take his eyes off them, even when she lowered the flask and passed it back to him. He leaned closer to her, and caught the trace of mimosas that he had come to associate with her.

'I think it's your scent.'

'It could be.'

She leaned in a little closer. Kit put his nose closer to the hollow of her collarbone and inhaled. Desire bowled him over, sending him spinning. He let out a soft growl and raised his head. Valentine was very still with an inscrutable smile on her lips.

'Is that how you bewilder people?' he breathed.

'It can be. But I'm not doing it to you.' She reached out a hand and touched his face, skimming it from his ear down to his jaw and leaving a trail of heat in its wake. 'Not intentionally, that is.'

She smiled. Kit's blood pounded as another spool of desire overwhelmed him. He was barely breathing. He swallowed, feeling a ray of sunshine pulsing within his chest. Valentine leaned forward and kissed him. He stiffened and she pulled back.

She sat motionless staring at him.

'You kissed me back before.'

'I shouldn't have.' Guilt wrenched him back to cold reality. 'I have a fiancée.'

'Yes, you do. If you're feeling guilt, then ask yourself why.'

'Because I'm promised to her.' His voice sounded hollow. Almost as hollow as the feeling that it had been the only reason he could convincingly summon.

'Even though she's let herself be wooed by Silas!' She tutted. 'Besides, it's common knowledge that what happens in a Safe House doesn't count.'

He would never have instigated a kiss himself, but he wasn't at all displeased when Valentine tugged his face around and pressed her lips to his.

The taste of Rosy Wine from her lips, coupled with the scent of mimosas, was dizzying. He took her face between his hands and slowly let his tongue trace the contours of her lips, exploring her parted mouth. When they had kissed before it had been full of surprise and anger, hate and mistrust simmering between them, but this was something new. She tugged at his lips with hers then bit down gently and at the same time she slid her hand up to cup the back of his head. Taking control of the pace. His pulse hammered in his ears and he got up from the bed, quickly turning away so that Valentine wouldn't spot how very aroused he was.

'What's wrong?' Valentine stretched out, throwing the eiderdown back so that one naked leg was visible.

'Why are you trying to seduce me?'

'What makes you think I am?' She crossed her other leg over the one that was visible. The silk nightdress pooled around her thighs, providing scant modesty.

'You kissed me,' he said. 'Wasn't that a prelude to … to something more?'

She gave a short laugh. 'It was only a kiss, and not even a very passionate one at that.'

It had been more passionate, by a number of degrees, than any kiss Kit had recently had. Possibly more than he'd ever shared with Adelaide.

'Don't play games,' he snapped. 'If you're not trying to seduce me, then what did you kiss me for?'

'Curiosity, mainly,' Valentine said. 'I wanted to see what you'd do.'

'Well, now you know.'

He sniffed and she rolled her eyes.

'What, are you offended that I didn't say that it's your rampant charisma or your handsome face that made you irresistible?'

'There's no need to taunt me.' He put his hand to his cheek, feeling stupid. It was the first time one of her references to his face had succeeded in wounding him and he was disappointed at himself for caring.

'I wasn't taunting you,' she said, shuffling so that she knelt upright.

'Really? That's not what it sounded like.' He began dragging the chair in front of the door. The scraping of the feet on the wooden floor was awkwardly loud and he hoped whoever was in the room below wasn't disturbed.

'What are you doing?' Valentine asked.

'Going to sleep,' Kit muttered, standing up and stretching out his spine to release the cricks. The swim, which had eased his tension, now felt a long time ago. He shook out the dressing gown, planning to use it as a blanket. 'Tomorrow is going to be another long day and I'm tired.'

'No, I mean, why there?' Valentine asked.

'Because it's a damn sight comfier than the floor.'

'But why not here? There's room in the bed for two.' She sat back and spread her arms wide to illustrate her point.

He faced her, crossing his arms, unsettled by the way his leg muscles had involuntarily twitched to walk in her direction. 'After what just happened between us, do you really think that's wise?'

He sat down, stretched his legs out and shook the dressing gown so that it billowed and settled over his legs. Ignoring Valentine, he folded his hands over his belly and closed his eyes. After a couple of minutes of silence, he heard her cough, then speak.

'I didn't tell you the complete truth before.'

'You surprise me,' he said grumpily. 'When exactly are you referring to? I'm sure I couldn't possibly tell which occasion you mean.'

She sighed heavily.

'I kissed you because I'm feeling melancholy and you were being kind to me,' she said quietly.

He opened his eyes. She was still sitting up but now her shoulders were slumped, and she'd gathered the eiderdown around herself and looked like a child hugging a soft toy for comfort.

'The bard's story reminded me of what I am, and it pains me to think of it. I feel cold where my heart longs to be. I want to feel some heat.'

She pressed her palm to her chest and gave him a smile that was edged with sheepishness, as if it pained her to admit it. 'I lied, too, when I said it wasn't passionate. It was, and it was very good. I did want more, but I won't take it from you. Come and lie with me for the night.'

'I really can't do that,' Kit said. Her honesty – and he had no doubt this was the truth – was disarming; more seductive than any kiss could have been. He understood. He longed for that closeness and companionship. 'A kiss is one thing but anything else would be completely inappropriate.'

'I'm not asking that of you.' She tilted her head on one side and gave him a grave look that reminded him of a little bird. 'I just think I'd rather not lie here alone. Please, come sleep beside me.'

She held her hands towards him, palms out in supplication and invitation. It was probably a bad idea, but Kit barely hesitated before tossing aside the dressing gown and joining her beneath the covers. The chair had proven to be less comfortable than he had anticipated, and it was that, he told himself as he lay beside her, that had been the deciding factor.

They lay rigid beside each other at first, but they both

began to grow drowsy and shift around the bed. There was a brief organisation of limbs as they negotiated positions that would suit them both. Valentine curled onto her side facing away from him with her back pressed against his side. Her frame went limp, and she gave a soft snuffling snore. Kit stared into the shafts of moonlight. This was a much more sensible way to spend the night if he wanted to awake ready and prepared. Tomorrow, he'd have to face the man who had abducted Adelaide and enslaved Valentine. The man who had committed grave wrongs against the woman he had long cared about and another he believed he was starting to.

He wriggled into a more comfortable position on his side and put an arm around her, aware of the rise and fall of her body against his chest. They'd shared the dodo shelter the night before, but being in a bed was altogether more intimate and pleasant. On the cusp of sleep again, he realised there was nowhere else he would rather spend the night.

~

Valentine woke to find herself face down. Her leg was crooked between Kit's and his arms were loosely around her back. Waking in a tangle of limbs in itself was not a new experience for Valentine. After all, she had courted and seduced many people and almost-people in her time at the behest of her master. He drove hard bargains when he bought and sold favours but wasn't above throwing her into the negotiation as a sweetener, and often the price included a night in her purchaser's bed.

One of her skills was to lock memories away in

compartments where they could not hurt the owner. She'd used the trick on herself more times than she could remember after a night she'd loathed, but she didn't feel the confusing lethargy in her limbs that accompanied a night she'd hidden away. It suggested that there was nothing she'd felt the need to obliterate, so she was fairly certain that she and Kit had not tumbled together. Somehow, that had not arisen, other than the brief and embarrassing moment he had accused her of attempting seduction.

Kit's head lolled over and he yawned, though didn't fully wake and Valentine closed her eyes, basking in the unaccustomed feeling of contentment. He had asked nothing of her, but had freely given comfort when he could have bargained for knowledge or favours.

He was too honourable to be true. He acted through compassion for her and the defence of his woman. It was torturous being unable to work out what she required of him and what would be the key to understanding him. In her time, she had played the part of the slut, the virgin, the wise woman, and the innocent waiting to be taught. None of the roles had ever failed but she suspected all of them would fall against Kit's fortifications.

Her lip curled with frustration. It pecked at her head that she hadn't yet found his weakness. No wonder she had failed to entice him when they were back in his world. She wondered if Valentin was the key but he closed himself off whenever there was any hint that he found men as attractive as he did women. How frustratingly stupid his world was!

He yawned again and stretched.

'Good morning,' she murmured, craning her head to look at him. She blew at the hair that had fallen across his forehead.

He leaned up on his elbow and blinked, bleary eyed, then smiled.

'Good morning, Valentine. Somehow I thought you might have vanished in the night.'

His nightshirt was untied at the neck, and she caught a glimpse of his chest as the loose garment flopped open. Smooth and almost hairless. She'd seen it as they'd sun dried by the pond and her hand twitched as her fingers longed to stroke it. The solidity of his body was oh, so enticing, and she grew hot, aware of his proximity and calling out to taste what he might offer. She laughed to cover her discomfiture.

'Where would I go? This bed is far too comfortable to do that. Also the company is pleasant.'

'I agree on both accounts,' he said. 'This was definitely a better choice than the chair or floor. Are you happier today?'

She looked inwards. 'Yes, actually I think I am.'

His eyes smiled and she glowed with pleasure. She rolled around to face him, leaning on her elbow as he did. He rested his hand on her arm. 'I'm glad to hear it. I hoped I helped a little.'

The attraction between them was immense; the raw sexual need in him as potent as in anyone she had encountered, and she couldn't believe he didn't feel it, too. She knew how men worked. All she'd have to do was slip her hand down between their bodies, take his cock in her hands, and he'd be incapable of turning her away. Would her master even know if they swived? It might be a risk worth taking.

'More than a little,' she breathed, sliding her hand onto his waist in a tentative exploration of his rection. She was more disappointed than she could articulate to feel the muscles stiffen, not with desire, but with awkwardness. The time was not right. 'We had better get ready to leave,' she said with some reluctance.

'Of course. Would you like to use the bathroom first?' Kit asked.

Reluctantly, Valentine pulled herself from his arms and wandered into the dressing room. Her clothes had been neatly laundered and lay folded in the pearwood chest, smelling faintly of lavender. Kit's clothes were there, too, with his vest and underpants on the top. She grinned at the sight of them, wondering how anyone could wear something so restrictive. She bathed in warm water, applied a creamy lotion to her skin and dressed.

'Your turn,' she said, coming back into the bedroom. Kit was still sitting in bed. Valentine had to resist the urge to clamber back on and straddle him. He climbed out and sauntered into the bathroom. He appeared more at ease with himself the longer he spent here and she wondered how eager to return home he would be.

He emerged shortly thereafter, dressed and with his hair slicked back. He picked up his bag and strode to the door to move the chair away. Valentine gathered her belongings and looked around to discover Kit staring at her with a hostile expression.

'The door is locked. What have you done.'

'Nothing. You locked it. What have you done with the key?' she asked, scowling at the accusation in his words.

'The key is in the lock. I've just tried it, but nothing

happened.' He demonstrated turning the key in both directions and lifting the latch.

'Let me try,' Valentine said. She turned it clockwise and anticlockwise hearing the tumbler fall in and out of place, but the door would not move. 'The key isn't the problem,' she said anxiously. 'Something is wedging the latch itself, or it's been bolted.'

'Who would do that and why?' Kit said, joining her.

'I don't know. Somebody who doesn't want us leaving.'

They stared at each other in silence then Kit turned back to the door and hammered on it with his fist. The wood was thick and he barely made a sound. He slapped it open-palmed and spun around.

'What are we going to do? Is this Silas's doing?'

Valentine exhaled loudly. 'Why would Silas lock us in a bedroom together? He doesn't even know where we are!'

'Then, who?' Kit demanded.

Valentine hugged herself defensively. 'I don't know, but someone is trying to stop us carrying on with our journey, and that's not in Silas's interests. He needs us there.'

Kit had caught a lot of attention the previous night. A young, handsome human who could create pictures with his words would make a valuable asset to any number of households, though she thought better than to tell him that.

His expression changed from anger to anxiety. She inhaled deeply and the smell of something familiar caught the edge of her attention. She dropped to her knees and sniffed along the bottom of the door. Citrus and almonds. She threw herself backwards.

'*Sour Sansevra*! Kit, cover your mouth quickly and your nose. Someone is trying to drug us.'

Even as she spoke, there was an increase of heaviness in her head from being so close to the source. Kit began to hammer on the door again, demanding to be let out.

'Save your breath and don't inhale it more than you have to,' Valentine snapped. 'This is intentional.'

'Is it gas?' Kit said. His face was a sickly, pale colour, except for the scarring which had not changed and now looked more prominent due to the contrast. 'Not that. I cannot be trapped. I just can't. There aren't any windows. We need to get out.'

He began to pace around the room then rushed to the door and beat on it again with his fists. Valentine seized him around the waist. He wheeled around, eyes wide and panicked.

'Kit, stop!' She released him and held her hands up in front of her. 'We'll find a way! It's not a gas but a soporific plant. When the leaves are burned, the smoke causes unconsciousness.'

'The same effect, though.' He closed his eyes and she feared he might pass out, but he shook himself from the stupor, ran to the bathroom and returned with the towels. 'Pull down the curtains from the bed,' he instructed, as he began wedging the towels at the bottom of the door.

Valentine obeyed, dragging the eiderdown, too. Kit grabbed the silk nightgown from the bed and began to rip it. 'Put this around your face,' he instructed. 'It will slow the gas down.'

'How do you know to do this?' Valentine asked as she wound the strip around her nose and mouth.

'From the trenches. I got caught—' He stopped winding

and put his hand to his cheek. 'How long should it take for our enemy to assume we'll be unconscious?'

'It's quick to work. The cloths won't keep it out for long, but it will buy us a little time. Perhaps ten minutes,' Valentine said.

If the intent was to capture not kill. Half an hour would be long enough to ensure they never woke from the sleep they would fall under. She had to hope it was the former.

'Then we'll just have to hope whoever is out there is impatient and we're not completely insensible when they open the door,' Kit answered, reaching for a candlestick from the dresser and squaring himself. His eyes had taken on a dangerous glint.

Valentine marvelled at the change in him. Jeopardy appeared to bring out his best side, though he would surely deny that if she mentioned it.

'If only the window was bigger,' he said, glancing at the gap in the eaves.

'Oh, Kit, you are an absolute marvel,' Valentine exclaimed. 'I'd forgotten all about the window.'

'It won't provide much fresh air,' he said with regret.

'No, but I can get out of it.'

He looked her up and down. 'You're small but not that small.'

She rested a hand on his arm, astonished that he still hadn't realised what she could do.

'I can be smaller. You might not want to watch this,' she said. She took a step back, preparing to change. It would come as a shock to him, but there was no time to prepare him or explain, not while the room was filling with the *Sour Sansevra* smoke. 'Do you remember when I said that I would be travelling as the crow flies to get my things? I wasn't lying exactly.'

She spread her arms out and concentrated, feeling for her other form, letting her fingers become pin feathers. The world was sharper through the bird's eyes, and she could read every creased line of astonishment written around Kit's eyes. He pointed at her dumbly, mouth opening and closing beneath the wound silk. She hoped there would be the opportunity for discussion later, but now she was feeling the effects of the soporific more acutely with her smaller frame. She flew clumsily up to the gap in the eaves and out into the fresh air.

Time was of the essence, she knew, but she darted higher to where the air was fresher, and as she did, she wheeled around and looked in the direction they were heading. They were so close to reaching the foothills of the mountains. Her resolve doubled and she flew down again tucking her wings and gliding into the open door of the inn.

The room was busy with travellers eating breakfast and having a drink before they set off and it was busy, so her arrival went unnoticed. The innkeeper was bustling around, talking to his guests. If only he was aware of what grave assault was being conducted beneath his roof, he would not be so cheerful.

She cooed a warning then flew up the stairs. At the top, she landed on one of the sconces that lit the corridor with a gently burning torch. A man was kneeling by her bedroom door, a long pipe in his hand as he blew the smoke into the gap between door and floor. She recognised him as the bard who had told her story the night before.

Anger seized her at his impertinence, but it was tinged with relief. This maggot was seeking not to kill, simply to drug them. Once he assumed they were both unconscious, it would be her that he carried off, not Kit. The feathers down at the band that encased her leg ruffled. She hadn't planned what to do once she had left the room, but now she acted instinctively. She stretched her wings to their full width and flew at her would-be tormentor. Her claws were short and blunt but his hair was long and loose, so as she reached him, she dived down and grabbed hanks of it, beating her wings and screeching.

As she had hoped he would, the bard flailed trying to swat at her. She was ready for the moment he let go of the pipe and released his hair, diving down swiftly so that she could seize it. Smoke trailed along the corridor, rancid and greasy. Too late, the bard realised what she was doing and tried to catch up but she was too high. That was one problem dealt with, now to free Kit. She flew back to the stairwell, suspecting rightly that the man would give chase and thinking quickly.

Valentin would be best now, she decided. He was slightly larger and stronger and marginally less at risk of rape. By the time he rounded the corner, he had returned to his human form and grasped a torch from the wall sconce. As the bard appeared, Valentin thrust the flaming torch into the assailant's face. He shrieked with pain and raised his hands.

'How dare you!' Valentin snarled. 'Whatever else I am, I am still a Gentle of my house. You dare to raise a hand against me and the one who is under my protection! In a Safe House!'

The man dropped to his knees.

'I was going to save you, my lady, my lord,' he whimpered.

'By drugging me?' Valentin stepped back in disbelief.

'I know the story. I told it last night for you. I would fight for your release and your hand.'

There it was: the reason for his actions. Not Valentine's liberty but a transfer of sale from their master to him. The conditions of their release from enslavement would be a different servitude. The flaming torch had been all but extinguished, so Valentin blew it out and beat him around the head with the smouldering end.

'You make me sick to the stomach.'

The uproar had finally been noticed. The door of the room next to Valentin's opened and the love-making trio stuck their heads out. The landlord and a handful of his staff appeared at the top of the stairs.

'Gentle, is there a problem?' he asked Valentin.

Valentin retrieved the pipe from where it had fallen. 'This knave was in the act of filling my room with *Sour Sansevra* smoke. He has broken all the laws of hospitality.'

The landlord's face darkened, and with good reason. If this became general knowledge his reputation as the proprietor of a Safe House would be in tatters.

'Then I will deal with him,' the landlord said. 'It's just as well you managed to escape.'

'Yes, I...' Valentin's stomach plummeted. 'Kit!'

He ran to the door. The latch had been wedged with a thick piece of wood. He tore it free and pulled the door open. Kit had pulled the chair over to the window and was slumped beside it on the floor in an odd reproduction of the scene in the plate room. Presumably, he had been attempting to breathe in as much fresh air as possible but had been overcome and collapsed. Valentin rolled him onto his back, pulling the cloth from his face. His lips were pale and tinged with blue and his head lolled like a puppet whose strings had been cut.

'Oh, breathe, please,' Valentin pleaded, slapping his cheek to try to rouse him. He groaned softly, proving that he was at least alive.

'Oh, thank Mab!' Valentin let himself sag down a little with relief.

Kit opened his eyes, which were slightly glazed, and smiled up at him with a stupid expression on his face.

'You're the most beautiful creature I've ever seen. The handsomest, too. Thank you for saving me, darling. My dear little dove.'

He reached his arms around Valentin's neck and pulled him down into a kiss. For someone who had been close to death only moments before, Kit showed more passion than Valentin would have anticipated him capable of. He began to kiss Kit back but tasted the citrus and almonds on his tongue. This was the *Sour Sansevra*, at work, not Kit. He didn't mean a word of it and would probably not even remember saying or doing it when he recovered. Even knowing that the passion was an enchantment, it took all of his to strength pull away rather than take advantage.

The room was still heavy with the scent of the smoke. Valentin stood up and tried to heave Kit to his feet but he might as well have been trying to drag a sack of rocks. Even in his male form, Kit was too heavy for Valentin, and in no state to help himself.

'Somebody, help me!' he called and presently one of the serving boys came in. Between them they dragged Kit downstairs and outside where they laid him on the grass. The innkeeper brought a pot of chicory tea and a mug containing a large lump of waxy honeycomb. Valentin poured the tea over the honeycomb and held it to Kit's lips.

'Drink this.'

He shook his head. 'Can't. No debts.'

'There is no debt involved in this,' the innkeeper said fervently. 'Your money is no good here, either, Gentle. Any debt you might have owed is paid by what almost happened to you.'

Kit nodded, but his mouth remained a tight line, Valentin wasn't sure he really understood.

'If you'd have died, his Safe House would have been forfeit.'

Kit reached for the tea and gingerly sat upright to sip it. He paused and looked at Valentin.

'I know you, I think?' he asked suspiciously.

Valentin smiled and concentrated, slipping back into her female form. Kit gaped.

'You were a bird,' he mumbled. 'And a man.'

'I was,' Valentine confirmed, waiting for disapproval or revulsion, but Kit gave her a lopsided smile.

'You saved my life,' he said.

'I did.'

'That's a debt I can never repay.' He took her hand and pressed it to his chest. The blood in Valentine's veins turned to liquid fire and an unseen fist punched her chest. It was unnerving.

'Gentle, what shall I do with the bard?' asked the innkeeper. 'He's bound and awaiting his sentence.'

When she didn't answer immediately the innkeeper coughed discreetly.

'Should we send him to your family?'

Valentine looked at him sharply. 'No!'

There was no one left to send him to that she still associated with.

'Do what you want with him. The trespass was against you as much as against me. I'll leave the matter in your hands.'

The innkeeper's eyes gleamed. 'Yes, Gentle, if you desire it. I think a couple of decades scrubbing the floors in my kitchens will be adequate.'

He bowed and went back inside.

'Who is your family?' Kit asked, clear interest in his voice.

She froze. 'No one I want to speak of.'

The innkeeper's boy had brought their bags out. She gestured to them.

'Are you fit to walk yet?'

Kit clambered to his feet. 'I think so.'

She regarded him thoughtfully, then strode back into the inn. The unfortunate bard was sat on the floor, his hands bound behind his back, while the innkeeper plaited leaves and raw wool into the charm that would hold him as servant.

'You trespassed against my friend, and he deserves recompense,' she said, kneeling down and pulling the boots from his feet. They were fine, fawn leather, looked about Kit's size, and the bard wouldn't be needing them any time soon. She walked back to Kit and held them out.

'Here, I said we'd get you some better footwear.'

He didn't take them. 'Do they belong to the bard?'

'Not any longer.'

He folded his arms. 'In my world it would count as looting to take the belongings of an enemy.'

'We're not in your world now. Put them on and let's go. We still have a long way ahead of us,' she said.

She put the boots on the ground and picked up her bag, wondering what he would do. When he sat down and began to unlace his shoes, she suppressed the grin of triumph and strolled in the direction of the mountains, knowing he'd be at her side before too long.

Chapter Fifteen

For all his reservations about wearing another man's shoes, Kit had to admit they were the most comfortable footwear he'd ever possessed. The boots looked odd with his trousers, but he didn't care. They were soft leather, laced to mid-calf and moulded themselves perfectly to the shape of his feet. He assumed there must be some sort of enchantment at play. It was good that he had something to think about because Valentine appeared shaken by the morning's events and Kit certainly was.

For the first hour neither of them spoke. Valentine had an angry look in her eye, the sight of which deterred Kit from broaching any of the subjects he wanted to. And there was a great deal he wanted to ask. The day grew increasingly hot but in an oppressive way. That, coupled with a stuffed head that felt like the worst hangover of his life, did not make for pleasant travelling. He couldn't really remember anything from Valentine transforming into a bird in front of his eyes to when he had woken on the ground in front of the inn and she'd transformed from a man to a woman before his eyes. He curled his nails into his palms, unnerved by how attractive the male Valentine had been.

By what he estimated was roughly eleven o'clock they reached the foothills of the mountain range.

Long ago – ages now it seemed – Valentine had described her homeland to him. He'd pictured the Italian Lakes, or the Pyrenees in all their splendour. But this country looked sick. A lake they passed had a brownish tint to it as if the water was filled with rust. The heathers and grasses were insipid greens and the clouds and mist that obscured the peaks had a sickly, sulphurous tinge to them. They passed a few hamlets and villages that looked run down. It could have been England, except women sat spinning in doorways on wheels that rotated by themselves and children played with spinning tops that rose high into the air with trails of sparks. They walked into one of the larger villages where it was market day. Again, it could have been Malton except for the stall selling dodo eggs and the stallholders and shoppers.

Kit doubted he would ever get used to the sight of people with ears that were too pointed or teeth that were too sharp.

'Stop staring,' Valentine said sharply as Kit's eyes settled on a tall, graceful woman with dark brown skin, white hair and a pointed white beard who walked arm in arm with an equally stunning man with green skin and wings folded at his back.

'I'm only looking,' Kit said.

'You're being rude. You look just as strange, though no one is staring at your face.'

'I'm not staring because they're strange, I'm staring because they're both beautiful.' He caught himself and stopped talking, aware he'd admitted to finding both of them attractive, though he suspected Valentine had already guessed his vice. 'What business is it of yours in any case?'

Valentine spun away haughtily and began to study the wares on a stall run by a man with skin marked like snakeskin. She sifted through rows of coloured glass beads that were shaped like scales and threaded onto fine wire. Or perhaps they were scales. Nothing would surprise Kit any longer.

Valentine picked up a bracelet with beads that were shaped like daisies but pale bluey purple with the sheen of dove's wings, and greyish green leaves. He couldn't suppress his questions any longer and at least Valentine was speaking to him now, even if only to admonish him.

He had so many questions but one direction would open him up to scrutiny that was best avoided so he chose the other. 'You can turn into a bird.'

She ignored him.

'I didn't imagine that did I?'

She gave no indication that she had heard him, but her hand trembled as she examined the bracelet.

'It wasn't the effects of whatever was drugging us?' Kit asked, determined not to be brushed off.

She sighed impatiently.

'You didn't imagine it.'

'You were the dove on my windowsill.'

'Yes, and the one who flew overhead while you and Adelaide were arguing in the maze on the night of the party, and I watched while you spoke with your father.'

'I feel so stupid!' Kit exclaimed.

'Don't. You didn't know about any of this at that time. It was before you'd seen your aunt's toad.'

She patted his shoulder.

'I almost had it when you said about going back to the inn. I think I was close to working it out, but then I lost the thought.'

She shrugged. 'Now you know.'

'Did you ever watch me getting undressed?' he asked, narrowing his eyes.

She sniggered and gently shook her head.

'Let's go.'

She hung the bracelet back on the hook, but her eyes lingered on it.

'Not for you, pretty lady?' the stallholder asked.

'Another time perhaps,' she said, and there was a touch of regret in her tone before she moved away that was familiar to Kit. Adelaide was the same when they'd been shopping and she was hoping that her parents (or sometimes Kit) would buy something for her.

'How much is it?' Kit asked, struck by the sudden impulse to make Valentine happy. The colours would go nicely with her pink bangle.

'What have you got?' the stallholder asked.

Kit patted his pockets. No wallet. Nothing to trade, unless the snake-man wanted his wristwatch, and he was reluctant to give that away as it had been a gift for his twenty-first birthday.

'Nothing,' he admitted.

'I'll take a truth in exchange,' the stallholder replied. His tongue flickered over his lips and Kit's skin crawled to see it was forked.

'Give me the truth of why you want to buy it. Is it for your companion? Your lady love?'

'Oh, no. It's for my friend,' he explained. 'The woman who was looking at it just now.'

The snake-man gave a loud, hissing, laugh of amusement. 'And she's not your lady love. Well, that's a bafflement indeed, isn't it. Then tell me why you want to gift it to her?'

Kit opened his mouth, but the man held up a hand.

'Wait!' He reached into his cash box and pulled out a small vial with a cork in it. 'Speak your truth into here. There's no point letting it go to waste.'

He removed the cork and held the vial a couple of inches from Kit's lips.

'Tell me, good son: why would you buy the trinket for the lady fair?'

'Because her eyes looked on it with longing and I would be the source of gladdening her heart,' Kit answered.

The words didn't sound exactly like his own, but the man appeared satisfied because he corked the vial and flipped the bracelet from the hook into the air. He caught it in a small velvet bag that had appeared from nowhere, while the vial balanced on the palm of his other hand, humming gently with what Kit assumed were his words. The man gave him the bag.

'Be the owner of the time and the purpose you gift it.'

Kit nodded at him and slipped the pouch into his pocket, where it felt surprisingly bulky. They exchanged pleasantries then Kit went to find Valentine. She was sitting on the steps of a fountain, drinking from the cup that was attached to it on a long brass chain.

'Where have you been?' she asked looking round at him.

Kit smiled. 'Just looking at things.'

The snake-man was wise to suggest he wait until she was in a better mood.

'At least I know how you got into my room. That's one mystery cleared up in any case.'

Her lips almost curved into a smile, suggesting the bad mood that had caught her was releasing its grip. He sat beside her and accepted the cup. As the water appeared to be owned by no one it was presumably safe to drink. As she passed it to him, her bracelet glinted in the daylight.

'I should have guessed. Your bracelet and the dove's ring are the same colour. I even noticed the ring on its leg and thought it must be tame. Of course, really that should mean the bracelet should be around your ankle, though I suppose birds use their claws a little like hands so—'

'Will you cease talking!' Valentine snapped.

Kit stared at her in astonishment.

'Are you intent on mocking me?'

'Not at all,' he replied. 'I was just thinking aloud. I didn't mean to upset you.'

'Well, you are only half thinking, aren't you,' Valentine said crossly. 'Babbling on like a child and letting anything pass your lips.'

'Probably,' Kit said. 'It's not so long since I was drugged, after all.'

He bristled and dropped the cup into the fountain where it

splodshed as it sank. His mood plummeted with it, and pent-up exasperation at a long line of unbelievable revelations came tumbling out.

'And before that, it's not that long since I found myself telling stories to an audience made of the fae and goodness knows what else. And it's not so long before that when I walked into a maze I've trodden a thousand times, lost my way and came out in broad daylight. And not so long before *that*, when I saw a living toad on my great-aunt's tongue, and today I've just had confirmation that the woman I've shared a bed with can change into a bird and a man, and I'm feeling rather stupid and more than a little overwhelmed. So, no, I'm probably not thinking entirely accurately nor considering my words carefully.'

He turned around properly to face her. She was sitting very still, listening to his outburst impassively, but her face was pale and mask-like. She dropped her head onto her hands.

'Will you please tell me what is upsetting you so much?' he asked. 'You saved me back there. That's wonderful, so I don't understand why you're so angry. You even had the choice of sending the culprit to your family but that appeared to upset you. In fact,' he added, modulating his voice to be less harsh, 'You've been in a terrible mood since last night.'

She looked up at him through the protection of her hands. He could see her bright eyes, peering through her fingers.

'See if you can work it out.' Her eyes were heavy and tired. 'Think about why birds have rings.'

She turned towards the mountains and they walked in silence for a while, Kit musing on her words.

Why did birds have rings, and why did that make her so angry? It gave him something to ponder as the climb got steeper.

Though Kit was quickly becoming out of breath, Valentine began to sing to herself as she walked. Her voice was low, and made Kit think of wintery twilights and honeyed milk in his nursery. Determined not to be outdone, he began whistling a marching song and hoisted his bag over his shoulder. He was under no illusion that his voice was anything other than dreadful, wavering around the notes rather than hitting them all (he had the distinction of being the only boy in Meadwell who had been asked not to join the church choir) but Valentine grinned at him, anyway.

'Very wise. It's worth a slightly more pleasant journey with feet that won't ache so much. Music has its own enchantments.'

'Really?' Kit raised his eyebrows.

'Of course. Even in your world that's the case. Haven't you ever been swept away by a piece of music and forgotten everything, or been brought to tears by a chord you've never heard before? Music can rouse anger or pity or desire.'

'Well, yes.' Kit swapped his rucksack from one shoulder to the other. 'I am not sure that's magic, though.'

'You don't have to be sure for it to work,' Valentine said. 'People didn't know why the sun came up for thousands of years, but it didn't stop it happening.'

Kit began to sing again and before he had reached the end of the first line, Valentine was harmonising with him. He almost stopped in surprise but she motioned with a hand for him to carry on and she fell in beside him. There were seven verses in the song, and though she didn't know the words, her vocalising blended astonishingly well with his. By the time the song came to its end, Kit was surprised to realise that his feet were crunching on packed snow and that they were approaching the peak of the mountains that had been miles away. He turned back to look down the road and saw that they'd climbed quite a long way already and the inn was a distant speck, glinting in the folds of the valley like a discarded sequin.

'I told you,' Valentine said smugly, as he glanced around him.

'But that's not possible.' He gaped stupidly. 'We've actually travelled a lot further in the space of ten minutes than we did all morning. Miles and miles. I didn't even feel the climb.'

'Well, perhaps now you will believe me,' she said. 'Though I don't think that would work in your world.'

'We sang as we marched and we never arrived at the battlefield any quicker,' he said. 'Though of course none of us were in any rush to get there.'

'But you are in a rush to meet Silas?' Valentine asked. She narrowed her eyes as she spoke.

'Yes. The sooner I find him, the sooner I can reclaim Adelaide and we can return home.'

They were walking on level ground now, on a pathway weaving its way between the two peaks of the mountains. The air was chilly and the sun barely broke through the bilious yellow fog that shrouded the tops. Patches of moss and heather claimed some of the rock but looked as if they were fighting a losing battle.

'But you'll stay and help us,' Valentine asked quietly. 'Look at the sky. The clouds should be snow white. The world isn't healthy.'

Her face was a study of misery.

'I don't know.'

Valentine unshouldered her bag and sat on a flat rock. 'That's better than no.'

He sat beside her, setting his bag beside hers. The bracelet in his pocket pressed against his leg as he leaned down. Now might be the time to give it to her, but what would a trinket do compared to helping her as she wanted? He leaned back and stared up at the sky. A pair of birds circled, hovering on the currents. Raptors of some sort, though without the jesses that allowed a handler to prevent them flying away. From the corner of his eye, he could see Valentine staring at them, too. He glanced down at her wrist where the bangle seemed to pulse from within and remembered the carrier pigeons.

'Birds wear rings to show who owns them,' he murmured.

She nodded and there was sadness in her eyes. 'Yes, they do.'

In his world, in the current century, the idea would have been incomprehensible. But here people did things differently.

'Is this a shackle not an ornament?'

Her head whipped up and her face was contorted with anger.

He bit his lip, then asked quietly, 'Valentine, are you a slave?'

She let out a sigh. 'I am bound to the service of the one who caught me. This band proclaims my status, and my shame.'

'Like in the fairy tale the bard told last night,' Kit pointed out.

He was unprepared for the ferocity his observation caused, though later he would kick himself for not having seen clearly.

'It wasn't just a fairy tale,' she spat, leaning forward. 'How dare he! For that alone, he deserved my wrath!'

She snarled the words, her deep voice guttural. Kit drew a sharp breath in.

'You're actually the sister in the story the bard told? The maiden who was tricked.'

Valentine drew her legs up so that she was sitting cross-legged and dropped her hands into her lap, one covering her bracelet.

'I don't want to talk about it,' she mumbled.

The sight of Merelda's toad sprang to mind.

'Don't want to, or can't?' Kit asked gently.

He lifted her hand and drew her round towards him so he could get a better look at the bracelet. He viewed it with revulsion, remembering the story of how the necklace had tightened as the woman had put it on. He thought of Adelaide and whatever means Silas had used to steal her way. What had he given her that she couldn't resist? It couldn't just have been a posy of flowers. The bitter taste of vomit filled his throat, and he swallowed it down.

'I'm sorry. I didn't realise. That's appalling. I'm so sorry.'

'I don't want your pity,' Valentine said, and sniffed.

'Nevertheless, I feel it.'

She hid her face behind her hands again, but he could see the flush of pink her cheeks had become.

'Don't. It makes my shame all the worse.'

'You have nothing to be ashamed of!' Kit fought the urge to take her in his arms and hold her close. Instead, he reached for her hand and held it tightly. 'Evil has been done to you.'

'Yes, but I was unwary and allowed myself to be tricked. I should have known better but I fell for the simplest of devices.'

'May I look at it?' Kit asked.

She nodded. He lifted her hand up onto his lap and ran his thumb over the smooth coldness of the carvings.

'I noticed this on the day of the fair when we walked together. I thought then that it looked impossible to remove, but I assumed it was the skill of whoever had carved it and there was a hidden catch and a hinge. There isn't, though, is there. It really does stay on permanently?'

'It won't come off until my master is dead, or the conditions are met to free me,' Valentine told him. She reached out her hand as if she was going to touch the bangle but surprised Kit by laying her fingertips on his hand, a simple gesture that caused him to tremble.

'How many years have you worn it?'

'Fifty-seven years. I was just seventeen, and stupid, when I was caught.'

Kit rapidly did the sum and gasped. 'You're seventy-four years old? You look no older than twenty-five.'

'We are a long-lived people. My grandmother lived to be two hundred.' She shrugged but her eyes glinted and Kit suspected she was pleased with his reaction.

'So, you might have to endure another hundred years or more of slavery? That's dreadful.'

'When my servitude has lasted for ninety-nine years and ninety-nine days I may ask for my freedom. My master might then set me a task or a quest which will allow me to win it.'

'How generous of him,' Kit snarled.

Valentine sniffed. 'There are worse people to be enslaved by. My master does not treat me with indignity or demand that I share his bed, which is something.'

Silas! Kit's jaw tightened. He had to remember he was holding Valentine's wrist otherwise he would have balled his hand into a fist. He'd speculated about their relationship, but he'd never imagined this. That he did not rape her as a matter of course was the bare minimum and was all that would stop Kit beating the fae to death with his bare hands as soon as they met.

'Will you tell me what happened?' he asked.

Valentine uncrossed her legs and twisted around to face Kit. She appeared to be thinking deeply.

'On one condition. I want to know about the scars you bear on your face and your heart.'

'That's something I don't talk about.' His shoulders tensed and a weight descended onto him. She thought being trapped was shameful but that was nothing in comparison to what Kit had done.

'You should.' She leaned against him and rested her head on his shoulder. Cautiously he put his arm around her shoulder. 'Ease your burden. I know you are brave. You won a medal.'

Kit's throat tightened. The same praise he'd endured and accepted since the damned night when he'd lost so much. He'd vowed never to admit the truth, but with Valentine, he came the closest to feeling the urge. It wasn't just his story though.

"Come with me. We'll go together."

'I can't. The shame is too much to bear and if you knew the truth about me, you'd deny our acquaintance.'

'Then it will eat you eventually,' she said. 'I will tell you one thing. You've been responsible for my only hope so far.'

'I have?' Something like pride flickered in his heart, and it made him realise why he hadn't immediately said he wouldn't help. He'd give anything to see her happy. Her contentment mattered a great deal to him.

'When you threw the iron key at me and it hit the shackle, the tiniest crack appeared. It was the first hope I had in all the years I've worn it.'

He hadn't felt any qualms about hurting her to test his theory then, but now remorse threatened to eat him alive. Her voice had been full of shock, and he'd assumed at the time it was anger that he'd damaged it.

'I was an absolute beast!'

She smiled tightly. 'You did what you thought necessary. I'm not sure I blame you for doing whatever you could to defend your love. If I'd had someone like you, perhaps I'd have been freed long ago.'

She put her hand to his cheek. Her eyes were inviting him to take a chance on a kiss. She'd kissed him back then, and that hadn't made sense, but now it did.

Kit swallowed. At the summit of a mountain, with clouds and snow surrounding him, it shouldn't be possible to feel so hot. He had to suppress the urge to unbutton his shirt.

'I hope Miss Wyndham knows how lucky she is to have a man with your courage and devotion, who loves her so deeply he'd walk into another world to get her back.'

He released his breath. Thank goodness she'd mentioned

Adelaide and brought him to his senses before he'd kissed her. It gave him the impetus to move, because as well as his grudge against Silas for taking her, Kit now had his enslavement of Valentine to add to his list of reasons to hate the fae. He promised himself that the reckoning would come soon.

Chapter Sixteen

'We should go,' Kit said, dragging himself back to reality and away from the too-tempting prospect of kissing Valentine.

'Of course.' Valentine lowered her eyes and took her hand away from his cheek. They both picked up their bags and began the journey down the other side of the mountain.

'Why did no one come to rescue you?' Kit asked. Valentine's story was like a scab he couldn't resist picking. 'The bard said you had brothers. Surely one of them should have come to rescue you?'

She kicked a small rock and sent it skittering ahead down the path. 'The oldest was a drunkard from the age he could first raise a glass, and he could barely focus on what was ahead of him. The second was too cowardly to risk himself in the service of a sister.'

'Was there a third?' Kit asked. When her eyes widened, he explained, 'I know in stories that threes are important. Isn't it always the younger son who wins the day?'

He briefly thought of Alfred, who would no doubt have rushed straight to follow the fae if he'd been asked. Valentine clapped approvingly.

'You do know some tales after all. Yes, there is usually a third and he succeeds where his brothers – or sisters – fail. My brother did try to free me. Often the prize is half a kingdom and the hand of the maiden. My brother wanted both. My master was not ever going to give him half a kingdom, and I emphatically did not consent to giving him my hand, much less the rest of my body with it.'

They'd reached the rock again, and she kicked it harder, sending it off the path and into the long grass that was growing at the side.

'He tried to take it anyway, so I wept until my tears formed a pool, I carried the pool to the coldest place I knew and formed an icicle. I used that to pierce his heart. I preferred my slavery to a tolerant master than life as the plaything of a lecherous brother-husband.'

'Yes, I imagine you would. As much as I love Addie, for most of our early lives we felt more like brother and sister.'

He turned away abruptly, finally giving words to his reluctance to marry Adelaide. The hesitancy when they kissed wasn't due to any aversion to her sex: his tastes for men were seen as criminal and shameful, but he was not so unnatural that he didn't find women equally appealing. He swallowed, feeling the hard thumping of his heart. Andrew's much-loved and much-missed face swam before his eyes. He blinked it away, not wanting to dwell on that pain.

No, his reluctance to marry Adelaide was because there was no passion between them, only the deep affection of siblings. They were too close. If the older generation had wanted them to have a happy and full marriage, they'd have done better to keep the two cousins apart so that familiarity didn't breed such awkward, incestuous feelings.

Kit had never considered that fairyland might have urban areas but just as he'd always been able to sense when he was growing nearer to a large city when on a train journey, he became aware they were approaching a town of some significance. The hamlets and villages got closer together, with more signs of businesses and industry and fewer single farms. The houses looked increasingly rundown, too. Paint was faded and gates often screwed together with mismatched planks of wood. The people, too, grew wearier looking and suspicious, stopping what they were doing to stare as Kit and Valentine passed, some narrowing their eyes, others bowing their heads.

Their clothing appeared to belong to earlier times – spanning centuries from medieval to the nineteenth century. Kit felt very conspicuous in his modern clothing and wished he'd thought to look for a cloak in the market instead of spending his time bartering for the bracelet.

Valentine was dressed in a long-sleeved tunic of subtly woven greys, with green braid at the sleeves and a purple scarf knotted about her neck. Dove colours. The realisation made him smile. With them, she wore a pair of closely cut fawn-coloured trousers and sturdy ankle boots. Her cap was pointed, making Kit think of illustrations of Robin Hood. All women should wear trousers, though of course Valentine wasn't only a woman and he supposed she needed to wear clothes that would pass on a man. He tried not to stare at her striding athletically along, but she caught him looking and stopped to twirl around.

'Do you like me in this garb? Your women don't wear trousers, do they. Unless they are riding a horse, of course. But I suppose a skirt would not be practical for that.'

'I don't know,' Kit said, relieved she had jumped to another subject before he'd had to admit he did like how she looked. 'In the past, women wore skirts and rode side saddle.'

'Very impractical,' Valentine said. 'Astride is much better. Have you ever tried side saddle? It's quite remarkably hard. All you have to grip between your legs is one small pommel. Can you imagine that? She burst into peals of laughter as he felt his cheeks colour.

'Kit, you are so demure, you make me feel quite evil, as if I was a villain in a mummer's tale trying to seduce the village maiden.'

She wheeled around, stopping directly in front of him so that he almost walked straight into her.

'You aren't a maiden, are you Kit?' she asked flirtatiously.

'Mind your own business,' he snapped. 'I'll take so much teasing, but there is a limit.'

Her expression of amusement dropped. 'I'm sorry, I didn't mean to offend you. I'm just teasing, as you say. Be friends with me. I don't want to draw attention to us.'

Her eyes darted around, and Kit realised they were being watched.

'Do they know you?' he asked her as a woman drew her children back.

'Some will,' Valentine said quietly. 'Some will never love me but will not recognise why. Others will know whose woman I am by the bond I wear. It's better if they don't know who I am or what my purpose is. There are always some who embrace their servitude, even if they are barely aware of being in it and wouldn't hesitate to inform him, I'm close to his stronghold. And while we're thinking such things...'

She stuck out her hand and a passing cart stopped. She spoke briefly to the driver – a small man who came the closest to Kit's view of what a storybook dwarf might look like – to ask if he was going to Fythcaster, and when he answered that he was, she paid him and clambered into the covered wagon he was towing, motioning to Kit to join her. They found space between boxes that contained glass baubles that looked to be filled with smoke and glitter. Kit reached his hand out, fascinated by the swirling contents.

'Shake one and see your future,' Valentine said darkly. 'But beware, they'll only tell you a half-truth and I'm not sure I want to know mine.'

He drew his hand back, certain that he didn't want to know his.

Kit settled back. Valentine had mentioned people being unaware of their servitude, but she clearly knew and resented hers. He should have told her that it was not only to free Adelaide that made him determined to confront Silas Wilde, but to liberate her, too. Whatever he threatened, he knew inside him that Valentine would never become his enemy. The thing that bothered him was that he was growing increasingly certain that the place that occupied such knowledge was his heart.

By the time the sun was dipping down, Valentine called out to the driver, and they clambered out of the cart. It continued and Kit looked around, expecting them to be in the town Valentine had mentioned. Instead, they were at a fork in the road and the cart had turned right towards the red stone walls of the town, while Valentine started down the left, leading away from it.

'I thought we were going to the city.'

'I never said that. We're going to find Silas. We're nearly at his camp.'

Valentine hugged herself, whether from cold or for comfort, he wasn't sure, but Kit suppressed the urge to wrap his arm around her. She had grown more serious the longer they had sat in the cart.

'Do you need to stop?' he asked. 'If you're tired or scared, you can compose yourself a little.'

'No, but thank you.'

She drank from her water flask and handed it to Kit. He put his lips to the rim with no hesitation then saw her looking, with an odd expression in her eyes.

'What's wrong? Do I still need to ask if this is unconditional?' he asked.

'No, you don't. It just made me think how easy it would be for someone to bewilder you but then you caught yourself and asked.'

'I wouldn't forget to ask if it was anyone else who offered,' he said. 'It's only because it's you that I almost didn't.'

She drew a sharp breath and blinked.

'How long before we reach his camp?' he asked.

She looked at the sun, which had a slight green hue now that the distant hills had almost bisected it.

'Another hour at most. It won't be long till you get Adelaide back.'

She sounded solemn. It rubbed off on Kit. He would've expected to feel more joy at the thought of seeing her and his quest being at an end, but the enormity of his task ahead was daunting. He had no idea how hard it might be to confront Silas and win her back.

As if she could read his mind, Valentine frowned. 'It's possible that Adelaide is enraptured with Silas you know. I should warn you of that. I don't mean enchanted or bewildered into thinking she cares for him. It's very important to his code that every lover of his comes of his or her own free will.'

'What do you mean?'

'I mean he wanted her to love him. He is very vain. Quite insecure, really. Don't worry, though, you're twice the man that he is.'

She blushed deeply as the words left her mouth, and Kit's heart flickered. It hadn't occurred to him in the slightest that Adelaide might feel anything other than hatred for Silas. Valentine clearly liked him, too, despite everything he'd done to her. It was troubling.

'Valentine, I find myself liking you, though I never thought I would.'

Her face melted into a smile and the sight was so poignant that Kit had to force out his next words.

'Don't think for a moment, however, that I will put up with you helping Silas against me when we meet. If you try standing in my way, then you will become my enemy.'

'That won't have to happen,' she said firmly. 'You'll see soon enough.'

Kit had expected the city. When that had not been the case, he had expected a castle or fortress – possibly something resembling the fairy-tale palaces that graced the Rhine built by the German king. What he found was a series of small walls that might once have been a medieval village, and inside that, a camp of shabby tents and caravans that had been erected higgledy-piggledy with no rhyme or reason to the positioning. The commanding officer from the training camp outside Harrogate would have taken one look before bawling every man out and making them start again neatly pitching in rows. There were people – and Kit had grown used to that description encompassing all kinds – milling around or sitting by various fires cooking food that made his belly rumble. He hadn't eaten properly since the previous night at the Safe House.

Valentine took him by the hand, weaving her way deeper into the camp until they arrived at a large tent, slightly grander than the others.

'Here we are,' she said to Kit, joy in her voice. She raised her voice and shouted, 'Silas, come out! We're here.'

Kit tensed. He released Valentine's hands, instinctively balling his fists. Silas appeared not from inside the tent, but from a smaller one to their left. He was carrying a green glass wine bottle in one hand and a wooden bowl in the other.

'Valentine!' He broke into a wide smile. 'At last, my dearest, you've arrived. And Mr Arton-Price! How wonderful to see you here.'

He spread his arms wide in greeting, his face as delighted

as if he was greeting his closest brother. Kit walked up to him, swung his fist back and punched the fae square in the belly.

'Where's my fiancée, you treacherous bastard!'

Silas dropped what he was carrying as he doubled over. He muttered something beneath his breath and waved a hand in a flourish. Kit flinched, anticipating a counterstrike, but the bottle and bowl simply floated to the ground and landed softly without breaking or spilling their contents.

Silas stood up. His expression grew serious, eyes and mouth narrowing into dangerous slits. Kit became aware that the familiar background hum of camp life had become muted and that he'd just been very foolish. He'd been in situations in the trenches where a single act or word could change the mood of the camp. He was deep in a world he didn't understand, surrounded by friends and followers of the man he'd just assaulted. Tension congealed around him. Nevertheless, he readied himself, fists raised in his best-approved manner, weight settled evenly.

Silas blinked slowly and his good nature asserted itself on his face.

'Yes, I rather thought you might want to do that. I'll give you that one strike for free, though you'll pay dearly for any more.' He spread his hands graciously and raised his voice. 'Let it be known that Christopher Arton-Price is welcome in my camp and is to be accorded every courtesy and civility, every freedom.'

The tension ebbed away and people began to go about their own business once more.

'Where is Adelaide?' Kit repeated trying to keep his tone more level. 'I want to see her. Don't make me ask a third time.'

'She's in her chamber,' Silas said. 'Are you sure you want to see her? She has changed somewhat.'

'Of course I want to see her. She's the reason I came here. Take me to her now.'

Silas bowed. 'As you demand.'

He walked to the doorway of the grand tent. Kit followed but Valentine caught him by the sleeve.

'Do you want me to come with you? You don't know what you're going to find in there.'

His senses fizzled. 'You're worried. Why? What has he told you?'

She shook her head. 'Nothing that you haven't heard.'

Kit's throat tightened. 'Thank you, but I think this is something I should do alone.'

He pushed back the curtains covering the doorway and walked into the tent, whereupon he was immediately overcome by a sense of disorientation that made his stomach churn. What had appeared small on the outside defied the laws of science, because the walls ascended upwards almost beyond view, spiralling away much further than the height of the tent should allow. The furnishings were reminiscent of a scene from a pantomime of *The Arabian Nights* that Kit had seen at school. Everywhere was plush and opulent, swags of burgundy and claret velvet and silks decorating the walls. In the centre was a large, double chaise longue, dressed in myriad shades of red. In the centre of it lay Adelaide.

She was not sleeping as Kit had feared but was as alive and awake as ever. His eyes swept over her looking for a sign of shackles of any kind or ill treatment, but there was none. In fact, she was reading a book and lazily plucking grapes from a bunch in a copper bowl at her side.

She had gone stiff when he entered, and her eyes had taken on that strange fuzziness that he remembered from when she'd spent time in Silas Wilde's company back home. Then she smiled widely and leapt from the bed crying Kit's name and flinging her arms about his neck.

'Oh, Kit, darling, you came. I knew you would. Have you seen Silas? He's been so keen for you to arrive.'

She kissed his cheek. She smelled of violet and almonds.

'You were eating,' Kit murmured.

'Of course. I was hungry. Would you like some grapes? They are simply divine.'

'Do you know what that means?' Kit asked, his stomach twisting with consternation. He doubted Silas had taken the care to explain the nature of obligations and enchantments to her. Like Persephone, she may have been trapped by her need for sustenance.

'It means that whatever they do to grow them here is something we need to learn. Papa's hot house never produces anything like this,' she said.

'Adelaide, look at me. You're not thinking straight.' Kit took her by the shoulders and jerked her round to face him. Her eyes widened, then she pouted.

'What's wrong? Why aren't you happy to see me? You've come all this way, and I missed you. I've been waiting for years to catch up with you. I thought you'd never get here.'

His legs went hollow, blood draining in horror at the implications of what she'd said.

'Years? Addie, it's only been three days since you went to sleep. Four at the most.'

'For you, perhaps.' She stroked his good cheek, letting her hand linger on his jaw and looked up at him. 'Look at you. Still as handsome as the day we danced at our engagement party.'

He took her hand from his face and held it tightly. Her touch was disturbingly seductive, and he was struck by how little he wanted that. Had he ever craved it?

'That's less than a week ago.'

'Look at me, Kit. I'm older than I was when we last saw each other.'

He studied her face. She looked healthier, which given that the last time he'd seen her she'd been lying comatose in her bed, was hardly a surprise. But her hair was longer and there were the slightest lines around her lips and eyes. Her figure looked fuller, too, in a way he couldn't quite define. Time had indeed passed for her.

'Wilde,' he bellowed. 'Get in here and tell me what you've done to Adelaide!'

'Keep your voice down,' she admonished in a low whisper.

She left his side and hurried to the chaise longue. Her gown was long and loose, silks and chiffons in purples and blues, gracefully falling and swaying as she walked, making him think of a moth. Her hair fell loose to her waist. He tried to remember how long it really was, but his brain refused to work. Silas walked through the curtains. Valentine followed him in, looking worried.

Kit grabbed Silas by the throat with one hand, and raised the other back in a fist.

'What have you done to her? You told me she was unharmed, but she's talking of being here for years.'

'Kit, let him go!' Adelaide shouted. A piercing wail rang out.

'Now look what you've done,' she snapped, her eyes accusing. She stalked to a rocking cradle on a wooden stand. The canopy over it appeared to be made from tulip petals held together by silver threads. From the cradle came the angry cry of a baby whose sleep had been interrupted. Adelaide picked up the bundle.

'He's only been asleep for an hour.'

She held the shrieking child tightly. It – he – had thick white hair and an indignant red face.

Kit's hand, still on Silas's throat, grew limp.

'Whose child…' he managed to blurt out.

'Give him to me,' Silas said. He shook Kit's hand from his neck as if swatting an irritating fly, then walked to Adelaide, took the child from her and jiggled it over his shoulder.

'Hush, Caelwen, my pup, Dada's here.'

Adelaide was gazing at the fae and the child with a look of adoration that could only mean one thing. The fullness of her figure made sense. Her belly hadn't yet shrunk back after childbirth and her breasts were those of a nursing mother.

Kit's legs wobbled. A growl rose in his throat and somehow he turned it into speech.

'Wilde, get out. Valentine, go with him please, I need to talk to my fiancée alone.'

'About that,' Adelaide said. She looked meaningfully at Silas, who coughed and jiggled the crying baby a little more gently.

'I'm afraid I must refuse your request for privacy,' Silas said. Until I know your intentions, I'm not prepared to leave my wife and child unprotected.'

'Your *wife*?'

Kit looked at Adelaide in disbelief.

'We've been married a year and a half,' she said happily.

'No, Addie,' Kit protested. 'We've only been here a matter of days, and even if we hadn't, he abducted you. If you've been forced into marriage, nothing can uphold it.'

'There was no force,' she said, only half meeting Kit's gaze. 'And perhaps you've only been here for three days, but I've been here much longer, I told you. It took us two years to cross through the forest but when we came out only three days had passed here.'

Silas gazed at her. 'It gave us time together that has been the most precious I could imagine. I would not wish back an hour of my life.'

The shock of realisation, coupled with a staggering sense of betrayal, made Kit's legs tremble. Adelaide had spent her extra time in a way he could never have contemplated. He took a deep breath, but the tent was stifling and the air tasted stale. The room began to spin. He felt himself losing control of his limbs and was suddenly very tired.

'I came for you, Adelaide, and you didn't wait,' he mumbled before he fell sideways and into blackness.

~

Valentine caught Kit before he hit the ground and lowered him gently onto the deerskin rug. Adelaide took the baby from Silas and rocked it over her shoulder.

'Silas, dear, go and help Miss Dove carry Kit to the bed,' she instructed.

Silas walked over and knelt beside Valentine. The sight of a lord of the Fae obeying a human woman without question was the most disconcerting thing Valentine had seen for days.

She hitched one of Kit's arms about her neck and motioned for Silas to do the same. Together they pulled him upright and settled him onto the chaise. Adelaide had put the now-sleeping baby back in his cradle and sat on the edge of the chaise looking at Kit with concern. It gave Valentine an odd feeling to see. Possessiveness. It wasn't nice and made her feel slightly like a dog protecting a bone.

'He's fainted. Nothing more,' she said then bit her lip. 'Let him sleep a little longer. He's had a hard couple of days.'

She cast a hand above his brow, murmuring a charm, and his eyes, which had begun to flutter open, closed once more. She was halfway to smoothing back the locks of hair that had fallen over his forehead but caught herself in time. Silas would surely spot an affectionate gesture such as that. She stood upright and folded her arms across her chest.

'Let us leave Mr Arton-Price in the capable hands of Adelaide and go and talk over there,' Silas said, pointing to the doorway and causing her to wonder if he'd spotted some sign of her affection for Kit. Never mind; she had plenty to say to Silas, in any case.

'What in Mab's name were you thinking, begetting a child on a mortal woman?' she demanded as soon as they reached the relative privacy of the doorway. She could barely contain her exasperation. 'Another half-fae?'

'Where did you get such a voice?' Silas looked taken aback at her vehemence. 'When I left you in their world you were the meekest, most compliant woman I know. Are you sure it hasn't been two years for you, too, for you to change so much?'

'For me it's been less than a twelve-night since you walked back to our realm and left me to fend for myself but if you thought I was always meek that's only because you've forgotten what I am, or you didn't bother to notice.'

'I don't like it.'

'Well, you'll learn to.' She tilted her chin up defiantly.

'Go back to how you were before,' Silas said petulantly, folding his arms.

'I most certainly won't! I was all alone. I was scared and lonely at first and I had to grow into myself. I like me now.'

She felt an unfamiliar throbbing in her chest, the sound of drumming in her ears. She hadn't been alone, Kit had been with her, and she had no doubt that it was his influence that had given her the confidence to use her voice. Though they had sparred and parried many times, his challenges had never been unfounded or unjustified.

'You brought Kit with you, I see. Well done. Is he making you happy?'

She didn't answer immediately. There were too many conflicting memories. She walked to the firebox that glowed gently in the centre of the tent and sat cross-legged on one of the large cushions in front of it, looking into the shadows that the glowing coals cast through the cut-out holes in the lid. Silas sat on his haunches by her side.

'We weren't talking about me,' she said firmly. 'We were talking about you getting Adelaide with child and how you had the time to do it. How did it take you two years to arrive here when it took us a matter of days? Was that your plan from the outset? How do you think another half-mortal will help matters?'

He looked embarrassed. 'It wasn't intentional. We got caught in a snicklegate as we came through Whenlock's Wood.'

Despite the complications caused by the new situation, Valentine threw back her head and laughed. Snicklegates were patches of land where time moved differently. It could take days, weeks or, as Silas had discovered, years to pass through them while no time passed outside. Or, of course, one second inside while the decades spanned. The Silas Wilde she had known for years would never have been clumsy enough to fall through one.

'You're losing your touch.'

He smiled ruefully. 'It was Adelaide's fault. She ran after a lightmare and I couldn't leave her to go alone. I'm glad I did, however, because it has given me two delightful years with her. As to how the child happened, in the usual way of things or course.'

His eyes glowed, the irises pulsing with mauve, as he looked over his shoulder at Adelaide. She smiled back at him with what looked like genuine affection.

'I can prove it, if you doubt me.' Silas held out his hand and she put her fingers on his wrist, feeling for a pulse. She gasped and tightened her hand.

'It beats! Oh, Silas! A heart? You? The being who has caused women and men to pine away with love sickness! The marble-hearted lord of a thousand yearning souls.'

Silas shivered and closed his eyes.

'For my great grief, yes.'

Valentine took her hand away. How odd that she'd been expecting to have to comfort Kit's injured feelings, but had never suspected that Silas might be afflicted.

'You know Kit is determined to take her back with him, don't you?' she cautioned quietly.

He opened his eyes again. 'I do, and it will break the heart I have so recently grown. I just hope he will join our cause now he's here, and not try to take her before we have freed our land. I would hate to have to kill him.'

'I won't let you do that,' Valentine warned.

Silas raised his eyes. 'It appears I'm not the only one to have become enraptured by a mortal.'

'I'm not enraptured.' She frowned. 'He trapped me in iron. I didn't expect that, and you didn't warn me it could happen.'

Silas reached for her hand and stroked it soothingly. 'Poor dear Valentine. Would you like me to inflict sores upon him? The inability to speak his esses? Breath that smells like dogs' farts?'

She smiled at the indignation Silas displayed. 'No. He was desperate to find out what was happening to Adelaide, so I don't blame him. And when he saw the effects, he freed me, so I don't think he understood the power of it at first.'

She stared over at the bed where Kit was lying. He looked so vulnerable that it was as if the string that had bound them as they crossed through the maze was drawing her towards him. When he woke, what would he think?

'He understands about iron now, though. Good. You've done better than I had hoped. We just need to convince him to help us and I'm sure he will, now that he's seen what our homeland is like,' Silas continued. 'When Adelaide adds her entreaties to ours, how can he fail to oblige?'

Valentine nodded doubtfully. Silas had a childlike mind at times. Now that Kit had seen that his fiancée had borne a child, he was less likely to want to help rather than more, but Silas appeared not to have considered that. He clapped his hands together.

'Let's put our minds to that and see what we can do. Adelaide, my love, you know him better than anyone.'

Adelaide stood gracefully and walked to them. She sat on the cushions, leaning against Silas, but with one arm pointing backwards towards the sleeping Kit in a way that made Valentine bristle. She hadn't cared a fig for the relationship between the two humans before, but now, seeing them together was painful in a way she disliked. The woman seemed to want a claim on Kit, even though she had chosen Silas.

'Tell me about your journey,' Silas prompted.

Valentine drew herself taller. There was plenty that she could share and much of it would send a clear message to Adelaide that she had passed up a man who was better than she deserved.

Chapter Seventeen

K it slid back into consciousness, hearing first. Low voices were talking urgently. Some sort of argument. He decided it was not his problem. The next sensation to return was awareness that he was lying on something far softer and more luxurious than he had slept on in the past few days. His limbs felt heavy, and it was pleasantly like the time he had woken up after the explosion to discover he'd been in hospital for three weeks. The revelations that had accompanied that awakening had been blows he had yet to reconcile himself to. The memories were a jagged knife through his contentment and dragged him fully back to consciousness.

'…was as squiffy as a marsh goose.'

That was Valentine talking, he was sure.

'Oh dear, you poor unfortunate thing.'

Silas Wilde's voice.

'You can go to the Maidens, Silas!'

Valentine again. Angry about something, which didn't

come as a surprise to him. Kit didn't have the energy to ponder what.

'You didn't even think to demand him as a bondsman for a year?'

'You know my feelings on enslavement.'

'I'm awake,' Kit murmured as he opened his eyes. The billowing velvet of Adelaide's tent stretched open to the heavens above him. The illusion (assuming it was) was still disconcerting and nausea-inducing. He shuffled himself into a semi-reclined position, saw a pewter goblet of water and reached for it. It was halfway to his lips when he cursed himself.

'Is this without obligation?' he demanded.

'Completely without. I said before that you have the freedom of my camp. That means all food and drink,' Silas said, crossing to stand beside him. Valentine joined him. Her eyes flickered nervously from Silas to Kit. He wanted to reach for her hand and reassure her everything would be fine, but he wasn't at all sure of that.

He took a long drink and discovered there was a slightly metallic taste to it but nothing unpleasant. Feeling a little more refreshed he sat upright and looked around.

'Where is Adelaide?'

A slight murmur of guilt tickled him that she hadn't been his first thought.

'I'm here.' The voice came from the corner of the room where the cradle stood. She was sitting in a large woven basket chair that hung from a hook shaped like a bird's talon. She was nursing the baby to her breast.

Their eyes met.

'I'm sorry, Kit,' she said. 'I can see that it was very unexpected for you.'

'You're damned right!' He swung himself upright. 'I would never have betrayed you if it had been me.'

He'd withstood the assault on his mind of adjusting to the reality of this world's existence and the fact magic was real. He'd endured the long hours walking and the dangers they'd faced, but to realise it had all been for a woman who had fallen into the arms of someone else was crushing. He walked out of the tent. The air outside was fresh and smelled like rain. A few people looked at him curiously but most just carried on with whatever they were doing.

'Where are you going?' It was Valentine who had come to ask him. Not Adelaide, who had wronged him. Somehow that didn't surprise him. He stuck his hands deep in his pockets.

'I don't know, but there's nothing for me here.'

'I'm sorry about what she's done. You must be heartbroken.'

'Yes, I must be,' he agreed absent-mindedly.

Curiously, heartbroken was low down on the list. Angry. Betrayed. Disappointed. Her infidelity crushed him. Hypocritical kisses with Valentine flickered past his eyes, luridly coloured. Kisses weren't the same at all.

'Now what are you going to do?' she asked.

'I'm not sure. I still need to take her home, though she might not be so willing to come now she has a child. I'll have to tackle Silas about that.'

'The child is only here,' Valentine said. 'Her living body is in her bed in your world. It has borne no child nor aged.'

'Then I can take her and leave now,' Kit said, reeling around hopefully. 'None of this is real.'

Adelaide was asleep in Meadwell. He might be there, too, despite what Valentine had assured him. It didn't matter what had happened here, because as soon as they went home they would wake up and everything would be back to normal. But Addie thought it was real and she'd still done what she'd done. They could talk about her infidelity once they were safely home.

'You can't go home without helping us,' Valentine said, her face dropping.

'Oh, yes, I can. Just show me the way,' he said bitterly.

She hugged him, as if she was attempting to stop him leaving.

'Silas come quickly,' she called.

'I don't want to see him,' Kit growled.

'But you need to,' she urged. 'Silas, quickly.'

'No!' He shook her free more roughly than he intended to. 'Don't you understand anything? I don't want to see him. I don't want to see Adelaide. I need to be alone. I need to think.'

He pressed his hands to his temples and closed his eyes. Tears leaked from his closed lids and he found it unbearable.

He drew a long, deep breath and forced his emotions back into their container, damned if he was going to give into them in front of anyone. He looked into Valentine's eyes and saw only the compassion she'd always shown. The kernel of blackness inside him softened slightly and he might have mastered his feelings completely if Silas hadn't emerged from the tent, blinking as he walked into the brightness.

'Valentine, you called me? Ah, Kit, we need to talk. Come drink with me!'

A burst of fury made Kit's cheeks burn. 'I have nothing to say to you, and I sure as hell won't drink with you. Send us home,' Kit demanded. 'Both of us.'

'No. Adelaide can make her own decision. You don't speak for her.' Silas's voice was like silk, presumably meant to be soothing, but it grated on Kit's nerves. 'I'm sorry, now isn't the time to send either of you home. My world depends on your help.'

Kit gasped at the audacity to assume he would still help with whatever Silas had in mind!

'Your world can go hang for all I care,' he snarled.

'You don't mean that,' Valentine said, her face twisted with an anguish that grabbed Kit by the throat and squeezed.

'Listen to yourself,' Kit exclaimed, shaking his head in disbelief. 'You're standing by the side of the man who enslaved you, and you're defending him. What are you thinking?'

'What are you saying?' Silas interrupted. 'I haven't enslaved anyone!'

'Really?' Kit reached for Valentine's hand and held it out, showing the bangle. 'What do you call this?'

Silas's face took on a dangerous expression. His eyes elongated and he looked less than human. 'I call it a wrong that should have been righted long ago. Valentine, did you tell Kit this was my doing?'

She tugged her hands free from Kit and hid them behind her back.

'I didn't tell him that … but I might have let him think it.'

'What?'

Kit and Silas both spoke together. They glanced at each other and for the first time ever, Kit felt a twinge of solidarity with the fae.

'I thought you hated Silas, and that he kept you prisoner,' Kit asked Valentine.

'Yes, I'm afraid I did give that impression. I couldn't do otherwise,' she said. 'Sorry. To both of you.'

Kit raked his hands through his hair in exasperation.

'This is one of those matters of constraint, isn't it? Like Merelda's toad. I never asked you if it was Silas by name, so you didn't have to correct me.'

'That's right.' Valentine looked sheepish. 'Silas is a good friend to me. He's a good man. I know you might not think so given that he left me in your world and has stolen your fiancée.'

'I do love her, though; I can vouch for that.' Silas leaned forward, his normal appearance reasserting itself, and with such keenness in his eyes that Kit was charmed, despite himself. 'It's true. I was a captivated man the moment I saw her. A lost man the moment she took my hand to dance. And since then, I have been steadily claimed by her each moment we spent together. I am utterly her slave.'

'Steady on,' Kit said, his jaw tensing. 'This is my fiancée we're talking about.'

He met Silas's gaze. The fae was standing like a pantomime villain, feet planted apart, hands resting on top of his cane, elegant fingers lightly gripping the silver wolfhound's head. He was utterly breathtaking. No wonder Adelaide had fallen for him. The sheer, seductive aura that emanated from him was enough to captivate anyone. If Silas had set his sights on Kit, he couldn't honestly swear he wouldn't have succumbed.

'Silas, don't you have any sense of tact,' Valentine snapped. She looked at him and there was the slightest hint of tears in her eyes.

'He has a heartbeat,' she said to Kit. 'That probably means nothing significant to you, but it only happens when our love is awakened. We really don't yield our affection easily and when we do, the effects are long-lasting.'

'And painful,' Silas whispered, looking once more human and vulnerable. 'For veins that are accustomed to perhaps one heartbeat a day, to feel the rapid surging of blood is uncomfortable, to say the least. Loving changes us.'

'Well, that's very romantic for you,' Kit snapped. He crossed his arms and looked away. Did Silas believe that he would revaluate his opinion on the grounds that his love for Adelaide was supposedly true? He swallowed down an uneasy lump of guiltiness as he considered whether his own heart would have started beating in the same circumstances. He wasn't sure Adelaide had ever inspired such devotion in him.

'I'll hear you out if you can be quick,' he grunted.

'The man I am seeking to overthrow is the one responsible for Valentine's captivity. If you help me free our land, it will free her, too.'

'Tell me more,' he said. 'I don't trust or like you, but Valentine has been a true friend and guide, so for her I'll hear what you have to say.'

'Walk with me,' Silas said. It wasn't exactly a command, and besides, Kit was curious enough to listen to what he had to say. They left the camp and walked for perhaps half an hour until they emerged on a ridge of grey marble overlooking the city and castle that the cart had been heading for. The pointed, red turrets glimmered like newly spilt blood in the sunlight and pennants billowed in the wind. The ground between it and where they were sitting looked parched, grass scrubby and unhealthy. It gave Kit a chill, reminding him too much of areas designated 'no man's land'.

'The town is Fythcaster. That citadel is the seat of the Faedemesne.' Silas pulled a leather bottle from a string across his chest and swigged. He offered it to Kit, who refused.

'This was to be mine, but the man who sits unworthily on the throne is called Caul Gilling. My uncle. When my father died, he claimed I was not worthy enough to command and usurped me.'

'Why?' Kit looked at him sharply. He had plenty of doubts about Silas's suitability for all sorts of things but the fae's regality wasn't one of them.

'My mother was of your world. A human. It should make no difference, however. I am perfectly worthy. Ordinarily, he would not have been able to even breach the defences of the citadel, as there is a rite involving blood that ensures the heritage is passed on accordingly, but things have become troubled and I have been unable to get close enough to the site of the rite to claim my inheritance.' Silas frowned. 'What has worked for centuries no longer appears to.'

He dropped into a seating position, legs dangling over the ridge, which dropped away sharply in front of them, and it crossed Kit's mind that Silas might have lured him here to his death. Conversely, if he pushed Silas, no one would be the wiser and he could take Adelaide and leave the whole matter behind him.

'Why has it stopped working?' Kit asked, brushing the thought away. He'd killed in the war but he wasn't a murderer. He cautiously lowered himself down too, thinking on what Silas had just revealed. He was part human. That was certainly unexpected.

'I have my theories, though I don't know if they are correct. I think it's to do with the amount of iron in your world. You saw first-hand how it affected Valentine. You must have considerable charms to still be in possession of your eyes after doing that, but that's by the by.' His mouth twisted into a smile.

'My theory is that the consequences of your wars soak through to my world. Your recent war across Europe, for example, has seen the ground rained down upon by bullets and shrapnel in a way previously unseen. The shards of iron from explosions, the weapons, never mind the blood itself, seeping into the fields.'

Kit flinched. 'I've seen it. I don't need to remember it.'

Screams of warning. Screams of agony.

'My apologies. My point is, that for whatever reason, the order of things here has become unstable and my uncle took advantage. He's taking advantage of your people, too. I want to rid our land of my uncle. I will be a better and fairer ruler than he ever would care to be. Let me show you more.'

He drew a brass telescope from beneath his cloak and passed it to Kit. The city was surrounded by walls, reminding him a little of York. The land outside was mainly farmland, with a few smaller settlements, and beyond the city was what appeared to be a quarry.

'The meadows surrounding it were once the lushest grass, the most fruitful fields,' said Silas. 'Now look at it, and look at the poor beings toiling away.'

There were people tending animals, digging trenches and engaged in sundry menial jobs, breaking rocks, mending fences, pushing ploughs by hand. Most of them moved sluggishly, heads down and bobbing as if they were half asleep. There was something … mundane about them. Something familiar. The clothes and hairstyles were not like any he'd seen since crossing through the maze.

He tore the telescope from his eye and cried out in shock.

'They're human!'

'Yes.'

'Are they asleep in my world, too?'

'Asleep, or moving as if they are. It depends on what their strength of will is like.'

Kit gazed at them, aghast. 'I thought Adelaide was the only one. No, that's not right,' he corrected. 'There's the boy from the fete, too. How long has this been going on?'

'Forever, when the sleepers are only one or two. This scale, on and off for a couple of years,' Silas said. 'There have always been cases, but my uncle discovered the way of gathering people in quantities.'

'It's horrific! All these people snatched from their lives.'

'Yes. This is what we are fighting against.'

'But you've done it, too!' Kit laughed incredulously. 'You're just as bad as he is.'

'No, I'm not.' Silas glared. 'Adelaide is the only one I have brought here. Do I make her toil in the mines or fields?'

Kit shuddered, thinking how Silas had tried to persuade him, and how Kit had endorsed him asking Adelaide. How many others were there? Who else had been taken?

'Valentine said she was sorry about the child at the fete and that it shouldn't have happened. Did Caul Gilling take him?'

'Yes. Stealing a child is one of the old ways that he wishes to hark back to. Of course, back then we'd leave one of ours in its place, or a rock.'

'Is your uncle the one who ensnared Valentine?' Kit asked.

'Indeed.' Silas's eyes flickered over Kit. 'You would like to be her champion, I think.'

Kit looked away, then back. Why should he hide the truth? It was nothing to be ashamed of. 'Yes.'

'Good. She's been waiting too long and deserves her freedom. It mayhap that when I defeat my uncle it will happen naturally, but it's better not to take a chance.'

Kit's belly tightened. 'I thought at first that you were her master.'

'Yes, that deception was rather unfair of her, but it spurred you on to come and find me, so I'll forgive her.'

'She said your uncle was a good master, despite her captivity,' Kit said.

He heard his words and stopped. No man who owned slaves and stole children could ever be described as good.

'So she believes.' Silas frowned and glanced over at the castle. 'He uses and bargains with her to gain favours from others. She has limited memories of those things because I try to hide them from her.'

Silas spoke earnestly. Kit was beginning to understand him a little more. He made bad decisions but it appeared he genuinely did believe that they were for the right reason.

'A person's memories shouldn't be taken without their consent.'

'Wouldn't you want yours taken away?' Silas peered at him, squinting, then sniffed. 'I don't know what causes its heaviness, but I can see your heart is burdened. Are you not tempted by an easy mind?'

The heart Silas referred to pounded unbearably.

"I love you."

"I can't do this anymore."

Of course it was tempting, but if he lost the heartache, would that diminish the cause and the memory of those caught up in it?

Silas gestured to the castle.

'Despite what Valentine believes, my uncle is not a kind master, nor is he a benign ruler, and the sooner he is deposed, the better it will be for everyone. He has no qualms about using anyone to get what he wants. Dictators rarely do. I know you owe me no affection, but you must see that I have asked for aid, which is different to abduction and forced labour.'

Silas spoke so earnestly that Kit felt himself weakening. He was enormously likeable when he tried to be.

'Yes, I do understand. But why do any of you need to involve us?'

'Why did your countrymen go to fight because a duke was assassinated far across the water? It's a philosophical argument we could talk about all day, but we don't have time. My uncle has eyes everywhere. Some willing, some unwilling.'

Kit frowned. 'What about Valentine? She belongs to your uncle. Could she be his spy?'

'No. He doesn't value her for her cleverness or her wit, only beauty and status.' Silas tilted his head. 'You're fond of her. I can see it. The pair of you wear the same colours in your souls.'

'Yes, I am, though I can't say anything about souls.'

Silas smirked. 'What fools these mortals be. And what fools us, too. William Shakespeare, you know. Now, he had some fanciful ideas, but he was before my time of course. It's practically slander, the way he described us. Horses head and revels in groves painted as barbarians. Ha! I'd like to think we have developed since those times.'

He stood and held out a hand to Kit.

'Come, you've seen what I wanted to show you. Now let's go back and eat. It'll be night soon and these woods are not the safe places they once were. Our camp is full of hope and fun, though, and I would like very much for you to see us at our best.'

Kit took his hand and stood. Silas held it for a beat longer than necessary, looking deep into Kit's eyes. Despite his animosity, he couldn't deny that he was charmed. Silas was so captivating. So attractive in every possible way.

'You don't want to trust me, but I wish you would because I like you a lot. I wish you would work with me on this,' Silas breathed.

'You haven't explained what you need me for,' Kit said.

'I'll be perfectly honest. I came for Adelaide. I didn't need you, but Valentine persuaded me that you had potential.'

'Oh.' Kit sucked his teeth and dropped his head. He was

surplus to requirements. Not Childe Roland. Not Orpheus. Not the hero of fairy tales after all.

'I mean no insult by that.' Silas touched him on the shoulder and Kit looked around. The fae's eyes glinted and he stepped closer to Kit, enveloping him in the scent of sage. He slid his hand down Kit's arm and rested his thumb in Kit's palm, moving it in small circles, then lifted it to his lips.

'You and I could do great things together, but only with your consent.'

Kit swallowed, his eyes dropping to Silas's lips. They were plump and ruddy, with just a hint of moustache, but the budding desire fractured when he thought of Silas and Adelaide together.

'I don't want to do great things with you,' he said, dragging his hand free.

Silas grinned and blew gently on the side of Kit's face, his breath warm and honey-scented. Kit groaned as a surge of desire spiked between his legs.

'Would you like me to conquer you, Kit? Would you like to conquer me, first of all?'

'Go to hell, Silas,' Kit growled. He stepped back, shaken by the strength of the craving that had awakened. 'I'm not here for your amusement. however attractive you might be, I don't like you. So no, there will be no 'conquering', no alliances of any sort. I will do what needs to be done and then get the hell out of here and back to my normal life.'

'Yes, that normal life, which is so appealing,' Silas said quietly. Kit looked at him suspecting mockery, but instead, the fae's face was solemn. 'The life that is so fulfilling that the lights surrounding you ebb to a dull mustard. Here, you glow vermillion.'

He gave a sigh that exuded disappointment then began to walk back in the direction of the camp. Having nothing else to do, Kit followed.

Chapter Eighteen

Halfway back they met Valentine coming from the camp. 'Did you sort out your differences?' she demanded. 'You've seen the castle and the sleepers.'

'I have. It's sickening.' He turned to Silas. 'I don't like you. I don't think you've dealt with either me or Adelaide honourably, and for a speck of dust, I'd call you out.'

'He's lying,' Silas said cheerfully. 'He finds me as beguiling as anyone does.'

The thump in Kit's heart was a traitorous witness to that.

'Don't confuse attraction with fondness,' he said through gritted teeth.

'You don't have to be fond of me to help me. Caul Gilling's actions won't just have implications for my world, but for yours, too. And who knows how many others that we have no knowledge of.'

'What do you actually want me to do?' Kit asked.

'I want what I told you from the beginning.' Silas cradled his hands in front of his heart. 'I need help restoring my land to its former splendour. To do that I need to proclaim my birthright. I wish you to lead the assault on my uncle. Command my army.'

'Your army?'

Silas waved his hand around imperiously in the general direction of the tents. 'My loyal nobles and their subjects who have resisted my uncle's manoeuvres.'

Kit stared at him, incredulous. The assorted men, women and creatures he'd seen looked nothing like an army and, if it came to it, he'd be hard pushed to tell which were nobility.

'You want me to lead those people in an attack on a castle? To fight against your uncle's army, including those he has plucked from my world?'

'Yes. I know you are brave enough. Your reputation is not unfounded.'

Kit's guts twisted at how little Silas knew.

'No.'

'No?'

'No. Your people aren't soldiers, and even if they were, they'd be fighting unwilling humans. Innocent people will be slaughtered. You're just as bad as he is.'

'Believe me, I take no pleasure in it. I had hoped that he might abdicate and let me take my rightful place,' Silas said. 'I would have settled for that, but he refused. And deposing him into exile won't work because he is strong and the land is too weak to resist, so it really is the only way.'

He put his hand on Kit's shoulder. 'Don't hate me for involving you. I see your potential. It warms my heart. Join me.'

'Even if they were an army, I'm not a leader or a soldier,' Kit said.

'But you have a medal,' Silas said.

'You're a hero,' Valentine added softly.

Kit put his hands to his face, feeling his cheeks heating. The roughness of his skin only served to illustrate their point. He couldn't bear it. He shook his head. Again, Silas put a hand on his shoulder.

'It seems daunting, but it won't be. You were a hero in your war. I've heard the tales and though I have not seen the medal – iron being anathema to me, as you know – I understand the significance of what it bestows.'

'It bestows nothing! Stop it,' Kit shouted. He raked his hands through his hair and glared at Silas. 'Stop talking about me as if I am a hero. I'm not. The whole thing—'

'What whole thing?' Valentine asked. 'Why don't you tell us what happened? It's going to consume you.'

She spoke so tenderly that sourness made Kit's throat cramp. If she knew the circumstances, what would she say?

'Maybe I should let it.' The combination of guilt and grief and shame was threatening to explode inside him. He ground his nails into his palm and turned on his heel.

'Where are you going?' Silas demanded.

'Away, for now,' he said tightly. 'Don't follow me. I don't want to see you.'

He walked blindly, not really caring which direction he went in.

Not a hero.

Shells descending.

"Don't leave me, Kit."

He sagged against a tree and put his hands to his face, giving a loud sob. Other, softer hands enclosed them and pulled them away.

Valentine had followed him.

'You didn't say that you don't want to see me.'

'I didn't, did I,' Kit said.

'There are things I can offer you to heal the pain in your heart.'

'I don't want spells,' he said, thinking again of Silas banishing her memories.

'Come with me,' Valentine said quietly. 'I might be able to help without be-spelling you.'

Silas was now hurrying towards them, but Valentine held a hand up to him. 'Go away. I'm taking Kit with me.'

Silas pouted. 'Where?'

'Somewhere he can find peace for a while.' She took Kit by the hand and laced her fingers through his. 'To see the unicorn.'

Kit had a hundred worries but they were all crowding his tongue and he couldn't decide which was most pressing, so he simply walked at Valentine's side in silence. They went into the thick forest and climbed upwards until they came to a level clearing.

'Sit down and be quiet,' Valentine whispered, indicating a slight mound where the grass was softer. Kit obeyed. The air smelled sweetly of recent nightfall, the scent of daylight flowers fading as they closed and the night plants took over. He wasn't yet at peace, but the subtle releasing of his muscles suggested to Kit that the tension was ebbing.

When the unicorn arrived there should have been a

thunderclap or a fanfare, but it simply ambled into the clearing, grazing on foliage. It was white and had a horn, but that was about as far as the resemblance went to the images he'd seen in books. Its hair was shaggier, and in stature it resembled a Welsh mountain pony rather than a majestic thoroughbred. The horn that grew out of its forehead was short and stubby – closer to a rhino's horn in size and shape – but, like the deer in the park at Meadwell, it looked to be covered with a velvety layer. It looked like it had evolved a single antler rather than a pair, and now that Kit had seen it, it did make sense as a species.

'It's not what I was expecting,' he whispered.

Valentine laughed softly. 'That's because you've seen medieval manuscripts. If you saw an elephant for the first time based on what you'd seen there, you'd probably say the same thing. She's beautiful, isn't she.'

She was.

'Go and say hello to her,' Valentine whispered, nudging him in the ribs and pointing to a thick patch of white blossoms. 'They like sand clover.'

Kit picked a handful then took slow steps towards the unicorn with his hand outstretched. It whiffled then trotted over with interest in its intelligent brown eyes.

'Be polite to her,' Valentine called. 'They're very bright.'

Kit bowed his head and scattered the blossoms on the ground. The unicorn bent to eat them. Kit stood perfectly still, aware of each breath entering and leaving his body. When the unicorn had finished eating, it lifted its head and stared at Kit with calm interest. He held his hand out, and after a dozen lifetimes, the unicorn lowered her chin onto it. Kit's heart swelled and he broke into a smile, exhaling softly, as he would with an unfamiliar horse. The unicorn's ears twitched forwards and then she blew out, covering Kit's hand and arm with warm, clover scented breath.

'Hello, lady,' he murmured. The unicorn whinnied then pressed her head heavily against him. He choked back a tear of happiness at the honour.

From the corner of his eye, Kit could see Valentine approaching. She reached out a hand and stroked the unicorn's other ear.

'Your heart aches so much. When will you believe that you are more than your face?'

She put her fingers to his temple and stroked gently down the side of his face to just above his ear. Her fingernails were short and practical, but nevertheless, he felt a quick trace of sharpness as they rubbed over the raised tendrils of his scar. It wasn't seductive but the intimacy made him draw a breath. He trusted her. He'd seen the male side of her and the enchanted side, the vulnerability that she hid beneath her flippant and spiky exterior.

'Everyone assumes I'm grieving for the loss of my face, but in truth I don't give a damn about how I look,' he told her. 'I did at first, of course. You'd have to be inhuman not to be appalled at such a change. It's how it happened that I can never be reconciled to.'

'The inner scars are often greater than the outer scars,' Valentine said. Her eyes flashed towards his. 'You have so much pain. Tell the unicorn. She'll listen. It's one of the things they do.'

Kit looked back at the unicorn who was standing patiently,

and gazed into her soulful eyes again. He stroked his hand down her neck. She twisted her head and butted against him, pushing the horn into his hand.

'She senses your nobleness,' Valentine said quietly.

He'd never been particularly religious, and the idea of a confessional was alien to him, but he suddenly felt the need for absolution, and to pour his agony out to the animal. He nodded and somehow the unicorn understood because she blew softly into Kit's hand. Kit knelt beside her and stroked her jaw as he spoke.

'I was awarded the Military Cross for sounding the alert and preventing a surprise attack from no man's land. I'd spotted something was wrong on my way back from the latrines and made my way across open ground to alert the right people.'

He kept his eyes on the unicorn's dark lashed, intelligent eyes but his words were for Valentine. He could stop there and that would be enough. He would never dream of telling anyone in the real world but this was a dream. Or if he really was in a world where the sexes could couple as they chose in pairs or threes, and no one condemned their wantonness, it might be his only chance to unburden himself.

'I wasn't just coming back from a pee. The reason why I was awake and out was because I was having a fight.'

He laughed harshly and glanced at Valentine. She nodded her head and placed her hand on the unicorn's withers.

'Isn't that absurd? A fight in the middle of a war. With a man. Who I loved.'

Kit pressed his lips together in a futile attempt to stop them trembling. He folded himself into a seated position and looked up at the unicorn.

'His name was Andrew.'

He tasted the word. The first time he'd spoken it aloud since the formalities were done with. Once it had delighted him to whisper it, but now it brought only grief.

'We met in the last week of 1917. He was an artillery observer for the battalion, transferred to us when the previous man—' Kit's belly filled with acid. 'You don't need to know the details. It's not important and I barely knew him. When Andrew arrived, he lit my existence after I had been grovelling in blackness.'

A cautious smile. "We could always try that tango again. If you'd like to, that is."

He smiled at the memory for the first time since waking up in the field hospital.

'For three months, we were everything to each other. We spent hours talking in the darkness of the trenches, holding hands, huddled together to sleep – nothing uncommon in that, you understand, all the men used what warmth and support they could find simply to stay upright, but the snatched kisses were enough to get us court martialled if we'd been caught.'

'Your world is unenlightened,' Valentine murmured.

Kit swallowed, unable to disagree.

'We used to talk of a future together. Not that we could ever have had one. It's a criminal act in Great Britain and what we did would see us driven from polite society, if not actually sent to Holloway for hard labour. He wanted me to go back to Canada with him. Told me we could live in the Rockies in a cabin and no one would know what were to each other. I said we would deal with it when the world was at peace once more. I put off facing up to it because I'm a coward.'

His lip curled as he thought back to the frantic nights when he'd dared to believe that after hellish months in the trenches, he would find a way to untangle the mess of his life and his feelings.

'So you parted because you could not be together,' Valentine whispered.

"Don't leave me, Kit. Please."

Tears rose in Kit's eyes, blurring his vision into smears of green.

'I've wished that every night since. Andrew was with me the night of the attack. We were quarrelling. Andrew had always known I was going to marry Addie but he wanted me to put an end to it even though it hadn't yet officially happened. He said I should write to her and break it off, but how could I do it in a letter rather than face-to-face.'

The unicorn rubbed her cheek against him. He swallowed and sniffed.

'Of course you couldn't. You're too honourable.' Valentine said. He didn't dare look into her eyes. His tears were falling freely now.

'He could be so bloody-minded at times. He absolutely refused to see it as anything other than a slight on him and we quarrelled. I said I was going to return to the dugout, but he caught me round the waist and kissed me again, and I couldn't resist him. He begged me not to leave him. And then the shelling started. Only a couple of grenades tossed in our direction, but he saw the movement first. He pushed me down. Sheltered me with his body. I lost half my face, though I didn't even feel it at the time, but it took his right arm and half of his torso—'

Kit sobbed and buried his face in his palms.

'He died in your arms?' Valentine asked.

He looked up at her bleakly, wondering how much more of the sorry tale he could bear to reveal. If he left it there, he'd still appear a hero, a notion that had been unendurable since he awoke to find himself praised.

'No. He died alone and scared. Weeping and begging me to stay with him but I couldn't. I needed to raise the alarm. He was half gone already, but he knew I was abandoning him.'

"Don't leave me, Kit. Please don't leave me."

'I left him and I'll never be able to forgive myself for that.'

'You saved more lives by doing so.'

Valentine put a hand on his arm, but he shrugged it off. He didn't deserve compassion. Streams of tears coursed down his cheeks. Green and purple lights bloomed in the darkness when he opened his eyes.

'No. I could have shouted from where I was to raise the alarm. Someone would have heard, but I couldn't stand to watch him die.' He put his head back and cried aloud.

'That's the truth. That's what makes me a coward, and of course, later I couldn't admit why I'd been out there or why he had, so I lied and let everyone assume he was caught in the shelling when it started. I should have been the one who died not him.'

Valentine stroked his cheek; the one which bore the

evidence of the night. He deserved the deformity. A grim memorial to the man he'd lost.

'I'm so very glad you weren't.'

'I'm not brave. I'm not the person Silas needs to lead anything. It was pure chance I happened to be there. But I accepted the praise as if it had been intentional. The mentions in dispatches. The medal.'

He spat the final word, the distaste for it causing a bad taste in his mouth.

'Every minute since, the truth has been trying to burst from my lips, but I kept it prisoner. I am a fraud.'

'What could have been gained by telling the truth?' Valentine said. 'Your lover would have died with a reputation for what your world sees as a perversion – though why they insist on that is beyond me – but this way he did not.'

Kit shivered. He hadn't thought of it in that way. He'd written to Andrew's mother and sisters as a friend, telling her comforting lies about the instant death that had taken her son and how bravely he'd fought in those last moments. What good would the truth have done her?

He grimaced and wiped his arm roughly across his face, streaking the tears. The unicorn shook her head gently and snorted warm breath across Kit's lap. He gazed at her, wondering what magic she exuded that could have drawn that confession from him and yet make the telling feel cathartic.

There was a rustling of leaves, then Valentine's arms came around him from behind. As she leaned her body against his back, he caught the scent of mimosa and tilted his head back to catch it better. She kissed his cheek.

A twig snapped behind them. The unicorn stiffened then

scrambled upright and galloped away. Kit turned to see what had disturbed it and saw Silas standing, half concealed in the bushes. Adelaide was at his side.

'Silas, I told you to stay away!' Valentine thundered, clambering to her feet and stamping towards him.

Adelaide's face was pale. Kit started to get to his feet but she shook her head and the curl of her lip made him hesitate. 'I heard what you said. You told me you would never have betrayed me, but you lied. I have felt dreadful about falling in love with Silas and now I discover you had a lover in France. A man! You disgust me!'

She gave a sob and ran back into the forest. Silas barely paused before dashing after her. Kit slumped back down, his guts too ripped up to have the energy to follow. He lay on his back on the moss and stared at the stars that dotted the sky. There were no constellations he recognised. It was the perfect symbol of how mixed up his life had become. He laughed.

Valentine settled on the ground beside him, lying on her stomach, arms beneath her chin. 'I don't understand why you're laughing.'

'Neither do I. Adelaide is furious with me and I never wanted her to learn about that side of myself. It's not like your world where we come from.'

'Why do you care? She left you for Silas and you've just told me you loved someone else anyway.'

Kit looked sidelong at her. She had such a simplistic view of the world. He was quite envious of it. He propped himself up on his elbows.

'It's possible to care for more than one person, in different ways. That's what Andrew could never understand. He wanted to be everything to me and for me to be everything to him. I couldn't give him that.'

He bit the inside of his lip so hard he tasted blood. 'I'm not sure I could give it to Adelaide, either. I'm pretty certain now that she doesn't care anyway.'

'Which part of you do you give to yourself?' Valentine asked him.

'I don't understand what you mean.'

She prodded his shoulder with a finger but it felt friendly rather than confrontational. 'Which part of you takes care of you? Which part puts your needs ahead of all? All you've told me and all I've seen of you tells me that you twist yourself in knots to please other people, but how many of them do the same for you?'

'I...' He floundered and lay back to look at the stars again.

'You spend so much of your life wondering how to make yourself worthy, but do you ever stop to consider whether you do it for people who are worthy enough to deserve you? What do you want? Look me in the eye and tell me what will make you happy?'

'Do I deserve to be after what I told you?' he asked.

She flicked his ear. It stung and he jerked his head up.

'Ow!'

'I'll do that every time you doubt it if that's what it takes. Yes, you do deserve to be happy. Now, tell me what will make you happy.'

Kit looked at his fingernails. They were grubby and chipped. It was better to focus on them than look at Valentine and risk his eyes revealing the truth.

'Time, maybe. Will that mend a broken heart? I don't know if mine will ever be completely mended.'

The skin around the nail on his ring finger was rough where he'd worried it with his teeth. He couldn't stop looking at it.

'Look at me,' Valentine commanded. When he didn't, she took him by the face and dragged his head around. 'What do you want?'

Her eyes were ringed with feathery lashes that he wanted to run his lips over. There was no judgement or pity in her eyes, only desire. More than there had been when they'd shared the bed, more than when they'd kissed.

'I want you,' Kit murmured. 'I think that will make me happy.'

Valentine smiled. 'That's the answer I wanted to hear.'

She wiggled her foot in between his and drew her leg up, running her bare toes up his calf. It was divinely erotic but he froze.

'We can stop,' Valentine said.

'I don't want to stop. Only, I've never actually made love with anyone. Not Andrew. Not Adelaide,' he admitted.

'I suspected as much,' she said. She straddled him and tugged him up into a seated position.

'Fortunately, I have, and by all accounts, I'm very good.'

She giggled and tugged his shirt from his waistband. He ran his hand over her tunic, felt the small mound of her left breast and gave it a tentative squeeze.

Valentine craned her head up to look at him.

'Was that wrong?' he asked.

'Not at all. I just wondered if you want me to be Valentin?'

He paused, hand still on her breast. 'Why would I want that?'

'Because of the man you loved.'

'I've loved women, too,' Kit said, pulling her close and trying to articulate his feelings. 'It isn't simply about bodies. I loved Andrew because of who he was, not because he was a man. I care for Adelaide not simply because she is a woman, but because of what makes her … her.'

He pushed Adelaide from his mind. This was no time to be thinking of her. He leaned forward, pulling Valentine closer and brushed his lips against her collarbone. He caught the scent of mimosa, and he groaned.

The desire was rising in unbearable waves and he was finding it hard to contain himself.

'I want you because you are *you*,' he whispered hoarsely.

Valentine put her hands to his waist, pushing them beneath his shirt and up to his chest, letting her fingertips dance lightly across his skin.

'Then you may have me,' she purred. She kissed him on the lips, but before he could properly respond she moved her mouth onto his jaw and then up to his ear. When she bit it gently it felt as if he'd discovered a previously unknown artery that ran between the lobe and his groin. He gave a strangled gasp and rolled them both over so that he was on top.

'What if someone sees us,' he murmured.

'They won't, unless we want them to.' Valentine waved her hand, muttered some words and drew a veil of night over the clearing.

Afterwards, they lay beneath a pile of discarded clothes. Kit understood why his trenchmates had called the climax the 'little death', because it felt like suspension between life and the afterlife, rendering his limbs languid and his mind like sponge. They didn't speak, but perhaps there were no words needed for what they'd done. He was exhausted, both mentally and physically but the heaviness inside him felt lessened.

The unicorn returned when the sky was starting to grow light at the edge. She stood over them, looking curious and blew warm breath on Kit's feet.

'Thank you,' Kit whispered. The intelligent eyes widened and she bowed her head then trotted away, moonlight falling on her flanks and turning them silver.

Valentine squeezed his hand.

'Thank you too,' Kit said.

She laughed. 'What an odd thing to say.'

It had been his first time, but for her there had been countless times and most of them under duress from what he gathered. It made her gift all the more significant. How could he possibly refuse to help her?

'I don't like Silas but I am going to offer my service,' he told her.

'Thank you.'

His fingers brushed against the bracelet and he tensed as it nudged something at the edge of his mind. Something useful. He almost had it, but Valentine kissed him. Something felt different and it took him a moment to realise he was feeling the scratch of stubble against his jaw and Kit realised with a start that she was now Valentin.

Valentin pulled away from the kiss and his eyes met Kit's. He raised his brows in a question. Kit swallowed and gave him a smile. Valentin's hand shifted against Kit's thigh and the resulting waves of pleasure left no room for thoughts of any kind.

Chapter Nineteen

K it woke when it was light with a sense of determination. He dressed, covered Valentin with his cloak and left him sleeping, then returned to the camp. His clothes were dirty, and he couldn't remember the last time he'd washed so when a woman with a mountain of washing and a copper pot offered him a fresh shirt of sky blue with yellow braid, he accepted it gratefully and changed. He found the bracelet from the market in his trouser pocket. He'd missed the chance to give it to Valentine, though maybe straight after sex wouldn't have been the best time in case she thought it was a sort of payment.

But then he had it. The solution he'd almost grasped before but lost.

Silas was sitting outside his tent. He was softly plucking a melody on an eight-stringed harp. Adelaide was presumably still inside. Kit's stomach churned. At some point, he needed to speak with her and thrash out everything. For now, though, it was Silas he needed.

'Walk with me,' Kit said, tilting his chin up and speaking firmly.

Silas looked surprised at the tone but laid down the instrument and stood.

'You aren't the same man today. What's changed?'

'Nothing that concerns you. Did you hear my confession to the unicorn last night?' Kit asked as they walked side by side to the ridge.

'I did. I know I shouldn't have followed but I know hearts speak the truth when they're present.'

'You shouldn't have brought Adelaide,' Kit growled. His stomach clenched at the thought of what she'd overheard. 'That's not how she should have learned what happened.'

'She chose to come. Do you think I can forbid her from doing what she wants?'

In that instant Silas stopped being a fae lord and became just a man in love with a determined woman. Kit softened a little more towards him.

'No. I never could, either,' he admitted, unbending slightly. 'She has that knack. I'd say it was magic if I didn't know better.'

'Would you?' Silas said, stroking his chin.

'In any case you know the truth. I'm not a fighter.'

'On the contrary,' Silas said softly. 'The conflict in your heart that holds you back also gives you life. I would not want a man who relishes the thought of slaughter.'

He leaned forward and touched Kit lightly beside the left eye. His fingers left a trace of coldness. Kit wondered whether Silas suspected what had happened after he had left the grove.

They sat on the ridge and looked at the castle and the camp where the humans were being kept.

'I won't lead my people into danger,' he said. 'The sleepers Caul Gilling enticed from my world have no stake in your fight.'

Silas let out a deep breath. 'I don't care how the aim is achieved. I care for the people of this world and would rather not see them die either.'

Kit drummed his fingers on his lap. 'I have an idea. It might not work but if it does it will save bloodshed. One person attempts to cut the head from the monster.'

'You're talking assassination?' Silas asked after a moment.

'Yes.'

Silas nodded thoughtfully. 'Without my uncle to lead them, I believe most of my subjects will be keen to live in peace with me as their leader. Assassination started your recent war. It seems fitting it will end ours.'

'I think it was a lot more nuanced than that,' Kit said.

'Of course. There are always layers to be uncovered. Nevertheless, I hope it will be enough to tilt the scales in my favour,' Silas said, enthusiasm radiating off him. 'It would be dangerous and almost impossible to get close enough to cut his head off. I wonder how… Perhaps a disguise of some sort?'

He started to rise. Kit pulled him back down.

'That's not actually what I mean. Would iron kill Caul Gilling if it tipped an arrow or spear? That could be from a distance. It came to me last night when I—' He shifted a little, aware he was skirting close to a subject that was intensely personal. 'When I thought of Valentine's bracelet. Iron damaged it. Iron hurt her, and I'll feel guilty for that for years to come.'

Silas's eyes gleamed with excitement. 'Iron would indeed kill him. You are a genius! I knew it was worth bringing you, too, the moment I saw you with the bow. You will be the one to do it, of course. You hit the centre of a target with three arrows in succession.'

'That's true,' Kit said. 'The colours stood out.'

'The fae I need you to kill clouds himself in dramas and dazzlement, hiding himself from my kind when he chooses, but you will be able to see him clearly. Tell me your plan.'

'Is it possible to bring iron here to your world?'

Silas looked to the sky. 'Very difficult, but it has been done in times gone by. You are a student of alchemy are you not?'

'We call it chemistry these days, but yes, I suppose I am.' Kit frowned as the unpleasant memory of a battle he'd lost came back to him. 'That is, it's always been a fascination of mine, even though my father refused to support me financially in reading it at university.'

Silas seemed both uninterested in and unperturbed by Kit's admission. 'Excellent. Then all you need to do is transform iron so that it may be brought across the thresholds and then transformed back.'

'How would I do that?'

'I don't know. That's for you to decide. Blend it with something then separate it again. I'm sure you will know.'

Kit sucked his teeth. He looked into Silas's eyes. It might have been an effect of the dawn light or the oddness in his vision, but the fae's irises glowed.

'I'll do my best. Then we need to get me close enough that I can have a chance of shooting him. I don't know how, though.'

'I think I can manage that,' Silas said.

'And if I do what you ask, you'll let Adelaide go free? She'll be able to return home. We all will?' he asked.

'If that is what she desires.' An emotion flashed across Silas's face that Kit had never seen there before, but he recognised it. He'd long been familiar with its company. It was sadness verging on the edge of heartbreak. Silas did not want Adelaide to leave. Kit hardened his heart. That was no concern of his.

They walked back to the camp, discussing, rejecting and fine-tuning a plan until they had something that Kit could believe would work. A figure was sitting by the fire, which was now blazing fiercely. Valentine was female again and was sharpening what looked like arrows with a short-bladed knife. She looked engaged in her task but as the men approached, she smiled at Kit, gazing at him from beneath her lashes in a manner that made him want to drag her off into the nearest tent—

At that moment, Adelaide emerged from inside the tent. She looked at Kit and her eyes tightened before she walked to the fire and sat opposite Valentine. Valentine looked at Adelaide with a slightly cool expression.

'I wondered where you were this morning,' Valentine said, smiling at Kit.

It occurred to him that he'd abandoned her sleeping after they'd made love. Leaving her to wake alone in the forest was definitely not the mannerly thing to have done.

'I was walking with Silas,' he said, determined to keep his mind on business.

'Then you are friends?' she asked, giving him a smile that was a bedazzlement all of its own.

'It's a little more complicated than that,' Kit said.

'But you have resolved your differences?' It was Adelaide now who spoke. She put a hand on Silas's arm and looked at Kit coldly. He vowed to speak with her alone later. They needed to discuss what she'd heard the night before, what she'd done with Silas, and where it left the pair of them and their engagement.

Silas looped one arm through Kit's and put the other around Adelaide's shoulder.

'Come, let's be friends together and eat.'

Silas led them to a large firepit over which an entire animal was slowly rotating on a spit, and Kit realised how hungry he was. They were presented with bowls of the meat and a vegetable-filled rice dish, and retired to a large rug beneath a canopy at one edge of the fire. The meat was beef – a variety called *ouroch*, according to Silas – and like everything he'd eaten since arriving, it was delicious, with a fearsome flavour of chillies. As his belly filled, Kit's temper evened out.

When they had finished eating, Kit put his bowl on the floor beside him. Soft music was being played somewhere, and the camp resonated with laughter and chatter. It seemed a shame to bring an end to the atmosphere, but he'd spent long enough being sociable.

'I've made my mind up. I'll do what Silas wants,' he said.

'You'll lead the army?' Adelaide asked. She lifted her chin. 'But after what you said last night are you brave enough?'

'Not that,' Kit said, trying but failing to brush off the way her judgement wounded him. 'I'll need to return back home and bring something made of iron with me, if I can.'

'Iron?' Valentine leapt to her feet. 'That is what has caused the harm to our world. Why would you want to bring more?' she demanded.

'Because sometimes a big solution is needed,' Silas said calmly. 'Iron is notoriously hard to bring through the barriers, but it will be enough to kill Caul Gilling.'

'A gun?' Adelaide asked.

'No. That would be too much. Too big.' Silas looked at Kit. 'Often knowing that you are carrying the iron is enough to make things alert. It's all wrapped up with perception.'

'Things?'

'Magic. The forces that guard the borderlands. I'm honestly not sure what to call it.'

'Well, I'm sure there's lots of iron back home,' Adelaide said. 'There must be hundreds of horseshoes or tools.'

'So, if I have iron that didn't look like it was iron, would that work?' Kit asked thoughtfully.

'It's a trick that has been used before, many years ago, I believe,' Silas said. 'If you had a piece of iron about which your feelings were so jumbled that any emotion was sufficiently clouded, that might be enough to disguise it. Can you think of such a thing, Kit?'

Valentine gave a tight smile. 'Speak clearly for once, Silas. You mean Kit's medal, don't you.'

'Of course. You hate it, Kit, don't you.' Adelaide looked at him pointedly. 'That's what Silas is thinking of. Aren't you, darling.'

Kit couldn't quite hear Adelaide referring to Silas with the endearment without flinching.

Silas smiled. 'Exactly.'

A sense of weariness threatened to overpower Kit, coupled with the desire to see events brought to a conclusion.

'If I'm going to go back and then return I want to do it now,' he said, standing and nodding at Silas. 'Tell me how to return home and I'll bring you your iron.'

'You need something to take you home and something to bring you back. I can give you a sprig of lilac to send you there.'

Kit looked at Valentine. Her eyes flickered up to meet his and the world grew distant and still for a moment.

'Can you take me?'

'She can, but I'm more reliable,' Silas said, before she had the chance to answer. 'I've been travelling between the worlds for longer.'

'Not with me,' Kit argued, 'and Valentine has never trapped me in slow time.'

Silas snorted and looked put out. Valentine's eyes crinkled.

'I can give you the means to return,' she said.

'Who will you choose?' Adelaide asked.

'Valentine,' Kit answered.

'Very well. Valentine, Beefriar's Arch, I think.'

'Of course. Give me a little time.'

She stood and began to transform, her arms becoming wings and her form changing. Kit heard Adelaide gasp in surprise as Valentine flew away.

Silas stared at Kit; his eyes narrowed in suspicion.

'You weren't surprised by Valentine's transformation.

You've seen it before. Yet you still appear to care for her. Humans are curious.'

'I've seen a great many things I thought I'd never see over the past few years, in my world as well as yours. Yes, I know about this,' Kit answered. 'And her other aspect.'

'Come, it isn't far to the gateway,' Silas said. He held his arm out for Adelaide, who refused it, grumbling slightly about how she would have preferred riding to walking, then deciding she would stay in the camp. Kit smiled to himself. She hadn't changed too much, it seemed.

'I'll check on you while I'm there,' he told her.

She hesitated then nodded. 'Tell Sarah I love her.'

He smiled at her, knowing that he needed to broach the subject of the night before and his revelation about Andrew, but she looked away. The loss hit him again, along with the injustice that, had he lost a female lover, the world would have been sympathetic.

He reached for her hand and she gave it reluctantly.

'It won't be long now until all this is done and then we can go home for good,' Kit said.

'Let's not make plans until everything is ended.' Adelaide pulled her hand free, gathered her skirts up and walked off to the tents. Kit watched her with growing apprehension. She'd said Sarah, not 'Mother'. She was pulling loose from the human world and it was troubling.

~

He followed Silas, and within an hour they arrived at what looked like the ruins of a medieval monastery covered in climbing plants. Valentine flew down from an archway as they arrived, gripping something in her claws. She uttered a cry then dropped it into Kit's hands. He looked down at what she'd given him and was unsurprised to see walnuts. Three of them.

'One should do the trick,' she said, returning to her human shape. 'Crack it to break the shell, crush the kernel and blow the fragments into the air.'

Kit pocketed them.

'Don't lose them,' she said urgently.

'I won't, but if anything goes wrong you can come and get me, can't you.'

'Of course.' She smiled bravely and Kit got the distinct impression she was holding something back.

'It can be cold. Can I offer you a cloak?' Silas held out his own, but the bright green and red garment looked so outlandish that Kit declined. Silas held out a hand. Kit took it reluctantly. Silas's grip was hearty, his hand warm.

'If you cannot bring the iron, no blame will be attached to you.'

Valentine approached, her hand outstretched, too. Kit moved in to hug her, resulting in her hand jabbing him in the ribs. They laughed, then he held her close. Warmth bloomed inside him.

'I'll see you soon.'

He walked towards the archway. Silas began to intone something that sounded almost like the Greek Kit remembered from school, except the vowels were stretched and twisted. A soft glow pooled in the archway and the scenery that was visible through it blurred. Kit walked towards it, paused only to check the walnuts were safely in his pocket, and walked through.

He wasn't in the maze. That was the first thing that became apparent. A gust of bitterly cold air ripped across his face, leaving the scent of salt and fish. Indecorous shrieks and squawks filled his ears and he tensed, wondering what unearthly creatures he was about to encounter, and he wished he had a weapon. He edged slowly forwards, feeling his way with his feet. The glaring light that surrounded him receded and the sky cleared. He blinked to clear the blotches from his eyes, and when he opened them it was early morning.

He looked behind him and gave an astonished cry. Until that point, he still hadn't been completely certain that he hadn't left his body behind, but he was nowhere near his bedroom.

He was standing on the West Cliff in Whitby and had emerged between the giant pair of whale jawbones erected some sixty years previously. The monstrous shrieks had been simply the cries of the gulls.

Through the weathered bones, the sky behind the old abbey on the East Cliff glowed in the rosy, dawn light and the harbour walls pincered the sea, shielding the harbour from the fierce crests that buffeted the stones.

'Impossible!' he exclaimed.

He looked down at himself. His feet were clad in the laced leather boots he had acquired at the Safe House. Combined with the blue and yellow shirt, he was an odd sight. Thank heavens he hadn't taken up Silas's offer of the cloak, otherwise he would have looked ridiculous. As it was, one or two people were staring at him. Townspeople, presumably on their way to work. He straightened his cuffs then walked off, skirting around the whalebones rather than passing through them again, just in case the gateway was still open.

'What are you doing?' asked a stern voice. 'There's no place for drunkards here. Staggering about hiding behind the whalebones.'

Kit turned and found himself face to face with a police constable.

'Sweet Jesus,' the constable exclaimed, pointing to Kit's face.

Humiliation seared him. He'd grown used to not being stared at, and now the experience shamed him. He put a hand to his cheek and felt the roughness of a few days' worth of stubble.

'The war happened, and no I'm not drunk. I need to get to Dalbymoorside. If you'll excuse me, I'll be on my way.'

'Is that right, sir?' the constable asked, following him.

'Yes. I've been away travelling and now I need to go home. Can you direct me to the railway station?' He patted his pockets and sighed. 'I seem to have come out without my wallet.'

'Indeed, sir. Best come with me then.'

The constable seized him by the scruff of the neck.

'Am I being arrested? What's the charge?' he demanded, wriggling free.

'Vagrancy and drunkenness,' replied the constable, reaching for the handcuffs that swung from his belt.

'I'm not a vagrant, nor am I drunk. I'll come to the station with you and then you can call my father. He will clear everything up at once.'

'Well, that's very civil of you, sir,' said the constable as he tugged Kit's hands behind his back. 'Much obliged. Come on, then.'

'Iron, I see,' Kit said. 'Well, I suppose there's poetic justice in there somewhere. I never thought of those, but of course, the medal will be better.'

The constable rolled his eyes and gave Kit a stern look. Clearly, he had decided he was some sort of imbecile.

'That's right, nice and safe. Don't you worry, sir. We'll have you in touch with your family in no time at all.'

He took Kit firmly by the shoulder and led him down the hill.

Ten minutes later, Kit found himself in Whitby police station. He reluctantly surrendered his stopped watch and emptied his pockets into a tray, conscious of the desk sergeant's eyes on him. The three precious walnuts, a couple of stray leaves that had worked their way in there at some point, and the velvet bag with the bracelet that he had bought for Valentine at the market. He still hadn't found the right time to give it to her and he broke out in a cold sweat at the thought that it might have melted away like Silas's coins and been lost to him.

The presence of a piece of jewellery caused a raised eye, as well it might, considering his state of dress. He muttered something about his lady friend, which resulted in knowing smirks between the constable and sergeant and Kit could almost see them adding 'Frequenter of prostitutes' to his charge sheet. He furnished the inspector with his father's telephone number and allowed himself to be locked in a cell (more iron, of course). He lay back on his bed and waited, trying not to let his frustration get the better of him. He was reasonably sure his father would come to collect him, and he was equally sure that he'd get the bracelet back, but whether the sergeant would think it worth keeping the nuts was anyone's guess, and without those he had no way of returning to the Faedemesne.

~

Silas clapped his hands. The archway shimmered briefly then the colours faded and the trees and derelict buildings behind it came into alignment with the surroundings.

'Well, I think that went rather well.' Silas beamed at Valentine.

She rolled her eyes. 'Do you really?'

'Yes. Kit has stopped trying to threaten me and he will bring us the means to end my uncle's reign. Well done, Valentine.'

'Well done?'

'Yes, well done. He has grown since I last saw him. His courage is more open and he walks with pride. I think that must be your doing.'

'Some of it is,' she admitted.

She stooped and picked up a few blades of grass beside her, concealing her face. Kit had gone from her world and she felt his loss keenly inside her.

'We've gone through quite a lot together,' she told him.

What an understatement! Never mind the adventures they'd had on the way to meet Silas, what they had done last night had been a revelation. He had been a little clumsy and she hadn't been surprised when he admitted it was his first time. It was far from being hers, but it was the first time she had been with someone who genuinely seemed to like her so that made it special for both of them.

'Yes, I can see he has had quite an effect on you.' Silas gave her a speculative look. 'Give me your hand.'

'You won't find a heartbeat,' she said hastily. 'There's no point looking for one.'

'No?'

'No. I am fond of him, but only fond.'

Her tongue thickened. She wasn't incapable of lying, though it didn't come easy to her. She didn't think she was in love.

Yet.

They sat on the grass waiting for Kit to return. Silas conjured a bottle of wine and two glasses.

'It doesn't matter how enraptured we are. We are only borrowing them,' she pointed out. 'We have to give them back.'

'I don't have to return Adelaide,' Silas said. 'She belongs here as much as she belongs there.'

He sounded so confident, and Valentine had to ask herself what made him so. She turned away and looked back at the arch as an excuse for hiding her face.

'Would you give up your longevity and your throne if Adelaide asked?'

'My longevity, in a trice. My throne? No. I will not abdicate the responsibility I have too long lacked. I hope she'll stay with me. Together, my bride and I will be able to claim the land in a way Caul Gilling never can. Once my child is grown he can take his place as lord. Then I can reconsider and Adelaide and I can be together.'

Kit would no doubt have things to say about that, but there were too many paths to walk down before that became a problem.

'Does Adelaide know what will happen to her child if she returns to her world?' she asked.

Silas hung his head. 'No. How could I explain it to her,' he whispered. Even if I could, that information would influence her. Any decision has to be hers without conditions.'

He drained his wine and pursed his lips as if it tasted bitter.

'If only I had brought her through entirely rather than just her spirit. The baby will vanish to a memory when – if – she returns to her body. The kindest thing I can do for her will be to charm her memory so she doesn't remember anything of this. I alone will bear the death of our child and I alone will mourn the loss of my wife.'

Valentine leaned her head against his shoulder. Her eyes pricked with sorrow, and she had never felt more stymied by the laws that bound their kind.

'You won't be alone. I'll be with you. We can mourn together for what we have lost.'

'Thank you,' Silas said. 'Of course, first we have to win our battle. Then Kit and I can have a reckoning regarding his intention to take Adelaide back with him.'

Valentine shuddered, anticipating the battle of wills that would ensue.

'I hope it won't come to a fight,' she said.

'So do I. I would hate to have to harm him. I wonder… An exchange could be brokered. If you are freed and we succeed, you could go with Kit and stay in his world. Would you do that?'

Valentine looked at the ground.

'I don't know. There's so much iron and I'd be mortal, wouldn't I? I'd only have another sixty years or so in a body that was growing older and weaker. I'd have to stay in one form forever.'

Her voice faltered at the thought of never taking to the skies again. She poured a glass of wine and drank it quickly.

'He could stay with you here,' Silas suggested.

'Only if he chooses to. And of course I can't ask.'

Valentine stared at the sky, drumming her heels on the grass in frustration. The sun was faint, hidden behind the miasma of grey that hung overhead. Kit should be returning soon. She'd enchanted the walnuts to return him to her side.

'What if he doesn't come back?' she muttered.

'He will.' Silas was sitting cross-legged, staring at the arch. 'If not to bring us what I need, then to take back Adelaide.'

Of course. She pressed her lips together tightly. Two reasons that were perfectly adequate. There was no need for a third. There was no need for it to be her.

Silas grew restless before Valentine did. Of course he did. He was never able to be still for long. He murmured a charm beneath his breath and cast it at the ground in front of the archway.

'I'm going back. I'll feel when the gateway opens and come back then. Are you coming with me?'

She shook her head and stretched her legs out. The weather looked to be good and her cloak was warm. She was used to sleeping outside, and if it got too cold, she could change form to keep warmer.

'I'll stay. He might not be long and I'd rather he didn't find himself alone when he returns.'

Silas nodded. 'As you wish. Keep checking for that heartbeat, Valentine. I don't want you to find yourself grieving too much when he leaves.'

Chapter Twenty

Within two hours of being arrested Kit was woken by the cell door being unlocked. He'd been soundly asleep so was rather thick-headed when he swung his feet to the floor and came face-to-face with his father and mother. Ellen flung herself on to his shoulders and clung to him.

'Where on earth have you been! My boy!'

His father looked sternly over his wife's shoulder. 'Three days we've been waiting to hear from you and there has been nothing. It's an absolute embarrassment.'

'Oh.' The pressure of Ellen's hand on his shoulder informed Kit that she was as taken aback as he was by Charles's attitude.

'I'm sorry, Father. I can explain,' he said.

Charles walked out of the cell. He said nothing to Kit until the formalities had been completed and Kit was released. He reclaimed his possessions, reaching for the nuts first and putting them into his pocket, relieved that he still had them.

It was only when the car had made the long, difficult climb

up Blue Bank from Sleights, and Charles's hands eased on the steering wheel that he began to speak.

'Your mother's been worried frantic. With Adelaide's illness, the last thing we needed was your selfish indulgence in traipsing off without telling anyone.'

'I am sorry truly. We left in a hurry.'

'We?'

'Miss Dove and me. Do you remember her? Mr Wilde's friend.'

'This is intolerable,' Charles railed. 'Your fiancée is in a state of coma, and you are traipsing around the countryside with another woman! I suppose that gaudy trinket you had is for her?'

It did look bad, Kit had to admit.

'She thought she might be able to help with Adelaide's condition. She was a nurse,' he lied. 'How is Addie doing?'

Ellen spoke. 'She woke once, but only briefly enough to take some broth. She's slept ever since.'

'Whatever it is, I fear it is spreading. *The Times* carried reports of similar cases throughout Europe,' Charles said gruffly. 'Did Miss Dove offer any solution?'

Kit smiled properly for the first time since coming back. 'I believe she might have done. Mother, Father, I'm so sorry for not informing you. I didn't have time.' It occurred to him that Merelda might have been able to offer an explanation but had chosen not to, or perhaps his parents hadn't even considered asking.

When they arrived home Kit ate his way through enough game pie, boiled potatoes, bread and butter and cold cuts to fill a man double his size. Curiously, even though he had eaten while he'd been away, his body didn't feel as nourished as he might have expected. He resolved that when he returned, he would pack a hamper full of provisions. He and Adelaide might want their own food for the next day or two, and of course, Valentine loved ginger biscuits.

He went to his apartment. While he ran a bath he rummaged in his bureau among the assorted pens, bottles of ink, and other detritus until he found the box containing his Military Cross. He weighed it in his hand. It was lighter than something that weighed so heavily on his mind should be. He took the walnuts out of his pocket and lined them up on the table beside the box. He leaned close to them and sniffed, hoping to catch a hint of the scent from Valentine's hand. There was the slightest trace of mimosa, but it was too faint for his liking. Now he knew she was on the other side of whatever boundary it was that he'd crossed, the gulf felt wider than the channel and the longing in his heart was physically painful.

He climbed into the bath and lay back to soak away the days of accumulated dirt. He closed his eyes, wondering what she was doing. He didn't mean to sleep, but woke as a mouthful of water brought him coughing back to consciousness. Drowning would do no good for anyone, though his father might be glad to see the back of him.

After dinner he paid a visit to Doctor Smith. News of his absence had reached that far, and the doctor subjected him to a series of questions regarding his absence, which Kit evaded and half answered as best he could, thinking wryly that he'd learned something from the fae after all.

'I fell in with some people who may have the answer to the problem of the sleeping,' he explained.

'Really?' Doctor Smith beamed. 'Come into my study. I'll get us both a sherry and you can tell me everything.'

While the doctor poured two delightfully large measures, he explained that more cases were being reported.

'Human nature is such that once one person talks of a thing, others feel emboldened to share their tales. I am sure there are even more cases in far-flung countries that have yet to come to light. If your friends have indeed found a cure, then I hope they will be able to put it into production very soon. These things can take a long time to manufacture.'

'It's not a medicine, I'm afraid.' Kit sat back and sipped the sherry.

'What then?'

Kit smiled. 'I don't think you would believe me if I told you. You would think I'm quite mad.'

'Or perhaps you would think me mad if I did,' the doctor answered, raising a brow. 'As I say, some things are not talked about until others raise the subject. I'll try keep an open mind.'

Whether or not Doctor Smith was merely speculating or genuinely knew something, he was, apart from Merelda, the only person who had shown any interest in solving the problem. Kit thought he was close to admitting to knowing something of the fae world.

'I travelled somewhere that I did not believe existed at first,' he said cautiously.

'I thought so.' Doctor Smith smiled. 'You have a look of the Changed about you.'

'I need your help,' Kit explained. 'I need a very sharp blade such as a scalpel. Would you have something like that?'

'Naturally.' Doctor Smith looked at him with open suspicion, perhaps wondering if Kit was intending to slit his throat.

'I need to open something and be able to seal it again. I can't think of anything at home that would do the job. I thought a doctor would probably have equipment.' He reached into his pocket for a walnut and held it out.

'I suppose there's no point me asking why,' Doctor Smith asked, clearly fishing for the answer.

'I need to hide part of my medal in it,' Kit confessed. 'Then I need to seal it again, probably with wax, and if you have any strong-smelling ointment, I could use some of that too.'

The doctor looked at him over steepled fingers. 'I was right. You've been Touched. I've listened to a lot of interesting stories over the years, and I have never been sure whether I was a believer or not, but it appears that I am. Come on through into the surgery and you can show me what you intend to do.'

With the aid of the sharp scalpel, the walnut split fairly easily into halves. Kit gathered the meat in a handkerchief and put it back in his pocket.

'I'll need that later.'

He took out the medal and reached for the small hammer and chisel Doctor Smith had provided, the usual use of which Kit preferred not to dwell on. He balanced the medal on the operating table.

'I need iron chips.'

He handed the doctor the chisel. 'Do you want to do it? I think that if one of us has to hold it steady and run the risk of losing fingers, that should be me. I don't have as much use for them as you do.'

'Very well.' Doctor Smith weighed the hammer in his hand, positioned the chisel and brought it down. A splinter of the medal cracked off. It was about fingernail-sized. Big enough to tip an arrow.

Kit gave a triumphant cry. 'Give me another just to be on the safe side. Actually, let's try for three. Three is an important number.'

'Is it?'

'Yes.' Kit shook his head with a laugh. 'I imagine if I was the third son I would find this all so much easier, of course. It's a shame Miss Dove didn't set her sights on Fred.'

'Would you like me to prescribe you a tonic?' the doctor asked, raising his wiry eyebrows.

'I'm not sure that would really help. I'm not mad, you know,' Kit said hastily.

'No, I don't believe you are. There are things, Horatio in this world, et cetera.'

Kit grinned. 'I think perhaps *A Midsummer Night's Dream* is more appropriate. Now let's get to work. I need two more chips and then I need to melt a candle.'

Ten minutes later, the job was done. Kit had wrapped the three shards of iron in a strip of bandage that had been dipped in mead. He'd added a few smelling salts and sealed it all inside the shell with candle wax.

Dr Smith led him to the door.

'I hope to see you again. How will I know if it works?'

'You'll know I've been successful when they start to wake up. If for any reason I don't come back…'

He faltered, thinking of the enormity of the task ahead of him. To walk into a vindictive monster's castle and try shoot him. 'If I don't return, please tell my father I'm sorry.'

~

Merelda was drinking cocktails with Sybil, Ellen and Sarah in his parents' sitting room. Alfred was lounging in a chair doing a jigsaw puzzle. Merelda gave Kit an excited wave.

'How lovely to see you again. Is everything well? I hear you've been travelling. Oh, the things you must have seen.'

'Wandering around Whitby and getting arrested?' Alfred scoffed. 'He saw the inside of a cell, I know that much.'

Kit ignored him.

'I'm finding a solution to all this. Mother, I need to go away for a couple of days again. Or maybe not a couple of days, I'm not quite sure. I'm going to take the Vauxhall if you don't mind.'

'Now? But dinner will be served in just over an hour. Where are you going?' Ellen asked.

The scent of curried lamb wafted through from the kitchen. Kit inhaled, his mouth starting to water. He was tempted to wait until he'd eaten before departing, but it would be too easy to find reasons to delay.

'I just have to take something to a friend.'

Ellen wrapped her arms around him. 'Kit, I'm worried about you. Your father thinks your mind is unbalanced. He wants you to speak to a doctor. You've never been right since you came back from the war.'

Kit straightened up. 'I feel better than I have for months.'

'Your father won't like it.'

'He'll have to just put up with that,' Kit replied briskly. He pecked his mother on the cheek and did the same to his aunt and grandmother. He walked around the table and took Merelda by her hand. The papery skin of her wrist sagged in his.

'Everything is moving,' he replied. 'I hope to have good news soon. I don't suppose Enid has any more mead, does she?'

Merelda beamed. 'Oh, yes! You have been learning. I'll go and ask her to bring some.'

She walked out, cane tapping on the floor.

'I'm going to go see Adelaide before I leave,' Kit announced, and left the room before anyone voiced an objection.

He entered Adelaide's bedroom with slight trepidation given the coolness between them but told himself not to be silly. He wasn't annoyed with this version of Adelaide and she didn't find him abhorrent.

She was lying in her bed, but dressed in a different nightgown to the one he'd seen before. Her hair was covered in a boudoir cap and she looked healthy. She was the age she should be, and her stomach was as flat as ever. Kit wasn't an expert but she didn't look as if she had recently given birth. Valentine had told him that was only in the other world, and it appeared so. He frowned. It would be a complication, when she returned home with a child. They'd have to concoct a story about the baby being abandoned and needing adopting.

On her bedside table was a carafe of water. Kit sat on the edge of the bed and wetted the sponge. He put it to her lips, wondering if he should try mead, but why complicate matters now?

'Hello, Addie. I don't know if you can hear me where you are, but I'm coming back now. Tell Silas I've got what he needs, and if I've planned well, I'll be able to bring it through. I'll see you soon.'

He didn't expect a response and of course there wasn't one. He leaned over and kissed her cheek, feeling a brotherly surge of affection.

He thought more carefully about his clothing this time and dressed in an old pair of walking boots rather than his brogues. He raided the pantry for two packets of ginger biscuits, a bag of apples and a small packet of tea, as well as sundry other things. His first days eating only berries with a hungry belly wasn't something he wanted to repeat.

Merelda and Enid were waiting for him by the door to the hall. Merelda took his hand and drew him close.

'Everybody tells me I'm away with the fairies but only you know they were all correct.'

'Have you ever heard of someone called Caul Gilling?' Kit asked.

Merelda dropped her face into her hands with a sob that pretty much answered the question. Enid hugged her and glared at Kit.

'That's a name we don't speak and neither should you.'

Kit nodded, glad to have some suspicions confirmed. 'He's the reason everybody is falling asleep. I don't know if killing him will break the curse on Merelda, but I'll do my best to break it.'

'Thank you.' Tears sprung to Merelda's old eyes.

Another thought crossed his mind. Silas had spent time talking to Merelda on the night the whole affair had begun. Was it possible that Merelda was the half-human-half-fae's mother?

Enid gave Kit a small bottle of mead. He put it in his inner pocket, checking the walnuts were there while he did so. He had three but one of them was surplus to requirements, so he gave it to Enid.

'Will you keep this safe for me? There may be a circumstance when it's needed.'

Enid closed her palm over it. 'I'm guessing we had better not put that with the Christmas nuts.'

Kit grinned. 'No. The last thing we want over carols is anyone unwittingly opening a portal to the Faedemesne.'

At night, the journey back to Whitby met with no traffic. He parked the car on the clifftop in front of the long rows of Regency houses. He'd heard once that Lewis Carroll had stayed in one and wondered whether the tales of Alice were based purely on imagination or whether the author had experienced something like he had. From now on, whenever he read anything with a touch of fancy to it, no doubt he would wonder the same thing.

He dozed in the car and woke at the first brimming of dawn over the sea. He had no idea whether he would emerge through the same gateway when he next returned, so he locked the car, put the keys in an envelope and wrote the telephone number of Meadwell Hall on the front, then posted it through the nearest door. He walked to the whalebone archway and pulled out the undoctored walnut, wondering whether he was wise to have left one with Enid, after all. If something went wrong and he was unable to get back through, he'd have to somehow get the keys back from the house, drive home and do the whole thing again.

He felt the nut containing the iron chips deep in his pocket, nestling next to the velvet bag and bracelet and whispered a quick prayer to any gods or supernatural influences who may be listening that his plan would work.

He cracked the walnut with the nutcrackers he had purloined from the dining room before leaving the house. The shell split into three, but the meat came out whole. He wished he had paid more attention now to what Valentine had done back in the gardens on their first journey, but back then he hadn't really believed it would work. He ground the meat between his hands, feeling the oil spurt across his palms as he crushed it. He closed his eyes then fixed them on the palm of his hand and opened them.

There was a glimmering of luminescent light. He raised his hands to his lips, drew in a breath and blew hard towards the whalebone archway. The fragments of nut pooled up, caught by a gust of wind far greater than the one he had blown, but nothing happened at first. He counted five faltering heartbeats and without any sort of fanfare, the colour of the dawn between the bones took on a slightly different shade to the horizon surrounding it. The waves on the sea inside were surging to the right not the left. A black-backed gull flew into his peripheral vision from the direction of the town but as it passed behind the whalebones it did not reappear.

Kit laughed aloud, not caring whether any lurking police constable might hear. It had worked. He had performed real, actual magic. But he had no way of knowing for how long! He strode towards the bones with a confidence that felt so unfamiliar it was like a stranger to him. He knew for certain it had worked when warm sunshine hit his face, but as he stepped onwards, his entire body grew heavier and his feet became hard to lift. It didn't make any sense; the journey to England had been easy so there was no good reason why the return should be so arduous.

He was smothered in a feeling of dread that he'd inadvertently been caught in a snicklegate and time would pass slowly for him. He'd arrive in the Faedemesne to discover that years had passed. The land would be ruined, Adelaide and Silas would have a dozen children and barely remember him and Valentine would still be in servitude to Caul Gilling. He couldn't let that happen. Redoubling his efforts, feeling he was dragging each foot from quicksand, he pressed onwards. He thrust his hands into his pockets and felt the nut with its contraband and everything became clear. That was the reason. He was trying to bring something across that should never be brought.

His fingers closed around the velvet pouch which held Valentine's bracelet. Her face rose in his mind. The glowing smile and look of delight as they'd kissed, and the look of disappointment she would bear if he arrived without the iron. He tightened the pouch in his fist.

'I'm coming back,' he shouted. 'Just wait for me.'

With her face floating in his mind, he began to sing the song they had sung on the way across the mountain. Three verses in, he tripped and tumbled forward landing on his knees. His hands were still in his pockets and he ended up in a heap face down before he could get them out to brace himself.

There was a laugh behind him, and when he turned his head, Valentin was sitting cross-legged on a rock.

'That was elegant,' He remarked, jumping down and coming to help Kit stand up. 'I thought you'd never come back.'

'How long was I gone?' Kit asked.

He looked at Kit solemnly. 'Six years, and I waited every day.'

Chapter Twenty-One

Kit's legs wobbled.

'Oh, God, no!' He clutched Valentin's hands, pulling him close. 'I'm so sorry, I was as quick as I could be.'

He tailed off, seeing laughter bubbling in Valentin's eyes.

'You're joking, aren't you, it hasn't been that long?'

'Not quite a full day,' Valentin admitted, laughing. 'I just wanted to see your face when I told you that.'

'You wretch, that wasn't at all amusing,' Kit snapped. 'I had dreadful worries about that halfway back through. It was like torture to imagine you'd think I'd abandoned you.'

Valentin stopped laughing immediately, his humour replaced with an earnest look.

'I'd never think that, and I would have come every day to wait, if necessary,' he said quietly. 'I'm so glad you're back. I did wait here the whole time.'

Kit drew him into a hug and Valentin's hands snaked around his waist. Kit rested his cheek against Valentin's and his heart began to beat faster. Something was different in the way they held each other but he needed time to ponder exactly what had changed.

Unfortunately, Silas galloped into the clearing on a black horse, Adelaide behind him.

'You're back,' Silas said, dismounting and lifting Adelaide down. She looked over at Kit and Valentin embracing and her eyes narrowed. She walked over to the gateway and Kit hastened to her side.

'We can go through it and go straight home,' he said.

'You know I don't want to,' she replied.

Silas waved his hand and the gateway stopped pulsating.

'I got what we need,' Kit said. He reached into his pocket for the walnut. The wax he had sealed it with had turned brown and the shell looked like it had been through a fire, but the two halves were still together. Silas and Valentin drew back, reminding Kit that what he'd brought had the potential to kill them. He hurriedly put it back.

'I don't want to bring this into the camp because of the danger to you all. I'll stay here and do what I need to do. Adelaide, do you think you can bring me three arrows? I know you'll be safe while I work.'

Their eyes met. It would give them the privacy to hold the difficult conversations he'd been putting off. She obviously realised that too because her lips turned down but she gave a brief nod.

'Of course. I'll be as quick as I can.' She took Silas's arm and he lifted her onto the saddle and swung himself up behind her. They trotted away.

'Three arrows?' Valentin looked at Kit sharply.

'That's how it works, isn't it? I don't expect the first one to work, or the second,' Kit said.

Valentin's mouth twisted. 'I hope the first works because once Caul Gilling knows what's happening his defences will be up.'

'Go now,' Kit instructed. 'I don't want anybody near me while I work with the iron. Once I'm done, I'm going to make my way down and try join the human workers. No one will notice one more sleeper shuffling around.'

He pulled Valentin into his arms, conscious of the walnut in his pocket and the damage it could do. 'You'll be free soon, I promise.'

'I believe you,' he said, and kissed Kit full on the lips. He stretched his arms and transformed into the bird, taking to the skies and flying ahead of Silas. Kit rested, relishing the solitude, until he heard the rustle of Adelaide trotting back into the clearing on the horse. She'd brought her baby, wearing him strapped to her chest with a length of wide silk. She dismounted and handed Kit a felted cloak with a rabbit fur collar and large hood, a bow and a quiver that contained three arrows fletched with greyish purple feathers.

'Valentine asked me to tell you she charmed them herself,' she commented as he examined them. 'That was Valentine before, wasn't it?'

'Sort of,' Kit said. He tried to ignore the expression of distaste on Adelaide's face.

He broke open the walnut and set to work binding the chips of iron to the tips of the arrow with silk thread. Adelaide unwound the baby from her front and spread the sling on the ground and sat on it. The baby began to whimper so Adelaide put him to her breast. It was the first time they'd been alone and the silence was uneasy.

'Did you see me while you were home,' Adelaide asked eventually. 'What about Mother and Father?'

'Your father has gone back to Halifax. Your mother looks as well as she could, given that her daughter is in an unnatural sleep,' Kit told her. He sat back on his heels. 'You're right, you are younger back there. The family think I'm going mad, and I'm not sure they're wrong.'

He sighed at the mention of the family, wondering what was happening back in Meadwell now that he'd left again, and how soon he'd be able to take Adelaide home. That was why he'd come here, after all. 'I'm not sure what they'll think when we turn up with a baby. We'll have to think of an explanation.'

'Of course.' She shifted the baby to her other breast and gave Kit a brittle smile, perhaps contemplating how she'd explain his existence. She gestured to the grass at her side and Kit sat, transfixed for a moment by the scene of maternal happiness; Adelaide's quiet stillness brought to mind a painting of the Virgin Mary and infant Jesus. This was not the woman he had known. The Adelaide who had longed for the theatre and nights of dancing would never have been content living in a tent, however luxurious, or feeding a baby in a forest.

'What happened to the woman who didn't want babies and who declared a life without trips to London wasn't worth living?' he asked, then immediately winced at what sounded like an accusation.

Adelaide looked at him. 'I changed. People change. Besides,

I never said I didn't want babies. I just didn't want them too soon.'

Kit hung his head. 'You mean you didn't want them with me?'

'No. I would have wanted them with you eventually. If we got married. I've discovered a lot about myself since I've been here.' She looked down at the small head nestling against her, white hair in a dandelion clock shock, then back up at Kit. Her lips turned down. 'And about you.'

'I'm sorry you heard the confession I made to the unicorn.' he muttered, remembering the look of revulsion on her face.

'Did you make it to the unicorn or to Valentine? Or is it Valentin?' Adelaide said with a barb in her voice that caused Kit's cheeks to flame. He glanced up and saw her eyes were filled with tears. 'I'm furious at you! How could you not have told me what happened to you while you were in France. To keep all that from me, your closest friend since we were little!'

'How could I tell you?' Kit turned his head away, unwilling to see the hurt in her face. 'I've lived with my shame ever since and it has been eating me but I accepted that as my penance.'

He rubbed his eyes. Adelaide's outline danced in red and gold. 'I told you I never wanted the medal. Now you know why. I wasn't the great hero.'

'Kit, I don't give a – a damn about whether or not you were a hero. Besides, you came here to rescue me and you went back through the pathways alone. That's quite heroic, you know. I wouldn't have been brave enough to do that. That's not what hurts. I always assumed there would be other women when you went off to war, but to discover you loved a man! That's so humiliating for me!' Her face twisted with distress.

'I know you must see me as an abomination.'

'Kit, you could end up in gaol. It's criminal. It's just – wrong!'

'It's criminal but it isn't wrong,' Kit snapped. 'At least it shouldn't be. It isn't here.'

He pushed himself to his feet and folded his arms, staring down at her angrily. 'You've been here for years, surrounded by people with tails and horns, who change between men and women, and you haven't learned to accept that a person can fall in love with anyone! I'm surprised you can't wait to get back to the real world.'

'If it comes to that, I'm more surprised that you would want to!' Adelaide glared then dropped her eyes. 'In an odd way this comes as a relief. If you wanted a man, you could never want me.'

'Yes, I could.'

It had been so easy to explain the distinction between body and, for want of a better word, soul, to Valentine, but that wasn't important now. Kit reached for Adelaide's hand but withdrew it.

'I'm sorry. For everything.'

She shook her head. 'Silas will be wondering what's happening. I'll go back to the camp, and you do what you need to do.'

She stood and walked to the horse which had been waiting patiently.

'Tell Silas I'll be listening for his signal in the morning,' Kit told her. 'Make sure you stay safely back in the camp when everything starts.'

'That's up to me.'

'I didn't come here to see you put yourself in danger.'

Adelaide narrowed her eyes. 'I'm not really sure why you came here at all.'

Kit turned his attention back to the arrows, grimly wondering the same thing.

~

It was easier than he anticipated to shuffle his way into the throngs of people working on the land surrounding the castle. He mimicked their slightly dreamlike, confused state and soon managed to get closer than he expected. The arrows were small enough to stow in his rucksack and the iron must have had an effect on the guards because they avoided him, possibly without knowing why.

He kept his eye out for the small child who had fallen asleep at the sack race, but there was no one he recognised. He watched the sun as it moved overhead, remembering the details he had worked out with Silas. When night fell, he followed the sleepers into the closest camp to the castle walls. The camp was similar to the one Silas was living in, except everyone here was a human. There appeared to be no guards. Kit joined the line for a bowl of stew and hunk of bread and found a place at a fire. He didn't eat, knowing that the food most definitely came with obligations.

He was hungry so he munched a couple of the ginger biscuits he'd brought, which caused a stir of interest from the people nearby. He offered them round, assuring everyone there was no obligation, and was delighted that the men and women who ate seemed to awaken slightly more. What magic did ginger contain? He'd have to ask Merelda.

'This isn't Kent,' one man said, looking around and blinking.

'Wo ist Stefan?' asked a short woman.

German? The enemy. Though perhaps not under these circumstances. He quickly surrendered the remaining biscuits to everyone close enough, and once he had gathered around a dozen people who seemed to be aware of who they were, he set about explaining what had happened to them.

'My name is Kit Arton-Price. I'm from the human world and I've come to free you.'

'I know you!' A young child pushed through the crowd. 'Mr Arton-Price, I'm from the village. I want to go home. I want my mother.'

Kit recognised the child, who crumpled in tears as he stood there. It was the boy from the sack race. He lifted him onto his lap.

'And I'll take you.'

The boy's sniffles subsided. He looked shyly at the onlookers. 'He's from the big house. He's a war hero. He got a Military Cross. He'll do it.'

For the first time, Kit heard those words without the sense of shame pulling at his innards. The medal would serve a better purpose and perhaps he'd finally earn the description.

'I hope it can be achieved without bloodshed, but be ready to run if it looks dangerous. I promise you this, every one of you will be returned to your real life when Caul Gilling is defeated. You will have Silas Wilde's assurance on that.'

There were a few cheers but not as many as Kit imagined

there would be, and he wondered if he hasn't made himself clear.

'I mean you'll all get to go home,' he said. 'Back to your bodies and your real lives.'

There was a shuffling in the ranks.

'What if we don't want to?'

The speaker was a squat, solidly built man, aged approximately forty. His hair was tightly braided in long plaits that fell halfway down his back. Both arms were bare and his deep brown skin was covered in intricate tattoos.

'I have nothing to go back to. Even though we're all free and supposedly equal now, too many white men seem to struggle to remember that. Here no one has called my race into question. Why would I want to return to that life?'

'I like it here better too,' another voice chimed in and Kit had to search to see this speaker. It was a young man. Barely a man, really, because the fluff on his cheeks and chin was still as downy as a duckling's first attempt at feathers.

Kit was starting to feel out of his depth. He hadn't suspected anyone would willingly stay.

The youth gave a giant sneeze. His body snapped and he vanished, replaced by a small boy who couldn't have been more than five. He looked very much like the boy on Kit's lap, but he was clearly undernourished and both arms were covered in bruises.

'Me mam and dad beat me. What chance do you give me of even making it to six? I'd rather stay here and work in the fields. I'd never seen the outside of Gateshead before I came here.'

Kit sat back on his heels. 'I didn't think of that.'

'Why would you. You're rich and grown,' the boy asked.

Kit looked at the child. Didn't he deserve to grow into the fine youth he'd chosen to be?

'I understand,' Kit said.

The braided-haired man curled his lip, though not unkindly.

'Not everyone has the privilege of growing up in a big house like you did. You will have a full life of luxury surrounded by those who care for you. A celebrated war hero.'

Kit couldn't meet his eyes.

'There is nothing here that could bind you?' a tall woman asked.

Kit stared at her. She was beautiful, with long sweeping hair and an olive complexion. Was that how she appeared in the real world? Was she even a woman?

'We're not talking about me,' he replied. He glanced at the child who looked dejected and physically small, holding a large wooden mug that was now too heavy for him. What better life did Kit have waiting for him? He had his affection for Valentine to hold him to this place, though he had no idea how one-sided that was. At home, he had a future wife who loved someone else and a father he disappointed. He had the knowledge hanging over him of years of duty and the secrets he had shared here, but which would forever have to remain concealed.

The child squeezed his eyes shut and gave another great sneeze, which saw him return to his chosen shape. He saw Kit looking and shrugged.

'I've got my own shoes and my own blanket here,' he said, before ambling off, presumably to take advantage of it.

The mood in the camp was sombre that night. Kit recognised it as the familiar, almost tangible solidity to the air that came before a battle. The anticipation of something that would change, and the knowledge that some would survive, and some would not. Different groups had gathered together around various campfires, bonded by some common ground known only to themselves. A small woman with short auburn hair and skin so pale it could have been carved from porcelain sat with a bald man whose black beard was woven into thick strands that reached to his waist. The manner in which they leaned against each other suggested an attraction that, if it had not already been consummated, would surely not be far away. Their affection raised no eyebrows, any more than the union of the tall woman dressed in a kimono and her lover whose hair stood in blonde spikes across his head. It gave Kit a pain in the stomach to see acceptance here that he could not imagine England allowing in fifty or even a hundred years.

He accepted a cup of warm, sweet wine after asking the usual assurances that he would be under no obligation, which seemed to surprise the young woman in charge of the barrel.

'We were told that to ask was rude,' she explained. A burst of fury blasted him. That's why there was no need for chains or walls to keep them in; the people here didn't know that their meals were keeping them trapped in slavery. They'd been tricked into surrendering their freedom.

He sipped it, tasting cloves and cinnamon bark, then found an empty space beside one of the fires.

'Your speech was very good,' said the woman he sat next to. Her hair was piled high on her head in a style that his grandmother might have worn. She stretched out long legs that were clad in laced boots and fawn-coloured trousers of soft leather.

'I suppose you'll be staying here, too,' he said.

'Why is that?'

He gestured at her trousers, and she laughed.

'Freedom is tapping at our window. I plan to return to Scotland and do my damnedest to ensure that women in our world can wear and do what we like. If we can in this world, just think what we can do in ours.'

They clinked cups and drank then Kit settled down to sleep, wrapping his cloak around him. The signal would come just after dawn, when Silas had judged the castle would be at the most vulnerable and he needed to be ready to play his part.

∼

Kit woke early and was already waiting, arrows and bow in his rucksack, when the smallest sliver of sun began to appear from behind the lower of the two mountain ridges. He made his way towards the moat that surrounded the castle and took up a position. The booming of Silas's voice took him by surprise, even though he had been expecting it.

'Caul Gilling, I am here to claim my birthright. Show yourself to me.'

Some magic must have been in play, because the voice echoed as if through a loudspeaker.

'Usurper. False ruler. Your time is done. I come to this place with the blood of my kin and yours. Surrender and you might live.'

Kit winced at the lie. Silas had instructed that he was to

shoot Caul Gilling whatever the fae did. He looked towards the forest and saw Silas emerge, leading the procession of his followers. The band of men, women and creatures from the camp carried weapons but were dressed in fine robes as if they were about to enter the House of Lords. It was a definite message to Caul Gilling that they viewed themselves as the rightful rulers. Silas himself wore a cloak of deep blue edged with ermine, flung back to reveal a polished breastplate. Valentine was on one side of him and Adelaide on the other, both wore scarlet cloaks that Kit hadn't seen before.

Kit swore under his breath. There had been no mention of Valentine being present, though he understood why she would want to witness the downfall of her captor. Adelaide should have stayed safely back at the camp as he'd told her.

There was no time to dwell on the matter, however, as a sound like a crack of lightning erupted from the castle. Kit moved further round. The drawbridge had a gateway with an open walkway above it. Silas had been certain that this would be where Caul Gilling would appear, and he was right.

The air grew heavy and the acrid smell of burning garlic filled Kit's nostrils. It reminded him of the trenches and mustard gas and he retched. A wizened figure appeared. He looked ancient and although he was physically unimpressive, he wore a white cloak hanging down behind him and a headdress of black gems on his brow. Even if Kit hadn't known he was important, he was accompanied by a dozen guards dressed in leather and chainmail, all holding bows or spears.

'I surrender to no one,' Caul Gilling called down scornfully. 'You haven't the means to complete the rite.'

He looked very similar to how Kit imagined Silas would

look in a hundred years, but with an unpleasant scowl. He leaned forward, hands on the parapet, and stared at Silas who was still walking closer.

This was Kit's opportunity. He half closed his eyes and stared at the figure on the parapet. As Silas had suspected, Caul Gilling had a slightly blurred glow around him. Kit notched the arrow, running his fingers over the fletch made of Valentine's feathers.

'This is for you,' he murmured even though she couldn't possibly hear him. 'I will be your champion.'

He pulled back the string, took aim and fired the arrow.

It fell short, bouncing off the stone, just short of Caul Gilling's beringed hand and fell back into the tangle of weeds at the base of the wall. He'd half suspected it would, and having two arrows left, he wasn't discouraged. The fae looked down to see where the arrow had come from and Kit met his eyes. The irises were milky, almost as pale as the whites, and they shone with malice.

'What are you?'

'I am here to free the Gentle known as Valentine,' Kit shouted, refusing to be cowed.

The fae burst into mocking laughter. 'One of the humans here to free my bondslave? Really? Can't you see I'm engaged in a greater matter than yours? Go back to your work and you can make your pathetic appeal when I'm done with my nephew.'

Without hesitation, Kit drew back the string and let the second arrow loose. The aim was better and this time it bounced off Caul Gilling's arm. The fae hissed and his pale eyes yellowed with fury.

'Iron? Here? You dare!'

He spat words that lifted Kit off his feet and threw him into the air. He landed painfully on his back with a jolt that knocked the breath from him and it was only with great effort that he managed to hold onto the third arrow and the bow. Through the pain he heard a roar, and by the time he had struggled to his feet he saw that Silas's company were approaching the gate. Caul Gilling snarled another spell, and a great wind arose, gathering soil and grit. Silas and his followers pushed on undeterred, Silas and others screaming words of their own.

The sleepers had been roused by the noise and were starting to appear. Hundreds of them making their way from the camps. Many looked confused but Kit recognised some of the ones he'd spoken to the night before. They were holding objects that could barely be described as weapons. He groaned. The plan was supposed to stop the need to involve anyone innocent and he'd failed.

Kit crept closer to the wall. Caul Gilling was distracted by Silas and one arrow remained. He gritted his teeth, thinking that he had suspected this the way it was always going to be. Threes in fairytales. Of course the first two had failed, so this one could succeed.

He drew back his arm, took a breath to steady his nerves and concentrated on the figure on the parapet, letting his eyes blur so that the world became grey with Caul Gilling a smudge of oily silver and sulphurous yellow in his vision. He let the arrow fly free, certain that it was travelling to the centre.

Without even looking, Caul Gilling waved a hand and the third arrow span away.

Kit dropped to his knees with a cry, barely able to believe he'd failed. Another cry came simultaneously, this one of triumph and Kit raised his head to see Silas, Adelaide and their followers swarming through the gateway and into the castle.

At the same time there was a fluttering of wings overhead, close enough to whip Kit's hair, and he saw Valentine flying in the direction of the arrow.

He scrambled to his feet and ran after her, shouting for her to stop, knowing that the arrow tip would wound or kill her if she touched it, but unable to match the speed she moved at. He saw her circle and dive. Saw her rise with the arrow. Saw her turn back towards him, falter and plummet groundward, the arrow still clutched in her claws.

Chapter Twenty-Two

The anguish Kit had felt at failing to kill Caul Gilling was bad, but it paled into insignificance compared to watching Valentine fall to earth. The ground loomed up to meet her long before Kit could reach her, but she thrashed her wings, and somehow managed to right herself before impact and rose clumsily again before dropping.

He slid and caught her before she landed in a manner that would have made his upper fifth-form rugby master proud. He rolled onto his back and cradled her in his arms. Her heartbeat was a faint fluttering in the palm of his hand but it was enough to know she was alive and he gave a sob of relief. He eased the arrow from her claws. He wanted to hurl it far from her but she'd sacrificed too much for him to let the second chance go to waste.

'What were you thinking?' he raged, far too loudly.

Panic slammed the dove backwards, beating her wings weakly. She tried to answer but the only noise that came out was a burbling cooing. Horrified at having alarmed her, Kit gathered her into his arms, making soothing, wordless sounds.

'You can turn back now,' he said.

She grew still and he braced himself for the change in weight and size, but nothing happened. She squawked, her tiny bright eyes fixed on his.

'Don't worry,' he said softly. 'You're just weak. Give it time.'

He tried to keep his voice level, not having the slightest idea whether she was doomed to remain in this guise.

'You're safe, my love,' he said soothingly. He stroked the glossy feathers of her neck and she grew calm.

'Come on. I have a job to do,' he said.

Holding the arrow in one hand and cradling Valentine in the crook of his other arm, he walked to the castle. The fields outside the castle were full of humans and fae alike, all mingling in confusion or seeing the opportunity for freedom from Caul Gilling's oppression. No one prevented him entering.

Silas's followers were fighting against Caul Gilling's soldiers. A handful of bodies lay bleeding or already dead. The spiky-haired man was clutching the body of his kimono-clad lover and keening. The scent of blood hit Kit like a punch to the face as he found himself back in the midst of a battle and the muscles in his legs tensed, ready to run. Silas and Adelaide were making their way stealthily around the inner edge of the courtyard. They appeared to be heading towards a large, grey marble statue of a woman with her head bowed and hands outstretched on a raised platform.

Caul Gilling presumably thought the same because he launched himself off the rampart with a cry. His cloak spread and belatedly Kit realised they were wings. He landed gracefully in front of the statue.

'What do you come here for?'

'I am Silas of the Wilde. My bride and I are here to fulfil our birthright,' Silas shouted. His voice rang with command. A significant number of Caul Gilling's soldiers paused their assault and looked towards their master.

Silas continued to walk towards the statue. 'If you accept me as your lord, stand down your weapons. This bloodshed will end now.'

Fighters on both sides let their weapons fall. Even Kit felt his fingers twitch to drop the arrow but he gripped it firmly. He made a nest by the wall with his cloak and lowered Valentine into it and as he did, he felt the small bottle of mead he'd asked Enid for. He uncorked it and poured some into his cupped hand then held it to Valentine's lips.

'It's mead.'

She pecked at it until his hand was empty. He stood. Her eyes followed him.

Don't leave me.

The voice in his head was a mix of Andrew's and hers. His stomach churned.

'I have to. You'll be safer here,' he whispered.

Silas and Caul Gilling were still facing each other, though Silas had been edging around so that he was closer to the statue. He had produced a dagger with a very thin blade and was holding it out. Adelaide held his hand and was glaring at Caul Gilling.

'My blood will speak to my ancestors,' Silas growled.

'Your blood will beg for death,' Caul Gilling sneered.

'Our blood does not fear death,' Adelaide spat.

Kit shook his head in irritation. He had no time for theatrics of this sort. He strode up, concealing the arrow behind his back. All three of them turned towards him causing a pit of fear to open in his stomach, and he had to force himself forward. If he was going to be a hero worthy of the iron he concealed, now was the time.

'I am here to demand you free the sleepers and the Gentle named Valentine,' he said firmly.

Caul Gilling curled his lip in contempt. 'You demand? A warped faced weakling who cannot shoot an arrow straight? You are nothing.'

A grey streak flew past Kit and the fae's laughter was cut short by Valentine launching herself at his face. As Caul Gilling held his hands up in protection, Kit lunged forward and stabbed the arrow upward. He'd loathed bayonet training for war, but was grateful for it now as the motion came easily to him. The tip of the arrow pierced Caul Gilling's chest. He uttered an unholy shriek and began to clutch at it.

Valentine circled away and when she landed beside Kit, she had transformed back to a woman. She held up the arm bearing the bracelet, and struck Caul Gilling across the face.

'I free myself,' she shouted.

She reached forward, drove the arrow further into Caul Gilling's chest, and twisted. He looked at her in confusion, then his milky eyes flooded with scarlet. Blood spread across his chest, and he fell forward, rust-brown tracks appearing on the back of his hands as they clutched the ground. Soldiers, sleepers and fae rushed forward, an uproar filling the air.

Valentine lifted her hand. The bracelet dulled to the faintest pink then broke into two pieces and fell to the flagstones, where it shattered into a dozen more.

'He's dead,' Valentine announced, her voice half a sob. 'I'm free.'

She flung her arms around Kit, clinging onto him and laughing wildly. He buried his face in her hair and held her close.

'Then there's only one matter left,' Silas announced. He walked past the body, pulling Adelaide after him to stand before the statue.

'Give me your hand,' he said to Adelaide. She obeyed and he held out the dagger.

'Stop!' Kit yelled.

He shrugged Valentine off and barged towards them.

'Don't worry,' Silas said. 'This is the birthright I told you of. The queen needs blood.'

'Yours, not hers,' Kit snarled.

Silas smiled infuriatingly. 'Ours. The blood we share.'

'Merelda's blood?' Kit asked. 'She always used to talk about how she'd had a baby.'

'She said that it was replaced with a stone, but no one believed her,' Adelaide confirmed. She bit her lip. 'We all thought she was mad.'

Kit's stomach squirmed, remembering the squat toad clinging onto her tongue. 'She's your mother, isn't she?'

Silas's eyes flashed with amusement. 'I'll never get tired of how humans jump to conclusions so quickly. Though I am half-human myself, my father loved and cherished my mother, and they lived here happily for a century. I'm not Merelda's son. Though it's true she had a baby, and it was taken from her.

'My uncle raped Merelda then cursed her. He tongue-locked her so that she could not speak of who had charmed her.' Silas's eyes flashed with anger. 'He was plotting his conquest, even then. If the child had been a boy, then he would have raised him as a successor, secure in the knowledge that he had a dynasty of his own. But it was a girl. She was brought here for a time, but then my uncle lost interest and returned her to your world. Unfortunately, by then Merelda had aged beyond that of motherhood, so the child was found a new mother.'

While Silas had been speaking, Kit had been studying Adelaide and a memory came to him – the moment he'd come across Silas sitting with Merelda in the maze and mistaken her for Adelaide.

Right mother, wrong child.

'Addie,' he said softly. 'You were adopted.'

'In Halifax.' Silas nodded slowly. 'You have to remember that time here can act differently. A day can be a week. Or decades.'

'But she's human.'

'Half human,' Adelaide murmured.

It made a strange sort of sense. The baby sent back to the family like a twisted version of the changeling stories. It explained Adelaide's knack for charming people. She was probably using bewilderments she didn't even know she possessed.

Silas took her hand and kissed it. 'My darling, you belong here as much as you do there. Half a fae. The blood of my family runs in your veins, too. Did you think I picked you by

329

chance to come with me here? I told you I needed your help to mend my kingdom and I meant it.'

'What do you need me to do?' she asked Silas.

'For twenty generations my family have sworn an oath to rule with honour and fairness. The blood seals the compact. To claim my throne and the responsibility that goes with it I must do the same. I only need a little of yours and you will be my queen. We will rule together.'

Kit jerked his head up.

'You don't have to do that,' he said. 'We can go home now.'

'Home?' she asked, looking confused.

'To Meadwell. You're half human, too.'

He suspected he knew the choice she'd make, but once she made it, she wouldn't be able to unmake it. He turned to Silas.

'Does this have to be done now? You should give her time to think about the consequences.'

Silas gave him a quick look of annoyance then shrugged. 'I suppose it doesn't. My uncle is no longer a threat and now I think of it, performing this ritual in front of his corpse is unseemly. At noon we'll meet here again. It will give my people time to spread the word and come from further afield.' He snapped his fingers. 'Where are my courtiers? My loyal advisors? Come, we have work to do.'

He swept off towards the double doors, waving his hand. They creaked open as he approached. Kit looked at Adelaide, then at Valentine, who was standing alone. She looked slightly pale after her exposure to the iron but she was looking at her wrist, which was now free of any shackle, and her expression was radiant. Both women called to him for different reasons.

He knew which one he wanted to see, and which he should speak to. But who first?

As he dithered, Valentine looked at him, nodded slightly, then extended her arms and rose into the sky. Not a dove now, but something with dark feathers above and pale below. It might be a merlin but Kit wasn't sure. She soared up until her silhouette was swallowed by the sun and vanished. He began to weep with the sheer joy of seeing her so free, and hastily wiped his arm across his eyes to hide the evidence.

'We have things to discuss. Will you come with me for a walk?' Kit asked Adelaide.

She looped her arm through his and together they strolled through the courtyard. They climbed the tower with its staircase spiralling around the outside and stood on the battlements where Caul Gilling had been. The failed arrows would be somewhere nearby, and he'd need to find them to return the iron safely back to his own world. He'd seen the effect it had on Silas's people – on Valentine, in particular – and had no desire to see it used again.

Only when Kit was certain they would not be overheard did he start to speak.

'Are you all right?'

'Why wouldn't I be?' Adelaide frowned in confusion.

'You've just seen your father murdered. Isn't that a shock?'

She leaned on the parapet, linking her hands together, the mannerism startlingly similar to Caul Gilling's.

'He fathered me, but I'd hardly count him as a father! He stole me and cursed my mother, then left me when I was of no use. I've spent the last two years witnessing the devastation caused by him. The world is better off without him.'

She had an edge of steel to her voice. She would make a strong leader, probably stronger than Silas would be, and the faedemesne would be better off for it. 'No, if anything it's Merelda I'll miss. I like her a lot. That's why I feel so content here, I suppose.'

He was right. She wasn't planning to come home. He could make it hard or easy for her. He took a deep breath. 'I do love you, Addie, just not in the way I'd need to for us to marry. You're beautiful and I find you absolutely beguiling, but I'm not *in love* with you. And, I know you're not in love with me, either.'

She reached for his hand and squeezed it.

'I love you too Kit, but like a brother.'

'Our engagement wasn't for us, it was for the families. It would be a terrible mistake if we go through with it.' He touched her shoulder gently. 'I came here to rescue you and take you home, but that choice isn't mine to make for you. You should stay here with Silas and your son if that's what you want.'

'I do. I am in love with Silas. I feel like I belong here. I know I do.'

'Then I formally release you from our engagement.' It felt like the rightful end of something that should never have happened. He pressed his lips together.

'Thank you, Kit, darling.' Adelaide pressed her hand to his cheek, her eyes growing moist. 'You don't know how happy this makes me.'

The relief in his heart told him that he probably did. She hugged him tightly then pulled back and looked at him anxiously.

'I'm not really here, though, am I? You said you saw me at Meadwell.'

'That's right. You need to wake up, then you can come through. I'm sure it can be done and your body and spirit can join together again. Silas will explain how, and I'll help as much as you need me to.'

She embraced him. 'Thank you, and then we can come back together. Oh Kit, we'll have a lovely life!'

'I'm not coming back with you. I can't. I have too many responsibilities and there will be too much to explain.' Kit grimaced at the thought of how he was going to finance the upkeep of the estate without Adelaide's money.

'You'll need money. I shall leave you everything,' she said. 'I won't be needing it. As far as I'm concerned you can sell my jewellery, and I'll even write you a bank draft for as much of my capital as I can access.'

'Your parents won't be happy about that,' Kit cautioned.

She laughed recklessly. 'I don't care, they'll be even less happy thinking I've eloped with a Hungarian nobleman.'

'Hungarian?'

'I just picked a country. One where they're unlikely to start checking birth records and identities. I'll pack my things, leave a note for Sarah and be back here before an hour is up.'

'You call her Sarah. I noticed that before. You'd already made your mind up to leave.'

'I can't stay at home just for my parents. No child should, and I don't think she'd want me to.'

She kissed his cheek and Kit knew just how much he'd miss her.

'Kit, I hope you find happiness. With someone. Whoever she – or he – might be.'

Her blessing, with all the acceptance that it involved, meant more than he could articulate. He hugged her tightly. A shriek came from above and he looked up to see the silhouette of the merlin. He waved but Valentine spiralled off again, black against the clouds, and he wasn't sure she'd even seen him.

'She's the one you love, isn't she. Or he is? I'm not sure I understand that.'

'Yes,' Kit whispered, 'but I don't think they know I do, and I don't know how they feel in return.'

'Then go and tell her and find out, idiot.' Adelaide prodded him in his chest and just for a moment they were children again, teasing one another. He hurried down the stairs as fast as he could, cursing whoever built a staircase on the outside of the keep without a railing. One wrong move could send him plummeting hundreds of feet to his death.

Silas emerged from inside the castle, looking every inch the king. He'd changed into a dark purple cloak and had the circlet of black stones around his head.

'Adelaide is yours. I've formally ended our engagement,' Kit told him. 'I'll be returning to England alone.'

'That wasn't necessary for our union to proceed. She has declared herself my wife,' Silas said. He dipped his head. 'But I appreciate the gesture.'

'You didn't need me at all did you. It was Adelaide all along,' Kit asked.

'It was Adelaide I needed because of whose blood she bears. It's fortunate for me that I also love her. As her fiancé I needed your permission to court her in the first place. I saw your skill with the bow, and I wanted your friendship and your courage.' Silas leaned over and kissed Kit beside the lips, leaving a trace of heat and the scent of pipe tobacco on an autumn night. 'And on that subject, are you sure you want to go back? There will always be a place for you at my court as an adviser, and a friend.'

Kit bit his lip. The world here seemed brighter already. Whether it was just his damaged vision, or his imagination, or whether the pall cast on the land by Caul Gilling was beginning to lift, the sky looked a paler grey, with hints of blue breaking through. Why shouldn't he give up the miserable existence of Meadwell and let Alfred take over as he so clearly wanted to? He sighed with longing.

'You're tempted, I can tell. Though I caution you to decide quickly,' Silas said. He put his hands behind his back and began to walk. Kit fell in beside him.

'I spent two years caught in a snicklegate, with time to think and plan. My uncle was right that, in some ways, my land is affecting yours, and as we've seen, yours affects us. I think the borders need to be closed permanently. No more crossing between. No more half-human children.' He blinked. 'No more iron seeping through the firmament.'

'That's very drastic. We use iron a great deal now but might not always,' Kit pointed out. 'Steel and other metals will be used.'

'That might harm us more rather than less,' Silas said. 'Who knows what else might be created; more destructive, deadlier. No, to keep safe my people – and yours – we need to close ourselves in.'

'What about progress?' Kit said. 'New ideas? You can't hope to pickle the world as it is.'

'That's true.' Silas smiled at him. 'Perhaps once a decade, a handful of brave souls may be permitted to pass across and gather or impart ideas. To keep the folktales stocked with characters. But no more than that. Are you not tempted to stay now?'

Kit ran his hands through his hair and grinned.

'Yes, and you know it, but I have to go back. Responsibilities, you know. A kingdom of my own to rule,' he said, trying to sound enthusiastic. 'Ask me again in a decade.'

'Then I shall grant you a bedazzlement. I would see your face be as handsome on both sides so that the world knows your goodness.'

There was a little tug at Kit's heart. It was tempting, though not too tempting. Because this was how the fae made bargains. There would be an obligation on him if he did that. Besides…

He shook his head. 'Thank you, but I earned my scars. I'll let them serve me as a reminder of what I did.'

'You're an odd man. Shouldn't the outward man resemble the inner man?'

'I behaved without honour in the field, as you know damn well. My heart bears the greatest scars, and I would not have you erase a single one of those.'

He bit his lip. Since he had bared his heart to the unicorn, it hurt a little less than he'd grown used to. Perhaps the pain and guilt Kit felt over Andrew's death and his abandonment of him was beginning to heal.

There was an expression of benign amusement on the fae's face.

'I talk not only of the valour in your own world but in mine. You are a braver man than you permit yourself to believe, and I would have you know your worth. Very well, keep your badge of disgrace if it makes you happy, but it is my wish that you see the world with clarity.'

He reached out and rested his hand upon Kit's forehead and began to speak in a high, rapid voice. Kit's head filled with a wriggling, as if a thousand worms of steel were burrowing into his brain. It wasn't painful as much as uncomfortable as the power surged into him and he became aware on a level that he had somehow previously not been that Silas was an extremely powerful being.

Silas pronounced two final syllables and withdrew his hand. Kit opened his eyes and gasped. The sight in both was clearer than it had ever been.

'What did you do?'

'I took the damage from your eye. You will always bear your outer scars but there is no reason why your sight should be obscured. And no, before you ask, this places you under no obligation to me. It is a reward freely offered in commemoration of the great services you have performed here.'

Kit's newly healed eyes filled with tears. He raised his eyes to the sky, blinking rapidly and caught a glimpse of Valentine circling on the air currents, her spread wings now the silhouette of a red kite. He sighed with longing.

Silas cocked his head and raised an exquisitely arched brow.

'I can call her if you like. No obligation. Regard it as a final favour.'

Kit didn't hesitate.

'Yes, please.'

~

High on the air currents, Valentine watched Adelaide and Kit speaking. Saw them embrace. Pain shot through her chest that she could no longer deny. She shrieked in alarm, at first not understanding the sensation, and then in despair and grief.

A beating heart now lay inside her, and the tragedy was that it was tied to the man now standing with his future bride.

She wheeled away, not wanting to see any more and flew towards the mountains. She intended not to return but heard a call that sounded like a bird of prey. Silas. She grew tense. Now that she was free, she would bend to no man's will. It was right and proper that no man had a claim on her. But when she saw that he was not alone, she felt the beat of that heart again and knew that she was only lying to herself. She circled about, then plummeted at speed, deciding as she dropped which aspect to be, before spreading her wings, and landing on the ground a bird, standing up a woman.

'You called me, my lord?' she asked bowing to Silas and contriving to face away from Kit.

'I did. You and Kit need to speak.'

He walked off in the direction of the tower where Adelaide waited.

'I thought the dove was your only form,' Kit remarked.

She flexed her fingers. 'For a long time it was. It is how my master preferred me. In my mildest and most submissive state.'

Kit grinned at her, his eyes crinkling with amusement. 'I don't think I would ever call you submissive. You're fierce and argumentative and downright rude at times.' He reached for her hand and ran his thumb over the palm. The little shocks of sensitivity that danced up and down her arm were torture.

'I think I shall miss your argumentative nature most of all when I leave,' he said. 'I'll be going without Adelaide. I've released her from our engagement.'

'But I saw you embracing. I felt the love radiating from you both,' she said quietly.

Kit smiled, a touch of sadness edging it. 'It is the love of a brother and sister for each other. Two hearts glad that our engagement is at an end. I'll return and she'll stay here.'

'You aren't coming back?'

Valentine's chest tightened in agony. Oh, her newly hatched heart would be unendurable if it could cause such poundings. How Silas must have suffered when his grew.

The sadness in Kit's face deepened, his eyes growing more sorrowful than she'd imagined possible. 'I can't. I have too many responsibilities at home, never mind the fact that I'll have to deal with the repercussions of Adelaide leaving. You could come with me if you'd like. Now I'm not going to marry Adelaide I'm free to look elsewhere and there's nowhere else I'd rather look than to you.'

She shivered remembering the oppressive weight of the iron bars crushing her in the room he had locked her in, and the pain and disorientation she'd felt when the tip of the arrow had screamed as she had carried it. She wasn't brave enough to go with him to that world.

'I can't. I'm so sorry Kit. There's too much iron now and it's only going to get worse. I could come and visit you, perhaps somewhere far from any towns, but I can never stay.'

'I understand. Silas said as much. He says he's going to close all the gates. For our safety as well as yours.'

'Forever?'

No more travelling through between worlds. Kit forever or Kit never.

Throwing caution to the wind she began to speak, to ask him to stay, but of course no words emerged. Even Silas Wilde couldn't break that magic and ask his love to stay. It had to be volunteered or requested and given entirely freely by the human. All that emerged from her mouth was a strangled sob and Kit, misinterpreting it, showed the compassion and tenderness she'd come to love. He enfolded her in his arms, burrowing his face into her hair.

'I shall miss you so very much, my love,' he said. His voice was thick with misery but not enough for him to ask to stay.

He bit his lip, and looked a little worried. 'I have something for you. I've been waiting for the right time to give it to you…'

He produced a small pouch from his trouser pocket and gave it to her. She tipped the contents into her hand and immediately recognised the flower beads as the bracelet from the stall in the market they'd walked through.

'Kit, what did you buy this with?' she asked.

'A truth. That I wanted to be the source of gladdening your heart. But now I'm not sure. You might not want to wear anything on your wrist now.'

She didn't wait for his answer, but wrapped the strands around her wrist in place of the shackle. The imprint caused by the magic binding was still visible, but the beads partly obscured it. For the second time in their conversation, she couldn't summon the words.

'You don't have to wear it like that,' Kit said. 'You're not bound to me.'

'I know I'm not and I shall never be bound against my will again, but I'll wear it there all the same, to remind me of what I've been and what you did for me. My champion.'

'You freed yourself,' he pointed out.

'With the means – and the courage – you helped me find.'

Kit gathered her in his arms again and kissed her. The wildness flared inside her. She could transform into an eagle with the power coursing through her veins. She kissed him back passionately, letting her desire flood out through her and into him, feeling his surging back into her. In her mind she could almost see it, a golden thread running through both their bodies. However long she lived she'd never forget this moment.

The bronze bell at the top of the castle tower chimed. Valentine looked up. The sun was overhead. Time for Silas and Adelaide to complete the birth-rite. She took Kit by the hand and led him back to the castle courtyard. It was already filled with people dressed in clothing of all kinds: rags, tags, velvet gowns, chiffon and silks, leathers and feathers. She hesitated at the back until it occurred to her that she was no longer a bound chattel, at which point she led him through the crowds until they were directly in front of the statue, along with the more grandly dressed fae. She smiled pointedly at a couple of horned men, daring them to tell her to move, but they must have recognised who she was because they fell back with sweeping bows.

'We deserve our place here,' she said firmly to Kit. 'I'm a Keeper of the Order of Thorns and I intend to make up for the time I've lost.'

Silas and Adelaide appeared, both clad in green robes that swept to the ground. They stopped in front of the statue and Silas began to speak, though Valentine let the words wash over her without really listening. Finally, Silas stopped talking and lifted his knife. He ran the long, curved blade over the mound beneath his thumb on his left hand and a drop welled up. Adelaide held out her right hand, sucking her breath in when the blade cut. Silas put his hand on the statue's right and gestured for Adelaide to do the same on the left.

Valentine held her breath. For forty years, since Caul Gilling had usurped the throne, the Elder Quene had bowed her head in grief, but as the couple touched her hands the statue's head lifted slowly until the face became visible. The smooth marble woman shared Silas's fine features and, Valentine realised, Adelaide's.

Adelaide beckoned and a young skorrig, short and hairy with a pronounced, catlike snout, stepped forward, holding the wrapped baby. The skorrig looked odd, but they made the best nursemaids or masters. Valentine looked at Kit from the corner of her eye and saw no surprise on his face. He'd learned well.

Adelaide pricked her son's finger, producing the tiniest drop of crimson blood and touched it to the statue's hand. A subtle sighing filled the air and a soft, cocoa-scented breeze caressed Valentine's cheek. It felt like a kiss, and when she put her hand to touch it, she realised she was crying. Tears were streaming down Kit's face, too, and she wondered at what point he would realise that his scars had faded almost completely to nothing.

After the ceremony, there was a feast. Valentine didn't manage to speak to Silas privately until the late evening when he had finished walking amongst his subjects and speaking with delegations from different communities who had gathered outside the castle grounds. They found a spot by the river that ran behind the castle and sat together.

'Silas, I know you have dazzled away some of my painful memories in the past. Don't bother denying it. I can always tell,' she added quickly, seeing his face taking on the expression it always did when he tried to deny something.

'I thought you didn't know. I did it with the best intentions,' he said. 'The indignities you endured at my uncle's hand were reprehensible.'

'I know. It's a kindness that I've never thanked you for properly.' She twisted her fingers together and her eyes fell on the daisy bracelet. 'If I did want something to heal my heart and make me forget someone completely, what would it cost me?'

'For you, absolutely nothing. There is nothing you can ask for that will ever repay the debt I owe you.' He lifted her chin. 'Is that what you really want?'

She blinked away the tears. 'The one thing I really want I'm not allowed to ask for. You know that.'

He put his arm round her and kissed her softly on the temple. 'I know. I won't grant your request now. Ask me again in a month, and if you still desire to forget Kit, then I will do as you ask.'

Chapter Twenty-Three

I t appeared there were very few who regretted the death of their previous ruler, even those who had fought in Caul Gilling's colours. The celebrations were like nothing Kit had experienced before. He thought his engagement party and the celebrations that ended the war had been extravagant, but the music and dancing and feasting went on for hours.

Kit's contribution was Figaro's 'Aria', followed by a recital of *The Green Eye of the Yellow God*, to wide applause from the crowd and complete glee from Adelaide. If he achieved nothing else, he could embark on a career as a music hall performer.

Silas was sitting beside the river with Valentine at his side, and his and Adelaide's child between them, wrapped in a striped woollen blanket. They were deep in conversation and didn't notice Kit and Adelaide approaching at first. He beckoned Kit and Adelaide to him.

'Tomorrow I'll start the task of returning the sleepers if they wish to go. Anyone who wishes to stay may do so. Some of them will doubtless try to find their way back here and I'll permit anyone who does to return.'

He coughed meaningfully and for a moment Kit felt the intense power that Silas had emitted when he'd healed Kit's eyes. The certainty that he was doing the right thing began to waver.

'I'll send you now with Adelaide to return to her body.'

'Can you send us straight to Meadwell? I left the car in Whitby, but I posted the keys through a letterbox so I'm not sure how we'll get it back.'

'Anywhere can be a doorway,' Silas said. 'I have a fondness for rivers, personally.' He gestured to the water they sat beside. In the moonlight it resembled a silver ribbon running through velvet fields. A marble bridge spanned it. Kit had hoped for a journey to delay reaching the gateway. Here and now seemed too soon, though the longer he stayed, the harder he would find it to go.

'Time is of the essence when you reach Meadwell. Adelaide's spirit will return to her body, then you can send her back. The longer she remains in your world the fainter the connection to my land and to our child will become.'

Silas handed him two pieces of lilac.

'I'll only need one,' Kit said quietly.

Silas gave him another penetrating look. 'It's best to have two. You never know when you might choose to use it. I offer you my hand and my blessing. Christopher Arton-Price, you are a free man here. No one shall or can place you under obligation.' He rested his forehead against Kit's 'Must you go? Just imagine what we can do together. You and I, and Adelaide and Valentine. Imagine the life we could share. The four of us united would bring such strengths to each other. We would be unconquerable. Undefeatable.'

'That means the same thing,' Kit said, his tongue feeling thick and dry. 'You don't need to say it twice.'

'You make a good point, but mine still stands.' He stared into Kit's eyes, so captivating that Kit's blood started to rush, his heart to pound. Kit shook his hand before he threw all his intentions away and stayed. While Adelaide and Silas kissed farewell, Kit turned to Valentine.

'I'll never forget you,' he said.

'Goodbye Kit,' she said quietly.

He leaned forward to kiss her, inhaling the scent of mimosas for the last time. She hadn't asked him stay. She was a free woman now, and whatever affection they had found clearly wasn't enough for her to want him that much. He released her, knowing that if he didn't he'd find it impossible, and nodded to Silas.

Silas tossed the lilac petals into the air and blew. They were slightly more elegant than the walnut pieces, Kit had to admit.

The arch beneath the bridge began to glow with a green light.

'I've tried to get you back as close as could be. We left Meadwell through the river. You should emerge back there.'

'As soon as you get there go up to my room and I'll be waiting outside,' Adelaide told him. She kissed her son on his forehead and handed him to Silas.

The petals were floating in the air and settling around the bridge. The luminescence began to pulsate. Kit took Adelaide by the hand, and they waded into the water. It was pleasantly cool, but the wind buffeted them as they walked into the mist beneath the arch and down the long pathway. As the sounds of celebration grew fainter and the mist rose around them Adelaide began to slow down, until she stopped altogether.

'I can't go through. What if something happens to Caelwen while I'm gone?' she groaned.

She let go of Kit's hand. It was the worst thing she could have done because when the mist cleared, she was no longer beside him. Kit cried out her name but to no avail and he had no choice but to continue forward, telling himself not to panic. Perhaps that was supposed to happen, perhaps she had returned to her sleeping body.

It was raining heavily when he emerged from the gate that led to the deer park. The pathway had sent him close but not exactly where he should be. The rain lashed down and he had no real idea of what season it was. The leaves were still lush and green and the grass was tall, which suggested it was still summer.

Running at full pelt only took him fifteen minutes to reach the house. He ran straight to Adelaide's room. He didn't bother to knock but went straight in.

Aunt Sarah was sitting by the bed reading.

'Kit! You've been gone four days! Where have you been?'

He did a quick calculation. That meant it was June the twenty-first. The longest night, and the summer solstice. Whether that was significant or not was something he could think about later.

'You're soaking wet!' Sarah exclaimed as Kit walked to the side of the bed.

Adelaide was still lying as she always had, her face pale and her eyes shut.

'But that's wrong,' Kit said. 'She shouldn't be like this.'

'I know. It's so hard to fathom,' Sarah said.

'No, I mean she really shouldn't be,' Kit said. 'She wasn't supposed to be like this now.'

Sarah rose from her chair and walked towards Kit with her arms outstretched. 'You're not well. You've been gone for days again. Your parents have been worried sick. Let me go get them.'

He was on the verge of protesting until it struck him that he needed Sarah to leave.

'Yes, go,' he said gently. 'Adelaide loves you and Richard very much, you know.'

Aunt Sarah's eyes crinkled. As soon as she was gone, he dropped onto the bed beside Adelaide.

'Addie, can you hear me? You should be awake by now. What's gone wrong?'

Her eyes fluttered open. She tried to raise her head, but it fell back weakly.

'Kit. I feel so weak. Take me to Silas.'

'I'll take you. We'll go now.'

He walked to her dresser and swept her jewellery into an evening bag and put the loop over his wrist. He felt for the lilac in his pocket then lifted her from the bed and into his arms. She weighed almost nothing. How long had she been surviving on beef tea and cornflour? It was no wonder she had no strength to walk.

They were halfway across the lawn before he heard his parents calling his name. It would be far too complicated to explain what was happening, so he ignored them and increased his pace. The deer park was too far so he headed towards the bridge where they should have emerged.

He laid Adelaide on the riverbank and jumped into the river. It was waist deep and freezing. The current was rapid and unseen fish and plants grasped at his legs unpleasantly.

'Can you walk at all?' he asked Adelaide, but she just sighed. He lifted her in his arms again but it meant he couldn't easily reach the lilac in his pockets.

'Come on Addie, you've got to try help me here.' He let go of her legs and caught her before she sank in a heap, throwing her arm around his neck and supporting her entire body weight. Her feet went from under her as they touched the slippery mud and they both dropped beneath the surface. Kit pulled her upright with difficulty and dragged her as he waded towards the bridge.

Aunt Sarah was shouting his name over and over, alternating with Adelaide's. He glanced behind and saw his parents, brother and aunt striding towards him.

'Kit whatever you think you're doing it isn't the answer,' his father cautioned.

'It's going to be fine,' he replied. He found the lilacs and crumbled the petals from the stems into his hand. 'I'm taking her where she needs to go.'

He threw the petals up in the air and blew. At first, he saw no signs of any gateway. He reached for the second lilac stem but from the corner of his eye he saw the pulsating glow underneath the bridge. It grew stronger as he reached it.

'Stop, please,' Aunt Sarah begged.

Kit smiled at her, wishing with all his heart that Adelaide was conscious enough to bid her mother farewell in person.

'Adelaide loves you very much and she wants you to be happy,' he said softly. 'We aren't going to get married because she loves someone else. She wants to go join him. She'll be so happy there.'

As would he be. Why was he choosing to stay here? Valentine might not need him but that didn't mean she wouldn't want him in the future. He'd have all the time in the world to wait, after all.

He waded towards the bridge. It was wide enough for a farm cart to cross, but when he reached it, he saw that the arch beneath it had become a tunnel that stretched much further.

As he stepped closer to the bridge Adelaide began to revive enough to take some of her body weight.

'We're nearly there. A few steps further,' he urged.

They were chest-deep now. From behind, Kit could hear the anguished screams of their family. It tore his heart. Addie might be content to leave without saying goodbye, but Kit couldn't.

'Addie this is too cruel. We can't just abandon them without a proper explanation.'

He had a second piece of lilac. He didn't have to go right now. Silas had been wise to give it to him.

'You go on. I'll go back and I'll try to explain as best as I can. I'll come through soon.'

Adelaide stumbled at first but as they walked further into the passageway her strength began to return. Whatever part linked her to the Faedemesne was reaching out for her body. A piercing wail echoed off the walls: a child keening for its mother.

'I'm coming,' Adelaide cried. She pulled away from Kit and ran. Unlike Orpheus she didn't look back once.

When she was lost from sight, Kit waded back through the tunnel and emerged into sunlight breaking through the rain. His father had removed his shoes and was about to climb into the river. Aunt Sarah was lying on the grass face down, being comforted by Ellen. Kit had never seen her in such disarray.

'Murderer!' she screamed, upon spotting Kit.

Charles grabbed him roughly around the waist and dragged him back onto the bank. The uproar had caused servants and members of the household to come running.

'Call the police,' Sarah screamed. 'He's drowned my daughter!'

'No,' he said. 'That's not what happened.'

But how could he prove otherwise? Two had gone into the water and only one had emerged.

Sarah pointed to the evening bag hanging from his wrist. 'That's Adelaide's. He's a thief too.'

'No, let me explain.' Kit looked around. Adelaide was beloved by the household. From the expression on the faces watching him, the servants would gladly tear him limb from limb!

'Better come inside before something bad happens,' Charles growled.

There was no love in his father's eyes. Explaining would be impossible.

He had only one choice. He needed to go join Adelaide, Silas and Valentine, as he should have all along.

He wrenched himself free and waded towards the bridge, reaching into his pocket for the final piece of lilac but before he could enact the magic, Crossle the butler plunged into the river beside Charles and the two men grabbed hold of his arms.

'He's a wrong 'un, sir. Locked a woman in the plate room, though I begged him not to. Left her to die.'

Crossle dashed the lilac from Kit's hand, flowers unstripped. They tumbled into the water and were washed away by the current under the bridge which, to Kit's dismay, remained just a bridge. The fight went out of Kit, seeing his way back lost forever, and he slumped, allowing the two men to manhandle him to the bank and restrain him.

~

'His mind is quite broken. It's not his fault. Sergeant Lawn, you must see that.'

Kit listened to his mother's pleas echo down the passageway and into his cell. He lay on the bed that was bolted to the floor; hands lightly clasped across his chest. His clothes were still damp, since he had not been permitted to change them before being taken to the police station in Helmsley. Now he lay on a mattress that was so thin it might better be described as a blanket, listening to his mother begging to see him.

He tried not to worry. Adelaide knew he should be coming and when he did not appear, someone would come looking for him but how could they imagine what he was going through? His skin grew cold. He had no idea how much time had passed in the Faedemesne. A day? A week? Was Adelaide and Silas's son now a strapping young man?

His mother's entreaties had no effect and now his father

was blustering and threatening. Demanding access to his son as soon as the family solicitor arrived. Time passed. It grew dark. His clothes dried. He was fed. Made use of the chipped pot in the corner. Lying down on the bed, he slept.

The next day was exactly the same. As night fell again, he allowed himself to give into his despair and weep. Bars of iron surrounded him. He'd been placed in iron cuffs while they brought him here. Even if his friends knew where he was, they would be powerless to assist him in escaping.

His father and the family solicitor visited the next morning and Kit was taken to a room with a table and chairs. Mr Lohan was the same age as Charles. They'd gone to school together. He was a local man and had returned to practice in York. That he had come over to speak to Kit personally was a great favour.

'Christopher, you need to tell us exactly why you did what you did. From the outside it looked as though you abducted Miss Wyndham and intentionally drowned her. Can you offer any alternate explanation?' Mr Lohan asked.

'Adelaide was planning to elope with a Hungarian nobleman. Father, you remember him. Mr Wilde, who was at our engagement party.'

'So you decided to abduct and drown her before she was able to break off your engagement.'

Kit jerked forward. 'No! I like him. I'm happy for them both. He was meeting us under the bridge. As Addie was too weak to walk, I had to carry her.'

Mr Lohan appeared unimpressed.

'Nobody was seen beneath the bridge before or afterwards.'

'They must have gone quickly while everyone was busy detaining me,' Kit suggested. It sounded feeble as he said it.

'They must have heard the furore, yet this alleged nobleman and Miss Wyndham left you to your fate.'

"Don't leave me!"

Kit bowed his head, seeing how bleak his future looked. Mr Lohan removed his spectacles and polished them on a handkerchief, looking up at Kit.

'In the absence of Miss Wyndham, or her body, the charge will be murder. Charles, I am very much afraid he will be found guilty, and the penalty will be capital,' he said.

Kit saw his father stiffen. 'But he's my heir. That can't be allowed to happen.'

'I find it very unlikely, given his inadequate explanation for events, that Kit will be able to convince a jury of his innocence. Surely, if Miss Wyndham and her lover were aware of your current predicament, they would come forward to prove that she is alive and well?'

'I don't know how to contact them,' Kit protested. His chest grew tighter by the minute. 'I had the means and I've lost it.'

Mr Lohan made a few notes on his pad of paper, the scratching of his nib being the only sound. He replaced the lid and put down the fountain pen. He looked at Kit almost kindly.

'Christopher, you have suffered a lot in the service of our country. It's possible that your mind has been damaged as a result of your injuries and your ordeal. I will represent you and I suspect the best defence will be insanity. An asylum might be your best chance.'

'I'm not going to plead insanity,' Kit said.

'Then you'll most likely hang.' Mr Lohan turned to Charles. 'I'm sorry, Charles, but as he's being this obstinate I can do very little. I will defend him, of course, and we could plead insanity with or without his consent.'

Kit shoved his hands deep in his pockets and his fingertips brushed against a single lilac blossom that had somehow escaped destruction. He took it out with excitement, threw it in the air and blew on it, hope rising that he would see the means of escape, only for it to fall to the cell floor as nothing happened. Charles and Mr Lohan exchanged a look that said everything Kit feared.

'I'm not mad,' he said urgently, but his words sounded hollow.

Was his mind damaged? He didn't think so, but he supposed that mad people didn't.

Charles looked at Kit. Kit stared back. His father appeared to have aged ten years.

'I'll speak to my son alone now,' he said coldly.

The solicitor left.

'I asked you not long after your engagement party whether your mind might have been affected by your ordeal. You swore it hadn't. But I cannot see any other reason for your irrational behaviour. Either way, you have left me no alternative but to disinherit you.' He pressed his hands together. 'Either they will hang you or imprison you or incarcerate you in an asylum. No outcome will leave you in a position to inherit Meadwell and you've shown me that you aren't capable in any case. Alfred will have to step up to the role.'

'I have no doubt he will do the job admirably,' Kit said.

Charles walked around the table and leaned close to Kit. 'It is my greatest sorrow that he was not the eldest.'

Kit gritted his teeth before answering. 'It is mine, too. I'm sorry, Father. I did what needed to be done.'

'And so shall I.' Charles knocked on the door. Just before exiting, he turned back to Kit. 'It will be better if they hang you.'

Kit put his head in his hands. Given the alternatives, it was hard to disagree with that assessment.

Chapter Twenty-Four

The case made the national papers. The rejected suitor who drowned his fiancée and attempted to steal her jewels. With Kit's inability to account for actions and Mr Lohan's clear reservations, the verdict was almost a foregone conclusion before the trial had even started. Mr Lohan's efforts to suggest that Kit's actions had been an act of mercy towards the catatonic woman – that he was unable to bear seeing Adelaide in her state – fell on deaf ears. Especially as reports of the puzzling illness suggested many sufferers were beginning to wake of their own accord.

Kit's declarations that Adelaide and Mr Wilde would appear at any time to prove him right sounded like the ravings of a desperate man and as the hours in court passed, his faith wavered until his repetitions sounded hollow even to him.

The judge's words echoed in Kit's mind as he was led from the courtroom, numbly putting one foot before the other.

Hang by the neck until dead.

They hadn't come.

357

'Well, this is a pretty pickle you've got yourself into,' Doctor Smith sniffed. He'd managed to wangle a visit to Kit in Armley Prison where he'd been taken awaiting his execution after the passing of three Sundays. That the entrance resembled a castle and reminded him of Silas's home was an irony Kit did not find amusing.

'I think that's an understatement,' he said wryly. 'I don't suppose you can vouch for me that I was trying to help Adelaide? Word of a medical man and all that.'

He sagged into the uncomfortable wooden chair.

They hadn't come and his hopes faded with each passing day.

'I wish I could help you, but it's beyond my capabilities,' Doctor Smith said. 'I don't blame you, by the way, for refusing to plead insanity. I don't think I could bear life in an asylum as a sane man. I don't think a person's sanity would last very long under those circumstances. A quick death is a much more attractive prospect. Assuming that is your only choice.'

'I think it is.' Kit dropped his head into his hands.

"Don't leave me, Kit."

Andrew's words echoed in his ears. Begging. Condemning. Mocking. He couldn't quite shake the idea that this was his punishment.

'I'm trapped here, and I don't even have a way of contacting them. It's too much to hope that somehow they'll find out. Silas gave me some lilac to use, but I lost it.'

Doctor Smith cocked his head. 'I thought it was walnuts you used.'

A hot sweat washed over Kit. 'You're a genius! I'm an imbecile!'

He sprang from his chair, causing it to clatter to the floor. 'I need to see my great-aunt Merelda. I left a third walnut in her keeping. It's always the third! Can you ask her to crack and seal it as you saw me do?'

'I will speak to her. I don't imagine we'll see each other again so let me wish you the best of luck. I truly hope you manage to escape to your fairyland.'

Doctor Smith stood and shook Kit's hand. 'Oh, I almost forgot to tell you. Do you remember the little boy who fell asleep at the fair? He woke a day after you returned, fought his father with strength and skill quite remarkable for a child of his age, then announced he was going to become a watchman and hasn't been seen since. Do you know anything about that?'

'I couldn't possibly say.' Kit smiled. It was good to know that at least one of the sleepers' tales had had a happy ending.

~

The days until Merelda visited were the worst of Kit's life. He could barely sleep and when he did his nightmares were plagued with the faces of those he'd loved and lost.

Her arrival was announced the afternoon before his execution was due to take place.

'I've been ill. I'm sorry,' she said, settling onto the chair that the warden put in Kit's cell. 'I have started to feel recently that I am almost done here.'

'You've got years left in you,' Kit said gallantly.

'I hope not. Oddly, now that my toad has gone I feel slightly bereft. I had not expected to be outliving you.'

'I'm hoping you won't,' Kit said. 'I mean that in the nicest possible way, because I intend to live for a very long time. Do you have the walnut?'

'Yes. At first, I couldn't think what you were asking for, but then Enid reminded me. She's so clever.'

'Yes, she is. You're lucky to have her.' Kit smiled. 'You're lucky to have each other. Not many people manage to find their heartmate and keep them.'

'I told Enid you knew.' Merelda's eyes crinkled then grew solemn. 'But then I think there are reasons you might be more aware of our situation than the rest of the family, my dear.'

'There are.' He told her about Andrew. Not the dreadful death, but the laughter and tenderness they had shared. Even under the dire circumstances, his heart felt lighter. If everything went horribly wrong and he died, at least one person would know the truth. When he had finished, Merelda had tears in her eyes.

She blew her nose then gave him the walnut. The shell had a faint shimmer to it that greeted Kit like an old friend. Silas had indeed cured his eyes and he had none of the blurred outlines on common everyday objects, so this little reminder of the Fae was quite heartening to his general despair. The two halves were sealed together with red wax.

'Red for luck. Do whatever it is you need to do and go be with them. That's what you're planning, isn't it?'

'Yes. There's nothing for me here.'

He took her by the hands. 'Merelda, you were right, you know. You did have a baby, and that baby was Adelaide.'

'Thank you, Kit. I'm so pleased to know that for certain. I always did like her.' Merelda's face cracked into a smile that was so like Adelaide's that it struck Kit as astounding no one had ever noticed the similarity. But who would have believed such a thing was possible?

'You didn't murder her, did you? I believed you didn't, and now I'm even more certain.'

'No, I didn't. I took her to where she wanted to be. She is the Queen of the Fae with Silas Wilde as her king and a son that will grow up to rule after them. She's happier than I've ever known her. I only wish we hadn't caused so much distress to the family in the process.'

Merelda brushed a tear from her cheek.

'There are always victims, however good the intentions. The recent war taught us that. Now, what about that troublesome little madam you locked in the silver vault?'

'I dare say she's happy, too. She's free from what bound her. She didn't ask me to stay,' he admitted in a small voice, feeling the wound so deeply he almost craved the noose.

'Did she not?' Merelda cocked her head and her birdlike eyes gleamed. 'And did Silas Wilde ask Adelaide that question?'

'I wasn't present at every conversation they had,' Kit said.

'Well, I'm willing to bet that request never came from him. They can entice and borrow but they can't ask to keep. It's one of the rules of that place. Oh, it's so good to be able to talk freely. I can't thank you enough,' Merelda said, licking her lips with a toad-free tongue.

'I think you just did,' Kit said. He squeezed the nut tightly. 'I asked Valentine to come here with me, but she said no, then she started sobbing. I think now that she wanted me to stay but she couldn't ask. I'm an idiot, aren't I!'

'The best sort,' Merelda said with a gentle laugh. 'You're

away with the fairies, or at least you soon will be. Do you want me to leave you alone while you do this? I suppose a mysterious escape from gaol would be better if there was no one to witness it.'

Kit weighed the walnut in the palm of his hand and glanced at the window. Through the grille the sky was dark with clouds. 'I don't think it'll work here. There's too much iron. For whatever reason, it stops magic working. Perhaps one day a chemist will discover why. I'm going to have to wait until I am somewhere without iron.'

Someone rapped on the door and informed them they had five minutes.

Kit helped her from her chair and escorted her to the door.

'Thank you,' he said.

'Thank *you*,' she replied. 'For taking the toad away and for telling me who my baby was. It's so good to know I'm not actually mad and never was.'

'You and Enid could come with me,' Kit suggested.

Merelda squeezed him tightly. 'Don't think I'm not tempted. But I think taking everything into account that we've learned, our lives have been long enough. I hope yours is as long as you deserve it to be.'

～

Kit was led to the prison courtyard at dawn. His hands trembled even though they were bound behind his back and his heart thumped as he walked the path that only led one way. Damp air hit him and he shivered.

'It's cold. I'm not afraid,' he told the guard at his side.

The guard shrugged as if he didn't believe Kit. 'Aye, many say that.'

He couldn't look at the scaffold, where a black-clad man waited and a noose swayed softly in the breeze. Outside the walls he could hear the singing of hymns from those hoping to save his soul, and shouts informing him he was a murderer and a monster.

In all honesty, he wasn't sure who was right. Perhaps they all were.

'Please give me a minute to pray,' he begged Warden Evans. The warden was a kind man with three young children. He must have seen hundreds of men who had done the vilest things, but he had treated Kit with more courtesy than many would.

With difficulty Kit reached around and took the walnut out of his pocket and squeezed the two halves together so that the wax cracked and the meat fell into his hand. He'd practised the movement long into the night until he could do it in seconds, knowing seconds would be all he had. He lifted his face to the sky.

'Silas Wilde, your man calls for aid,' he called.

Warden Evans looked at him suspiciously.

He flicked the crumbs upwards with difficulty.

'Valentine, Keeper of the Order of Thorns! Adelaide, blood of Fae and Meadwell!' he called.

The wind swept upwards, catching the shards of nut and swirling them around Kit. He laughed, seeing it was obviously working.

'What's that?' Warden Evans stepped towards him, alarmed.

Kit backed away and glanced around, desperately searching for the luminescence that would lead him to the Faedemesne. When he saw it, his knees went weak. In a cruel trick, the gateway had formed in the only circle available: the noose that awaited Kit's neck. It pulsated with an indigo light, but it was too small and too high, and with his hands still bound, he had no way of clambering through it.

As he stared at it in dismay, a word echoed around the yard.

'Sleep.'

The warden's eyes took on a glossy look and he began smiling benignly. The other guards and the executioner appeared to be under the same enchantment. Kit wasn't certain whether the spell extended to the crowd at the other side of the wall, but the songs and shouts grew fainter.

A grey streak shot out of the glowing hole and circled around Kit's head, then a dove perched on the wall. Around one leg was a blue ring. The bird dropped from the wall, and as it landed, Valentine took her female form. She stood with her hands on her hips looking at Kit. Hands bound and wearing prison uniform, he stared back, a sweaty mess of relief.

'What have you got yourself into?' Valentine asked.

'Everything went wrong,' Kit said.

'Adelaide told us she didn't wake up, but you obviously got her body through,' Valentine said.

'Yes, but without her body, everyone thought I'd murdered her.'

'Of course, now you're about to be executed you want to

come through,' Valentine said. 'You're lucky Silas hasn't sealed the ways yet.'

'I was going to come anyway, straight after taking Adelaide, but the lilac was taken from me.'

'You were going to come back?' Valentine looked into his eyes. He'd forgotten how thick her lashes were. How green the irises.

'I'd have come sooner but I'd forgotten I had the means.' He stared around him. 'And there's been quite a lot of iron in my life recently.'

'Yes. I can feel it.' Valentine shuddered.

He stepped towards Valentine. She held out a hand, and on noticing his hands were bound, she waved a hand and said a few words. The ropes fell away and he rushed to her, gathering her into his arms. Warm and soft. The smell of mimosas filled his senses, causing his throat to seize.

'I finally took time to think about what you're not telling me as much as what you are. You couldn't ask me to stay, could you? I thought you didn't want me to and it never occurred to me to ask.'

Valentine scowled. 'One day, I'm going to be very angry with you that you doubted me so much.'

She buried her head in his chest. 'Today is not the day, though.'

'I've missed you so much,' Kit said, gazing down at her. 'I love you, Valentine. I want you, and I want to be with you. I want to sing songs and recite poems by campfires, and make love in the woodlands, and bathe in streams. And I want to marry you.'

He took her hands in his and ran his thumb over the bracelet.

'If you don't want me, then I'll accept that, but if that's the case then you might as well go back through the gateway and let me hang because I'd rather die here than live without you.'

'Well, then, since you have asked me so prettily, I shall consider your request.'

She burst into peals of laughter that Kit considered highly inappropriate given his situation, then threw her arms around him.

'Kit, dearest Kit! Did you ever believe the answer would be no?' She put her hand to his cheek and gazed into his eyes, all merriment gone. 'I wept solidly for a week when you left and didn't come back. I was close to asking Silas to bedazzle away my memories of you, but I couldn't bear it in the end. The pain of losing you was nothing compared to the joy of having known you. Of course I want you to come with me.'

She tilted her head towards Warden Evans who was staring with a glazed expression in his eyes and a rictus smile. He looked as if he was trying very hard to speak.

'We need to go now; these people won't stay befuddled for much longer.'

She fumbled at her wrist and undid the clasp of her bracelet. The skin where the shackle had rested was almost healed. She met his eyes.

'I wear it constantly to remind me that it's something I choose to do.'

She looped it around his wrist and held his hand. The frisson of desire that the touch of her skin gave him told him he was doing exactly the right thing. He looked at the noose doubtfully. It was big enough for a head but no more and he really didn't feel too keen on putting his neck through it.

Valentine leaned in and kissed his cheek. 'Have you ever imagined being a bird?'

'Not really,' Kit answered honestly. He grinned. 'Though there's a first time for everything.'

'I can't promise the magic will last for longer than will it take to get through the gateway, but we'll have plenty of time for me to teach you.'

Kit's heart soared. He had no idea how long his life would be but he had no doubt that every moment with her would be exciting.

He had no doubts about anything any longer.

Valentine murmured some words and Kit felt his body shrinking. There was a tightness that was not exactly unpleasant, then he felt himself soaring towards the purple haze and the world was left behind them.

∾

Jeremy Evans considered himself a kind and fair man, even though his job was guarding evildoers and guiding them to their deaths. Moreover, he was a Methodist and couldn't even blame it on the demon drink, so until his dying day he kept the secret of what he'd seen in the yard that morning.

One bird flying through the noose from nowhere, and then two birds flying back through to nowhere, all within the space it took to sneeze.

It was preposterous. Besides, as quickly as it had happened, they hanged the prisoner who had drowned his fiancée in a fit of madness or jealousy.

If it felt to Jeremy Evans that the prisoner felt too rigid and showed no emotion, or even many signs of life as he walked up the steps, that was something Jeremy also kept to himself.

Who would believe him?

After all, condemned men do not turn into birds and fly away, leaving wooden puppets in their place and a lingering scent of exotic flowers.

That sort of thing only happens in the stories he read to his daughters at bedtime.

And everybody knows fairy tales aren't real.

Author's Notes

I've explored the meetings between humans and fantasy/folklore characters in *Daughter of the Sea* and *The Promise Tree* but those stories took place in our world. I knew that in my next book I wanted to send my characters off to weird and wonderful places (through the maze, at the back of the wardrobe and down the tunnels you've been told to stay away from), but I wasn't sure what would send them there.

I first came across Encephalitis Lethargica, or the 'Sleeping Sickness', years ago, thought it was interesting then forgot all about it. When I was researching the First World War for the chapters of *The Promise Tree* where Edwin is in France, it cropped up again and it seemed the perfect explanation for vast numbers of people to fall asleep without explanation. The Fae as creatures who steal people away has been a staple of fairytales for as long as they've been told.

Most of my books have a song that I listen to while I get into the writing mood. This one has *Rhiannon* by Fleetwood Mac and *Thomas the Rhymer* by Steeleye Span.

Thanks to Avril and Mairibeth who explored the Cabinet of Curiosities in Haworth with me where we looked at skulls and potions.

Thanks to my kids who encouraged me to include more queer representation in my writing.

Thanks to my editor Charlotte who, as always, gives me brilliant advice, loads of support and took me out onto the roof terrace in London to look at the view!

I hope you enjoyed reading this as much as I enjoyed writing it.

ONE MORE CHAPTER

YOUR NUMBER ONE STOP

FOR PAGETURNING BOOKS

The author and One More Chapter would like to thank everyone who contributed to the publication of this story…

Analytics
James Brackin
Abigail Fryer

Audio
Fionnuala Barrett
Ciara Briggs

Contracts
Laura Amos
Laura Evans

Design
Lucy Bennett
Fiona Greenway
Liane Payne
Dean Russell

Digital Sales
Lydia Grainge
Hannah Lismore
Emily Scorer

Editorial
Kara Daniel
Charlotte Ledger
Ajebowale Roberts
Jennie Rothwell
Caroline Scott-Bowden
Emily Thomas

Harper360
Emily Gerbner
Jean Marie Kelly
emma sullivan
Sophia Wilhelm

International Sales
Peter Borcsok
Ruth Burrow
Colleen Simpson

Inventory
Sarah Callaghan
Kirsty Norman

Marketing & Publicity
Chloe Cummings
Grace Edwards
Emma Petfield

Operations
Melissa Okusanya
Hannah Stamp

Production
Denis Manson
Simon Moore
Francesca Tuzzeo

Rights
Helena Font Brillas
Ashton Mucha
Zoe Shine
Aisling Smythe

Trade Marketing
Ben Hurd
Eleanor Slater

**The HarperCollins
Distribution Team**

**The HarperCollins
Finance & Royalties
Team**

**The HarperCollins
Legal Team**

**The HarperCollins
Technology Team**

UK Sales
Isabel Coburn
Jay Cochrane
Sabina Lewis
Holly Martin
Harriet Williams
Leah Woods

eCommerce
Laura Carpenter
Madeline ODonovan
Charlotte Stevens
Christina Storey
Jo Surman
Rachel Ward

**And every other
essential link in the
chain from delivery
drivers to booksellers
to librarians and
beyond!**